The Six-Year-Old Hobo

The Six-Year-Old Hobo

Happy reading !

David W. Goodwin

David W. Goodwin

Library of Congress Control Number: 2014903539
ISBN: Hardcover   978-1-4931-7686-1
                 Softcover   978-1-4931-7685-4
                 eBook   978-1-4931-7687-8

Rev. date: 06/02/2014

To order additional copies of this book, contact:
Xlibris LLC
1-888-795-4274
www.Xlibris.com
Orders@Xlibris.com
550804

ACKNOWLEDGEMENT

THE SIX-YEAR-OLD HOBO was inspired from an article I read called "Confession, a Roman Catholic App." One thing led to another and without much thought, the seed for this story was planted, the characters emerged, got inside my head and helped to guide the story.

I have a lot of people to thank for their helpful comments and review. Family members include my partner and first reader, Suzanne Ryan, who, as a pre-school teacher, gave me many great insights into kids and their remarkable intellectual capabilities. Above all, she assured me that there are many six-year-olds out there capable of Zeke-like adventures, thoughts, feelings and verbalizations. I also had fantastic, thoughtful reviews and critiques from my daughter, Hannah, an English teacher in Thailand, and my quasi-stepdaughter, Clare Ryan, a visiting assistant professor in Political Science at Macalester College. Hannah, now known to me as the "Comma Queen," gave me invaluable grammar and punctuation corrections, as well as countless suggestions for improvement and some wonderful ideas. Clare, given her stellar background in law, provided advice on shoring up the legal framework of the story to make it as factually correct as necessary. My mother, Mary, read my first draft, caught a few ugly errors and "liked it better than *Slave Camp Nightclub*."

Several friends also helped considerably. Two policemen-buddies of mine (who also happen to be awesome cyclo-cross racers) graciously agreed to read my first draft and provided judicious comments. I'd like to thank both Matt Domnarski, a trooper and pilot with the Massachusetts State Police and Greg Wise, a detective with the Amherst Police Department. In addition, my friend-since-college, Christopher Curtis, provided helpful feedback and encouragement, and helped to tweak the cover photo that I created, taking it from good to stunning.

Thanks everyone!

CHAPTER 1

THE NIGHT THE six-year-old became a hobo was a lot easier than he expected. He knew that hobos rode the rails so after he slipped out the back door of his house, walked to the end of his road, went downhill on Velta Drive and continued in a zigzagging manner across South Main Street and the full length of Baca Avenue, he was right smack dab at the edge of the Burlington Northern Santa Fe trainyard. Whenever a car drove by, knowing full well that a six-year-old toting a hobo stick walking down the street in the middle of the night would arouse a lot of suspicion, he was careful to duck behind a bush or one of the low adobe walls that lined the streets of his upscale neighborhood. The last thing he wanted was to get caught and sent back to Confessionville.

Since his hometown was located at a major interchange for several railroad lines, he was plenty familiar with the comings and goings of freight trains and the sleek New Mexico Rail Runner Express commuter rail. He also knew exactly where the chain link fence topped with razor wire ended along South 1st Avenue and was easily able to slip into the trainyard without any trouble.

The hardest thing about riding the rails, he soon found out, wasn't finding the right train car, it was getting up into one. Tank cars, hoppers, flat cars, piggy backs, gondolas, refrigerated cars, engines, cabooses—he knew the names of all of them from his favorite book, *Charlie the Caboose and the Great Divide*. He noted, though, with some six-year-old nostalgia, that most trains these days consisted of flat cars loaded with huge freight boxes, some stacked on top of each other or loaded with semi-trailers being hauled someplace to a waiting truck tractor to be driven somewhere on the road where the railroad didn't go. These weren't appropriate for hobo transportation but the trains pulling the more traditional train cars were, especially the boxcar if the sliding door was open. Walking around the switchyard for a while, dodging railway workers who were easy to spot from the bright lights put out by the huge flashlights they carried, he was able to locate a few empty boxcars with open doors that stood idle waiting to get hooked up to a locomotive. Walking over to one with an open door, in the shadows of the freightyard, he tried climbing up inside but got his arm somehow stuck on a metal bar just inside the door. He was able to get free without too much trouble, but in the process, it sounded like he might have torn something. Getting inside was probably going to be a bigger challenge than he had anticipated.

On the tracks behind him, he heard an engine backing up to a row of cars and he knew his time had come and he had to act immediately. Walking towards the sound, he saw another open boxcar and tried again, this time using a different strategy. Since the six-year-old could barely reach the first rung even with his outstretched arms, he was again thwarted in his attempt to get onto the train and sat down beside the tracks and yelled out loud, "This really stinks! How's any kid supposed to get on a train?" Perhaps he yelled a bit too loudly because he heard a man's voice coming from above. Perhaps God wanted to hear his Confession now for real this time, not just through some idiotic confess-your-sins-or-God-will-punish-you sort of smartphone app that his parents had recently downloaded and made him do with them.

"What's got yer diapers in such an uproar, Angelina?"

The kid looked up and saw a grown up hobo standing in the shadows of the boxcar peering down at him with his face lit up from the harsh bright mercury vapor lights of the freightyard. His jaw was full of whiskers and his eyes shone like sparks, even over the lit stub of a cigar clenched between his worn down teeth.

"You lookin' to flip this boxie or you just hopin' to get both of us nabbed by the Bull?" Not knowing how to answer either of these questions, he told the man that he just wanted to get away on an adventure. "Well, you've come to the right boxie there, Angelina, 'cuz I ain't no jungle buzzard. If we hurry and get you into this here car, it just might take you away on the trip of a lifetime!"

"Why are you calling me Angelina?"

"Hey, be happy I don't call you Maeve!"

"Is that worse?"

"Yessir. You're a boy, right?"

"Yes, but my name is Zeke, not Angelina."

"Right, which is why I didn't call you Maeve."

Zeke saw the man's outstretched hand just as the boxcar lurched from the impact of the backwards coupling of the train cars in sequence as the

DAVID W. GOODWIN

locomotive made all the necessary connections down the line. Within a few more seconds, he could hear the loud roar of the engine as it started pulling away with all the cars in tow.

"Throw me your bindle stick so we don't have to do this on the fly," the old man instructed when he saw Zeke's hesitation. "And see that stirrup down there by the wheels? That's your first step. Step onto that one, take ahold of this here grabiron and the rest will be easy."

The six-year-old hobo did as he was told, gave his worldly possessions to the man, grabbed his rough and calloused hand with one hand and the metal handhold on the inside of the boxcar with the other and climbed into the car just as the train started getting some forward momentum. It was a moment of pure fear and exhilaration, like the first step over a cliff, not knowing what was below, how far down it was or if he would splash safely into water or smash into bits on the rocks. There was no turning back as he was pulled onto the train with his new friend.

"I was worried you might grease the tracks there, Angelina, err, um, I mean, Zeke. I've seen bunches of punks and rum dums fall under the wheels tryin' to jump a southbound. But now you're aboard, safe and sound. This here cannonball's headin' all the way to Shakeytown so let's get you settled in. Yessir, you just boarded yourself a rattler. It doesn't look like the pussyfooter saw you nail this one-eyed bandit so let's get inside and lay low for a minute until we clear the lights."

The newest and youngest hobo eyed this man with a mix of suspicion and gratitude from the floor of the sweltering boxcar where he landed when he was pulled inside. His parents always told him to be careful around strangers and never get into a vehicle with people he didn't know, under any circumstances, unless, of course, they were Facebook friends. They never said anything about trains, however, so he was thinking that maybe this wasn't such a punishable sin and he could get by on a technicality.

Looking around the stark confines of the boxcar, he couldn't make out a single thing since they had now traveled far enough to be away from the freightyard lights and were clearly hurtling out into the dead of night. Zeke couldn't tell where the boxcar walls began or even where the open door was that led back out into the void. The movement of the train made it tough to even stand up and was making his head dizzy, although the moving night air made the temperature inside the boxcar much more tolerable.

"Um, sir," he asked in a voice that was timid but loud at the same time, in order to be heard over the wall of sound the moving train was making, "where's Shakeytown?"

"Well, son, Shakeytown is the City of Angels out in Caly-forn-eye-aye. Yessir, that's where this hot shot is a-headin'. This here is one of the many stops this rattler makes before we hit the golden coast. Isn't that where you wanted to go, kid?"

"I guess so. I'd be surprised if my parents even noticed I was gone. And besides, they want me to go to Confession with them this weekend."

"Well, that's the darndest thing I done ever heard. How old are you, kid?"

"I'm almost seven."

"Why in the name of blasted bullets and beans would parents make a kid as young as you go to Confession? When was the last time you went, squirt?"

"Never, that's the problem. I don't think that I have anything bad to confess and besides, I thought maybe we were Jewish or didn't have any kind of religion. My dad has a few statues of that smiling fat guy around in the yard and calls him 'Buddy' and then sits beside him like he's pretending to be him or something. I just don't know what he's doing."

"Well, that's the craziest load of cow crap I done ever heard, if you'll pardon my French. I can't blame you for hittin' the rails. Have you ever broken any of the Commandments?"

"I'm not even sure what they are. My parent's just asked me a bunch of stupid questions that really didn't make a lot of sense."

"To tell you the god lovin' truth there kid, I don't know what they are either. Anyway, that's neither here, there or anywhere else on this crazy planet for that matter so let's just get you settled in for the trip west into the night."

The man slowly walked over close enough to Zeke so he could make out his outline in the faint light from the moon and stars that filtered in through the slats of the boxcar and the open door. His eyes were beginning to adjust to the darkness and he could make out a few piles of stuff inside the train car. He wondered about a lot of things and was formulating a handful of questions but felt this might not be the best time to ask.

"My corner's over there," the old hobo said pointing in the direction the train was heading. "I like my space, 'specially if another 'bo jumps on and even more 'specially if he's covered in crumbs. That happened to me

DAVID W. GOODWIN

once last year and I had to take a special bath at a free clinic in 'Toona and even had to boil up all my clothes and such."

"Couldn't you just have brushed them off?" the six-year-old asked.

"The crumbs? Ha! Oh, I see. I thought you was makin' a joke there, kid. No, crumbs ain't pieces of food. When a 'bo talks about crumbs, he's talkin' about bugs, the kind that get in your hair and other places that we don't like to talk about. So anyway, as I was sayin', my corner is over there and that means you can choose either that one or that one. You might not be able to tell in the dark but that corner's already taken by Burrito Betty, she's my road sister, my girlfriend if you will, but kind of a boozehound if you ask me. She's a bit elevated right now on account of, uh, let's say a trade she made for a bottle of moonshine a while back and now she's out like a rum dum, if you know what I mean."

"No, not really but that's okay. Sometimes my parents take naps in the middle of the day on Sunday, even though Grandma and Grandpa don't call them up and tell them that it's their naptime. I think they're a little too old for naps anyway."

"I hear ya, sport. So, man, which corner's it gonna be?"

Zeke slowly got up onto his feet and swayed a little as he got used to the rhythm of the rocking boxcar. Once he felt steady enough, he took a quick tour by walking around in an oval, trying to figure out if there were any advantages to choosing either of the two remaining corners.

"I think I'd be more comfortable in the corner near you."

"Well, I'll be! Not too close though, okay? I guess I would have done the same thing unless someone offered me a berth on a Pullman. Since it's unlikely that's gonna happen, that corner is probably the next best thing."

Zeke went over to the corner with the old hobo who was carrying the kid's bindle stick. Right at that moment, the train's locomotive took three long pulls on its very loud whistle, which almost caused him to jump out of his shoes. It startled him so much that he started to cry, even though he tried with all his might to hold his little tears inside his eyes.

"Now now, sonny, that's just something you're gonna have to get used to. Trains blow their whistle for lots of different things but three toots means the entire train has cleared the outer edge of the yard. That's good for us because it means that one of them nasty galvanizers ain't gonna fire us off this hot shot. You're gonna hear a lot of that so you'd better get your ear bones warmed up and used to it. Did you bring yourself anythin' to sleep on?"

"No, I forgot about that part. I'll just curl up here on the floor," Zeke said as he patted a tear off his cheek that managed to escape with the bottom seam of his tee shirt.

"No need to be uncomfortable or get dirty so soon. You'll get dirty enough after a few days of ridin' the rails. Here, you can have some of my Caly-forn-eye-aye blankets," the old hobo said as he handed Zeke a stack of newspapers. "You'd be surprised how cozy you can get with a pile of these."

The man took the papers back and showed little Zeke how to arrange them for maximum coverage. "See, you're so small that it doesn't take many sections to lay out a proper bed. We should probably get some shut eye now while the train's movin' 'cuz when we get to the next stop in a few more hours, we got to have our wits about us in case the Bull's in an ornery mood and tries to kick us off."

"Thanks," the little hobo said as he tried to settle down onto the makeshift newspaper bed. "Mister, just one thing before I try to go to sleep. What's your name?"

"I'll warn you that it's gonna sound kinda funny. I can't tell you my given name but 'bos have a funny way of namin' other 'bos. It may sound kinda weird to you but my full hobo name is Captain Bix Pickles Haskell, the Human Stinkbomb."

Zeke started laughing, a little at first, but then once it got rolling, it was also riding the cannonball straight out to the coast. It quickly escalated into a full six-year-old belly laugh and then transitioned into an all out laugh riot. He was having a hard time catching his next breath and began gasping for air during his full body laughing experience. Captain Bix Pickles was used to such a reaction, perhaps not quite to this extreme, but waited quietly in the corner for the boy to calm down. Eventually, when it seemed like that wasn't going to happen, he involuntarily joined the laugh fest as the sight and sound of this little kid, so clearly amused by his hobo name, became infectious.

"Is that really what other hobos call you?" Zeke was finally able to say out loud when his giggles eventually started to run their course and begin to evaporate into the night air rushing by the two open doors of the boxcar.

"Yep, purty funny, wun't you say? I wonder how you'd feel about my friend, Corn Dog Dougie, the Underpants King? Maybe my name isn't so bad after his! My road sister's full hobo name is Burrito Betty, the Princess of Poots, and I guarantee that you'll understand her name within ten minutes of meetin' her. It's perfect! After we get a little shut-eye, I can tell you about the 'Code of the Road.' This is very important and you'll have to learn about it sooner or later. Every hobo uses a monika to hide their real name."

"I know a girl named Monica. She's in my class. Do you know her too?"

"Probably not unless she's a 'bo. Sorry, I was speakin' hobo talk, you'll get used to it. A monika's a nickname or a moniker if you've ever heard that word before. You'll hear all sortsa funny monikas when you're livin' the hobo lifestyle, like, um, let's see, um, well, like All-tests-are-negative Dewey Cookie Dough."

This started Zeke off on another laughing jag. He had never heard such a pile of funny names in his entire life. He and his friend Warren sometimes made up funny nicknames for each other but none of them were even half as funny as these. They also made up nicknames for some of their other friends and some kids they didn't like all that much, like his classmate and occasional nemesis, Nicole. Warren's the one that came up with the idea to call her "The Nicoleinator" but they never called her that to her face because she'd probably haul off and smack them. When Zeke had heard that some of the kids on his soccer team called his mom "Foxy Roxy," he wasn't all that upset but it did make him a little uncomfortable. One day, when he and Warren were playing FIFA Soccer 13 on his PlayStation, Zeke kept getting called for handballs and it would give Warren a free kick. This gave Warren the brilliant idea to start calling "handballs," "Zekeballs," and he eventually started calling him that. Their other friends must have thought the name was a little too risqué for first grade so would only use this name when they were out of the earshot of adults. However, Zekeballs couldn't even begin to rival Captain Bix Pickles, the Human Stinkbomb.

"You know, Zeke, you don't really look like no Flintstone Kid. I don't see no tattoos or nuttin'. Heck, you ain't even draggin' one of them monster skateboards around," Captain Bix said, as Zeke was trying to get comfortable on the newspapers while rocking around from the rhythmic swaying of the boxcar and steady beat of noise from all the trains moving over the tracks. "You musta gotten one heck of a strong case of railroad fever to run away from your home in this nice little town."

"I've seen the Flintstones and the Flintstone Kids before. Are you talking about Pebbles and Bamm Bamm from the old cartoon or the series about Fred, Wilma, Barney and Betty when they were kids?"

"Slow down there, peewee! I ain't talkin' about no cartoon characters here. Flintstone kids are what us older 'bos call the younger kids that seem to be ridin' the rails these days. They've usually got some strange color of hair or dirty matted long hair in these crazy clumps that look like fuzzy turds and all kindsa weird metal objects pierced through their skin. Lots of 'em got some god-awful tattoos, too. Maybe you're too young for all that nonsense. Mostly, I think they just get them a screamin' case of Jack Wanderlust and have to follow it."

"I don't have any tattoos right now but sometimes at birthday parties we get fake tattoos that we can rub on. I've seen some older kids at the high school though, that look like what you're describing."

"Yeah, there's somethin' for you to look forward to, I guess. But here's the deal, sport, we need to come up with a hobo name for you since you're a gunsel and this is your first time ridin' the rails, right?" Zeke nodded. "Usually it takes a while for a name to develop as we get to know you, and then clear out of the blue, bam, the perfect name appears. How about your parents - do they got any nicknames for you?"

"My mom calls me Little Zekie sometimes and my dad will call me Mr. Zeke or ZZ or Devil Boy."

"Okay, that ain't much to work with. If you was missin' a leg, we could work limpy or gimpy into it but you seem to have everythin' intact. If you was blind or missin' an eye, we could call you Blinky or somethin' like that. If you was a foreigner, we've got all sortsa nicknames that could become a part of your monika. Are you from another country?"

"No, we've always lived here in New Mexico."

"You thought that maybe you were Jewish? Don't ask me why 'cuz I don't know but for some reason sometimes 'bos add the monika Trombenick into the name of some Jewish 'bos."

"I said I don't know if we're Jewish. I thought we might be but then Mom kept talking about the Catholics. That was the first time I'd ever heard about that. My dad talks a lot about some of his grandparents living in Ireland a long time ago, so maybe we're Irish."

"Oh, flannel mouths! I'm a flannel mouth too, since my parents came from Ireland a long time ago. That could work! Are there any special foods that you like?"

"My two favorite foods are ice cream and ham."

"You're probably not Jewish then!" Captain Bix Pickles said chuckling. "Let's just come up with somethin' now and we can work on it over time, just so's we can leave Zeke far behind at the station. How about Flannel Freddie, the Deviled Ham?"

Zeke wasn't entirely thrilled by the name but decided to keep his opinion to himself for the time being. Taking on a new identity all of a sudden made his impulsive decision to run away from home and hop a freight train seem a little more serious. Things weren't really that bad at home but sometimes his parents seemed a bit too preoccupied with their jobs and didn't often have a lot of time and patience for having a kid around. In some ways, he liked the freedom he had. He'd come home from school and his nanny, Pamela, was always waiting for him at the front door as he got off the bus. She could be a lot of fun to be around, if she wasn't totally preoccupied with staring at her cellphone like his parents did a lot of the time. On a perfect day, Pamela would have a nice snack waiting for him, they'd hang out for a while talking about some of the pressing issues in young Zeke's six-year-old life, then he'd change into his play clothes and run off with Warren or one of his other friends in the neighborhood. He'd always try to make it home by six when his parents would usually come home from work and Pamela would leave. She always gave him a big embrace when she left and he loved to feel her strong body wrapped around him. It made him feel that she loved him and he always wished his parents would hug him like that more often.

Weekends weren't a lot different. His mom often went to her office in Albuquerque on Saturday mornings or went out to meet with clients. When she would come back home, usually around lunch time, but sometimes later, it was his dad's turn to do his thing, even though he'd already spent most of the morning working in his home office. This usually meant going into his office for three or four hours, which was also in Albuquerque about a half an hour up the highway. They almost always went out for dinner on Saturday night as a family, unless his parents had a cocktail party to go to, in which case he would have a babysitter. Sundays were usually sleep in days for Zeke's parents so he was on his own until the late morning. Occasionally he'd use this time to watch things on his computer that his parents wouldn't normally let him watch. Vacations were a lot of fun but they usually only took one or, at-the-most, two family trips a year. As the end of each trip neared, his parents would finally start seeming more like normal parents again and they'd have a lot of fun, at least until they got back home and fell back into their typical work routines.

Sure, Zeke wasn't too happy about this new Confession thing and the frequency with which he got sent to time-out, and a few other things, so he felt that taking a break from that life for a while and living as a hobo could be a lot of fun. There were only a few days left of first grade, before their long summer vacation began, so he was thinking that the timing was probably pretty good. And besides, Captain Bix Pickles Haskell seemed like a pretty good traveling companion, not to mention that he was highly entertaining and seemed to speak a foreign language.

Zeke was starting to feel a bit sleepy from the warmth of the boxcar, the rocking of the train and the fact that it was the middle of the night and he was up way past his bedtime. Captain Pickles broke the silence and asked, "Hey Flannel Freddie, one thing I should know. How strong are you?"

"I'm pretty strong. I can do three pull-ups, about ten push-ups and can lift my friend Warren off the ground."

"That's purty dang good! Actually, I was askin' if you have any money with you 'cuz it might come in handy. If you're flat busted, you know, on the nut, we're gonna have to figure out how you can get some greenbacks. Some rec riders or scenery bums that I've met over the years was so strong they stunk, if you're catchin' my drift, because they're just ridin' the rails for a thrill even though their pockets are stuffed silly with toadskins."

"Really? Toadskins? No, I just grabbed a bunch of coins out of my parent's coin jar. I don't know how much I got but we can count it up in the morning when there's enough light to see."

"Sounds like maybe you just got yourself a buncha thin ones. That might not get you too far but we'll figure it out later. Let's just prone our bodies now and rest up," the Human Stinkbomb said. "Our next stop is Gallup and there are some fuzztails there that might be tryin' to get on. We're gonna have to keep a sharp eye on things when we pull into that yard."

Captain Haskell was talking like he expected Zeke to understand what he was saying. He was feeling a bit uncomfortable asking for an explanation every time he heard a new word, which was in almost every sentence. And the truth of the matter was that since Bix Pickles seemed so comfortable with his language, he resolved to try to figure things out on his own. He wasn't sure what "thin ones" or "toadskins" meant, assumed that "proning our bodies" meant to lie down since that's what he did after he said this, but he had absolutely no idea what "fuzztails" were. Maybe he was referring to raccoons and Captain Bix was afraid of them due to a bad experience with a rabid one. He had heard all about rabid raccoons on *Wild Planet* a few weeks ago.

Within a few minutes after Bix and Zeke had proned their bodies, Bix was in a deep slumber and was making some pretty remarkable snoring sounds to prove it. Even over the clatter of the train it was noteworthy. He decided to move a little further away from him in case he turned out to be an acrobatic sleeper, like his friend Warren. Zeke learned early on from having sleepovers with him that he needed to keep a certain distance away when they were sleeping in the same bed to avoid getting conked on the head from one of Warren's wayward arms while he was acting out something from one of his highly animated dreams. Sometimes he was on the receiving end of a kick to the side. It was possible that Captain Bix Pickles was one of those kinds of sleepers.

Just when it seemed that maybe he was also going to fall asleep, he heard some movement and mumbling coming from one of the other corners of the boxcar. He had almost forgotten they had another boxcar-mate and it seemed that perhaps Burrito Betty, the Princess of Poots was coming back to life. It sounded like she was rummaging around trying to find something. Maybe she needed to get up to pee. This raised an interesting question that he hadn't yet considered.

"Hey, Stinkbomb!" the Princess of Poots yelled out into the darkness over the train noise. "Where'd you put the number ten gunboat can? I need to take a leak or hurl, I'm not sure which one, maybe both. I need the can in a hurry!"

Stinkbomb was too far off in dreamland to hear her and Zeke was worried that she might come over and start feeling around and she'd get a big surprise when she discovered a young boy riding in the boxcar with her. Maybe he should talk to her before this happened, or worse yet, before some of her bodily functions kicked in. Did hobos actually use the full names of the other hobos when they were talking to each other? Were nicknames of the full hobo nicknames acceptable? In the end, he decided to err on the side of formality.

"Hi Burrito Betty, the Princess of Poots, my name is Zeke, um, I mean Flannel Freddie, um, the Human Deviled Ice Cream Cone, or something like that, and I'm lying on some newspapers over here by Captain Bix Pickles Haskell, the Human Stinkbomb. I just hopped the train back in Belén and am riding it out to Shakeytown. Can I help you find your can?"

Betty started making what sounded like growling noises followed by some gurgling sounds as she struggled to her feet. She then produced a few deep guttural pronouncements followed immediately by the unmistakable sound of throwing up. It sounded like it was coming from the other side of the boxcar and since he didn't feel anything splatter on him, he was grateful.

"Who the hell are you, Flannel Frankie, or whatever the hell you said your name was? And when did you join us in this boxie? You sound like a gay cat!" Burrito Betty said with a lot of effort and considerable slurring after making a bunch of throat clearing sounds followed by a long, almost never-ending sequence of spitting noises.

"I sound like a what?"

"A gay cat. I said you sound like a gay cat."

"Um, I'm not sure I know what that is. I boarded the train about half an hour ago. Mr. Stinkbomb told me that I could sleep over by him and he's now fast asleep. I'm almost seven. Does that make me a gay cat?"

"Sure does. Is Stinkbomb your jocker?"

"Is he my joker? Like from a deck of cards? No, he's not my joker."

"Not your joker, your jocker, you know, your protector. Is he taking care of you? How do you know him? I've never heard him talk about having an Angelina." It seemed that Betty's voice was beginning to return to her so Zeke could now understand her a little better.

"We just met when I hopped on board but now I'm beginning to get to know him a little bit."

"So you're his road kid, huh? Well, I'll be. Old Stinkbomb has a road kid! That's a good one. In all the years I've known that 'bo, I've never known him to have himself a road kid. You've just met yourself a real, honest-to-goodness angel. He's a dyed-in-the-wool hobo, that much is for sure, but I've never thought of him as the jocker type. Let me tell you there, Frankie, Stinkie ain't no wolf, he's just the opposite and that's a good thing for you. There are a lot of wolves and hooligans out there that would love to pick up a gay cat such as you and take advantage of them. Not Captain Bix Pickles though. He's A-number-one in my book. But why did you decide to get in the world quick? I can't say as I've ever met a breshen as young as almost seven years old. I'm coming over to sit with you so we don't have to yell across this boxie."

Zeke said that was fine, although given her recent actions, he wasn't too sure how pleasant it was going to be. Burrito Betty started shuffling over in his direction but got tossed onto her butt when the train lurched sideways as it began to round a bend in the track. She managed to get back on her feet and as she got closer, he caught a serious whiff of her aroma and could make out her outline in the faint moonlight that was now coming in through the open sliding door of the boxcar as the train changed its direction slightly. He also was able to see some cliffs and mesas illuminated by the bright full moon off in the distance and wondered where they were. None of this landscape now looked familiar to him as he was mostly used to the irrigated farms, open rangelands and desert grasslands that surrounded Belén or the forests that grew on the Sandia Mountains when they went the long way through Madrid to visit his mom's favorite place, Santa Fe. Zeke was rocketing along through the night towards a place he had never been and began to feel a shiver of excitement tingle through his entire tiny body.

As Betty approached, he could see that she was dressed in what looked like a pile of tattered and filthy rags that were draped around her in a seemingly haphazard manner. Her hair looked like it had been in a blender on high speed with various bits and pieces of trash mixed in.

"Oh, there's my number ten," Betty said as she got close enough to see things in the corner that Zeke and Bix occupied. "Excuse me, kid, while I tend to some business. I'll be back quicker than you can say 'Hey 'bo!'"

Betty grabbed the can and moseyed off to one of the unoccupied corners, falling another time before disappearing into the darkness as the can clanked its way off to the side. Zeke could hear her locate the can and then relieve herself into it. He began to get a rough idea of how she had gotten her hobo nickname. After letting out a large sigh of relief, she slowly made her way back over to Zeke's corner without falling a third time.

"Hey 'bo!" Zeke yelled out as the Princess of Poots sat down next to him. Betty cackled so hard it was punctuated with several loud farts.

"Oops, excuse me, but that's a funny joke! Oh, my head. What have I done? Don't make me laugh anymore, Frankie! I don't think my head can take that right now. I might have had a bit too many adult refreshments last night, if you know what I mean."

"Like at a cocktail party?" Zeke asked.

"Yes, like at a cocktail party. How do you know about cocktail parties?" Betty asked suspiciously.

"My parents go to them sometimes on weekends. They never let me go, even though I want to. I usually stay home with a babysitter but sometimes I have a sleepover at one of my friend's houses."

"So you've got parents? Tell me again, why did you decide to get in the world quick? I don't believe you've answered my question yet. Just say it softly so my brain doesn't explode, okay?"

Zeke, in a whisper loud enough to be heard over the ambient train noise, told Betty a condensed version of his life, including some details about his busy parents and the time they spent commuting to their jobs and attending their various meetings. He also mentioned the Confession app and confided to Burrito Betty that he sometimes felt kind of lonely and thought it would be better to have parents that were around more and liked to play with him and do cool things.

"Oh, that's so sad," Burrito Betty said and began to blubber uncontrollably. When she was finally able to stop the flow of tears and sop up all the mucus with one of her sleeves, she said, "What the fuck is, um, wait, sorry, um, what the heck is a Confession app? Some sort of dessert?"

"No, it's a program they loaded onto their smartphones," Zeke explained and he could tell by her silence in the darkness, heat and aroma of the boxcar that she had absolutely no idea what he was talking about.

"Okay, forget that I asked. Anyway, I'll help Pickles look out after you. Maybe we can get you back together with your parents and they'll realize what a treasure they've let slip through their hands."

"But I don't want to go home right now. So far, this has been the most fun I've had since we went camping on Cape Cod in a hurricane last summer."

"Aw, that's so cute. Don't worry, I won't rat you out for now. You kind of remind me of my own son who I haven't seen for a long, long time. You can think of me as your temporary mommy if you want. By the way, do you have a cigarette I could bum?"

Before Zeke could answer, Burrito Betty, the Princess of Poots, seemed to lose consciousness in the blink of any eye, fell over sideways onto Captain Bix Pickles Haskell, the Human Stinkbomb, and was immediately sound asleep again. Flannel Freddie, the Deviled Ham decided to curl up in the space between these two hobos and fell asleep before he could say "Hey 'bo" for a second time.

CHAPTER 2

THE SIX-YEAR-OLD'S PARENTS were new to the whole parenting thing, since Zeke was their first and only child. Maybe if his parents hadn't been so quick to jump on the technology train, so to speak, his stint as a hobo might not have ever happened. First, they went through a big Facebook phase when he was three and all he ever heard about were wall postings and how many friends each of his parents had and who got poked by whom. Then, of course, there was Twitter, which came along when they transitioned into a major smartphone obsession a few years later. Naturally, they had to have the latest and shiniest phones and he remembered well the night the three of them stood in line with him on a kid-leash for hours while they waited at BestBuy in the dark to get their hands on the new iPhones. It was kind of like living on planet Dork, in his mind. Once they had their phones in their eager hands, of course, they had to download all the coolest apps.

The very first one they got was the "Baby Shaker." They amused themselves trying to shake their phones in such a way to get the app baby to fall asleep. The point was to get two red X's to appear on the baby's eyes and then his crying would finally stop, or not, depending upon their shaking skills. They liked to tell him as they gyrated their phones around that it was a lot easier to get the app baby to sleep than it ever was when he was an infant. They would have to sing, rub his back and get all of his favorite stuffed animals lined up just so and even this wasn't a guarantee that he would stop crying and head off to Sleepyville. It was especially hard on his parents because they both had demanding and time consuming jobs and often worked at night, too. Since his nanny left at six every night, they were usually pretty anxious for him to fall asleep after dinner.

One of their most successful nighttime strategies was to read him his all-time favorite story about the talking caboose that wanted to grow up to be a sleek, powerful engine and pull a half mile long train up over the Rockies from Denver to Salt Lake City. His parents read the story to him so many times that all three of them had every word memorized. Almost without fail, by the time they came to the last line of the story, which was "and so the railroad company gave him his final wish," the boy was fast asleep. His parents took turns reading and honestly, both grew so tired of the story and came to dread this ritual, even though it had the highest success rate. One time, his father got the idea to record himself reading the book on his iPhone and the next time, when it was his turn to read, he started the story, switched to his phone as Zeke started to drift off and then simply let the recording finish up. This worked fine for a few times until once, midway through the recording, Zeke woke up and asked a question. Getting no answer, he sat up in bed, saw his dad's empty chair and started crying when he realized he was alone and being read to by a phone. His dad never tried this trick again, especially after Zeke found his dad in his office working on some sort of PowerPoint presentation.

Their next app proved to be a really bad idea given his parent's competitive nature. They each ended up breaking their iPhones a few times, which almost made Zeke happy. It was called "HangTime" and the whole idea of it was to throw your phone up into the air and the app would measure how long it was suspended in space. They went to extraordinary lengths to set the family record, including using a water balloon slingshot launcher, which resulted in a hang time of an impressive 10.45 seconds. His dad went to register his time on the HangTime record site and was dismayed to find that the current record was a seemingly impossible 1,026.10 seconds by someone named Cody Wattigny on August 15, 2010. He figured Cody must have convinced someone who was heading into outer space to drop his phone out of their spaceship before they got out past the troposphere where there was still just barely enough gravity to pull the phone back to earth. Finding it, however, must have been a bigger challenge but apparently he succeeded and set the current HangTime record.

Once, when Zeke was having some trouble with his math homework, he asked his mom to help him with a multiplication problem. He was pretty good with addition and subtraction but wasn't quite grasping the concept of multiplication. While they were sitting at the dining room table, he read a word problem to her that he just couldn't get.

"So, if I have to ride my bike three miles from point A to point B, two miles from point B to point C and then four miles from point C back to point A and then repeat the loop three times, how many miles will I have to ride? Our teacher says that she wants to see the equation written out using a plus sign and a multiplication sign. I don't get it."

His mom went into a long explanation that was not helping Zeke at all. When the boy asked a follow up question, she repeated her unhelpful answer like she hadn't really heard anything he had said. He looked under the table and saw that as she was giving her answer, she was also texting someone on her phone.

"Mom, I need your help with this! Can you pay some attention to me for a second?"

"Oh, sorry, honey. I was just sending a quick little message to one of my partners about a client we just agreed to represent."

"I wish for once you could forget about work for a minute and help me with this problem!"

The straw that broke the camel's back was the day his parents downloaded the new Confession app marketed by the Roman Catholic Church. His parents weren't even Catholics, for God's sake. The Confession app might make sense for some people but what, really, does a six-year-old have to confess? Maybe the time he stuck his hand in his pants and fiddled around a bit but it's not like that's a huge sin or anything. His parents were having fun seeing who was the biggest sinner (his mom usually won) when his dad got the idea for Zeke to log in and see how serious his sins were by comparison. It was right after coming out of a ten minute time-out for "accidentally" knocking his pickled beets on the floor of the kitchen because, quite honestly, he couldn't even stand the smell of beets, let alone the taste and there was nothing his parents could have done to make him eat beets, not even promising to take him to the train museum in Las Cruces.

"Hey, Devil Boy!" his dad called out as he went to retrieve him from the time-out room which doubled as his mom's office, "your time in prison is over. Come here and let's do your first Confession. I'm sure you've got some sins you'd like to get off your chest and I'd guess they might involve beets."

He was instructed to sit next to his father at the kitchen table and stare at the little display on his dad's phone. He entered in the six-year-old's user information while saying aloud exactly what he was doing for the kid's benefit (like maybe he'd want to repeat the process some other time on his own). His mom came over at this point and joined in on their fun, and in this case, the word "fun" was being used rather loosely.

"So, let's put in your name," his dad began. "And we know that you're a male, right?"

"Of course I am, Dad, you know that," Zeke responded in a voice devoid of inflection. His dad often asked rhetorical questions and wouldn't continue before he answered, so he was used to just going along with him. This was also a recurring jab his dad liked to make since Zeke's hair was a little longer than most of the boys his age.

"And now your date of birth. You know your birthday, don't you?" his dad asked looking at him. He nodded and asked if his dad knew it. "Yes, I do. I was there. It was a dark and stormy night as I recall and your poor mom was in labor for what seemed like half of our married life. You were finally born at the stroke of midnight so we got to choose which day was your birthday. It could have been October 31st or November 1st. Aren't you glad we chose Halloween for your birthday?"

"Yeah, I've heard that story about a hundred times. It might have been more fun to be born in November so I wouldn't always have to have a Trick-or-Treat birthday party. But at least this way, it's easy to remember."

"I'd personally love to have my birthday be Halloween, but I hear you. But don't you really love dressing up like a devil each year?" his dad asked, looking at Zeke who nodded because, in reality, he really did like all the great devil costumes he had worn in the past. "Okay, this is going to be a tough one. What was the date of your last Confession?"

"What's a Confession?"

"Right, I guess you wouldn't really know what that is," his mom noted. "Confession is a thing that Catholics do that make them feel better about doing bad things. They can go running around all week doing mean or disrespectful things and then at the end of a week of sinning, they go talk to a priest and tell him all the bad things they've done. He makes them say a few little prayers, they promise to behave better and then they get to go on their way feeling great. It's a remarkable system, don't you think?"

"I guess so but if I do anything naughty, I get sent to time-out. If I do a Confession after I do the bad thing but before I get caught and sent to time-out, do I still have to go to time-out?"

"Good question! Now you're thinking like a good Catholic!" his dad exclaimed. "I'd say the answer is no, you'd still have to go to time-out. What do you think, dear?"

"I would agree with your father."

"Okay, then, in that case, I choose not to do the Confession."

"Ah, c'mon, Zeke! It will be fun, I promise. How about we come up with a compromise? If you agree to do this Confession, we'll agree to give you one 'get out of time-out' card? Does that sweeten the deal a little for you?" his mom asked.

"Well, I guess so. I get to chose the time though."

His parents agreed and then his dad entered into the app that his last Confession was the day he was born. After entering the rest of Zeke's user information, he gave him a password of 1031, logged in, tapped on "Examination" and then the Ten Commandments popped up. His mom followed along on her phone so she was able to laugh and be a part of their shared fun experience. As they tapped on each Commandment, a list of strange questions appeared.

"Okay, let's skip over the First Commandment since none of those questions really apply to you and go straight to the second. Let's see, here's a good one. Have you ever wished evil upon another person?" his mom asked.

"Does it count if I wanted someone to get in trouble for something mean they did to me?"

"Yes, I suppose it does if you wanted them to get into trouble. Have you ever done this, little Zekie?" his mom asked in a soft voice with a kindly smile on her face as she slowly rubbed his back.

"Well, a few weeks ago, I was standing in line to come back into the school after recess and that bratty girl Nicole stepped on the back of my shoe so that when I took a step forward, it came off. She's always doing mean stuff like that and if I tell her to stop, she just keeps doing it even more. This time, I told her that if she did it again, I was going to tell Danny that she liked him. Danny's the biggest dope in our class."

"I think that's a yes," his dad responded, looking at his wife who was nodding slowly as she checked it off on her phone.

"Honey, you shouldn't say things like that about the dopey kids," his mom said. "I think maybe Nicole likes you and that's just her six-year-old way of showing it."

"I think that she's actually already seven because she had to repeat kindergarten last year. How would you like it if some stupid girl always did things like this to you?"

"You're right, nobody would like that," his dad admitted. He continued, looking down at his phone and after mumbling to himself for a while, eventually said, "Oh, here's another good one. Number three; do you do needless work on Sunday?"

"What do you mean by 'needless'?" Zeke asked, starting to sound a tad bit exasperated and hoping this whole thing was going to end soon.

"I think what they're getting at here, honey, is do you find other things to do to keep yourself busy so that you run out of time to go to church?" his mom paraphrased. She was probably pretty used to doing this given that she was a personal injury lawyer and spent a lot of time in court interrogating plaintiffs and defendants.

"We don't ever go to church so the answer is no."

"Fair enough," his dad said. "I think we can skip over the rest of the Third Commandment. Onward to number four! I think this one might apply to you, Zeke. Do you try not to bring peace into your home life?"

"I don't understand the question. If they're asking, 'do you try to bring peace into your home life,' why don't they say it that way?"

"Because they're looking for negative answers, not the positives, so you check off the things that you've done that don't necessarily live up to the Catholic standard," his mom explained.

"Then no, I don't try not to bring peace to our home."

"That's a clever answer there, ZZ!" his dad conceded proudly. He and his wife loved to argue the subtle nuances of words and phrases amongst themselves so he was pleased to see that Zeke was continuing this tradition. When his parents argued, it was often based on the phrasing of certain questions and comments. Recently, his mom asked his dad how he liked a fancy dress that she had just bought for a banquet they were attending. He responded that it made her look zaftig, thinking it was a compliment. She disagreed, consulted her dictionary app to see if that was what he meant, and things kind of went downhill from there.

"Let me ask the question a little differently then. Do you ever try to drive your parents a bit crazy? In fact, I think this was why you just got sent to time-out. Do you think that throwing your beets on the floor might have caused some problems in our home? Maybe you could have come up with a better way to let us know that you didn't like beets," his mom suggested.

"I've told you more than a few times before that I don't like beets. I accidentally knocked them off with my elbow when I was reaching for the salt. I know you want me to eat vegetables but I hate beets. Maybe I should make a list and write down the vegetables that I like. In the meantime, here they are—corn, peas, tomatoes, asparagus, ham, scallions and broccoli, that's it."

"I'm not sure when ham became a vegetable, but nice try, Mr. Zeke," his mom responded, secretly proud of her son's cleverness. "Honey, I think you need to check that one off for him."

"I agree. However, ignoring the beet-knocking-off incident here for a moment, let's think back a few days when you were getting ready to catch the school bus. We heard it coming up the street and you knew you had less than a minute to get out the door. Do you remember the incident I'm referring to?" his dad asked with a knowing, superior sort of half smile on his face, like he had just set an inescapable trap that he knew Zeke wouldn't be able to get out of without gnawing off a limb.

"Yes, but you and Mom didn't listen when I told you that I forgot to finish my math homework. Mrs. Edelweiss never listens to any of our excuses, even though you made me go to the Apple store at the mall with you the night before to pick up your repaired phone. It wasn't my idea to drop it from Aunt Lorraine's hot air balloon last weekend, was it? By the time we got home, you made me go to bed. All I needed was ten minutes. Besides, I thought you liked driving me to school sometimes."

"We do, honey, but again, maybe you could have told us what was going on instead of hiding in the garage behind the freezer until the bus had passed. Anyway, a yes on that one," his dad reiterated.

"Zeke, have you ever been angry or resentful? Have you ever physically harmed anyone?"

"Angry or resentful? Sure, who hasn't been? I'm feeling kind of angry and resentful right now that you're making me do this. Check that one off. I'm also kind of angry that you make me wear this watch all the time. I hardly ever need to know what time it is and if I do need to know, I can always check the cellphone you got me for my last birthday. Plus, it makes my wrist itch and it's really big and heavy. What was the other question?"

"Have you ever physically harmed anyone?"

"No, never, at least not on purpose or that I know about. Does it count that I ran into Nicole during kickball a few weeks ago when I was running to first base and she was blocking the path and wouldn't get out of my way? It shouldn't, especially since she had her leg out to trip me."

"Andrew, maybe its time one of us went in and had a little talk with Mrs. Edelweiss," his mom said. "It sounds like there's some tension between Zeke and the little brat Nicole that should get resolved. I think

I remember her from the 'Miracle on Main Street Electric Light Parade' last fall. Wasn't she on the same float as you, the one with the big lit up bull whose head went up and down, Zeke?"

"Yes, but luckily I was throwing candy from the front and she was in the back pretending to clean up the bull's poop which was really just little cut up glow sticks that Jill was throwing out of a little hole from inside the bull. I was wishing it was real poop."

"You're right, dear, I think it might be a good idea to arrange a conference with Mrs. Edelweiss. Let's get back to Confession now, Zeke. This is going to be a little tricky," his dad said with a little bit of hesitation.

"Don't you dare ask him about masturbation or homosexual tendencies! Zeke, pretend I didn't just say that. Oh, we can ask this. Have you not sought to control your thoughts?" his mom asked.

"Yes, I've not sought to not control my not thoughts—not! What does it actually mean to control your thoughts, really? Thoughts are thoughts. If they're not thoughts then what are they? How can anyone control their thoughts?" Zeke asked hoping it would send his parents on a tangent that might take their attention away entirely from the Confession app. Not only was his mom a lawyer, but his dad worked as a resource planner for the Bureau of Land Management and he dealt with deep, nuanced issues involving conflict and the greater construct of crafting some sort of resolution between people that were completely polarized. Zeke felt there were pretty good odds that they'd bite on this philosophical question, chew it up and then swallow it down without so much as blinking an eye.

"Good point," his mom responded. "Here's my interpretation of this one. I think it's pretty safe to say that everyone has a dark thought from time to time. That's normal, wouldn't you agree, dear?"

"Absolutely," his dad answered. "Let's say that I was having a dark thought. Let's say that I was upset about the Lowenthal's barking dog because, quite honestly, she can be pretty annoying. Now, if I were to control this thought, I would just let it go and realize that even though their dog's barking is a bit bothersome, they probably get annoyed when I go out with my leaf blower and blow pine needles around the yard for a few hours, so it sort of evens out. However, if their dog started its infernal barking again and I wasn't able to control my thoughts about it, I might decide to jump up, grab my rope out of the garage, stomp over to the Lowenthal's yard and tell them that if they don't either shut their blasted

DAVID W. GOODWIN

dog up or lock him inside their house in a soundproof box, by God, I was going to use this rope to tie his yapping trap shut, hog tie him, toss him in a burlap bag and then drag him off to the pound!"

"Honey, maybe you should take a few breaths and calm down for a minute," his mom said slowly and softly. "In this case, your thoughts turned to action so I don't think this is quite what the question is getting at."

"Ah, yeah, you might be right. I just downloaded the Cowboy Team Roping app a few days ago and I must have gotten a little carried away there, sorry. But now, maybe, you see what I'm talking about, eh Zeke?"

Zeke nodded his head. He was used to seeing his dad get worked up like this on occasion. It was kind of funny the things that could set him off. He knew the Lowenthal's barking dog was one of those things but it could just as easily be some sort of injustice he heard about on the TV news or when he went to brush his teeth and couldn't get enough toothpaste out of the tube or if their wireless internet was responding too slowly or if a driver in front of him didn't properly use their turn signal. His mom could be like this too, he just figured that all adults had somewhere along the line forgotten how to sit back and just enjoy life without getting their undies in such a tight bundle. If he ever got upset about something, he often ended up in time-out. Why didn't the same rules apply to grown-ups?

"Zeke, are you always careful to dress modestly?" his mom asked, seemingly out of the blue.

"That's a good question, Mom. When I get invited out to a party, which isn't very often, by the way, since I'm a six-year-old kid, do I put on a dress that seems to be missing a lot of material on the upper part and also seems like maybe it shrunk up a lot on the lower part so that most of my bare legs were showing and sometimes even part of my tummy?"

"That's enough of that sassy talk, mister!" his dad responded with a chuckle and mock anger. "Just because your mother dresses like that sometimes when we're going out to a cocktail party, it doesn't mean that it's okay for you to describe her outfit that way. That's just how some grown-up women dress when they want to show off a little. Ain't nuttin' wrong wit dat."

"How would you answer that question, Mom?"

"I suppose I'd have to check that one off if I was being completely honest."

"Well, don't check it off for me. I almost always wear enough clothes to cover my body unless it's really hot out. How much more of this do I have to do? I'm getting pretty bored and want to go play outside."

"Just a few more questions. Let's skip over the seventh, although I know for a fact that you waste time at home sometimes," his dad stated.

"Duh! I'm a kid, remember? We're supposed to waste time. That's what being a kid's all about! Maybe you should try wasting some time every once in a while. It's fun!"

"How about number eight? This is one that I think everyone struggles with sometimes. Have you lied since your last Confession, Zeke?"

"Nope."

"So, you're saying that from the second you were born until right now, at this very moment, you've never told a lie?" his mom asked incredulously.

"Never. Have you?"

"From the moment I was born?"

"Yes, have you ever told a lie any time during your entire life?"

"Probably. I can't think of one off the top of my head though."

"How about during a trial when you're defending someone that you know is guilty but you convince the jury that he's innocent. Isn't that lying?"

"No, definitely not. That's one thing we're taught as lawyers. Never lie. It will almost always come back to haunt you."

"So, by not telling all of the truth, isn't that a form of lying?"

"Zeke, I think you're going to make a great lawyer someday," his dad remarked and it wasn't the first time either of his parents made this observation. "You've got a good point there. Clearly, there are shades of gray between the truth and a lie. Remember last summer when you and Warren were out in the back yard playing stickball and the ball went through the Lowenthal's garage window? They came over the next day after coming back from vacation and asked if you broke it. You said no. Don't you consider this a lie?"

"No, I answered their question honestly. I didn't break their window. Warren was the batter and he hit the ball that broke the window, if you want to know the truth."

"See, this is the same sort of thing your mother does in court."

"So is this a lie?"

"Not technically," his mom answered, "but it's not the entire truth."

"I still stick by my answer which is no." Zeke said emphatically. "If they had asked if I knew anything about how the window got broken, I would have answered differently."

"Okay. I won't check that one off. We'll skip over number nine and just go straight to the Tenth Commandment. Here's the last one I'll ask. Are you jealous of what other people have?" his mom inquired.

"Like jealous of their stuff?"

"Yeah or other things," his mom responded.

"I sometimes wish I had a brother. Even having a sister wouldn't be too bad if she wasn't too much of a dweeb or too girly or took my things without asking or ate all the ham before I got any. Is that being jealous?"

"No. I think the question is more about other stuff. Do you ever feel jealous when one of your friends has something that you don't have but you really want?"

"Not really. You and Dad pretty much get me anything I want. I would like a rope's course set up in my bedroom but I don't know anyone that has one that I'm jealous about."

"Alright, we won't check that one off," his dad said. "I think we're done. Let's submit all your answers and see what the damage is."

"Wait! You forgot the Custom List. We can make up a bunch of questions that might be a bit more relevant for a six-year-old," his mother added.

"Oh, yeah. I guess I didn't scroll down far enough. What might a few good questions be? Let's see, how about - do you ever think that maybe you're adopted?" his dad asked.

"That's a good one," his mom said as she started pecking away on her little display screen. "How would you answer that one, honey?"

"No, but sometimes I wish I had been and that my real family would come get me and not ever make me do a Confession again."

"That's funny! Do you ever make up unflattering nicknames for us?" his mom asked after she had finished entering the information from the previous question.

"Yes, definitely!"

"You do? Like what?" his dad asked a bit surprised.

"Well, not me so much as a few of my friends. Are you sure you want to know?"

"I think so. What do they call us?" his dad asked.

"Well, not you, Dad, its Mom. Some of my friends call her 'Foxy Roxy.' I didn't make it up and don't ever call her that but they think it's really funny."

"I can see that," his dad said with a laugh while giving his wife a wink. "She's pretty foxy. Alright, we'll stop torturing you and ask one last question. Do you have one that you'd like to include, Foxy Roxy?"

"Well, I was thinking of one that might have larger theological implications, one that was more in line with the whole concept behind this app. How about—do you think that Jesus loves the little children, all the children of the world, yellow and red, black and white?"

"Yellow, red, black and white? What the heck does that mean?" Zeke asked as his voice went up higher into his already high six-year-old register. "Are those different cartoon children like Smurfs or something?"

"Yeah, it's kind of an outdated racist song that I'm guessing you've never heard. Yellow kids are Asian, red kids are Native American, black kids are African or of African descent, and white kids are Caucasians, like you," his mom explained.

"What about kids from Mexico, like Antonio in my class. Does Jesus love him? He's not any of those colors. And I'm not really white for that matter."

"Okay, stupid question. Let's forget about adding another one and just submit your answers and see where it goes," his dad said while tapping away on his phone. "All right, now we're getting somewhere! Looks like this app actually works. Zeke, repeat after me—'In the name of the Father and the Son and the Holy Spirit, Father it has been three hundred and forty-seven weeks since my last Confession . . .'"

"I'm not saying any of this stupid crap!" Zeke uttered angrily.

"Zeke, honestly, where do you hear that kind of language? Certainly not around us! Please don't talk like that! Dear, just skip that part. He doesn't have to actually say all this right now. Maybe some other time. Why don't you continue on to the next step?"

His dad reluctantly did what his wife suggested, went to the next screen and reviewed all the questions that Zeke had previously answered "yes" to, hit the "next" button and said, "Zeke, here's another thing for you to say, 'My God, I am sorry for my sins . . .'"

"Dear, let's skip that part too. Clearly Zeke isn't up for this right now."

"Nope, this was your idea, not mine. I'm not going to repeat any of that stuff."

"Okay, but now it's giving a list of prayers to say in addition to the first two things that I tried to read and it says to go visit a real priest for final absolution."

"Okay, first thing tomorrow, we're going to Google the nearest Catholic church and all three of us are going over to Confession," his mom informed him. "I think there's one near that new juice bar over on Becker Avenue. Oh wait, you've got school tomorrow. We'll do it on the weekend."

"Today is Friday, Mom. I don't go to school on Saturdays, remember?" Zeke said and immediately realized that clarifying the day of the week would probably mean that they might try to drag him to a church for Confession tomorrow.

"Oops, you're right Zeke. I lose track of the days sometimes."

"Oh, to be young again and have weekends free," his dad lamented. "Honey, remember when our jobs weren't so demanding and we could actually take weekends off?"

"Seems like a long time ago. Sometime soon things will get back to normal. I've just got to wrap up this trial and you've got to get through those public meetings and then we can get back to being one big happy family."

The six-year-old soon-to-be hobo knew that he had a short window of opportunity to get out while the getting was good. That night, after his parents were sound asleep (he wore them down by requesting many successive glasses of water after staying up late watching one of his favorite *Three Stooges* episodes on Hulu), he found a long stick in his closet, pulled out a big scarf from the basket in the hallway and tiptoed into the kitchen to stock up on snacks. He stacked up the food, some spare change from the jar on the counter that he put in the toe of a sock and a change of clothes, all on top of the spread out scarf and tied it to the stick (just like he'd seen Moe, Larry and Curly do). After taking one last look around, he snuck out the back door. With that first step out into his backyard and into the still hot New Mexican summer midnight air, he was on his way to living the Confession-free life of the world's youngest hobo.

CHAPTER 3

A S THE SUN rose up over the distant horizon, filling the master bedroom of the six-year-old hobo's house in Belén with glorious summer New Mexican sunlight, his parents were sound asleep curled up with each other, just like Zeke and his new hobo pals. His parents were blissfully unaware of the most recent events that were soon to change their lives forever. At the stroke of 7:30, his mom's cellphone alarm started playing that all-too-familiar snippet of marimba music that had become the soundtrack to her life and the beginning of another day of her fast-paced, high profile profession. Today, she was meeting with her new clients who lived in the affluent and upscale community called High Desert; one of the many new planned developments that had sprung up around sprawling metropolitan Albuquerque. The husband and wife had been injured when the hot-air balloon they were in hit a high-tension wire and caught fire, causing them to fall almost twenty feet to the ground, injuring them both, but not too seriously. Roxanne had arranged to meet with them this morning at ten to discuss some of the details of their upcoming hearing. Roxanne's husband, however, had other plans for her.

He snuggled in closer behind her and began a slow, gentle massage of her shoulder with his left hand, which then seemed to migrate down her arm and predictably found its way around to her front and by front, it meant his hand found its way to her goodies. There, his hand seemed to take on a greater sense of urgency as he caressed her belly and then worked his way slowly and deliberately up to her breasts. He used his arm as leverage to pull her back into him tenderly and then began a slow rhythmic gyration of his hips, which was his not-so-subtle indication that he was in the mood for something other than more sleeping and running off to their job responsibilities.

"Honey, what do you think you're doing?" his wife asked with fake naiveté, which only served to get him more aroused as it sounded super-sexy to him. They had been together for ten years, married for eight and as with most couples, they had their own set of actions and responses that each of them fully understood. The fact that she responded this way meant that she was seriously considering his overtures.

"Oh, nothing much. I was just thinking that since I don't hear any sounds from Zeke, he must still be asleep so this might be a good time for a little wake up sex. What say ye, Your Honor?"

"Sounds delicious, but it has to be quick because I've got to be out the door by nine-thirty at the absolute latest."

"No problemo, Foxy Roxy. I've got that one covered."

Foxy Roxy then slowly rotated around out of their bed, planted both feet firmly on the rug and reached over to her nightstand where she kept her cervical cap and spermicide, took both objects out of her drawer and placed them on the top of the table. As was their ritual, her husband got out of bed and went to the bathroom to wash his hands thoroughly before he took over the responsibility for the cap's insertion. Roxanne then prepared the beige device with a reasonably sized squirt of the jelly, the sound of which meant sex and had a very pleasant connotation for both of them.

When he returned, he sat down next to his wife, took her hands in his, looked her straight in the eyes and said, "Honey, maybe we shouldn't use it this time. Maybe we should seriously consider giving Zeke a little brother or sister. You heard him last night. This might be a good time to give it a go. What do you think?"

Roxanne's jaw dropped, literally, her eyes got as big as a pandas and she inhaled a short, sharp breath. She was clearly surprised and startled by her husband's comment. "Andrew, we've had this discussion before and I'm sure we'll have it again but I don't think this is the time or place for it. You know how busy we both are and I'm not sure that we've even got enough time for one child, let alone two."

She handed Andrew the cap full of goo like it was a fancy dessert with a deadly topping and he went about his task with relish, but if he was being honest with himself, he would admit that it was mixed with a little sadness. After all, it was Roxanne who first came up with the idea a few years ago to try to have a second child. He thought she would absolutely jump on both the idea and his baby-making appendage with that suggestion. Anyway, he focused back on the cap's proper placement and was eventually satisfied that he had gotten it situated just right inside her. They got back into bed and reestablished the position that had gotten him so worked up a few minutes ago. Ever mindful of his wife's schedule,

Andrew kept the foreplay to a minimum and they made love quietly from start to finish in about ten minutes, making sure both of them were ready to face their Saturday refreshed and satisfied.

"Hmm, that was nice, honey. That's a great way to start the day and I don't think we woke Zeke up," Andrew murmured. "How about I make you some breakfast while you shower?"

"That would be great, sweetie."

They slowly parted ways and set about their tasks in that delicious post-coital haze. Andrew walked quietly down the hall towards the kitchen, past Zeke's closed bedroom door, which implied that he was still asleep. Ever since he was big enough to sleep in his own bed in his own room, he insisted on privacy and liked to sleep with the door shut. He also asked that his parents knock before they came in, which they both generally respected. His dad gave the door a quiet little rap to see if maybe Zeke was awake and reading or something. When he didn't answer, he assumed he was still asleep and continued on his way to the kitchen.

As Roxanne showered and got dressed, Andrew made a beautiful breakfast for all three of them and even went out to the garden to cut a few fresh flowers. He set the table and was just pouring the cups of coffee when his wife appeared.

"My, look who's in a great mood! No signs of life from the little man?" she asked, tossing down a big bite of fried egg and Fakin' Bacon followed by a gulp of coffee.

"Nope, I knocked but there wasn't an answer. I think he was up late watching shows on his computer again. We might want to set an actual bedtime for him because if he's left to his own devices, I think he'll often stay up later than us. I'd hate to see him sleep half the morning away."

"Yeah, you're probably right. I have the feeling that perhaps we're a bit too lenient with him on certain issues. I know when I talk to other parents about bedtimes for their kids, they're all pretty incredulous that we don't have one for little Zekie. Maybe we should rethink this policy."

"I'd hate to become a typical parent that feels it necessary to control every aspect of their kid's life because I think Zeke makes pretty good decisions for himself. Even though he's only six, he seems a lot more mature than most other kids his age. Think about his friend, Warren. Now there's a kid that I think needs a lot of rules," Andrew observed.

"Maybe we should talk more about this later. I need to go but thanks for breakfast," Roxanne said as she took the last bite. "I've got to meet

DAVID W. GOODWIN

with those folks who had the hot-air balloon accident and are suing Mr. Lawrence X. Filborn, the balloon tycoon. I hope to be back by early afternoon, if all goes well. You've got another meeting Monday night, right? Are you ready for it or do you need to go into your office when I get back?"

"I think I could get by with just making a few phone calls to touch base with some key stakeholders. I should be able to hang with you and Zeke this afternoon. We could all use some quality family time."

"Okay, that would be great. Maybe we could do that Jeep tour this afternoon that he's been talking about."

Roxanne left the kitchen, got herself ready and went roaring away in her little red Mazda Miata convertible. Andrew cleaned up in the kitchen and gave another little knock on Zeke's door. Satisfied that he was still sound asleep, he tended to his needs with a shave and shower and figured he'd use this time to make some of those phone calls. He went into his little office, grabbed his work briefcase, another cup of coffee and went out on their back deck with his cellphone.

These meetings were proving to be not only tricky but also rather contentious. The challenge was to come up with a plan that everyone could agree on *and* was a sensible approach for how the area would be managed for the foreseeable future. The meeting that he ran on Thursday night, which was the first one in a series of seven across his district, didn't go very well and, in fact, the state police needed to be called in to diffuse a really tense situation. There were well over a hundred people in attendance and each and every one of them seemed to have an axe to grind and a different idea on the way to approach it. Given the wide diversity of interests in this region of New Mexico, which covers almost ten million acres or two entire states of Massachusetts as he was fond of reminding folks, many of whom were east coast transplants like himself so they could relate pretty well to this statistic, it was no big surprise. The issues ran the gamut—from forestry to range management to wildlife habitat to recreation to fire control to land disposal to energy development to geology to water to mineral leases to archeology, just to name a few. Even within each major issue, there were sub-factions that were fighting tooth and nail for a voice and a foothold. Andrew's job this morning was to talk to some of the energy stakeholders to try to get them to build a consensus of support for the plan that he had spent the last two years of his life working on.

Sitting in the morning sunshine on their back deck, Andrew pulled out some notes from his briefcase and rummaged through them until he found the sheet with names of the various stakeholders that had been meticulously recorded from Thursday's meeting. With his yellow marker, he highlighted all the names of the energy folks that he wanted to contact. As he started punching in the numbers of the first person, he looked at his watch and realized that maybe calling them at nine forty-five on a Saturday morning might be too early and would possibly increase the chances that his call might catch them in an ornery mood. He'd give it another half hour or so. In the meantime, he decided to take the initiative to call one of the Jeep tour companies.

"Hello, Big Air Off Road Adventures. This is Chip Brockaway. How can I help you?"

"Hi Chip, my name is Andrew Wappinger. I work for the BLM. I think you attended the Rio Puerco RMP meeting a few nights ago, right? Am I thinking of the same Chip Brockaway?"

"Yep, that was me. There aren't too many other, you know, Chip Brockaway's around that I'm aware of. Say, are you calling to tell me we can't drive our ATVs on BLM land anymore? 'Cause if you do, we will raise holy hell to fight it! I'm going to get all the other off road businesses together for your next meeting so you can, you know, hear exactly what we think of your crazy ass plan."

"No, no, calm down there, Mr. Brockaway. You do what you think needs to be done, although I'd love to talk to you more about that some other time. This, however, is a business call. I'm calling to see about going on an off road adventure this afternoon with my wife and six-year-old son. I realize this is really late notice but do you have anything available?"

"Well now, that's an entirely different story. I'm sorry for, you know, comin' on so strong there. I'm still feelin' a bit riled up about your meeting Thursday night, but I feel pretty strongly about keepin' my business afloat. It's tough enough with all them, you know, fly-by-nighters that have recently purchased a fleet of yellow Jeeps and feel they can just invade my turf without knowin' jack shit about the area. Hell, I've been doin' this now for nine years and I know the backcountry like, well, the back of my country, if you hear what I'm sayin'. These interlopers—heck, if they didn't have, you know, a GPS, they'd be gettin' lost or stuck out there in the pucker brush even more than they do now, which is a lot. I have to tell ya, I ran across this guide with a Jeep-load of, you know, New Yorkers last week up at Cabezon Peak that

DAVID W. GOODWIN

thought they were in Bandelier, if you can picture that. When I told him he was about ten miles west of there, he went roarin' off without even a thank you."

"Yeah, that's kind of rude. But that's one of the reasons why we're going through this entire planning process so we can sort these kinds of issues out, maybe not to everyone's satisfaction, but we're certainly going to try. So, about a tour this afternoon, tell me what you've got available."

"Sure thing. We've got your typical, you know, three-hour tour and we've got ten or fifteen routes you can choose from out of our Albuquerque office. We've got the overnight tour and that's a blast for, you know, a family. We take care of everything from soup to nuts. We've got the archeology dig tour where you visit a bunch of ancient sites but we can't take any kids under sixteen. We've got the Jeep and bike tour if you're into that sort of thing. We can also, you know, customize anything to suit your time and budget constraints. Now, I'm assumin' your pretty familiar with the area given your job. Do you have any preferences, Andy?"

"It's Andrew. Listen, I'd love to get out into a different area since I spend so much time in the Rio Puerco district. How about a trip down south into the Sevilleta Range? We live in Belén and they're only about ten miles south of here. Maybe you could send a Jeep down this way and pick us up. Is that a possibility?"

"That's entirely do-able Andy. I could do that myself since I haven't booked anything yet for this afternoon. Give me your address and a time and I'll be there. The whole thing will cost, you know, somewheres around three ninety-nine for the three of ya. You'd be payin' for somewhere around four hours, which includes my travel time, you know, to Belén, so how abouts I come meet ya right around one? I'll have y'all back by dinnertime."

"Better make it two. My wife's working this morning and I don't expect her back until later."

After ironing out the rest of the details with Chip, Andrew realized he'd better jump on the stick and deal with some of the remaining details. He sent a text to Roxanne ("Got a surprise. Can u b back by 1:30?") and then went back into the house to see if Zeke had gotten up yet. He figured once his son heard of this plan, he would go absolutely nuts with excitement. He'd been bugging him for weeks to do something like this.

To his surprise, Zeke's bedroom door was still closed. It really wasn't like his son to sleep in so late, especially on a Saturday when he usually got up at a reasonable hour and was chomping at the bit to have a friend over or tried to drag him away from his work to do something. After filling up his mug with some fresh coffee, he figured he'd take advantage of a continued lull in Zeke's activity level and decided to get his phone calls out of the way while he had the time. As he was sliding the glass door open to the back deck, his phone made the familiar text message sound. Andrew looked down and saw that Roxanne had responded with "I'm excited! C u then."

Andrew started thinking about the upcoming meeting on Monday and tried to hash things out in his head. You would think that companies that had some sort of energy interest in the region would present a unified front and support a plan that promoted all kinds of energy development and exploration, even with the minor restrictions he spelled out. Andrew worked hard with his staff and his colleagues at the Bureau as well as folks over at the U. S. Department of Energy and the Natural Resource Conservation Service offices to come up with a plan that he thought was downright generous to all parties. He thought all the non-renewable people would band together to protect their interests while the renewable crowd would come together with their own agenda. Boy, was he wrong! He vaguely understood it when the oil and gas people didn't want to give the solar people a seat at the table, both literally and figuratively, but they also seemed to be in direct competition with the uranium people. The uranium people distrusted everyone—stakeholders, the government in any form, private landowners and especially other uranium companies. Some speakers from one company even seemed to be in competition with people from their own company. This was the kind of thing that got Andrew so frustrated that he often thought about giving it all up and starting his own white water rafting business. So much of his professional life and energy had been invested in coming up with this plan, a plan that seemed like the ultimate compromise and still it was being trashed by people at the very first meeting. He was hoping to turn this around bit by bit throughout the long and torturous upcoming public meeting process.

He thought he'd call the renewable energy proponents first and dialed the number to one of the solar stakeholders. After he identified himself and asked for Janice Mitchell, he was told, in no uncertain terms by a male sounding voice, that this was not a good time to call her. "Yeah, how about during the week when she's at work," was his angry response to Andrew.

Undaunted, as was his general approach to his profession and life in general, Andrew picked the next name on the list and had a similar reaction. The third and fourth names didn't answer but he left messages on their voicemail. Finally, by the time he reached the fifth caller, a Mr. Alan Leach, who was the president of one of the four geothermal companies in the region that were in the exploratory phase of building a steam powered turbine geothermal power plant, he was able to engage him in a rational conversation.

"I was hoping that you would support our RMP and maybe, in the process, convince not only others in the energy industry to support it but also help drum up support from the private sector for the plan. We clearly need the energy but we also need wise resource management. You probably remember one of your competitors at the meeting on Thursday, you know, that guy from Dharma Drilling? He really just managed to make those in attendance think that we had some sort of diabolical plan to run roughshod over the environment and the only reason was to benefit the oil and gas companies."

"Yeah, that's what I would have expected from him. They've got connections to an oil shale company, which is owned by Shell. Even though he claims to be a geothermal guy, his bottom line is to promote oil shale and hydrofracking. You know, Andrew, is that what you said your name was? You've got to repackage your message. You should tell everyone that BLM is gonna close down all their current leases - oil, gas, solar, wind, pretty much everything - and then when you throw a few bones their way, they'd be a lot happier. As they all see it now, they've got nothing to gain and everything to lose."

"Kind of late for that tactic. Our approach has to be transparent which is why we're holding these meetings, to give everyone a chance to review the full plan. Have you taken a look at it?"

"No, can't say I have. I don't really have a spare six hours."

"Well, yeah, it is a bit voluminous."

"Hell, I'd say. It's a freakin' encyclopedia!"

"There are a lot of issues in the Rio Puerco District that need a thorough discussion. It's a pretty complicated cast of characters and a tangled network of interests."

"You're right about that. Listen, I need to go now but I'll give your proposal some thought," Alan Leach said, but Andrew could tell by the tone of his voice that he was just blowing smoke.

He looked down at his notes and thought about calling some more people but seeing as though it was closing in on ten-thirty, figured he'd better go wake up Zeke so he could be ready in time for their awesome Jeep experience. Walking into the slightly darkened house and down the hallway, he was still surprised to see his son's door shut. After a gentle knock followed by a harder knock and still no response, he decided to go inside.

"Hey, Devil Boy! It's unlike you to sleep the day away. Wake up, buddy! I've got a surprise for you!" As he carefully moved close to the bed, he reached out into the dark where he knew the bed was and started feeling around, fully expecting to find lumpy body parts under the covers. Of course he found nothing other than rumpled sheets and blankets. He made his way to the windows, pulled open the heavy curtains and was shocked to see an empty bed, an empty room and some of Zeke's clothes scattered around on the floor next to his Batman dresser with open drawers.

"Zeke, where are you?" his dad yelled. It was unlike his son to make such a mess of his clothes and not to make his bed. Maybe he was already in the kitchen eating breakfast. Leaving Zeke's bedroom, Andrew did a quick survey of the kitchen, bathrooms, both offices, and everywhere else for that matter, including the basement and garage. Nowhere. Maybe he was out in the yard. Nothing. How could this be? Retracing his steps, he called out his son's name, more urgently this time. Going back to the garage, he saw that Zeke's shiny new little bike was still there. He ran out into the street in front of their house expecting to see him running around with some of his neighborhood friends. Still no sign of his son. He ran back inside, grabbed his phone and looked up the number of his friend, Warren.

"What the hell is Warren's last name?" he said out loud. He couldn't think clearly enough to pull it out of the air so he reviewed his recently made and dialed calls to see if he could figure it out. Finally, he located what he thought was the right number.

After a young girl's voice answered, Andrew said, "Hi, this is Zeke's dad. Can I speak to either one of your parents?"

"No one's home right now. Umm, wait, no, oh, I mean, they can't come to the phone right now. Would you like to leave a message?"

"Can you tell me if Zeke is there this morning?"

"Who's Zeke?"

DAVID W. GOODWIN

"Warren's friend, Zeke. Small kid, big smile, smart as a whip, shaggy hair. Have you seen him today?"

"Warren's not here. He went with Daddy to the hardware store."

"Okay. Listen then, please. Ask your parents to call Zeke's dad when they get home. Can you remember to do that? Please? It's really important."

"My mommy doesn't live here anymore. She went off to live with Uncle Raul." Andrew remembered Zeke telling him a while ago that Warren's mom had run off with her Zumba teacher last year, leaving his dad and two younger sisters to get on with their lives without her.

Andrew hung up the phone and true panic began to set in. Should he call his wife? Should he call 9-1-1? Should he look around the neighborhood more? It was unlike Zeke to just take off without telling anyone first. He tried to calm himself down for a minute before he took action. Maybe he's somewhere close by. Andrew decided to jump on his bike and take a quick tour around the neighborhood. He couldn't have gotten too far, could he? After circling the three or four blocks that formed their immediate neighborhood and not finding Zeke or anyone else out on the streets or in their yards for that matter, he was thinking clearly enough to realize that he had to call Roxanne and the police. Time was probably the most critical element in locating his son and he had wasted enough of it already.

After getting back to their house, he ran through the house screaming Zeke's name. Grabbing his phone off the table on the deck, he was thinking more clearly and got the idea to call Zeke's cellphone. Unfortunately, his call went to voicemail so he left a message to call home immediately. Taking a deep breath, he then tapped on his wife's name.

"Hello, this is Roxanne Wappinger. I can't answer the phone right now but if you leave your name and a brief message, I'll call you back at my next available moment. Have a glorious law-abiding day!"

"Honey, it's Andrew. Please call me back ASAP. It's an emergency!"

Before he went out for his bicycle reconnaissance mission, Andrew had been on the fence about calling the police since he was holding out hope that he would find Zeke and this entire nightmare would simply vaporize. Now, he realized that the entire nightmare was a lot closer to being reality and he couldn't put off calling 9-1-1 any longer.

"9-1-1. What's your emergency?"

"My son is missing! I can't find him anywhere!"

"Sir, what is your name and address?"

"398 Ladera Drive, in Belén. My name is Andrew Wappinger."

"What is your son's name and how old is he?"

"His name is Zeke Wappinger and he's six years old."

"And when was the last time you saw him and where?"

"Last night at our house before he went to bed, probably around eleven."

"What was he wearing, sir?"

"His soccer pajamas."

"How tall is he and how much does he weigh?"

"Um, I don't know. He's average height and weight for a six-year-old, I guess. Maybe four feet tall and forty pounds. I don't know, maybe more."

"Sir, could you please describe him in detail?"

"Sure, he's got dark brown hair that's a little long at the moment, brown eyes, he's missing a couple of baby teeth and has a cut on his elbow from a little bike mishap a few days ago."

"Okay, any other distinguishing features?"

"Nope, he's just an average kind of kid. Pretty clever with words, I'd say. He can outsmart most adults if he wants to."

"Are you at 398 Ladera Drive right now?"

"Yes, I'm waiting to get a call back from my wife."

"Is there a chance that your son is with her or at a friend's or relative's house?"

"My wife is in Albuquerque with a client right now. She's a lawyer. I just called his best friend's house and he doesn't seem to be there. I'm not sure where else he could be."

"I'm sending over an officer right now. Do you keep your doors locked, sir?"

"Usually. I'm pretty certain they were locked last night before we went to bed."

"Alright. Please stay at your house until an officer arrives. Any other information you can supply?"

"No, that's about all I know right now. Thank you."

"Good bye Mr. Wappinger. We'll do our best to find your son."

Andrew didn't know what to do at this point since sitting and waiting wasn't really in his nature. He took another lap around the yard and then took another lap inside the house yelling out his son's name. He also added a mild reprimand that if this was a little joke he was playing that it wasn't funny. Zeke had been known to hide from his parents and Pamela more than a time or two. His cellphone started vibrating in his pant's pocket and since it played Lee Price's "Woman Like You," it meant that Roxanne was calling.

"What's the big emergency, Andrew? You gotta make it quick because I'm trying to wrap this meeting up!"

"I'm afraid it's Zeke. I can't find him anywhere!"

"What do you mean? I thought he was sound asleep when we were eating breakfast! Did he disappear after that?"

"No, I don't think he was there even though his door was closed. When I finally went into his room, it was empty. His bed wasn't made, his clothes were on the floor; he simply is nowhere to be found!"

"Did you call his friends? Did you call Pamela? Did you call the police?" she asked while the tone and volume of her voice rose exponentially as the short sentences were spoken.

"Yes to Warren. No to Pamela and yes to the police. They're on their way right now."

"Holy shit! I'm on my way home. Make more calls. I'm sure he's around somewhere! Look everywhere!"

Andrew hadn't thought about calling Pamela and he wasn't sure what other friends to call. He called Pamela's number but only got her usual voicemail message and asked her to call him immediately without revealing the reason for his urgency. Suddenly, he remembered that the phone and email listing from Zeke's first grade class was on the bulletin board in their kitchen and went over to see if any of the names looked familiar. As he was scanning the list, he heard the wail of a siren coming towards their neighborhood, getting louder as it got closer to their house. Andrew couldn't believe how all three of their lives had just gotten thrown into such disarray in the blink of an eye. Wasn't it just an hour ago that he and Roxanne were snuggling in bed and life didn't seem like it could be much better and he tried to talk her into having another baby?

As the siren approached, Andrew walked out the front door to meet the police car as it pulled into their driveway. The officer got out of his squad car and met Andrew half way between the car and the front door along their rather long circular driveway. Officer Ramirez introduced himself, looked around the yard and neighborhood briefly without saying anything and then asked if he could come inside to get some additional information. Andrew noticed some of his neighbors either standing out in their front yards or looking at him through their windows from the comfort of their own homes. Having a police car in the neighborhood wasn't an unusual event but having one pull into a driveway with a clear purpose was, especially since a policeman got out and was now going inside his house.

"Have any of you seen Zeke this morning?" Andrew yelled out to his neighbors. All of them just shook their heads or ducked behind their curtains out of sight. Andrew led Officer Ramirez through the front door and guided him into the living room. He took note of the policeman's substantial outfit that consisted of various communication devices fastened to his shoulders and more than a handful of items hanging around his sizeable black leather belt, including two holstered pistols, one on either side, a billy club, a canister that he guessed was mace, a set of handcuffs, badges on his breast pocket and shoulders, a nameplate, a shirt pocket crammed with pens and a Belén Police Department hat. It was a wonder that anyone could function with all this extra weight in the intense summer heat. He must be in pretty good shape to be able to walk and move like he was padding around his bedroom in his pajamas. He also made a lot of noise when he walked and Andrew wondered how he was going to sit comfortably but this, too, didn't seem like much of a challenge for him.

Officer Ramirez asked all of the questions that the 9-1-1 operator had asked and then some more as he jotted down some notes on a pad that he pulled out of one of his many pockets. He wanted to get some of Zeke's recent photographs, see his bedroom, take a tour around the house (including the basement) and then wanted to see the entire yard and garage. When he was finally satisfied that Zeke wasn't anywhere to be found and seemed to be convinced that Andrew's concern for his missing son was genuine, he said that he wanted to go back into the house to discuss the next course of action to take.

"Standard procedure in the case of a missing child under the age of eighteen is to assess the situation and immediately file a missing child report, if appropriate. I will need to disseminate this information to all on-duty officers, other law enforcement agencies, the National Crime Information Center, and the New Mexico AMBER Alert Network. I will also coordinate the appropriate search effort. And just so you know, I'm legally obligated to file a report with the New Mexico CYFD, the Children, Youth and Families Department. They'll want to interview you and your wife and your son when we find him at some point during this process but we don't need to worry about that right now. Finally, I need to search your residence and the last known location of your child, which we just did. You should file a report with the National Center for Missing and Exploited Children so we tap into every conceivable avenue of help possible. One more thing I recommend you do is to create a Facebook page for your son and get the word out that he is missing. Do you know what Facebook is?"

"Of course. I've got over three hundred and fifty friends at the moment. I can set up a page for Zeke in a matter of minutes."

"Alright, the sooner I file this report, the sooner we can find your son. I'm going to call in the K-9 Unit immediately and we'll start tracking him as soon as possible. Sir, do you have any other questions?"

"What do you think the chances are that we'll find my boy?" Andrew asked as his entire body assumed a cringing posture and he seemed to shrink in place.

"It depends on many factors, sir. We will need a lot more information before I'll be able to answer that question. The good news is that most kids that are reported as missing usually are found within twenty-four hours and were never abducted or kidnapped in the first place. Some just wander off on their own and show up back home in a few hours. For this reason, I would like you or your wife or trusted friend or relative to always be at home so that if your son returns, phone calls can be made to everyone immediately. Here is my business card. Call any of those numbers at any time if you hear anything. In the meantime, I'm going out to my squad car to file my report and call in the K-9 Unit. Until they arrive, you should do those things we just talked about. Remember, the National Center for Missing and Exploited Children."

Andrew went into his office and opened his laptop. He did a search for their website, found it immediately and quickly scanned through it before calling the 800 number listed. Their immediate advice was to look in closets, under beds, in laundry piles, inside large appliances, the trunks of vehicles and any other place a child might crawl into. Some of these seemed rather unlikely places that Andrew would have thought to look but felt like it was necessary to leave no stone unturned before he called. He systematically went through the entire house for the third time and paid special attention to all these potential hiding places and of course, found neither hide nor hair of his son. It was time to take the next painful step and call the National Center where he gave the person that answered all the same information he gave to Officer Ramirez and sent them a photo of Zeke from his iPhone. After hanging up, he logged into his Facebook page and began the process of creating a page for his missing son when he heard another vehicle pull up to the front of the house. Walking to the large bay window in their living room, he saw that a Belén Police Department K-9 patrol car had just parked in the street in front of their house. The officer got out of the vehicle and opened the rear door to let the search and rescue dog out and it immediately peed against a cactus in the front yard as Andrew walked outside.

"Mr. Wappinger, this is K-9 Officer Cellucci and Police Dog Bullet. Mr. Wappinger is the father of our missing person, a six-year-old male Caucasian named Zeke Wappinger."

Andrew bent down to pat Bullet's head but Office Cellucci immediately pulled back on the dog's substantial harness and said that the dog was on duty and not to be played with. He was a bit taken back by the reprimand until she explained that a police dog needs to focus one hundred percent of their time on work and that playtime comes later when he wasn't on duty.

"The first few hours are critical. Bullet's a bloodhound and can follow a scent for several days but as time goes by, that scent gets harder and harder to track," Officer Cellucci explained. "With a sense of smell that is about fifty times more sensitive than humans, with these long ears, highly developed nasal passages and all that extra skin around it's mouth and neck, it can funnel up smells from around it like nothing you can even imagine. Our first step is to locate some 'scent articles' that will have your son's smell all over it. Can we go inside and get a few articles of Zeke's clothing?"

Andrew led all three of them into the house and into Zeke's empty room. Bullet started getting really excited when he entered the boy's bedroom and began sniffing all around. Andrew handed Officer Cellucci a pair of pants that were on the floor.

"Undergarments are the best since anything that has been in direct contact with your son's skin will have the most concentrated smell on it. It's best that you not contaminate it with your own scent," she explained as Andrew was about to root around in the pile of clothes on the floor. "If you could use a plastic bag on your hand and pick up a few items for me to take with us along with a few photos of your son, I would appreciate it."

Andrew disappeared to attend to these tasks and came back a few minutes later with the bag and some recent photos that he printed off his computer, while Bullet was busy continuing with his sniffing festival. Officer Ramirez had gone back to his squad car and came back with a printed report in his hand and gave it to Officer Cellucci. With two Target bags on his hands, Andrew sifted through the pile of Zeke's clothes and selected a few choice items. As he turned one of the bags inside out and transferred both clothing items into it, he noticed Zeke's cellphone near the bottom of his dirty clothes pile.

"Damn, that kid never wants to keep this phone with him. This is the kind of situation we have it for. I just called it a few minutes ago. No wonder I didn't hear it ring, it was under all these clothes. Maybe there are some recent calls he made or received that might give us some idea about where he is."

Officer Ramirez asked Andrew for the cellphone and quickly reviewed the activity logs. "The last call he made was about a week ago to 'Mom,' the last call received was three minutes ago and was from 'Dad.' His last text message was to someone named 'Wildman Warren" this past Wednesday and it says 'Want to ride our bikes to the Harvey House Museum and then get ice cream?' Apparently Wildman Warren never texted him back. It's too bad your son didn't take his phone because we'd be able to track his location down pretty easily. Would it be alright with you Mr. Wappinger if we kept this phone and have our lab do a more thorough analysis?"

"Sure, that's fine. We can never get him to take it with him. I never go anyplace without mine."

"Most six-year-old kids don't even have their own cellphones. Most aren't really responsible enough at that age for such a delicate and pricey device."

"Zeke's a pretty mature kid for six and he's usually pretty responsible. He just doesn't really seem to like to keep his new phone with him. I'm sure that will change as he gets older."

Officer Cellucci was showing signs of impatience as her dog was getting rather agitated. "I think we've got everything we need here and clearly Bullet is ready to get to work." She leaned in close to Andrew and assured him that the two of them would do everything in their power to track down his son.

Seeing her up close and looking directly into Officer Cellucci's eyes, Andrew blushed a little when he realized how attractive she was and even though she seemed to be wearing the same uniform as Officer Ramirez, she certainly seemed to fill it out much differently. It was almost as if the material was being stretched beyond its normal limit in a few obvious places. On top of all that, he thought she looked rather familiar, like maybe their paths had crossed before. "Were you at my Rio Puerco RMP meeting a few nights ago? You look very familiar to me."

"No, I wasn't there but maybe you've seen me on TV a time or two. I've got a part time job as one of the ballgirls for the Albuquerque Isotopes."

"That's it! I'm a big fan, of the baseball team, I mean," Andrew stammered. "But you do really good ballgirl stuff too, like catching and throwing. You're really good at that. And I think your uniforms are really nice too, kind of like your police uniform, which is pretty nice too, but I think I like your ballgirl uniform even better. Anyway, um, where do we go from here?"

"If you'll pardon us now, it's time to turn Bullet loose on your son's trail. It seems like he's ready to go!"

"Thank you so much and good luck!"

They walked out the house and into the front yard and watched as Officer Cellucci was being pulled along by the very excited and anxious Police Dog Bullet. Andrew and Officer Ramirez watched as Bullet and his sexy handler took off, almost at a run, down the driveway and down the street like a heat seeking missile that nothing was going to prevent from meeting up with its target. Both men stood on the front steps of Andrew's house mesmerized.

"Kind of makes you want to become a K-9 officer, doesn't it?" Officer Ramirez asked.

"Or a ballboy."

When they were able to draw their attention away from the K-9 Unit, Officer Ramirez reviewed the report with Andrew to make sure he had gotten all the details right. A little while later, Roxanne came blasting up the street and squealed the tires of her Miata while turning into the driveway behind Officer Ramirez's cruiser. She slammed it into park and ran up to where the two men were still standing.

"Any good news yet?" Roxanne asked anxiously.

"Nothing yet but the K-9 Unit just left. We'll find our little boy," Andrew said with a ton of worry in his voice.

"Have you checked his location yet on Google Earth?" Roxanne asked anxiously.

Andrew just gave her a blank look and shrugged his shoulders while shaking his head like he didn't understand the question.

"From his GPS enabled watch that we got him last year for his birthday! Remember?"

CHAPTER 4

THE ROCKING OF the train and comfort of his new, aromatic friends had finally put Zeke into a deep sleep. After all, he'd been up the entire day and most of the night. Both Bix Pickles and Burrito Betty were deep sleepers and the rhythm of their snoring combined with the rhythm of the train was relaxingly hypnotic. Maybe it was the increasing amount of light entering the boxie, maybe it was the slow, gradual deceleration of the train or maybe it was the increasing temperature inside the boxcar, but something caused all three members of the new hobo family to begin the process of coming back to consciousness from their pig pile heap in the corner of the train car.

"Must be comin' into Gallup," Captain Bix Pickles Haskell, the Human Stinkbomb observed in a quiet but coarse and raspy waking-up sort of voice. "I think we've already blasted through Grants in the middle of the night. The train barely slows down much goin' through there. Remember what I told you about the fuzztails, Flannel Freddie?"

Still mostly asleep, Zeke tried to remember why he wasn't in his nice warm cozy bed in Belén and instead was in this strange place with these strange people. It took a few moments for him to remember the events that led him here and he was eventually able to respond, "You said we should watch out for rabid raccoons, right?"

"No, I definitely said fuzztails. You know, greaseballs, bad actors, scalawags, rat crushers, bo's to watch out fer," he explained and Flannel Freddie started to get the idea.

"What can we do about them?" he asked innocently.

"Keep them out of our boxie, for starters. After the train stops, we need to work together as a team to keep our eyeballs open in all directions for fuzztails and the Cinder Dick."

"Is the Cinder Dick the same as the Bull?"

"Now you're gettin' the hang of it, kid!"

Burrito Betty, the Princess of Poots, started making a different set of groaning sounds than Zeke had heard previously, followed by some moans and ended with a massive phlegm clearing ejaculation. She rolled slightly away from their family heap and was attempting to get herself into a more upright attitude, which was eventually successful when Captain Bix facilitated her journey by using his foot to give her a firm yet gentle power assist on her buttocks region.

"Thanks, honey," Betty slurred and fell more-or-less back where she came from but this time with her arm around Bix and then tried to give him a big smooch to show her appreciation. "You're the best damned hobo I've ever met. You are my Emperor and don't you deny it because I'll knock your freakin' block off if you disagree."

"That's enough, you loo loo," Captain Bix said with a little snigger. "Did you know that we've got company? Have you been properly introduced to my new breshen, Flannel Freddie, the Deviled Ham?" he asked as he extricated himself from Betty and pulled himself up to his feet.

"Yeah, he's so sweet. We had a delightful evening after you proned out. I've always wanted another kid. Well, no, not really, I guess that's not true - no offense, Frankie. I screwed things up so bad with the one I had that I'd hate to be responsible for screwing up another. You seem like a good kid, though, and like I think I said last night, I promise that I'll take care of you like I'm your mommy. A good one though this time."

The train was decelerating now so the rocking was at a slower frequency and it marked a clear transition between being out on the open rails without any serious worries, other than tending to one's personal needs, and the pure danger of being at a train switchyard replete with its own set of challenges. As the Deviled Ham was about to discover, the hardest part of the life of the hobo wasn't riding the rails, it was being back in civilization.

The two grown up hobos took turns using the number ten gunboat can off in the far corner and encouraged Zeke to do the same once they completed their task. He tried to avoid looking in their direction to give them as much privacy as possible but the idea of using the facilities on a moving train in the company of two relative strangers made him feel a little anxious. Bix must have recognized this and encouraged him to pretend he was in his own private bathroom and that he'd have to get used to this fact of life quickly because it was the only option "short of hangin' his little joint or rump out the door and hope there was nuttin' in the way." He had to whiz really badly so was eventually able to do what he had to do. When he was done, Betty grabbed the can and dumped it out the door right before they got into the outskirts of the railroad yard in Gallup.

"This here's a hot yard so lemme tell ya what our strategy's gonna be. Poots will keep an eye peeled on this side, I'll look out the other side and I want Freddie to pull all our turkeys, balloons and bindles together close to Poots' side in case we need to make a quick getaway. If either of us say to jump, we need to go to the opposite side, throw our junk out through the door and then get the hell outta here. I'll go first and help you two out if need be. Bulls will usually be on the side closest to the station but sometimes they'll surprise you by bein' on the other side and sometimes I've seen 'em double up on both sides in which case we need to hunker down in a corner and hope they don't check our boxie. We'll go past the station but the train won't stop there, it'll just keep goin' to the freightyard. Our best hope is that we don't see nobody and can just stay on this rattler and continue on to Winslow. If another 'bo tries to flip this boxie, we'll just say there's no room unless it's one of our friends. I think Yodelin' Slim might be in the area 'cuz I saw his name-de-road and yesterday's date over on one of them barrels in the yard in Belén."

The train was slowly coming into the station area and Zeke's two new buddies were keeping a watch out in all directions. He looked for turkeys and balloons, but only seeing their various piles of belongings figured this was what Captain Pickles meant. Sometimes he and his friends called things by nicknames but this hobo language thing seemed somewhat excessive. Maybe they did it to confuse non-hobos. His parents would often use code words or expressions in front of him, thinking they were pulling a fast one, but it was usually rather obvious what they were trying to avoid saying. A few days before his birthday last year, they were driving into Albuquerque on a Sunday to "go see a man about an armadillo," as his father explained. Zeke knew it was clearly a disguised trick so that he wouldn't suspect that they were actually going to a bicycle shop to pick out his very first bike without training wheels. He knew what they were up to since they had been asking him a whole variety of bicycle-related questions for weeks. They must think that he wasn't very bright.

Zeke looked out and saw the Gallup Amtrak Station go slowly by, bathed in deep orange early morning low sunshine, while Bix and Betty were half hiding behind the boxcar door and scanning their surroundings. They must have done this before since they almost looked like mirror images of each other. This was the first time Zeke had seen them in the light of day and the stark reality of these two hobos almost made them seem like characters right out of *The Three Stooges* episode he had watched the night before, seeing as how they were dressed and the way they were moving in unison. After clearing the station, the train veered sharply to the right and was in the switchyard with five or six sets of track to the station side and a long raised platform on the other side. The platform was filled with a lot of heavy-duty machinery, like big and small forklifts, some large cranes as well as an assortment of trucks. Burrito Betty told him that this was where the train cars were loaded and unloaded. Very slowly, the brakes started their high-pitched squeal and their train came to a full stop. Once all the braking noise ended, the entire train seemed to let out what sounded like a huge sigh and the three hobos involuntarily did the same thing.

"Looks pretty good on this side, how about your side Poots?" Bix asked.

"I'd guess that our boxie might be one of the cars that's gonna get loaded," Betty responded as she assessed the activities on her side.

"Like you did last night?"

"Very funny you layabout. Listen, I offered you some hootch but since you only took a few pulls, I had to finish it off myself. Hell, they're getting closer, closer, crap, they're comin' our way with two forklifts. Let's ditch this train while we got the chance!"

Captain Bix Pickles Haskell, the Human Stinkbomb, immediately sprung into action. He quickly started grabbing some of their stuff and began heaving it through the open door while Burrito Betty, the Princess of Poots, slid their belongings over to where Bix was and he then threw everything out. He then effortlessly maneuvered himself out the door and onto the tracks below. There was another freight train parked beside them so the narrow alleyway between the two trains was pretty tight. Betty was next and Bix helped her down to the ground in the space of only a few seconds. Flannel Freddie stood in the now empty boxcar alone and only saw the tops of his friend's heads. The sound of the forklifts was getting louder and louder and he looked over his shoulder expecting to see them appear in the other door.

"Jump!" both the Captain and the Princess yelled in unison, so Zeke launched himself out the door without even looking. Luckily, he didn't overshoot his catchers or slam against the tank car that was only a few feet away on the next track.

"Quick, get under the train before they see us!" Bix said in a really loud whisper. They had gotten out just in time because right above them,

DAVID W. GOODWIN

they heard the forklift enter their boxcar and felt the vibration from its weight and the way it caused the entire car to jerk all around. "Pull all our stuff under and stay away from the tracks and the wheels. If the train starts movin' before we can get out, be sure to lie face down flat in the middle and don't move until I say so. We can't stay here long but since we're right up next to the loadin' platform, it's either underneath or risk runnin' into the Bull in broad daylight out in the yard!"

"Holy mother of mercy, that was close," Betty whispered, which didn't really seem necessary given all of the racket that was now surrounding them. The loading dock had become a beehive of activity with the sound of diesel engines firing up, the beeping sound of vehicles getting thrown into reverse, men yelling instructions to each other and the occasional train whistles being blown from both near and far away. They could hear and feel a bunch of the train cars being loaded and unloaded from their position underneath, and it sounded like a well-orchestrated train symphony. "We need to be extra aware when all the noise ends because that's when the train might start moving again and we don't want to grease the tracks, now do we little Frankie?"

"No, we certainly don't." The three hobos sat still for a while and eventually felt comfortable enough with their hiding spot underneath the train for Zeke to say, "Hey, can you tell me something? When do hobos ever eat? I'm getting pretty hungry since I haven't eaten in a while."

"That's a good question. I guess it depends on a few things. First is what you got packed in your bindle. You can eat that stuff whenever you want. Second is what any of your travelin' companions have that they might share 'cuz that's kind of the hobo way. We share and share alike. Third is where you are when you're hungry. Most stops have any number of places where you can get some grub if options one and two don't pan out," Bix explained.

"Oh, right! I forgot that I packed a few things before I left home last night."

"Whaddaya got, kid?" Mr. Haskell asked.

"I kind of forget. I just threw some things in my scarf once I heard my parents snoring. If you pass me my bindle, we can take a look."

There wasn't a lot of room underneath the boxcar so they had to move carefully. Betty reached into the pile of their ragged belongings, pulled out Zeke's blue scarf that was still attached to his stick and handed it to him. "I pretty much ate all my road food last night while I was drinking but I might have a few saltines left that you're welcome to."

Zeke thanked her as he carefully untied and unrolled his worldly belongings, revealing a paltry collection of odds and ends. His new world consisted of a few baby carrots, a toothbrush, an apple, a pair of Bart Simpson underwear, a light sweater, a pack of gum, one pair of socks, a mini flashlight, a few apricot fruit roll-up and $2.38 in coins.

"That's an interestin' collection of goodies, Freddie. I expected to see more cookies and candies and less fruit and veggies," Bix observed.

"My parents hardly ever buy cookies or candy. About the only time I can get any is either when I'm over at a friend's house who have parents that buy that sort of stuff or if I sneak out and buy it myself. They only shop at the Whole Foods in Albuquerque so I'm lucky to even get the fruit roll-ups. Sometimes I can sneak some Two-Bite Brownies into our shopping cart but I usually get caught at the check out."

"You poor little bambino. I can't believe your parents don't buy you some of the good stuff! When my kid was your age, I made sure he never ran out of Coke, cookies, Pop-Tarts and Sugar Pops. Those are the foods that he wanted so I could always use them as bribes. Don't your parents ever bribe you to do something you don't want to do by offering you some soda or sweets?" Burrito Betty asked.

"No, never, although sometimes I wish they would."

Zeke grabbed his apple and was about to take a bite when he realized that if he was going to honor the Hobo Code, perhaps he should offer some to his travel mates, especially when he saw the two of them rummaging around in their bags for their own food. Betty produced her saltines while Bix found a hunk of questionably aged cheese and a Slim Jim.

"It looks like if we combine everything we got here, it's almost a meal!" Freddie exclaimed proudly throwing the carrots and fruit roll-ups into the middle on top of his bandana along with his yet unbitten apple.

"Ain't that the truth, brother!" Bix responded, doing the same thing with his items.

"Looks like breakfast to me!" Betty added and put her packet of six saltine squares into the pile. "I've even got a bottle of water."

The three hobos ate their breakfast in silence, all the while trying to maintain hyper-vigilance to the activities that surrounded them on all four sides and above. There even seemed to be action below since the rails, ties and sharp grey gravel chunks that it all rested on also seemed to be a vibrating living thing. The cacophony of voices, machines, railcars and engines made an almost pleasing sort of music. If it all hadn't been such a stressful situation that could possibly end in the hobos getting caught by the Bull or run over by a train, Zeke probably would have been having the time of his life. Even as it was, he was pretty excited about this new escapade.

Since their collective edible odds and ends were not very substantial, their breakfast was over before his belly was completely satisfied. Zeke began to wonder how they would get their next meal if this represented the sum total of their food stash. Before he had a chance to voice this concern, however, Burrito Betty spoke up.

"As I recall, the next stop is Winslow and that's about three hours of traveling from the time this rattler starts moving again and there's no telling when that will be. Maybe we should think about stocking up on provisions for the next stage of our trip. Unless there's been a mighty big development boom in Winslow since last time I was there a few years ago, we'd probably do better here in Gallup. Besides, I've got a few friends here that I might be able to call in some favors from. We've got to make sure that our little fella here gets his vitamins. What do you say, Captain Bix, honey?"

"I'm thinkin' you might be on to somethin' Betty. Are we talkin' the usual kind of favors that you usually get?"

"Maybe, but let's not get too specific on account of the tender little ears we now got with us. Let's just say that it might be worth following up on. And I think having a gunsel with us would allow us to work a few angles we don't usually get to work."

As they were debating their next move and where they might go, a pair of heavy work boots that were connected to a pair of very dirty jeans that were connected to half of a tee shirt with half of a reflective orange vest appeared standing next to the boxcar in the space between them and the tanker car, right behind where Captain Pickles was sitting. They couldn't see the man's shoulders or head but clearly heard his voice.

"Well, what do we have here? Looks like a cozy little spot for a picnic. Not a spot that I would choose but you people must not know you're trespassing. Get up here this instant!" the man said loudly as his hardhat topped head and scruffy face now appeared before them.

There really was no other option other than to do as they were told. All of their other escape options were blocked so Pickles nodded his head to the others and said very quietly that we should do as he says.

"Damn it, Poots, I thought you was on the look out! Now we're in dutch," he said in an angry whisper.

"I didn't see him coming. It's like he appeared out of thin air."

Zeke realized the trouble they could all be in and his first thought was that they would get thrown into jail and that his parents would be notified and he would be in the longest time-out of his entire life. He immediately felt kind of sick to his stomach, like he could throw up at any moment. As the hobos quickly gathered up all of their balloons and bindles and even the turkey, as Bix seemed intent on calling his battered suitcase, the railroad guy told them to make it snappy.

"We're comin' as quickly as we can," Bix called out. Leaning over close to Burrito Betty's ear, he whispered, "You might want to consider chuckin' a dummy."

Once they were all out from under the train and standing next to the railroad worker, Zeke was a bit overcome by the excitement, fear and maybe even the mixture of his culinary intake and started to show signs of tossing his cookies. Burrito Betty, the Princess of Poots, tried to comfort him and appear as motherly as she could but Flannel Freddie chose that moment to hurl and it caused all of the contents to splash in the general direction of the worker's shoes.

"What the hell are you doin' kid?" the guy yelled out once he realized what was happening and also when he realized that he couldn't get out of the way of it's trajectory. He tried to back up but was constrained by the tanker and by Bix and Betty, who were flanking him on either side. Most of the volume splashed near his feet but the initial spew landed right on target.

With this disturbance at full throttle, Betty chose that time to "chuck a dummy," which consisted of a full on fainting spell where she crumbled in a heap, in a carefully choreographed and controlled fall, onto their pile of possessions. Captain Haskell, apparently playing his part in this performance, bent down to administer to Betty while Freddie straightened up and tried to clean himself off, unsure what strategic gain was to be made by Betty's fake fainting spell. However, it seemed to get the desired result because Railroad Ralph took pity on them.

"This is one weird little family you've got here, mister. Listen, I'm gonna send you all on your way, just do it quickly because the railroad security folks will be coming through in a few minutes to do a complete search of the entire train before it heads out. Just don't try to get back on if you know what's good for you."

"Thank you, sir. We was just about to head into town and scrounge us up some grub. We appreciate you not turnin' us in to the pussyfooter,

DAVID W. GOODWIN

I mean, railroad police. Much obliged, sir. Thanks for the heads up. You have yourself a good day now," Bix said turning on as much charm as he could while Betty slowly came back from her fake unconsciousness. "You okay, honey? You okay, son?"

The three of them gathered up their belongings and started heading down the track away from the direction of the station they had recently passed.

"Go that way," the railroad guy said pointing in the opposite direction. "Security is coming from the other way. Make it quick! There's an opening in the fence just on the other side of the tracks once you get around this other train."

"Thank you, sir," Bix repeated as they scurried down the tracks sticking to the shadows as much as possible.

It seemed like none of the other railroad workers on the loading dock saw them so they managed to get around the train and through the fence without any further detection. They followed Bix through an overgrown field strewn with litter of all types, small rusty appliances and the scattered remnants of fire pits. One fire pit was still smoldering and Zeke thought they might set up a little campsite here but Bix kept walking through the field and towards an abandoned brick warehouse. Most of its windows were missing and weeds circled it like an ineffective green security fence.

"This here is one of the most famous hobo jungles of all in this neck of the woods. Why, on any night a few years back, when the hobo nation was as thick as thieves, you could often find twenty or thirty rail riders congregatin' here for a regular luau, makin' up batches of Skinner's Delight, drinkin' up some mighty tasty WPLJ's and white puke and maybe even meet up with a few road sisters or even better yet, some bims or hoboettes in heat and eat and drink and dance and love the night away. I tell you, those were the days! Ain't much of that happenin' anymore. The man is comin' down hard on us 'bos, makin' life tougher than it already is. Feast your eyes on this place here, Flannel Freddie. You might see just an old beat up field with a few old fire pits, but this is one of the greatest places in the whole dang world, if'n you're a hobo. Ain't I right, Burrito Betty?"

"Ol' Stinkbomb is right on about that, Frankie. But what he's not saying, because he's way too modest, is that he is the top hobo, the Jungle Cat, not some glass-jawed-wandering-willie-idler-who-thinks-the-world-owes-them-a-living type. But enough of this testimonial, right now we gotta figure out where we're going, where we're staying, what we're gonna be eating and what we're doing. And we gotta make sure young Mister Deviled Ham is alright before we go dragging him off to some new destination. You got any ideas there, Mister Haskell?"

"I'm okay now that I threw up," Zeke said meekly before Bix Pickles could answer Betty's question. "I just all of a sudden got really scared because I thought maybe we'd get put into handcuffs and taken to a dungeon somewhere full of rats and only be given a plateful of grub-infested garbage once a day to eat."

"Where do you get crazy ideas like that, squirt?" Bix asked.

"I watch a lot of old shows on my computer and sometimes that's what happens when people get caught doing things they shouldn't be doing. Although maybe if I was a Catholic, I could just go to Confession and not have to get thrown into a dungeon."

"Just so's ya know, the Bull usually doesn't haul hobos off to the slammer when they catch us. They usually just give us the boot, but not always, so we need to keep our eyes open. Oh look, Yodelin' Slim, the Pride of Nowhere, was here yesterday, too. See his name and yesterday's date on that rock? We must be movin' in the same direction. Maybe we'll meet up with him. Anyway, let's go over to that buildin', get out of sight and discuss our next step."

The three hobos trudged over to the building on the other side of the hobo jungle field. Zeke tried to picture it full of thirty ragged rail riders and could almost make out in his imagination a bunch of Bix and Betty look-alikes, huddled around a fire, cooking up some sort of weird and nasty tasting food concoction and drinking a shared bottle of some sort of booze. He thought about his parents and how they hardly ever wanted to go camping, even though Zeke dropped a huge number of hints that it would be great to take off and head into the mountains for a weekend of living out in the wilderness. Warren's amended family did this sometimes and Zeke was always jealous because, from his description, it sounded like a blast. When Zeke tried to get his parents to take him camping, they usually told him they didn't have the proper equipment, but he knew what they were really saying was that they didn't have enough time.

Last year, however, he finally convinced them to go on a camping vacation to Cape Cod. He found a campground on state land and through the on-line campsite reservation system was able to see that there were a few open slots in late August, a week before he had to be back to start first grade. He convinced his dad to use his credit card to reserve a spot and then they got three airline tickets to fly from Albuquerque to Boston. His dad was pretty excited about the trip since he was from the east coast and hadn't been back to visit for years; his mom was less than excited having grown up in the urban, but privileged, confines of Los Angeles. When they eventually got to the Cape, she became even less excited when the reality of sleeping in a tent on the ground, eating food that they cooked over a campfire and battling the mosquitoes became their new reality. Zeke, however, had a great time, exploring the big and little freshwater ponds and, of course, there was the lure and uniqueness of the ocean. As a kid growing up in New Mexico, being able to hang out at the ocean was a big thing. Sadly, when Hurricane Irene came barreling through midway into the week, his mom took off for the nearest luxury hotel, while Zeke and his dad weathered the strong winds and rain for another day eventually joining his mom at the hotel in Hyannis. Their vacation was disrupted even further when the entire Cape lost power. His mom was in heaven when they ended up spending their final few days at the Boston Waterfront Hotel. Maybe the hobo life was more conducive to camping and his new pals would show him a good time.

The old building had a huge boarded up wooden door and a big brick, stone and concrete stairway and porch with enough room for the three of them to comfortably sit down with all of their worldly possessions in the fresh morning sunlight. Captain Haskell rummaged around in one of his many pockets and produced a handful of cigar butts, offering one each to Ms. Poots and Mr. Deviled Ham. Ms. Poots snatched hers up while Zeke declined.

"I'm too young to smoke," he said as Captain Haskell produced a match and lit Betty's cigar and then his own.

"You're probably right about that but I had my first coffin nail when I was about your age," Bix said with a slight hint of regret. "I'll smoke just about anythin' I can get my hands on. Kinda hooked on these pimp sticks now."

"Yeah, me too," Burrito Betty added. "That and a buncha other things."

Since this was the first time he'd actually been with these two hobos when both were awake and they didn't have to yell to be heard above the sometimes deafening railroad noises, Zeke took the opportunity to review the list of ever-growing questions and observations that had been forming in his mind during the last ten hours or so. They were far enough from the switchyard that the train noises were somewhat muted although the morning air was punctuated by the occasional loud metallic crash of something train-related. However, all three of them failed to hear the approach of another hobo until he was standing right in front of them with a crazy wild-eyed look about him.

"Well, if'n it ain't that ol' zook, Burrito Butty," the man said as he took a few steps towards them.

"Don't you dare call her a zook," Bix Pickles yelled and his voice was all business as he stood up and got between Betty and Zeke and this dangerous looking hobo. "I was hopin' we'd never see your ugly yap again."

The two men got up into each other's faces and Betty made sure Zeke was behind her, just in case things got ugly. "Nickles Von Stupidoff, what brings you here?" she asked, trying to diffuse the sudden tension.

"You know my real name, Butty, and it ain't Stupidoff. Hey, looks like you two got yourself a little gay cat. What's his monika?" Nickles asked, ignoring Betty's question.

"None of your damned business, Stupidoff," Bix snarled as he used his body to push the menacing hobo back away from the building and put more distance between him and his family. "In fact, I'm gonna ask you to ambulate the hell outta here. We was just havin' a peaceful little rest after ditchin' that rattler and don't need no bad actors like you around."

"I ain't no bad actor, you flim-flam man!"

"Listen, Stupidoff, we're not lookin' fer any trouble so I'm gonna ask you to just move on and leave us alone. Got it?"

"I'm just lookin' for a little jazz, maybe your girlfriend here will let me put the boots to her like I did back in El Paso a few years ago."

That put Captain Bix Pickles over the edge and he put a quick half-nelson on Nickles Von Stupidoff and escorted him around the corner of the building while he was screaming and calling Bix all sorts of nasty things while in his tight and inescapable grapple hold. Eventually Zeke and Betty couldn't hear him anymore as both men disappeared from their sight.

"I'm sorry you had to witness that Frankie. Nickles is definitely a bad actor, a bad man, and we try to avoid him whenever possible. He's mostly harmless but he's a layabout and a backslider so we don't ever want to associate with him. You might have already guessed this but not all hobos are good people."

"Why did he say he was looking for some jazz? Is there a hobo band that plays around here sometimes?" Zeke asked.

"No, it's not a band he was looking for," was all Betty said before Bix appeared, looking a little flushed as he smoothed out the sleeves of his rumpled jacket.

"Good riddance to that stew bum. He won't be botherin' us again, I promise," Bix said, winking at Betty.

They all settled back onto the landing at the top of the stairs and got themselves comfortable, now that Zeke was confident in Bix's ability to protect them from bad actors. He started asking about the man but Bix said it was best not to talk about him right now. Instead, Zeke changed the topic and asked some of the questions that had been building up inside his head.

"How long have you two been hobos?" Zeke asked softly after some time had passed.

Pickles and Poots exchanged glances, like they were silently negotiating who would tell their story first and maybe even how much of their story they were willing to share with Flannel Freddie. Eventually, Poots gave Pickles a little nod and he started in with his story.

"To answer your question, sonny, I've been a hobo for a purty long time, yessir. It's kinda hard to even remember a time when I wasn't one, even though I was once married and had me a really good job. I even had a kid with a girl I knew in high school but I never had a chance to be a father. Her parents just up and moved away before she graduated; I guess they was ashamed for what we had done. I never saw her again after that. Then, one day about fifteen years later when my life seemed to be about as good as it could be, the bottom just fell out on me. I lost my job, I lost my wife, I purty much lost everythin' I once owned. My friends stopped bein' my friends and I didn't even have a roof over my head anymore. Not even havin' any close family members to fall back on, I became homeless without as much as a couple of thin ones to my name, only the clothes on my back and no real destination other than to leave the place where I was once happy. That place was now just a sad reminder of my own failures."

"What happened, Captain Haskell?" Zeke asked in a voice that was beginning to tremble ever so slightly. "It sounds really sad. What did you do that caused all of those terrible things to happen?"

"Captain Haskell was what we call a Boston bum, a mouthpiece, in his former days," Burrito Betty said. "Do you mind if I fill Frankie in on the details, Bix?"

"His name's Freddie, by the way and it's fine with me. You probably know the story by heart now anyway, since you've heard it probably more than anyone else. But that means that I get to tell your story," Captain Bix responded.

"What's a Boston bum and a mouthpiece?"

"A Boston bum is a 'bo that is either from the Boston area or is kind of a know-it-all with an attitude. Captain Pickles is a little of both, but in a good way. He actually does know-it-all, or at least most of it, but he has a pretty good attitude most of the time. And to answer your other question, a mouthpiece is a lawyer in hobo talk."

"My mom is a lawyer."

"She is? Well, I'll bet she's a really good one, right?"

"I guess so. She told me last night that I'd probably make a pretty good lawyer someday because one of the Confession questions was about lying. I asked her if she ever had to lie when she was defending someone that was guilty."

"Well, isn't that innerestin'," Bix exclaimed. "Funny you should say that because that's kinda what got me into the hobo world quick."

"Yeah," Poots said, wrestling back control of the story. "You see, your new hobo father was a lawyer once back in Brookline, which is a hoity toity suburb of Boston where all the rich boobs live. He was one of 'em. Country clubs, fancy dinners, cocktail parties, expense accounts, BMWs, beautiful wife. You name it, he had it, ain't that right honey?"

"I sure did, you bale of straw! Here one day, gone the next."

"Well, that one day was the day Captain Bix was asked to be a mouthpiece for an associate of the head of the prestigious law firm that he was working for at the time. The boss's friend had been charged with fraud, embezzlement and probably a whole buncha words that I never even heard of before. According to Mr. Pickles here, he was about as guilty as the day is long. His firm's partners had fabricated a bunch of phony witnesses and evidence and when Bix found out what they were up to and how they were setting him up to take the rap, he tried to tell the truth but only succeeded in getting himself disbarred when the full weight and resources of both law firms came down on him. It also turned out that his wife was in heat and had been having an affair with his boss and Bix ended up being the fall guy instead of being made a partner, which is what he was hoping would have happened. The boss went off scot-free, his wife filed for a quickie divorce, managed to get everything in the settlement and even ended up marrying the sleazebag boss. The other law firm took on his wife's case, *pro boner*, as Bix is fond of saying, as a way of paying his firm back and poor ol' Captain Pickles here didn't even stand a mud chicken's chance in Hades for a positive outcome to that set up."

"Well, that's all over and done with. Been about twenty-five years now since they booted me out of Brookline and I say 'good riddance you suckers!'"

"And that's when you became a hobo?" Flannel Freddie asked.

"Well, not quite. Once I was out in the world, essentially homeless, I moved in with a friend of mine who lived in Arlington. Nice neighborhood but I definitely wasn't in Brookline anymore. He had been an old pal from Yale and specialized in disability law, with a primary focus on railroad accidents. Given the dense network of aging railroads and rail lines in that part of the country, as well as a high population, he kept pretty busy. He knew a lot about the railroad industry and, since I had been disbarred from practicing law in Massachusetts, I became his lead investigator. I started spending more and more time around trains researching various cases and became quite enthralled with the whole train culture, both the passenger and freight sides of things."

"So what happened?" Zeke asked, noticing that for the first time since he met Mr. Pickles, he was talking like a normal person rather than using his hobo-talk.

"There was one particular case that I was researching. It was a remittance man who had lost both of his legs while riding as a dangler and was suing the railroad company for gross negligence and wanted them to pay all his medical bills and potential lost wages. Guy didn't stand a chance on several counts. First, he was trespassing. Hell, all of us are trespassers riding illegally so we don't have a leg to stand on, if you'll pardon the pun. Second, he had never had a job in the first place so to sue for potential lost wages was a long shot at best."

"Frankie, just so you know, a remittance man is a hobo who gets money from his family to stay away from them. In this guy's case, he was such a bad apple and lowlife that even his own family couldn't stand the sight of him. Can you imagine that? I wish someone would give me some nickel notes to stay away from them!" Burrito Betty observed. "And a dangler, or a trapeze artist, as some folks call them, is someone who rides the rails underneath the boxie or the reefer or any other kind of train car. Really dangerous. Only the really stupid people do this. I guess he felt it was safer than mixing it up with other hobos."

"Anyway, one day I was down at the freightyard investigating what the conditions were for the dangler and decided, spur of the moment, to flip a boxie myself, just to see what it was like, and here I am. I guess you could say that the hobo life just sort of appealed to me and I've been doing it ever since. So that's my story."

"Do you miss your old life?" Freddie asked. "That would make a really sad movie but I'd watch it."

"Sure, in some ways I miss my old life. But, you know, the truth of the matter is that I had to work so hard for that life that I almost didn't have time to enjoy it. I hardly ever saw my wife because I was always at the office; I had to hire people to do all the things that normal people do themselves like gardening, house repair projects, shopping, you know, stuff like that. My former wife was so busy with her activities that our schedules rarely had us in the same place at the same time so it was almost like not being married anyway. When I became a hobo, all that changed. I had a change of clothes, a few possessions and all the time in the world to experience life. In that way, I don't miss my old life but figure at some point, when the time is right, I'll settle down again."

"How did you get your hobo name?" Zeke asked.

"I was wonderin' when you were gonna ask. Let's see, the 'Captain' part is easy since I'm usually the one in charge, you know, callin' the shots when a bunch of hobos gather. The 'Bix Pickles' part used to be 'Bad Pickles' 'cuz once I found a jar of pickles in a trash can and ate 'em. Not a good decision, seein' as they were bad but I just love pickles, 'specially kosher dills. Those danged things made me sick and over time, 'Captain Bad Pickles' just became 'Captain Bix Pickles.' I don't know why, to tell you the honest-to-God truth. So the 'Haskell' part just got added to sorta round out my name and in Brookline, where I used to live, I owned a house on Haskell Road."

"And the Human Stinkbomb?" Zeke asked.

"Yeah, I'm not so sure I can tell you that one right now. Let's just say Burrito Betty gave me that name a long time ago on account of a rather delicate subject that you're too young to understand. It's a compliment though and I use the name proudly."

"And what about you, Burrito Betty? Why are you a hobo?"

"I guess that's a story that I'm supposed to tell," the Captain responded. "Your new temporary hobo mother, Burrito Betty, the Princess of Poots, followed a very different route to become a hoboette. Unlike me, Ms. Poots started life on the wrong side of the tracks, so to speak, and it was almost like she was born to be a 'bo. She never knew her parents, was raised in an orphanage and when she was finally adopted at the tender young age of twelve, her new parents were lookin' for someone to help out with the family business more than they were lookin' for a daughter."

"What was the family business?" Zeke asked innocently.

"They ran a very unsophisticated dognapping ring," Betty said. "My job was to identify wealthy looking older ladies in New York City out walking their dogs in Central Park. I was really young and cute and I pretended that their dog was one that I had lost. I was told to make a big fuss over the dog, call him 'Rascal,' pretend that he recognized me and was supposed to ask the woman her name and where she lived. They almost always told me way too much information. My new parents made me stuff my pockets with raw hamburger in baggies that were slightly open and the dog would almost always go nuts with excitement for me. When the thoroughly confused dog owner saw what was happening and began telling me that she had owned the dog since it was a little puppy, my parents would come running up to us exclaiming 'Rascal!' and take the dog from her owner before she even knew what was happening. We would then run off with their dog back to our apartment and then contact the owner a few days later demanding a large ransom for their dog's return. It was really easy to find most of them in the phone book from the information I managed to get from them in the park. It worked every time except once, when we were set up by the cops. My parents were hauled off to the Big House. I made a beeline for the train station near our house in Newark because I knew that with my parents gone, I'd get hauled off back to the orphanage and that was not a place that I had any intention of going back to."

"So you hopped a train and have been riding the rails ever since?"

"Yep, pretty much. It's taken its toll on me, that's for sure. Do you have any idea how old I am?"

"You look a little older than my mom and I think she's thirty-eight so I'd guess you're about forty or forty-five."

Burrito Betty lips started quivering and she began a soft sort of whimpering cry. Zeke immediately felt like he had said the wrong thing but noted to himself that she actually seemed way older to him than his mom. Nobody said anything for a while but Bix put his arm around her and the silence became deafening, filling the space around them with a thick, heavy layer of sadness.

Bix and Betty probably hadn't thought about their old lives in years and it undoubtedly brought back some painful memories. Poots had heard some version and various details of Bix's story numerous times but it still made her feel really melancholy and gave her a deep empty feeling in her stomach. Telling her own story only added to this emptiness and Zeke imagined the same was true for Captain Haskell. Zeke wondered if this little train ordeal of his might mean that he would spend a large chunk of his life riding the rails and end up like the Human Stinkbomb and the Princess of Poots.

When Bix Pickles Haskell had been telling his story, Zeke had been watching him carefully. There was something familiar about the way he pursed his lips when he said certain words, the way that his nose crinkled when he laughed and a certain way that he used his hand to emphasize a particular point. It kind of reminded him of his father and it suddenly made him a little homesick.

"I'm kind of missing my parents," Flannel Freddie, the Deviled Ham said shattering the silence, bursting into tears which didn't really surprise either of his traveling companions. Both of them noticed that he had been starting to well up a bit while he listened to their stories and knew it was only a matter of time before his floodgates opened.

CHAPTER 5

"OH MY GOD! I completely forgot about Zeke's GPS watch!" Andrew exclaimed when Roxanne reminded him of his son's birthday present from last fall.

"I tried to track him on my phone but wasn't getting enough bars until I pulled into our neighborhood," Roxanne said. "Quick, let's go inside and do it on the computer!"

As they were about to walk into their house, Officer Ramirez received a call on his police phone. Looking down at the caller's name, he told Zeke's parents to wait a second and then said, "Hello Officer Cellucci. Do you have any news to report?" He put his device on speakerphone so all of them could listen in on the conversation.

"We tracked young Mr. Wappinger's scent down to the train tracks off of South 1ˢᵗ Street at the very end of Baca Avenue. His trail ended there. I'd say there is a one hundred percent chance that he hopped a freight train because there was no other scent trail at all after that, in all directions," Officer Cellucci reported.

"Alright, good work Officer Cellucci. The boy's parents are both here with me now and apparently had outfitted their son with a GPS tracking watch. They are about to go call up his location on their computer. Come on back to their house as soon as you can."

"On a train? Our son? This can't be! There is no way he hopped a freight train! The frigging dog's got to be wrong. Maybe he followed the wrong scent," Roxanne wailed.

"You know how fascinated he's always been with trains. He loves going to each and every train museum in the area and constantly wants to read that damned book. How many times has he dragged us down to that bridge overlooking the freightyard? If we let him, he would just stand there for hours watching the trains coming and going," Andrew noted.

"Mr. and Mrs. Wappinger, can we go inside and see what his tracking device says? Every second is critical in getting your son home safe," Officer Ramirez gently suggested.

Inside, Roxanne sat down at their desktop computer. She pulled up the website of the company that made the GPS enabled watch from her list of bookmarks. When prompted for their user name and password, she paused and looked sideways over at her husband.

"You set up this account. What user name did you use?"

"Um, that was a while ago. I'm not sure I remember. I've never had to use this account before and quite honestly, I never thought I'd have to. Why don't you try 'FindZeke'? I'm pretty sure I set it up with something like that. Uppercase F and Z," Andrew suggested sheepishly.

Roxanne typed this in and then asked what password he might have used.

"I'm sure it was something with ten thirty-one. Why don't you try one zero three one."

"Invalid user name or password," Roxanne said, reading from the login screen. "Damn it, Andrew! This could take hours. Didn't you write this information down somewhere or memorize it? This is our son's life at stake here!"

Andrew tried to defend himself but couldn't come up with any excuse other than the fact that he had just forgotten it. They tried a few other combinations of names and passwords and still came up short.

"Call this number," Roxanne said, reading from the website in a barely controlled shout, her frustration level about to blow through the roof. "Explain the situation and find out how to log into their goddamned website."

He dutifully did as he was told and was immediately shunted off to their voicemail. He angrily left a message about the emergency and gave his phone number.

"What? Voicemail? Are they fucking nuts?" Roxanne shouted. Andrew had never seen her like this before.

"Calm down, sweetie. They said they'd get back to us as soon as possible."

"That's total bullshit! The reason we went with these morons is they promised us twenty-four-seven coverage in case we ever needed their services. Well, for Christ sake, we need their services now and what do we get? A damned voicemail? I can't fucking believe this! They are going to be hearing from me once this thing is over. That is totally unacceptable! Our son is out there somewhere on a train! A train, Andrew! God only knows what's happening with him. He could be in the company of some pervert. Did you hear anyone in our house last night? I swear, someone must have broken in and abducted him. This is crazy! Did you lock the doors last night? And this morning, when our son was already being swept out of our lives on a train, you decided you had to have sex with me! Was that really necessary?"

"Okay, I know you're upset and I am too, but this is nobody's fault. Let's just put all of our energy into finding Zeke rather than playing the blame game. Don't turn your anger onto me. We need to work together here and we need to figure out where Zeke is."

"I'm sorry, I just can't believe this is happening."

Andrew's phone started playing a really loud blues guitar riff, which meant that an unknown caller was calling him.

"Hello, this is Andrew Wappinger. Who is this please?"

"Hello Mr. Wappinger. This is Veronica Schleck from the Happy Blooming Lotus Company. We just received an emergency call from you concerning a problem logging into your account with us. Can you please verify your date of birth please?"

"October 5th, 1977."

"Can you please answer the following question? What is your favorite food?"

"Lobsters."

"If you could be any animal, what would it be?"

"A dolphin."

"Which of your siblings was your parent's favorite?"

"Me, I'm an only child."

"What was the name of the person you lost your virginity to?"

"Is this really necessary? My son is missing and we need to find him immediately. Come on! I've answered all these security questions properly. Let's cut to the chase here!"

"One minute, sir. One of your answers was incorrect."

"Which one?"

"If you could be any animal, what would it be? You said a dolphin."

"Oh, right. I probably said golden eagle, right?"

"Close, sir, you said bald eagle. But I'm willing to verify your identity. How may we help you today, sir?"

"Like I said, our son is missing. He is wearing a GPS tracking watch that we bought from you a few months ago and I can't seem to login to my account. We need your help immediately! Time is of the essence!"

"Please be patient, sir. I will do everything possible to help you find your son. One second please while I pull up your account information. Are you in front of a computer?"

"Yes."

"Are you at our website?"

"Yes."

"Okay sir, please enter the user name 'LostZeke' with an uppercase L and an uppercase Z."

"Okay, we've done that."

"Alright, sir, now for the password, type 'S' in uppercase, 'o' and 'n' in lowercase and then one oh three one. Got that?"

"Yes, we're in! Thank you Ms. Schnauzer."

"That's Schleck, Ms. Veronica Schleck, sir. Is there anything else I can help you with today?"

"No, thank you."

Roxanne began navigating through their website and clicked on the button that said "Locate Person Wearing Tot Tracker GPS Enabled Watch." This launched a Google Maps application and in the space of about five seconds, the State of New Mexico appeared and then started zooming into a red balloon that appeared on the map with the letter "A" and off in the left column in bold blue letters were the words "Person Wearing Tot Tracker GPS Enabled Watch."

"No freakin' way!" Roxanne exclaimed, looking over her husband's shoulder as Officer Cellucci and Bullet came into their room. "It shows him moving at a high rate of speed towards Tucumcari, right along the railroad! I guess he really did hop a freight train!"

"Well, I'll be!" Officer Ramirez exclaimed. "I guess those things really work. I've never actually seen them used in real life, only in demonstrations. So, now that we know where your son is, let's discuss our plan of how we're going to bring him home safely and as quickly as possible. I want one of you stationed here at your faster computer where you have good internet access to report on you son's movement. I want one of you to come with me with your smartphone so we can also track your son if we have a decent cell signal, to be certain to cover all bases. Be sure you have the right login and password. I'll notify the New Mexico State Police headquarters in Santa Fe, the Tucumcari Police dispatch center and the BNSF to let them know they've got a missing child on board one of their trains. This will make sure they stop the train in Tucumcari. I think it would also be a good idea to bring Officer Cellucci and her police dog, just to play it safe. Officer Cellucci, I'll talk to the captain and make sure we've got clearance to do this."

"I'll volunteer to drive there with Officer Cellucci," Andrew let slip out without thinking it through first.

"Sorry, they travel alone, police policy for the K-9 Unit. No distractions while Bullet is on duty, remember? You'll be traveling with me if your wife is willing to be the one to stay here and track your son. This is probably the most important job right now," Officer Ramirez stated.

"To be honest, I'd rather be the one to go get Zeke, if you're willing to stay here," Roxanne said.

After some further negotiations, it was decided that Andrew would stay at home, but only after Roxanne made an unkind comment to her husband, after her introduction to the part time Albuquerque Isotope's ballgirl, about his hyper susceptibility to being led around by his manhood.

"You can be so freakin' transparent sometimes, Andrew. I can't believe you're thinking about a ballgirl at a time like this," was her parting comment to him on the topic. "Can we get on the road soon? I'll be ready to roll in a few minutes. Approximately two hundred miles. It usually takes us about three hours to get there. Can we drive faster than the speed limit?"

"Yes, are you okay with that?" Officer Ramirez asked.

"Absolutely!"

Officer Ramirez excused himself to make some calls and get clearance to leave his district. Once this was approved by his commanding officer, he called the state police to notify them of his plan and they said they would meet him at the on-ramp to I-40 east from I-25 north and convoy out to Tucumcari together. Officer Cellucci asked if she could "freshen up" inside as well before they headed north. While the ladies were going about their business, Officer Ramirez called up the BNSF office in Belén to notify the Tucumcari switchyard and railroad police what was happening and ask for their cooperation. He checked in one last time with Andrew to see what Zeke's current location was.

"About three quarters of the way between Santa Rosa and Tucumcari. At the rate of speed they're traveling, it looks like they'll be in Tucumcari within, I'd guess, about fifteen or twenty minutes," Andrew reported. Officer Ramirez concurred with his assessment.

"Perfect. Be sure to check in with me whenever you have any updated information. You've still got my card, right?"

"Yes, right here," he responded pulling it out of his shirt pocket. "Should I call the National Center for Exploited Children and withdraw my report?"

"Not until your son is safely back in custody. Just in case something unexpected happens. It's probably better if you keep in close contact with your wife since she'll be in my cruiser anyway and that way I can keep all my other lines open."

"No problem, officer. You can count on me. Roxanne, remember the login name is LostZeke and the password is Son1031. You have their website bookmarked, right?"

"Yeah, I'd like to bookmark you right now, with a baseball bat," Foxy Roxy said under her breath but clearly intending her husband to hear her. "Can we get going now?"

The foursome headed out the front door into the two squad cars. Roxanne and Officer Ramirez were going to ride in his cruiser where Mrs. Wappinger was relegated, against her will, to the back seat. The part time Isotope ballgirl settled into her K-9 cruiser where her canine passenger was already waiting for her in the caged back seat. Their sirens went on in unison, creating an eerie sort of harmony, which was made more apparent as they drove away. The Doppler effect caused Andrew's perception of the sound to remind him of the theme from the Twilight Zone, which was fitting considering the current circumstances of his life, since it had gone from sort-of-normal to bizarre to frightening in the last few heartbeats.

As the K-9 patrol car went from local back streets to the busier main road to interstate highway, Officer Cellucci started up a conversation with her best friend and almost human partner, who had once again, tracked a scent to it's logical conclusion, even though it just led to a dead end. At least it gave them an idea where the young boy might have gone. The dog knew there must be a treat waiting for him soon, in addition to the one that he received at the switchyard, so was waiting anxiously with his mouth pressed tightly against the metal screen divider. Officer Cellucci reached into her little bag of treats that she kept hanging from her massive police belt and feed the anxious dog two of them through the steel protective mesh.

"Who's the best police dog ever? Yes, it's my best buddy in the whole wide world, Mr. Bullet! I'm so proud of my little snookums wookums.

When we get back home, once we retrieve this little boy from the train, you're gonna get another special treat. Yes, I'm talking to you, sweet doggie do! You did such a good job today the way you followed his scent the entire way to the railroad. Such a good, good boy!" Officer Cellucci would never talk like this in front of her fellow officers or anyone else while on duty but used her special goofy sing-songy voice only when she was alone with her dog, despite all the K-9 officer training she had previously received that frowned heavily on this sort of behavior.

Officer Cellucci had to get to Isotopes Park by six-thirty that night for a game with the New Orleans Zephyrs. She decided to call one of the backup ballgirls, Lola, to see if she could fill in for her, just in case she wasn't able to get back in time.

As the two police cars roared north on I-25 towards Albuquerque and the I-40 intersection at close to one hundred and twenty miles per hour on a stretch of road with a seventy-five mile per hour speed limit, they came upon a lot of panicked drivers who were probably going eighty or eighty-five and were also probably certain that they were getting pulled over for speeding. Their reactions were almost all the same; a quick letting off of the accelerator, a quick tap of the brakes, a quick swerve in their lane or a quick lane change to the slower, right lane and a lot of anxious head turning and mirror checking. It was almost comical to be in a police car going this fast and see the near heart failure that it caused each and every driver on the road. As the driver of a police car going this fast and under these dangerous conditions, Daria Cellucci was one of the most confident and, in her opinion, one of the best drivers on the entire force—full time or part time. She was a good driver even before spending time at the police academy and all her extra driver training really helped to hone her skills. As much as she liked the thrill and attention of being an Albuquerque Isotopes ballgirl, she was hoping that her job with the Belén Police Department would soon be upgraded to full time when the City Council voted on the new fiscal year budget next month. If not, she would be disappointed but, just in case, she had a few other irons in the fire.

Officer Ramirez and Foxy Roxy were in the lead car and he knew not to make idle chit-chat with the mother of a missing child. Assuming she was in her own world of fear, worry and anxiety, there wasn't much that could be said at this point to make their time together any easier. If she wanted to talk, it was going to be on her initiative. However, with the rush of noise created by a vehicle doing sixteen percent of the speed of sound even with the windows closed and the occasional crackle and communication traffic on the two-way police radio, they wouldn't have been able to carry on much of a conversation anyway. Besides, he noted that Mrs. Wappinger was busy staring down at her phone most of the time. They arrived at the I-40 interchange in about fifteen minutes and picked up two state patrol cars as soon as they merged onto the interstate heading east towards Tucumcari. As they blasted through the far eastern outskirts of Albuquerque, they climbed through the beautiful forested slopes of the Sandia Mountains.

"Any new developments on your son's location?" he finally asked as he accelerated up to full speed again while the other three police cars fell into a paceline behind him.

"Looks like the train just passed the Route 129 intersection in New Kirk," she responded. "Google maps says thirty-three point six miles from there to the train station in Tucumcari. I sure the hell hope they'll be able to stop the train."

"If it will make you more comfortable, let me call the station myself to make sure all the proper lines of communication worked out. If you can look up their number, it would save me a call to dispatch."

Before Roxanne could look up the BNSF office in Tucumcari, however, her phone started playing a reggae beat and a Rasta-influenced guy started singing, "It's your husband, oh yeah, yes your husband is trying to get through, it's your husband, oh yeah, and he has got a message for you, whoa whoa whoa whoa . . ." and it startled her so much that she dropped the phone by her feet and accidentally kicked it. The song might have continued indefinitely if she hadn't been able to grab it by almost crawling under the front passenger seat where it ended up.

"Hi Andrew. Any news?"

"Still tracking Zeke eastbound. Just passed the Route 129 intersection. Where are you?"

"I've been able to follow him as well. We just got onto I-40 east and are absolutely flying," Roxanne shouted into her phone. Turning her attention to Officer Ramirez, she asked how long he expected it would take to get to Tucumcari.

"A little over an hour," he responded, anticipating her question.

"We'll be there in a little more than an hour," she told her husband. "Have you heard anything from Warren or Pamela yet? I'm wondering if either of them know anything about this or can shed any light on his disappearance."

"Nope, I've got messages in with both of them but haven't heard back yet. Wait, there's someone knocking on the front door. Let me go see who's there. Can you hold on for a few moments, honey?"

"Well, certainly. It's not like I'm going anywhere," she said testily, making Andrew feel that, for some reason, she thought their son's disappearance was all his fault.

Andrew walked to the front door and made eye contact through the full glass side panel with a rugged looking, heavily tanned man dressed to almost resemble Crocodile Dundee, only with shorts and Tevas. He quickly ruled out Halloween given the time of year until he noticed a totally tricked out and jacked up yellow Jeep parked in his driveway with a logo that said "Big Air Off Road Adventures" on the door. There was also a silhouette of a Jeep filled with party people and their arms in the air (except the driver, Andrew noted) while flying off a large rock looking as if they were riding the New Mexico Rattler roller coaster at Cliff's Amusement Park in Albuquerque, a place Zeke had been asking to go for the last year. He signaled with his finger for the man to hold on a second while he quickly returned to his wife on the phone.

"Shit, honey, I completely forgot about our Jeep trip this afternoon. The guy from the company just showed up. I'll call you back in a little while."

"Come on in," Andrew said, opening the door and waved Mr. Dundee into his spacious living room. "I'm sorry to say that we've had a bit of an emergency since we talked a few hours ago. My six-year-old son disappeared in the middle of the night and we have reason to believe that he's on a freight train at this very moment about to arrive in Tucumcari. We're going to have to cancel our trip. I completely forgot about calling to tell you with all that's happened."

"Disappeared in the middle of the night?" Chip Brockaway asked incredulously. "How the hell does something like that happen, Andy?"

"Damned if I know. Listen, I've got to get back to tracking him on my computer so please just send me a bill for your time. Sorry. Hopefully we can do this trip some other time."

"How you gonna track him on your computer?"

"He's wearing a GPS watch."

"That's cool. Can I come see it in action? I've never actually, you know, seen one of these new-fangled devices work before," Chip said with an extraordinary amount of enthusiasm.

"Well, I guess so but I don't want to keep you from conducting your business if you've got somewhere else to be," Andrew said, kind of hoping that this guy would get the hint.

"No, I expected to be doing this trip with you guys all afternoon so I've, you know, got some time. That kinda sucks, though, havin' your son hop a freight train. Isn't he kinda young for that sorta thing? I did that a few times as a teenager and it was, you know, kinda fun although it could be downright scary too."

"Listen, Chip, it's Chip right? This is stressful enough at the moment without adding your comments into the mix. My number one priority right now is to find my boy and get him home safely. The Belén Police, including the K-9 Unit and the state cops, are on their way to Tucumcari right now and my job is to make sure we know where he is. Their job is to make sure the train gets stopped and that he is taken safely into their custody. You're welcome to take a quick look if you'd like but I really need to give this my full attention."

The two men went into Andrew's office and watched while the little red balloon with the letter "A" on it slowly moved east. From the map scale, Andrew estimated that his son was now about twenty miles west of Tucumcari. Chip was absolutely mesmerized by what he was watching.

"That is so freakin' cool!" was about all he could manage in the moment but eventually was able to ask another question. "So anyone that wears one of these, you know, watches can be tracked from a computer?"

"Well, yes, I suppose. You need to buy the watch, sign up for an on-line account, pay a monthly fee, you know, that sort of thing. It's not like anyone could track my son. Just us, unless you know our login and password of course."

"No, that's not what I'm after Andy. I'm thinkin' more like, you know, puttin' a bunch on my fleet of vehicles and bein' able to see where they all are at any given time. That would really be awesome!"

"Sure, that's do-able although they have special tracking GPS units designed specifically for vehicle use. The watch is designed for personal use, like in my son's case. Listen, Chip, I don't mean to be rude but I need to be able to concentrate on this. I've got a few phone calls to make and while I share your interest in the technology, I need to get back to work here."

"Yeah, yeah, I understand. Listen, I'm sorry about your son. I hope everything works out in Tucumcari. If there's anything I can do to help, let me know. Here's my card. If you need any other off-road services, I'm

DAVID W. GOODWIN

available for that kind of work too, you know, back country search and rescue stuff."

"I think we have it under control. I'm expecting everything will be fine and Zeke will be back safely in a few hours. Sorry about this afternoon. Thanks for coming down," Andrew said, wrapping up the conversation and corralling Chip towards the front door.

"Oh, Andy, one more thing," Chip said, halfway out the door, "it's one thing if he hopped a train by himself and is riding solo but it's another thing if he's, you know, riding with some other rail riders. Some of those guys can be a bit nasty, if you know what I mean."

"I don't need to be hearing that sort of thing right now," Andrew barked while closing the door behind Mr. Brockaway. "What is it with these morons sometimes? Do they think I want to hear that sort of shit?" he muttered to himself as he walked back to his computer.

He checked Zeke's location and got back on the phone with Roxanne. In the meantime, she had found the phone number for the BNSF Yard Office and Officer Ramirez was on the phone with the supervisor there. Roxanne told Andrew that she'd call back in a few minutes.

"Hello, this is Officer Ramirez from the Belén Police Department. I'd like to speak with the yard office supervisor, if I could please."

"That would be Mr. Joel Juanes. He's kind of busy at the moment with all that's happening around here but I'll be happy to connect you with him or his voice mail," the person answering the phone said. "One moment, please."

"Joel Juanes speaking."

"Mr. Juanes, Officer Ramirez from the Belén Police Department. Just checking to make sure you got the message that one of your trains is carrying a six-year-old missing child. We're pretty certain that it's currently about twenty miles west of Tucumcari."

"Yes, affirmative. We currently have two eastbound trains between Santa Rosa and Tucumcari and have instructed both of them to stop when they get to the station here. Do you have any additional information that would help us identify which is the one that contains the missing child?"

"I believe we do. I'm with the boy's mother and she's following his location from a GPS tracking watch. Please hold a moment." Officer Ramirez turned to Roxanne and asked for the latest update on Zeke's position.

"Right at this moment, he's just passing something called 'Quay Road Bk' on the map," Roxanne said and Officer Ramirez passed this information along to Joel Juanes.

After a few moments, he said, "Okay, that would be BN 9482643. I will immediately notify the conductor, a Ms. Priscilla Barbados, who is on her first solo run since going through our conductor-training program, and make her aware of the situation. She's hauling sixty-six cars and has instructions to stop, as does BN 4826483, which will arrive ten minutes earlier and is hauling ninety-seven cars. For your peace of mind, we have also been contacted by the New Mexico State Police and our central dispatch office in Fort Worth. Additionally, the Tucumcari Police just sent down a couple of cruisers. They arrived a few moments ago. The state police out of Clovis are sending another officer. When do you expect to get here?"

"Our ETA is currently 14:39. This will put Mrs. Wappinger's mind at ease a bit. Thank you Mr. Juanes."

"You're welcome. I'd like to get both of your phone numbers so we can communicate since the train will be here before you arrive. Does the mother have any special instructions or information we should know about?"

After the two concurred, Officer Ramirez simply asked that Mrs. Wappinger's son get home safely and quickly and he gave him both of their numbers.

The four police cars, traveling towards Tucumcari at an even higher rate of speed now that traffic had thinned out, had changed their positions slightly as the two state police cars assumed the lead position, as was protocol in a situation like this. Traffic, after they cleared the Sandia Mountains, was very light, dominated mostly by single and double tractor-trailer trucks that stuck mostly to the right lane anyway so they only had to contend with a few nervous drivers every few miles. The landscape went by in a blur but if she focused off into the distance, Roxanne took note of the transition to the flat, mostly barren terrain and the stark absence of trees but did notice a lot of tumbleweed stuck into the fences lining the highway in the foreground, trying to occupy her mind with anything but worry about her son.

Meanwhile, the first train, BN 4826483, began slowing down as it hit the western outskirts of Tucumcari, population 5,363 according to the 2010 census. Given the iconic nature of Tucumcari in both song and on the silver screen as one of the quintessential "old west" towns, the classic surrounding cowboy and Indian landscapes and the fact that "tukamukaru" is a Comanche word that translates to "lie in wait for someone or something to approach," it was the perfect location for Zeke to be met by the large cadre of local authorities and returned happily ever after to his remorseful and soon-to-be repentant mother and father. Sadly, all of their efforts were going to be for naught as young Mr. Flannel Freddie, the Deviled Ham was clear across the state in Gallup, hanging out with Captain Bix Pickles, the Human Stinkbomb and Burrito Betty, the Princess of Poots.

BN 482683 arrived at the switchyard and was immediately shunted off to the farthest rail line north that paralleled North 7th Street, just in case Roxanne's locational information was off a bit in accuracy and Zeke was actually on this train. It was immediately surrounded by police and railroad workers and all ninety-seven cars were given a quick inspection which failed to produce any six-year-old boys. When Zeke's alleged train, BN 9482643, arrived ten minutes later, it was also diverted off to one of the northern rail lines next to the other train and all sixty-six cars received even more attention, especially the six that were open boxcars. After another ten minutes of searching and finding no evidence of any unexpected cargo of the human hobo variety, the state police officer in charge of the investigation consulted with Mr. Joel Juanes and asked to speak with the officer from the Belén Police Department who had the boy's mother with him.

"Officer Ramirez speaking."

"Hello Officer Ramirez, this is Lieutenant Forsmark of the New Mexico State Police out of the District 9 office in Clovis. We are presently conducting a search of the BNSF freight train believed to be carrying a six-year-old missing person named Mr. Zeke Wappinger and have not yet located said person. We have both suspect trains now in the railyard and would like to speak to the boy's mother about her tracking information."

"I'll put her on the line," Officer Ramirez said, handing his police phone through a small sliding screen that was a part of the bulletproof polycarbonate window between the front and rear of the police car. "It's Lieutenant Forsmark from the New Mexico State Police. He'd like a word with you."

"Hello, this is Roxanne Wappinger. Have you found my little Zekie?"

"Not yet, ma'am. We have both trains in custody here in Tucumcari. A preliminary search has not yet turned up your son. I've been informed that the child is wearing a GPS tracking device and that you are able to locate the device on your computer. Is this correct, ma'am?"

"Yes, I see his location right now. My map shows three railroad lines oriented in a northeast to southwest alignment. My son is right now on the middle line, right where North 6th Street ends at the railroad. He should be pretty easy to locate."

"That's excellent information Mrs. Wappinger. I will dispatch officers to that location immediately."

"Can't you tell me anything else? I'm dying here!"

"Nothing else to report yet, ma'am. We've only conducted a preliminary search so far and hoped to locate your son without having to do a car-by-car search. With this information, we will be able to concentrate on a few cars. Can you tell me where you are and how soon you will arrive on the scene?"

"We just passed a sign saying that Tucumcari is the next exit, three twenty-nine. Two miles. We should be there in less than five minutes."

"Alright then. Please come immediately to the railyard when you arrive at the station. We may need your tracking information."

The high-speed caravan was at the exit in about a minute, took I-40 Business through the center of town and then turned on a side road to get to the train station. It was hard to miss, as there were three other police cars, an ambulance, a fire truck, a *Quay County Sun* news car, several BNSF company cars and a crowd of about thirty people gathered in the parking lot. Roxanne's heart sunk when she saw this circus. Their four vehicles pulled into available spots, turned off their sirens and lights and assembled around the person she assumed was Lieutenant Forsmark, who had just come out from the train station to meet them.

"Any good news yet?" Roxanne yelled as she jogged quickly over to him.

"Mrs. Wappinger, I presume?" he asked.

"Yes. Have you found Zeke yet?"

"Not yet but if you'll come with me, we'll be able to see exactly which train car he is in."

Their entire entourage, including Officer Cellucci and her dog, as well as all the various officers, railroad employees and two members of the press, fell into formation behind Roxanne as she was led by Lieutenant Forsmark through the train station and down the tracks while looking down to follow Zeke's red balloon on her smartphone.

"It still shows him on the middle track about a hundred feet in this direction," she noted as she walked very quickly, making sure not to trip on any of the railroad tracks and ties that made fast walking rather challenging. Within five seconds, she was standing in front of an open boxcar while everyone else caught up to them, even the local news reporter and cameraman, who was busy filming the action. "This is the train car." Roxanne peered inside the boxcar and yelled out her son's name while five police officers jumped up into it, while Bullet was going nearly ballistic with excitement.

"I'm afraid it's completely empty," Lieutenant Forsmark said while standing in the open door of the boxcar. "But I did find this on the inside door handle."

"Zeke's watch!" Roxanne cried out over the loud, excited barking of Bullet.

CHAPTER 6

THE THREE HOBOS were sitting on the front steps of the abandoned building in the early morning sunlight, contemplating their next move, just outside the BNSF property boundary at the Gallup railyard as the drama with Zeke's parents on Ladera Drive in Belén had all began. At the very moment that Flannel Freddie told his two pals that he was missing his parents, his mom and dad still didn't even know that he had run away in the middle of the night. However, Zeke's sudden case of homesickness presented a few challenges for his traveling companions.

"Well, son, that kinda puts us behind the eight ball. First off, Poots and me, well, we're used to doublin' up sometimes but since you've joined our little family here, I have to say that I feel somewhat responsible for you. Now, it was bad hoodoo for us to have to ditch that rattler but I'd have to say it was good luck that we was given a free pass out of Dodge by that cinder skipper. I think Ms. Poots will agree with me that maybe havin' you with us might lead to some more good fortune."

"I agree with Captain Bix. I always agree with Captain Bix because, dammit, that hobo is always right! But if you're thinking that you want to go home, well that's a horse of a different color. Maybe pink, maybe green. Heck, Frankie, have you ever seen a pink or a green horse? I know I haven't and maybe that's all for the better because who wants to see crazy lookin' horses anyway?"

"I think what the Princess is tryin' to say, Freddie, is that we're all free range chickens right now and since we ain't really got no place that we have to be, we could purty much go wherever we want to go, do what we want to do. You catch my drift, son?"

"Yes, I think so. Are you saying that you would might consider taking me home?"

"That's what we're saying. Just as long as you're not out to hunt a wampus!" Burrito Betty said, trying to reassure Zeke.

"It doesn't have to be right now, I just know that I want to go home eventually. But I know for certain that I don't want to kill any wampus because I love animals, even the ones that I've never heard of before. Is hunting wampus something that hobos like to do?"

"No, we're not talking about killing any animals. We just don't want to go to all the effort of getting you back home and then have you change your mind at the last minute, you know, like taking us on a wild goose chase," Betty explained while trying to stifle her girlish giggles.

"Or get arrested because your parents think that maybe we've kidnapped you," Bix said looking Zeke right betweens his eyeballs and nodding his head with a tight smile on his face.

"I would tell them the truth so you wouldn't get into any trouble."

"I hear what you're sayin' but John Law might have some other ideas. Believe me, I know a lot of innocent people that are livin' in the pisshouse for ten to fifteen years," Captain Bix explained. "Listen, we don't need to be rushin' into any decisions right now. Why don't we use the day to get some grub, maybe even find ourselves a cage or munie for the night since we'd have a tough time nailin' any train in this town at the moment, and let things cool down for a while. Betty, I know you've spent a fair amount of time in Gallup. What are some places you've grabbed some chow and rolled out in around here? I don't wanna have to carry the banner all night."

Burrito Betty looked like maybe she had just started to doze off because she jerked back to an upright position when Bix pulled away as he twisted his body to look directly at her. He was supporting most of her weight since they had been sitting side by side. She made a few guttural sounds that included an odd combination of throat clearing, burping and maybe even a hiccup thrown into the mix. Zeke thought it sounded like maybe she was trying to say a few words made up entirely of consonants and he knew from first grade that every word needed at least one vowel, even if it was only the letter "y" that could go both ways. The elementary school he went to only had one first grade class, which meant that he and Warren had the same teacher. Last weekend, out of boredom, they tried to come up with words that didn't have any vowels or "y's." They tried to convince Mrs. Edelweiss a few days ago that "brrr" and "nth" were words since they were in the *Official Online Scrabble Dictionary*. She didn't buy it.

"Um, well, my go to place to get a lump in this town is a few blocks behind us at some church called 'Our Lady of Something or Other and Saint What's His Name,'" Betty said pointing backwards over her shoulder. "They run a pretty sweet soup kitchen there. There ain't no Salvies in Gallup but one of my favorite places to flop for the night on the cheap is over by that lumber yard which also happens to be right near a thrift store up on one of those streets called 'Ghetto Fabulouz.' I can get there; I just don't remember street names. My girl, Marlene, works there and she sometimes puts some clothes aside that she thinks I'd like in a special box. Bix, you and me have crashed at the lumber yard before, if I'm not getting my towns mixed up, right?"

"Yep, we did that a few years back but I'm thinkin' we might want to go upscale a bit seein' as we're travelin' with Flannel Freddie this time. I seem to remember a flophouse one of them Catholic churches run clear out towards the edge of town. All you have to do is attend one of their masses and they'll give you a dinner, a shower and a bed for the night but sometimes they want you to help out with some chores, like bein' a pearl diver in the kitchen, washin' up after everyone done finished eatin'. It's not a big deal, I don't mind washin' a few dishes and it's a small price to pay for that sort of hospitality, I'd say."

"A Catholic church?" Zeke asked with a touch of fear in his voice. "That's what got me into the hobo world quick in the first place on account of having to do a Confession on my parent's phone!"

"Now, don't worry there, son. They won't make you do a Confession, at least they didn't the last time I went there," Captain Haskell said somewhat reassuringly. "Although, one time, they tried to get me to accept Jesus Christ as my savior. Call me a Doughnut Christian or a Mission Stiff if you want, but I'd have agreed to almost anythin' durin' that time of my life. It was when I first became a rail rider and I wasn't quite as savvy back in those days. Hell, I would have accepted Muffin of Destiny or her kid sister, Doornuts Sue Piglet, as my personal savior if it meant gettin' a meal, a hosin' down and a bunk for the night."

"You've talked a lot about other hobos but I haven't seen any on this trip so far except for that guy who was just here who wanted to listen to some jazz with his boots on or something," Zeke observed. "Where are all of the rest of them?"

"That's a good question Mr. Ham," Mr. Stinkbomb said. "The good ol' days of the hobo world seem to be fast fadin' into the past although there are still a lot of us. Not like the old days, of course, but if we were all to assemble in one place at the same time, I think you'd be surprised. A lot of our brothers and sisters fly north for the summer to avoid the heat down where we are. You felt what it was like in our boxie last night.

It can get pretty hot inside one of them coffins, especially if some 'bo chaser comes along while you're in a railyard and closes the door of the car you're in. That's why we all carry one of these rail spikes with us at all times to jam in the door so we don't get locked inside and cooked like a goose. That happened to Gopher Bazoo Brains a few years ago in Winslow, the poor bum. He was such a cabbage head that he passed out on a red ball up from Mexico and the heat got 'em. You've also got your family of coast tramps and beachcombers that just travel the rails along the ocean when the weather is warmer. Some hobos will eat snowballs in the winter and travel the northern routes but that takes a special breed or a trainload of hootch or canned heat to drink so you don't notice the cold. Most hobos, seein' as they're a rather mobile bunch of bums, are snowbirds in the winter and plan their travels accordingly."

"So why are you and Burrito Betty in New Mexico in June?" Flannel Freddie asked the obvious question.

"Maybe it was our destiny to be here so we could look after you," the Princess of Poots suggested. "Maybe this is God giving me a second chance to get motherhood right, or at least to do a better job of it."

"Or maybe it's because Poots and me decided to take a trip to Shakytown from where we was a-stayin' in Hannibal for the last couple of weeks 'cuz some of my friends was already there and I heard through the hobo grapevine that they was settin' up a jungle beanery near the beach and was lookin' for some warm bodies with talent to help set it up."

"If I change my mind and decide not to go home quite yet, could I come with you?"

"Sure, if that's what you want to do but I have the feeling that your mom and dad are probably going nuts right now wondering where you are. Maybe you should try to contact them and let them know you're alright," Betty suggested.

"I left my cellphone at home. Do either of you have one that I could use?"

"You have your own cellphone?" Betty asked.

"Most kids do but I intentionally left mine at home because it's kind of like a kid can't ever just go off and be by themselves without his parents or nanny or someone always checking up on them."

"Seein' as we're hobos and all, neither of us have ever had our own phone but we'll occasionally run across some rec riders or Flintstone kids that have 'em. We was ridin' on a piggy-back on the way down here somewheres when this young bozo bull artist flips the flatty we're ridin' on the fly while it was workin' it's way up a steep grade. This kid spent almost all of his time talkin' to friends, takin' pictures, and tellin' us that he was gonna twat them or something that sounded kinda stupid and stick them on some other place that didn't make no sense to either of us. Instead of talkin' to us and bein' a good hobo, he was on this damned mini phone the whole time. We gave him the name Phoney Phil from Philadelphia."

"I think he said he was going to stick the photos on Bookieface if I remember correctly," Betty said. "If it was ten years ago, I'd suggest we could go find a pay phone somewhere and you could call your parents collect but it seems like all of 'em have disappeared. Maybe we could find someone that has a phone that would let you borrow it for a few minutes. I suppose we could go to the police station and tell them our story but I think that would get all of us into more trouble than we could imagine."

"You're right about that, Poots! We're definitely not going to report this to the police," Bix Pickles stated emphatically.

"Good, because I don't think that's a good idea either. I know that I want to go home at some point but I also know that it's not right now. Maybe I could send my parent's a text message telling them that I'm okay so they wouldn't worry and we could still travel around and have some really cool adventures."

"What's a test message?" Burrito Betty asked.

"It's when you tap out a message on your cellphone and send it to someone else's cellphone. They get it almost instantly. It's how almost everyone communicates these days, sometimes even when they're in the same room."

"Instead of talkin' face to face?" Bix asked.

"Weird, huh? It's pretty handy sometimes though. Every once in a while, I'll send my friend Warren a text message in class since he's on the other side of the room. We just both need to make sure we have our volume turned off because if Mrs. Edelweiss catches us using our phones during class, we have to write a one page report on a current event."

"What sort of thing would you write in a test message?" Betty asked.

"Oh, I might text that I saw Nicole cheating on a spelling test or that maybe his dad would take us to see the Isotopes sometime since my parent's never seem to have the time to do fun things like that."

"Hmm, sounds like you can do a lot of things on one of them phones. Phoney Phil seemed to use his as a camera and to see where he was on a map as we was movin' on the train. He showed us but I thought

DAVID W. GOODWIN

maybe he was makin' some of this stuff up. A lot of the time he was playin' some sort of game rather than talkin' to us or watchin' the world go by," Mr. Pickles said.

"Yeah, you can do all that stuff. Smartphones also have a GPS in them so you can see where you are if you have service. In fact, Warren tells me that unless you turn your location services off on your iPhone, it's possible that others can figure out where you are. So if I send any text messages to my parents, they'll be able to figure out where I was when I sent the message. One thing I could do is only send a message or a photo when we're about to leave that place otherwise they might be able to catch me."

"Whoa, slow down there, Frankie. You're using some words there that I've never even heard before!" Burrito Betty said. "You're talking a language that almost makes you sound like Phoney Phil from Philadelphia. I love saying his name!"

The sunny morning was starting to turn into a sunny, warmer midday and Captain Bix Pickles suggested that maybe this would be a good time for a nap since none of them had gotten much sleep the night before and this was as good a spot as any "to jungle up even though there weren't much of a jungle here at the moment." They all relocated to the shady side of the abandoned building where there was another large porch. It was on the opposite side of the trainyard so they were out of sight and the train noise was muted. They were now facing the elevated interstate but at least that noise was more predictable and soothing and it quickly lulled the hobo family into a deep sleep as soon as they had all gotten comfortable on their newly arranged pile of bodies, bindles, turkeys and balloons. Zeke started to feel a little guilty that he left his home and parents in the middle of the night and began feeling some sadness to be away from them but fell asleep with a deep comfort knowing that his new traveling companions were good people in their hearts and were willing to look out for him. Plus, they had agreed to eventually take him back home so what would be the harm in having a little fun first?

The deliciousness of a midday nap, where the constraints of reality are sometimes suspended for whatever time the nap eats up, had infused the minds and bodies of all three hobos. The events of the last twelve hours surely had inspired dreams in all of them; dreams that none of them probably had for a long, long time. Burrito Betty went back in time to the last time she saw her young son. He was just a wee toddler back then. In her dream, she was able to change the outcome that had resulted from her making that one tiny decision that caused her to lose him. In real life, she had been hanging out at a bar in Memphis at a time when she was a homeless person taking a short break from being a hobo when she and the boy's father were making an effort to settle down and start a better life for themselves. While she and her boyfriend were busy pounding down some shots at the bar, their son was being entertained by a waitresses off in one of the sticky corners of the seedy bar. In real life, Burrito Betty (who was also known as Tiffany when she wasn't in the hobo world) started flirting with one of the motorcycle gang members that had recently roared into the bar. He had taken the seat next to her that had been recently occupied by her boyfriend, who was too drunk to defend himself or fight the effects of gravity when the motorcycle guy tipped the stool sideways and slid him to the floor like a beanie baby. The motorcycle guy used his large boot to push his body out of the way, had another drink or two with Tiffany, threw her on the back of his hog and blasted off into the night. Tiffany was so wasted that she forgot all about her son for a few hours and when she finally sobered up enough and told her new boyfriend to take her back to the bar, the place was closed and there wasn't any sign of her son or her boyfriend.

In Betty's dream, however, these events took a different trajectory. When the motorcycle thug slid her boyfriend off his stool, Tiffany bent over to help him back up. When the gang member sat down on the now empty stool, Tiffany got off and grabbed his stool leg and with considerable effort, but with great effect, pulled the stool out from under him and watched with great delight as he made a significant thud when he, too, crashed to the barroom floor. In the melee that followed, with various motorcycle gang members, bar patrons, barroom and kitchen staffers, and one extremely beefy bouncer with a baseball bat, order was quickly restored, the motorcycle gang was sent on their way and Tiffany's life with her son was back on track to survive the next test of time and lifestyle which she never got to experience. The Princess of Poots let out a celebratory poot in the midday shade of Gallup, which no one heard unless they had been walking by within about a hundred feet. A passer-by might have also noticed the large grin on her face, too, if they had been close enough to look.

Zeke's dreams were of quite a different nature. He dreamt of railroads, of baseball, of Nicole and Warren and, naturally, of hobos. However, the dream that was the most vivid involved having two parents, dressed like his real parents but with the faces of a cleaned up and groomed Bix Pickles and Burrito Betty. They were all living together in Belén, had a lot of free time to spend together and they were always waiting for him when he came home from school. They even took him down to the trainyard to watch the trains come and go. While they were standing by the chain link fence along South 1st Street, a train pulled up and out from an open boxcar jumped his actual parents, dressed in Bix and Betty's clothes. His dad asked him if he knew anyplace where they might get a bite to eat or if he knew where the nearest hobo jungle was. In an act of pure generosity, Bix and Betty invited them back to their house on the nice side of town where they all shared a great meal.

Captain Bix Pickles Haskell's dream was of his days as a successful lawyer in Brookline. His wife at the time was very clear early on in their marriage that she wanted to have kids and she wanted to raise them in the picture-perfect Brookline style. Back then, before Bix was Bix, he simply kept putting her off, eventually hoping that her biological clock's alarm would ring before she managed to get pregnant. In his dream, she actually did get pregnant and their son came into the world as the six-year-old hobo, Flannel Freddie. Bix felt like he was the luckiest person alive, much to his career-driven surprise. He woke up from this dream, looked at Freddie sleeping next to him and had the not-so-fleeting thought that dreams were often pretty powerful things.

It was still early in the afternoon when the three hobos awoke. They began talking about venturing out into the real world of Gallup, New Mexico to see if they could rustle up some food and something cold to drink since they were completely out of everything except for half a bottle of warm water. The day had become very hot, as was typical for the middle of June, and the waves of heat coming at them from their surroundings must have felt like someone had turned the oven up a few notches. Even the shadow of the building they were curled up in couldn't protect them from the effects.

"Do you know about the little cut-through tunnel? It'll save us about a mile of walking to get to the other side of the highway," Burrito Betty said to Bix Pickles as she stood up and surveyed their immediate environs.

"Yessir! Taken it many a time. Just gotta watch out fer slow movin' trains that might be comin' or goin'. Oh, and we'll pretend we can't read the 'Danger' and 'No Trespassin'' signs all over the place. Just be careful when we cross this railroad bridge to use the little wooden walkway instead of walkin' over the tracks. If a train were to come through here while we're on it, we'd have to jump over the side into the arroyo below. All we have to do is follow these picnic table symbols like you see drawn on that concrete abutment."

"What are those?" the Deviled Ham asked.

"Hobo code," the Princess answered. "There are all sorts of symbols that mean different things. The picnic table means that if we follow them, we'll find our way to a place where we can get some free grub."

There really was no other word that the casual observer of the hobo family on the move into civilization could use other than "motley." Burrito Betty's fetching rag-based outfit had not been improved with the passage of time. Flannel Freddie was wearing the same outfit he had on when he snuck out of his house in Belén the night before. It consisted of an Albuquerque Isotopes tee shirt with an image of their mascot Orbit swinging an oversized baseball bat, silky black basketball-style shorts, Nike running shoes and a baseball hat with the New Mexico Railrunner logo on it that his mom had bought for him this past Christmas. Captain Haskell had on an outfit designed for coverage and comfort rather than aesthetic appeal. He wore a weather-beaten porkpie hat with a few feathers stuck into the band, a striped, heavy cotton jacket covered with stains and rips, over a frayed and equally dirty tee shirt that had a picture of a young bejeweled girl riding a unicorn that said "Daddy's Little Princess," plaid pants that looked like another person might be able to fit inside with him and heavy lace-up boots with pieces of string that were only long enough to reach a few of the eyelets. It was also probably obvious to the casual observer that Zeke didn't fit in visually with Bix and Betty but after a night on the road, dirt and grime were beginning to accumulate on his clothes and body from his new lifestyle. After a few more days riding the rails, there was no doubt that he would look a lot more like them.

Once they crossed the bridge and quickly walked through the tunnel, they emerged out into the world of people, which included cars and honking horns, buildings, traffic laws, traffic lights, and the rules of a society that was increasingly alien to most dyed-in-the-wool hobos. Zeke had never been to Gallup before and immediately found himself smack dab in the middle of a demographic that he wasn't that familiar with. Gallup is a railroad town, like Belén, only much larger, more ethnically diverse and a bit lower on the economic spectrum. The part of the city they came out into definitely had a pretty large percentage of its population living below the poverty line as was evidenced by the ramshackle houses they saw and the look of some of the storefronts. As the hobos followed the route of picnic table symbols scrawled on telephone poles to the church that had a soup kitchen, they got a lot of second looks from the various people they passed on the street and who drove by in cars.

As they ambulated through this part of the city, as Captain Bix might have said, Zeke noted pawn shops, instant payday loan storefronts, small convenience marts, gas stations, liquor stores, churches, auto repair and tire shops, appliance repair shops and an occasional school or church. What surprised him, however, was that even though the three of them stood out like sore thumbs and people initially looked at them funny, nobody gave them any grief. In fact, most people eventually smiled and said hello after giving them the once over. Zeke noted to himself that in Belén, the homeless were basically invisible and people tended to ignore them completely, although he wondered if perhaps his new circumstance had given him a different perspective.

After walking for several more blocks, the hobos came to the place they were searching for. There was a massive church in a state of mild disrepair that took up the entire block with an ornate sign out front proclaiming it to be "Our Lady of Saint Jorge and Geronimo de Gallup Catholic Church." Underneath the gold painted letters was a message board with black moveable letters that said, "¿Cansado de ser un perdedor? ¡Se dirige a Dios!" It listed the dates and times of the Masses and Reconciliations at the bottom and also said that the Parroco was the Reverend Gaagii Jesus el del Dingo.

Since Zeke had a first grade class back in Belén that was somewhat bilingual, all of them spoke a little bit of Spanish. Not only was it unavoidable given the New Mexican cultural makeup but was also highly encouraged. He knew some of the words on this church sign but he wasn't totally clear about the message.

"I know that perdedor means loser and cansado means tired and Dios means God but do either of you know what that sign means?" Flannel Freddie asked his traveling companions.

"It's all Greek to me," Burrito Betty responded. "But I know Captain Bix is fairly fluent in Español."

"You've got the gist of it Freddie. I've spent a buncha time with some fruit tramps over the years so I've learned some of their lingo. If'n I'm readin' it true, it roughly translates to 'Tired of bein' a loser? Turn to God!' Now, I'm not feelin' like much of a loser at the moment but if I can get a good warm meal out of the deal, I'm happy to turn to God to get it. One thing to remember, though, is that we shouldn't tell the people inside too much about who we are, where we're headin' or what our story is. Understand? Let me do most of the talkin'. Whaddaya say, wanna go in?"

On the side of the church was an alleyway that had a telephone pole nearby with one of the picnic table symbols and an arrow pointing towards a door with a big colorful tile sign saying "Bienvenida." Bix opened the door like a true hobo gentleman and bowed at the waist as Burrito Betty and Flannel Freddie filed past him, quickly transitioning from the blazingly bright sunshine into the darkened confines of a hallway. All three had to stop for a moment to allow their eyes to adjust to the dark interior. Down the hallway, they saw a room filled with garish fluorescent lighting and heard the noise of clanging pans, silverware and plates. Bix re-established his leadership position and led the way towards the artificial brightness, sound and delicious smell of food.

Once inside the small church dining room, they saw an interesting mix of down-and-out soup kitchen patrons, a worker hustling around with food, as well as a few of them working in the cramped, adjoining kitchen and a person in church garb. The man who stepped up to greet them had on a black short sleeved shirt with a white clerical collar, very dark skin, jet black hair pulled back in a tight, long braid and a big smile on his face.

"Welcome to Our Lady of Saint Jorge and Geronimo, brothers and sisters!" the man said in perfectly enunciated English and an outstretched hand. "You folks look like you might be a little hungry. Can I interest you in a late lunch? You got here just in time as our kitchen closes every day at two o'clock sharp but I think we still have enough food to feed the three of you." He turned back towards the kitchen, visible through an opening in a dingy yellow tiled wall and yelled, "Got three more customers, Ramon. Do we have enough food left?"

"Last three servings, comin' up, Father!" he responded.

"Gracias! Why don't you folks sit down over here next to my friends, Ethel and Ernest?"

The three hobos were a bit overwhelmed with all the hospitality and sudden change of scene and were doing their best to make the transition from the world of the rail riders to the world of bright lights, friendly people and food. Burrito Betty looked like she had become a deer-in-the-headlights so Zeke followed the Human Stinkbomb's lead.

DAVID W. GOODWIN

They were led over to a large circular wooden table with a vinyl red and white checkered tablecloth that covered about half the table, surrounded by eight battered grey folding chairs. They sat down across from Ethel and Ernest, as instructed, while the other two groups of diners said their thanks to the staff and left the room, exiting out into the world through the same hallway. Zeke noted that Ethel and Ernest sort of looked like hobos themselves but were a little less grimy and the man barely looked up when the three of them sat down. The woman, however, couldn't take her eyes off of them while she was eating and had a big smile on her face, just like the Reverend. She was wearing a fancy, flouncy sort of party dress, a little worn around the edges, and the man was dressed in some sort of coveralls and had something on his head that kind of looked like an old-fashioned leather football helmet.

"My name is Father el del Dingo but most people call me Father Gaa Hey, derived, as you may have guessed, from my first names of Gaagii and Jesus. My mom is full-blooded Navajo and my dad was Mexican so I got a little bit of both. It's kind of evolved over the years since I've been up here in Gallup. What are your names and where are you from? I have a sneaking suspicion that you're not from around here. Am I right?"

"You'd be right about that Father. My name is, um, Alan, Alan Wilson and this is my wife Annie and our son, Flip."

"Alan, Annie and Flip Wilson?" Father el del Dingo asked with very wide eyes and a bit of surprise in his voice.

"Yeah, we get that reaction a lot. A lot of people don't remember him from the 60's. Flip's just a nickname. His real name is Brian."

"Like Brian Wilson from the Beach Boys?"

"Wow, you're up on your 60's trivia, Father!"

"Yes, I am. One of those crazy idiosyncrasies, I guess. Ask me about any Latino band from the 50's onward, that's my real specialty."

"I'll have to pass on that one," Captain Haskell said.

"One of my favorite YouTube videos is of Los Teen Tops doing their song 'Popotitos.' My friend Warren and me like to watch that sort of thing all the time. Do you know them?" Flannel Freddie asked while Bix gave him a look that tried to remind him not to give out too much personal information.

"¡Ay Dios! Los Teen Tops were one of my favorite bands growing up. I knew their singer, Enrique Guzmán because his family moved from Caracas to Mexico City. That's where I met him. We went to the same secondary school together, well, actually I was in grade seven and he was a junior in high school. He was a few years older than me but he was really popular and his band had a huge following. Where did you say you folks were from?"

"We didn't," Captain Bix interceded before Zeke could spill any more of the beans. "My family and me are just traveling through the area on our way to the artichoke harvest in Southern California. We're based out of Gainesville, Florida but during the warmer months we travel around kind of like migrant workers following the harvest."

"What about your son? What does he do for school?"

"He goes to school during the year in Gainesville and he's home schooled during our summer travels, I guess you might say. My wife here was a schoolteacher for about ten years before we decided it was time for a change. Ain't that right, honey?"

"Yep, that's right Bix, honey."

"Bix? I'm sorry, I thought you said your name was Alan?"

"Right, Alan. It is. Bix is my nickname. I go by either name really. Kind of like you, I suppose, people call me all sorts of different things."

Their conversation was thankfully put on hold as Ramon and another helper came over to the table with a big platter of food, glasses, silverware, napkins and pitchers of ice water and ice tea. While they all served themselves, Father Gaa Hey excused himself and tended to some business back in the kitchen. The three hobos thanked their servers and devoted their full attention to the meal and cold beverages at hand. They ate and drank like they hadn't had a full meal like this for ages, which was probably mighty close to the truth. Captain Haskell, in a very soft whisper, reminded his two dining buddies to keep from bumping their gums too much around the church workers. Zeke noted, yet again, with wonder, how easily Bix was able to sound like a hobo one minute and turn it completely off the next when the situation called for it. It was almost like he was trilingual.

The cold drinks were a godsend. The food consisted of rice and beans, a small green salad and chicken stir-fry. Even accounting for his current circumstance, it was probably the best meal Zeke had ever tasted. His parents rarely had time to cook regular meals so either they ate out at the same assortment of restaurants in the Belén area or one of his parents grabbed some take-out Chinese or a pizza on their way home from work. This meal seemed like something that a normal family might eat. Maybe this was going to be his new normal family and this might become one of their normal meals.

"Where did you folks say you was a-headin'?" the man sitting across from them mumbled, looking up from his plate with a mouthful of food, startling all three of them out of their food and drink stupor and celebration.

"To the artichoke harvest in California," Captain Bix Pickles Haskell, the Human Stinkbomb answered, pronouncing California the non-hobo way and sticking to his made-up story.

The Reverend el del Dingo returned at this point and sat down at the table with the remaining five diners at his church's soup kitchen. He made small talk about the meal, the history of the church, the neighborhood, their mission to provide for the needs of the homeless and those who were temporarily down on their luck. He asked Ethel and Ernest if they knew where they were heading after their meal, which only produced a few vague and muffled words from the man, Ernest, about here and there and the name of some town that Zeke had never heard of before. The woman, Ethel, however, became very chatty and talked about some travel ideas she had. He then turned his attention back to the Wilson family and tried to pin them down on their plans for the night and how they were going to get themselves out to California.

"Well, that's a good question, Father Gaa Hey. You see, we was travelin', that is, we were traveling west along Route 66, kind of taking the scenic route, when our car broke down right near the Continental Divide after we passed through Thoreau. Funds are a little tight at the moment and we didn't have the kind of money we needed to fix our cracked engine block so we sold the car to a junk yard for chump change."

"I'm sorry to hear that, Mr. Wilson. But I'm curious, how did you get to Gallup?"

"We were lucky, lucky to have friends who lived nearby who offered to drive us here. My hope was that seeing that Gallup is a decent sized city, we could all find some temporary jobs so we could earn enough money to buy an old jalopy and then continue on our way out to the harvest. Do you know of any places that might be hiring?"

"Good question. Things are a bit tight at the moment. There are lots of folks like yourselves looking for work but let me ask around at a few places. What sorts of things can you do?"

"I'm kind of a jack-of-all-trades, you know, carpentry, plumbing, window washing, truck driver, things like that. My wife, Annie, like I said, she's a teacher but can also cook and clean, even had a stint or two as a dancer."

"Is that so?" Father el del Dingo asked.

"That's right, Father. Naturally, that was back in my younger days when I was in a little better shape. I don't suppose you know much about that kind of dancing though. Anyway, I can do just about anything if I set my mind to it," the freshly dubbed Annie Wilson declared emphatically.

"I suppose you could, ma'am. And what about you son? How old are you?"

"I'm almost seven. I can mow lawns, rake leaves, run errands, do a little computer work. I designed my own web page a few weeks ago."

"You're kidding me, right? You designed your own website? I wouldn't expect a child who is six going on seven to have to go out and get a job."

"No, I like to do things like that, especially if it helps out my family. You hardly need to know anything. There's a lot of free software out there that you can get and the rest is easy. Anyone could do it, even my parents."

"Do you have a laptop with you that you use to show me how to do it?"

"No, I don't have one with me. We stopped at my cousin's house in Texas on our way out here and he showed me how to do it on his computer," Zeke said without a moment of hesitation. Bix was impressed that little Flannel Freddie knew his geography well enough to know that Texas was along the route they might have traveled from Florida to New Mexico.

"It's funny you say this because we were thinking of creating a website for the church that has links to the various programs we run and other information that might be useful to the community but nobody here knows the first thing about how to create one. Maybe we should talk later about this, that is, if you're interested."

"Sure, I could do that. I'm not a whiz programmer or anything but I know how to do some of the basic things."

Father Gaagii Jesus el del Dingo had apparently finished up with his small talk and launched into a discussion that Bix Pickles had warned Freddie about before they came in for their free lunch. He talked about sin and salvation, about heaven and hell, about prayer and good deeds, about being a good neighbor in the eyes of God and wrapped it up by asking each of the five diners sitting at the table if they would consider receiving Christ as their personal Savior. The four adults each gave their own non-committal response and Zeke asked if it would require going to Confession.

"No," Father el del Dingo responded with a hearty chuckle. "There are no rules that young children have to go to Confession. We generally wait until they're old enough to fully understand the difference between right and wrong and I find that's usually when they're seven or eight, sometimes older. Of course, anyone is welcome to the Confession booth at any time. Is this something that you're interested in?"

"No, thank you. I was just curious."

"I'd be happy to talk to you more about this at some other time if you'd like. For now, however, I've got an addiction group meeting to run so you'll have to excuse me. Before you leave, would you please clear your plates over into that tray? We're open for dinner starting a six this evening and you're welcome to join us. We have a little service afterwards which we would like you to be a part of as well. And, Flip, if you come back for dinner tonight, I'd like to talk to you about web design for a few minutes if that's alright with your parents, of course."

Captain Haskell, now also known as Alan Wilson, nodded his head while the Reverend said his goodbyes and left the dining room. In the meantime, Ernest seemed to be emerging from the haze he had been under throughout his entire meal and started a whispered conversation with the Wilson family.

"Are you folks really heading out for the artichoke harvest or maybe you're really on your way to Roswell?" Ernest asked in a vaguely accusatory and doubting tone of voice.

"You bet your ass we're going to the artichoke harvest. Why would we want to go to Roswell?" Burrito Betty said in a half-snarl.

"Well, either you're kind of late or kind of early. We used to be migrant farm workers too, and know from years of experience that the artichoke harvest happens in the spring and fall, not in June, so I'm not sure your story holds a lot of water," Ethel challenged, but in a nice way, if that was possible. "Is it also true that your car broke down?"

"Yeah, I wish it hadn't but thems is the facts," Captain Pickles stated.

"Listen, you folks don't need to feed us any stories. Maybe Father Dingo will buy it but we're not that easy. It looks to me like you're all in a bit of a mess right now and your story doesn't quite add up. Am I right?" Ethel asked kindly and her smile never seemed to waiver. "What's the real story?"

"I might have made up a little of it," Bix admitted, realizing that the time had probably come to level with these people.

"So, as one traveler to another, I think you folks should know about something we overheard in the jail this morning. Ernie and me was locked up overnight because I guess there's a law around here that says you can't be out on the streets at night celebrating with any alcohol, if you can imagine that. Well, perhaps we got a little carried away with ourselves but, none-the-less, somehow found ourselves in matching side-by-side cells this morning. As they were processing our paperwork to release us on our own recognizance, as they usually do since they know us pretty well down there, we heard something come through on the police scanner about a six-year-old boy missing from his home in Belén who might be riding a train. Now, I'm not saying anything to the nice reverend here about nothing but we've got a reason to believe that you folks might know a thing or two about this. You seem like nice people and all so I just wanted to give you a quick head's up," Ethel said in a loud whisper, not in a threatening way but more as partners in crime. She then pulled out a cellphone, fiddled around with it for a few seconds and showed them the AMBER Alert message about Zeke Wappinger. "See?"

This news sent the Wilson family into a full high alert panic and all eyes went to Captain Bix Pickles. Bix and Betty then looked at each other, then at Freddie and were so stunned that they didn't know what to say or how to react. Freddie, however, knew exactly what he wanted to do.

"Could I borrow your phone for a second and send a text message to my parents to let them know that I'm alright?"

"Sure thing, honey. Are you alright?" Ethel asked with a kind smile.

"Oh, definitely. These people are my new best friends. They are dyed-in-the-wool hobos, A-number-one, the best, nicest people you'd ever want to meet. They're taking excellent care of me," Zeke said to reassure her. "I just wanted to get away from home for a little while."

"I believe you, Flip, I mean Zeke. Here's my phone. We're not gonna get in any trouble for this, I hope," Ethel asked.

Zeke took the phone from her, spent a moment trying to decide which parent to text and what to say. He eventually decided that he would send a message to his mom and it simply said, "im fine dont worry will be home soon love zeke" and handed the phone back with a word of thanks. The former Wilson family quickly vacated the soup kitchen by way of the door they had recently come through and were back out onto the streets of Gallup without clearing their plates first.

"I guess you know that we've got to get out of town quick now because that message will be traced back here," Zeke announced to Bix and Betty once they were safely out of sight of the church. "I'm sorry but I had to do that. My parents are probably pretty upset at the moment."

CHAPTER 7

"I GUESS IT'S BACK to the drawing board," Officer Ramirez said to fellow Belén police officer and part time Isotopes ballgirl, Daria Cellucci, who in turn commiserated with Lieutenant Forsmark, BNSF switchyard supervisor Mr. Joel Juanes and naturally, Roxanne Wappinger. Mrs. Wappinger looked like an Isotope's pitcher who had just taken a hard line drive directly to her noggin off the bat of a burly power hitter. Meanwhile, the crew from *Quay County Sun* continued capturing video footage of the now cheerless scene while the various emergency personnel began walking back to their respective vehicles.

"Can I see that watch for a second?" Officer Cellucci asked Lieutenant Forsmark, who had just jumped down from the boxcar with all of his fellow patrolmen in quick succession. "I want Bullet to confirm that this belongs to the young boy."

"Oh, that's his alright," Roxanne sadly confirmed. "Maybe he's still on this train. Maybe he jumped or climbed over to another car. He's got to be here! Why else would his GPS watch be in there?"

As soon as Officer Cellucci brought the watch near her dog's powerful snout, he started barking in a staccato rhythm, brought his front legs and chest to the ground with his hind legs still extended, his tail looking like a helicopter propeller and then began making a high pitch crying noise. "Yep, this is his alright. Good dog, Bullet!" As expected, he received a few treats out of her doggie treat bag. "Officer Ramirez, I would like to do a complete walk around the entire train with Bullet to see if little Mr. Wappinger might be on or in another car, as Mrs. Wappinger has suggested. With your permission." She opened the plastic bag of Zeke's dirty clothes to refresh the dog's memory even further.

"That's a good idea. I think we'd all like to make a closer inspection."

The two Belén officers, Roxanne Wappinger, Bullet, Joel Juanes, two members of the press and Lieutenant Forsmark's crew started making their way slowly down the line of train cars. Roxanne said that she needed to place a call to her husband to relay the bad news. The entire entourage gave her some space and some time to make the call in private as they waited together off to the side of the railroad line.

"Andrew, we found Zeke's watch but we haven't found Zeke yet so I'm afraid I don't have any good news to report. We're about to do a full search of the train. Is there anything happening at your end?"

"Damn! No, nothing! I haven't gotten any calls other than from you. He's got to be there somewhere! I can't believe this! Why would Zeke run away from home? Call me the second you know something. I'll continue to monitor things here at the house. Good luck, honey!"

The small cluster of people then continued down the line of trains. Since there were sixty-six cars to search and a lot of them were tankers or refrigerator cars, the search party only looked below or on the top of those. As they came to each one, a police officer climbed up the metal ladder at one end and quickly scanned the top and the ones around it. The Belén officers and Bullet concentrated their efforts on the boxcars and flat cars and the two groups would leap frog each other down the line. When they arrived at the caboose, they made a U-turn and then started working their way back up the other side, eventually arriving at the two engines at the front of the train. They stopped briefly to talk with the rookie engineer, Priscilla Barbados, while she was standing outside near the front engine scrutinizing her travel log.

"I went through my full check list at each stop, everything was fine when we left the Belén yard right on schedule at 01:15, switched tracks in Vaughn, had a three hour layover to unload and load some new freight, left there on-time at 07:38, had another scheduled stop in Santa Rosa for some more freight transfer, left there two minutes late due to some track work that was just finishing up at 12:20 and then got the call from the BNSF dispatch in Fort Worth for a required unscheduled stop here in Tucumcari," Ms. Barbados recited while reading off her log book. "I didn't get any report from any of our railroad staff about any illegal riders. Generally, if the brakemen, switchmen, firemen, section hands or yard clerks see anything unusual, I'll know about it. Sorry not to be of any more help. I can't believe this is happening on my first solo run!"

"Thank you, ma'am. We appreciate your information. We'll clear your train for travel once we complete our search," Lieutenant Forsmark said kindly.

The group continued back down towards their starting point and had almost completed the full circuit when Roxanne heard that she had gotten another text message. She let out a big sigh thinking that it was yet another work related message that only served as an unwelcome distraction at this point.

"I wish these damned bozos would leave me alone," she said loudly while looking down a bit reluctantly at her phone. "Oh my God! It's a text from Zeke! It says, 'im fine dont worry will be home soon love zeke'! I can't believe this! Holy crap!"

Lieutenant Forsmark came running over and asked to see the phone. He examined it carefully, wrote down the originating phone number on a notepad, ripped the sheet off the pad and gave it to one of the officers with instructions to find out who it belonged to and where the message was sent from while Roxanne started crying and laughing in an almost comical, yet highly hysterical manner.

"My son is okay! Oh, what a relief! I'm so happy! But where is he? Who has him? Can we call the number back? I need to see him!" she called out in rapid-fire succession.

"Let's just wait for a few minutes. If we call the number back immediately, it might scare them off. Let's see what Officer Dumbrowski finds out. This will probably only take a few minutes," Lieutenant Forsmark said, hoping to reassure her. "I understand what you must be feeling right now but trust me on this. Just hang on for a moment, if you can."

The group walked down the tracks to the train station and through to the parking lot where Officer Dumbrowski was talking on his two-way police radio with the driver's door open, one leg hanging out and his black police boot firmly planted on the asphalt. Against her natural inclination to go over and take control of the conversation, Roxanne kept a respectful distance while he finished up talking with the dispatcher. She used this time to call her husband again to fill him in on the latest developments. After a few more minutes, the officer wrapped up his business and came over to address the small group.

"Headquarters has identified the phone owner as a woman named Sally Santorini whose billing address is a post office box number in Matamoras, Pennsylvania. The good news is that the FBI shared an app with us that makes it possible to send a text message to any phone number and get a current location back almost immediately. Ma'am, the message you just received was made from inside a church in Gallup, New Mexico, on the corner of Wilson Avenue and North 4th Street."

"A church? In Gallup? How can that be? That's clear across on the other side of the state! I thought he would be somewhere between here and Belén! Can I call the number now?" Roxanne asked in rapid-fire succession.

"We already have, ma'am. No answer but her voicemail message said that her name was Ethel so I'm not sure what's going on with that. It could be a stolen phone, it could have any number of other logical explanations, we just don't have any answers yet. We left a message telling her to stay right where she is because the state police want to question her. Officers from the NMSP District 6 office have already been dispatched to the location."

"Can we go to Gallup? I need to find my son!" Roxanne implored.

"At this point, ma'am," Lieutenant Forsmark stated, "it's a matter for the state police. Officer Ramirez will take you back to your home in Belén and we'll be taking over the investigation. I would like to get Officer Cellucci's commanding officer's permission to join our response team with her dog, that is, if she is willing and able to do this."

"Absolutely, I just need to call Lola to see if she can take over for me tonight at the Isotopes game," Officer Cellucci responded. "Let me call Lieutenant Swazee on my police radio to get permission."

"Oh, that's right! I've heard about a police dog officer that's also a ballgirl for the Isotopes. That must be you," Lieutenant Forsmark remarked.

"You're right about that, sir. There aren't too many other women around that fit that description, wouldn't you say?"

"How would you feel about having some company for the long drive over to Gallup?" Lieutenant Forsmark asked.

"We'd have to take my K-9 cruiser, Lieutenant, for Bullet of course," she reminded him. "And I'm driving. You're welcome to ride shotgun if you'd like. I'm capable of handling this on my own though."

"I'll bet you are. Let me call this in to let our officers and staff know what's going on," he said. Calling over to Officer Ramirez, he asked that he be notified immediately if any additional text messages were received from the missing boy.

Everyone scattered to do what he or she had to do. Roxanne, very reluctantly, realized that she was being relegated to watching the action unfold from the distant sidelines, even though it was her son out there. And, if the truth be told, Officer Ramirez felt like he had just been put back into his place as a small town cop, narrowly missing his chance for some real police work for a change instead of the usual traffic detail or occasional stolen goods investigation. It was fun while it lasted, he thought, and at least he got a chance to mix it up with the state police and drive really fast on the highway. His drive with Mrs. Wappinger back to Belén wasn't going to be nearly as exciting but he was feeling optimistic that the story might just have a happy ending.

Meanwhile, Officer Cellucci and Lieutenant Forsmark made their respective calls and prepared for the three hundred mile drive ahead of them. Since Daria Cellucci was eventually going back to Belén, she made arrangements with Lieutenant Forsmark to meet at the NMSP barracks in Albuquerque so he could drop off his squad car there and save her some time by not having to drive all the way back to Tucumcari. Before they all left the train station, they met as a group one last time to make sure they had each other's contact information and discussed communication protocol, to insure that everyone stayed in the news development loop. Lieutenant Forsmark said that he would be the primary point of contact with the NMSP District 6 office in Gallup and would share any information he received with the others.

"Things could happen mighty quickly," he reminded them all.

The three police cars all left the Tucumcari train station parking lot at the same time but the Ramirez cruiser quickly fell off the pace once they hit the interstate. As much as he wanted to, he couldn't justify driving back to Belén with his flashing police lights on at the same rate of speed that the two other vehicles were soon driving.

The drive to Albuquerque would take a little under an hour and a half. The Belén K-9 cruiser would follow the NMSP cruiser the entire way, keeping about ten car lengths between them for safety, as Officer Cellucci was taught in her police driver training. She decided that Lieutenant Forsmark must have been trying to impress her with his driving skills since it seemed to her that he got a little too close to vehicles as he approached them before veering out into the passing lane. She made sure to anticipate passing a little sooner than he did. When you're driving close to a hundred and thirty miles an hour, you want to give yourself as much of a safety buffer as possible, she thought to herself. However, based on the vast majority of male cops she knew, his driving style was entirely consistent with that of the others and probably extended to all other macho aspects of their police work.

The drive to Belén in the other vehicle was almost the mirror-opposite. Sure, they were able to drive faster than the seventy-five mile per hour speed limit, but without their flashing lights on, Officer Ramirez had a professional obligation to drive at a safe speed. Roxanne was understandably agitated in the backseat and made frequent phone calls to her husband back home and, unknowingly, was still clutching Zeke's GPS watch in her left hand.

"Andrew, we're on our way back to Belén. We'll be there around four-thirty or maybe a little later. The state cops wouldn't let me go out to Gallup with them but they did decide to take the ballgirl and her dog. Go figure! Listen, I was thinking that when I got home, maybe you and I should head out to Gallup on our own. Wait a second, Andrew, Officer Ramirez is shaking his head. Hold on."

"I know you want to do all you can to help, Mrs. Wappinger, but assisting the police in this investigation may not be helpful and might even be counterproductive," Officer Ramirez said, trying to choose his words carefully. "Perhaps the best place for you and your husband would be at home where we know we can find you. Being available by phone is critical in a situation like this. Understand?"

"Right, but if it was your child out there, you'd want to be there too. Right?" she challenged.

"Hard to argue but I just needed to say what I said. I can't physically make you stay at your house."

"So Andrew," she said, turning her attention back to her phone, "we'll talk more about this when I get home. Could you get some food and beverages together? All of a sudden I'm famished. Oh, and make sure your phone is fully charged. See you in about an hour."

The situation at the New Mexico State Police District 6 office in Gallup was one of routine calm at the moment. They had jurisdiction over a large geographic area and prided themselves on being the "Gateway to the Navajo Nation," as well as a busy tourist hub for both the Historic Route 66 and Native American artifacts crowd, in addition to the more adventurous and outdoorsy crowd interested in hiking, camping, visiting ancient ruins and cliff dwellings, hunting, off-roading and general sightseeing in the rugged and scenic backcountry. As such, they were very well prepared for the call that was about to come into their central dispatch communication center.

"District 6 dispatch, over," said Ellen LaToya, the operator on duty nearing the end of an otherwise uneventful shift. Her mind was beginning to imagine what the first strawberry margarita was going to taste like at the happy hour she and many of her fellow office workers regularly attended each Saturday during the warm months in Gallup, which was about half the year. Hopefully, the manager at the City Lights Bar and Grill made the effort to have the karaoke machine hooked up this week as she had requested the previous week when it was just sitting idle in the corner, much to their dismay.

"District 6 dispatch, this is Colonel Morgan from Headquarters. We have information to pass on to you concerning a missing child, a six-year-old male Caucasian by the name of Zeke Wappinger from Belén, New Mexico who was reported missing this morning and is currently in our AMBER Alert network. You'll see it come through over the network in a few moments. We have reason to believe that he sent a text message to his mother at 14:26 from a cellular telephone. We have identified the origin of the message to be at the Our Lady of Saint Jorge and Geronimo de Gallup Catholic Church at the corner of Wilson Avenue and North 4th Street. From our location services, it appears the call was made from inside a connected side building approximately twenty feet north of the entrance off of Wilson Avenue. Do you copy, over?"

"Yes, sir, I copy. I will dispatch a patrol car immediately. Can you tell me the suspect phone number, over?"

"Better make it two patrol cars, if possible," Colonel Morgan suggested and gave her Sally Santorini's cellphone number. "We have Lieutenant Forsmark from District 9 Clovis and K-9 Officer Cellucci from the Belén Police Department on their way from Tucumcari but they probably won't arrive in Gallup until 17:30 and will report immediately to your commanding officer. Officer Cellucci's dog has been tracking the boy's scent and could be invaluable help, over."

"Let me confirm that I've written down all the information correctly," Ellen said and reread the details back to the captain.

"That's correct. I will be checking back with you for a status update periodically. 10-4."

The Hobo Family Wilson beat a hasty retreat out into the street and quickly ran back through the railroad tunnel under the interstate and to the relative safety of the abandoned building near the BNSF railyard where they had just recently taken a long midday siesta. Once they were able to catch their breath, the urgency of hatching a new plan on the fly was apparent.

DAVID W. GOODWIN

"If what yer tellin' me is true about those little telephones, Freddie, and if what those folks back at the church soup kitchen say is true, then near everyone and their brother will be lookin' fer ya. Maybe sendin' a message to your mom and dad weren't such a good idea after all," Captain Bix Pickles admonished.

"Now, now, don't be picking on the boy," Burrito Betty said as she put her arm around him. "He did what he thought needed to be done. His parents must be sick with worry. We'll figure out something here."

"Well, it better be quick. Maybe we should just turn you over to the authorities and get this thing over with now," Bix suggested. "We've got a perfectly solid explanation, even though I'm ninety-nine percent certain it won't work out well for us. I'm not willin' to be pinched and sent upriver to the slammer again, this time for kidnappin'. The authorities don't take too kindly to folks like us Betty, you know that as well as me."

"You're right, but I think we should hear what Frankie has to say. What do you want to do, honey?"

"This is the most fun I've had my entire life so far! Maybe you two could come home with me. We've got lots of room in our house. My mom's a lawyer, she could find you a job, Captain Haskell, and I'm sure there's something out there for you, Burrito Betty!"

"Hold on there a minute, kid! I'm not innerested in bustin' a gut again. I did that for a lot of years and that's kinda why I'm a hobo now. I was tired of that rat race. Besides, I earn what I get. Nobody's gonna give me the works!" the Human Stinkbomb said emphatically.

"But we all just got a free meal. Doesn't that count as something you didn't earn?" Zeke asked.

"Well, I 'spose you got me there, Freddie. It's not too often we have ourselves a setdown like that. Most of the time me and Poots get our food by spearin' a biscuit, you know, dumpster divin'. But like I said yesterday, you'd make a darn fine lawyer someday. You seem to have a pretty good way of cutting through all the crap. Anyway, we need a plan and we need it now. What's it gonna be, Freddie? And don't say go back to your place and play house 'cuz that ain't gonna happen."

"Wait, let me weigh in on this," Betty offered. "First off, you don't need to be so hard on the boy. He's just throwing out some ideas. Second, I know we had a plan to hit the coast but it seems like that's all been thrown under the train for the moment. How about this Frankie, how about we find a bull local that's heading back to Belén, we get you back safe to your neighborhood and then Bix and me skedaddle our butts the hell outta Dodge? But we probably got to wait till it's dark because pretty soon this place will be crawling with pussyfooters, galvanizers and John Law."

"That sounds like a pretty good idea but if what I know about phones and the police is true, they're going to track us here in the next hour, if not sooner, and it partially depends on how quickly they find those folks we just ate lunch with," Zeke said.

Ethel and Ernest Gamble were just finishing up their free meal at the church a few minutes after the Wilson's left and Ernest, especially, seemed to be rather confused about all the events that had just transpired at their lunch table. It wasn't the first time they'd run across hobos and it wasn't even the first time they'd run across hobos on the run but it was definitely the first time they'd run across hobos on the run with a reported missing child. The seriousness of what just happened seemed like it was starting to sink in.

"Do you think there's any way that the government could trace that message back here?" Ernest asked Ethel. He had been conditioned to defer to her on most matters like this since she clearly was the brains behind their somewhat dysfunctional relationship.

"Oh Ernie, you're always so paranoid. That's the kind of stuff that only happens on Star Trek. I doubt technology is so advanced that the government or phone companies can do that sort of thing," Ethel said, trying her best to reassure him.

"I'm not so sure. How do cellphones work anyway? Far as I can tell, it's some sort of magic, like maybe there's a buncha invisible aliens all around us that somehow deliver all these messages at the speed of light and can perfectly mimic everyone's voices. I wouldn't be surprised with some of the shit they can do. I don't even know why you own that thing. It just seems to get us into trouble."

"I think it means a lot to my kid sister. She likes to know that I'm okay so she just pays the bill each month. All she asks in return is that I answer it when she calls every few weeks. Whoops! There it goes. I wonder who's calling me now?" Ethel said, trying to recover from the startle she always got since it rang so infrequently. "It says 'Restricted.' I don't know anyone named 'Restricted,' do you Ernest?"

"Don't answer it!" Ernest cried out. "It might be the aliens!"

"It's not the aliens, honey. Don't you want to know who 'Restricted' is?"

"Not really and if it's really important, they'll leave a message in Obama's voice or something."

"Obama's voice?"

"They can imitate anyone they want to," Ernest said knowingly. "Hell, they could make you think that one of them astronuts that landed on the moon was calling to tell you that they really did land on the moon instead of it all bein' staged on some Hollywood set like most sane people know is the truth."

Ethel decided not to take Ernie's bait this time and waited for a minute or so, staring down at her phone on the table until it made the sound that she had a voicemail message. After exchanging frightened looks, Ernest said she might as well find out what the bad news was. She picked it up, tapped on it a few times and leaned her head against Ernest so they could both hear the message together. There was so much clatter coming out of the kitchen that no one in there could have heard the message anyway, even if it had been put on speakerphone.

"This is Major Queznal from District 6 of the New Mexico State Police. Your phone was used a few minutes ago by a confirmed missing person as part of the New Mexico AMBER Alert system. We know your location. Officers will be meeting you there shortly. Please do not leave your current location. Thank you for your full cooperation. If you have any questions, you can reply to this message."

"Now we're fucked!" Ernest cried out loud. "Those whack jobs found us! That's the last thing in the world we need right now! Why did you let that little brat use your phone? We're in a fuckin' heap of trouble now! You said they couldn't do this sort of thing, Ethel!"

"Calm down, dear, and watch your language. We're in a church, for Christ sake! We didn't do anything wrong. We simply let someone in need use my phone. There's not a law against that, is there? So, what do we do—stay or run?"

"I say we run and the sooner the better!" Ernest said as he quickly got up from the table.

"Okay, but if we run, we are definitely doing something wrong and then we really would be in trouble," Ethel reasoned. "I say we stay and talk with the nice police when they arrive. That sweet little boy's life might be at stake. I think we owe it to him to be reunited with his family. You can see that, can't you? "

Before Ernest could answer, they heard the outside door open with a violent thud followed by the sound of heavy footsteps walking quickly down the carpeted hallway accompanied by lots of things jangling around getting louder as they got closer. Within a few seconds, two uniformed state police officers came striding into the dining area with their service revolvers drawn in front of them.

Ethel and Ernie Gamble froze in place. Now, given the fact that they had lived most of the last five years or so on the streets and were rather well acquainted with the police and the judicial system on account of their lifestyle and massive consumption of alcohol, they were, for the most part, friendly, passive people. The times they had been hauled into the slammer were mostly times when the police were doing so for their own protection, either to keep them from falling over into the path of an oncoming vehicle as they tried to wobble across the street or to keep them from becoming victims of some less savory individuals who might want to take advantage of them. Never, in all of their sorted and sordid experiences, however, did a police officer get in their face with a drawn gun.

"You ain't takin' me alive, copper!" Ernest yelled out, maybe from some primeval urge that told him it was time to go out in a blaze of seriously misguided glory. Standing beside the table, he tried to pull it up and knock it over between himself and the police but since it was too big and heavy and he was a tottering old psychotic drunk, he only succeeded in wrenching his back and slightly jostling the things on the table. Seeing that this gave him only one other option, he tried to make a dash for the door but, unfortunately for him, both officers were blocking the way and he only managed to bounce into them and then fell backwards onto his butt.

"Now, now, Ernest. Calm down, sir," the first officer said chuckling when Ernest first started running towards them and both officers had put their guns back in their holsters by the time the initial contact was made. They were used to dealing with Ernest. "Howdy, Ethel."

"Good afternoon, officers. Ernest, I'll be. What gets into you sometimes?" Ethel said with a half laugh while getting up to help Ernest off the floor. This now required the help of one of the other policemen as Ernest was having a tough time getting back on to his feet. He would have had a tough time anyway but now with his back tweaked a bit, it became even more of an ordeal.

"Let's get you settled over into this chair," the cop said. "We have a few questions we'd like to ask the two of you."

"I need to be reminded of your names," Ethel said, slowly walking over to them to read their name badges while making a show of pulling on her reading glasses that were hanging around her neck on a dollar store special oversized gold colored plastic chain. "Officers Starsky and Hutch, I see."

"That's right, ma'am. I'm Starsky, he's Hutch or as we're known when we're not starring in our own thirty-year-old TV show, Officers Gonzales and Hanover. Can I see your cellphone please, Mrs. Gamble?"

The phone had been resting on the tabletop when the policemen came into the room but Ernest's less-than Herculean effort to topple it failed to create the effect he had hoped for. He did, however, manage to send the phone sliding off the table top, which propelled it spinning in slow motion across the shiny and worn linoleum floor and off into a far corner of the dining room, visible to all four of them and the two workers watching the drama through the opening in the tiled wall from the kitchen. Through the door on the opposite side of the dining room, at that moment, walked the handsome Reverend Gaagii Jesus el del Dingo.

"What phone?" Ernest asked from his chair.

"I think they see the phone over in the corner," Ethel conceded sweetly, even going so far as to bat her eyes that seemed to be covered in at least two-day-old makeup. Her mascara was so heavy and coagulated that it looked like the blackened branch of a tiny Christmas tree plastered onto her eyelids complete with even tinier black ornaments hanging off the ends in a very random pattern.

"Officers, can you tell me what's going on here?" Father Gaa Hey asked.

"Sure thing, Father. Why don't you all have a seat over here? Listen, time is critical so we need to cut to the chase," the older and shorter policeman, Officer Hanover, who had been doing all of the talking so far, said while Officer Gonzales walked over to the corner to retrieve the phone. "We just traced a text message that a missing six-year-old boy sent from this location about ten minutes ago so we know he's in the vicinity. The owner of the phone is a person named Sally Santorini from somewhere in Pennsylvania. Ethel, did you steal this phone?"

She explained her connection to the phone, which seemed to satisfy the state police officers. Then Officer Hanover asked the three witnesses what they could tell them about the little missing boy named Zeke Wappinger.

All three started talking at the same time, all were saying different things so Officer Hanover asked them to stop for a second while Officer Gonzales put on a pair of blue latex gloves from one of his pockets, bent down to pick up Ethel's phone and looked at the recent messages sent.

"This is the one, a text message was sent at 2:26 pm," he reported. "I'm fine, don't worry, will be home soon, love, Zeke."

"Father, you go first. What just happened in here?" Officer Hanover asked.

"Three people walked in here about an hour ago. Never seen them before. A dad, a mom and a young boy that was probably the six-year-old in question. Said their names were Wilson, ironically just like the street name outside that door—Alan, Annie and Flip Wilson. They all seemed friendly enough, more talkative than most folks we get in here."

"You sure it wasn't the Jacksons—Michael, Janet and Tito?" Officer Gonzales said breaking his silence for the first time. "Can you describe them?"

"Yeah, I guess their names should have given me a few suspicions. I hate to stereotype but the parents looked like hobos. Filthy mismatched clothing, looked like they hadn't had a bath for weeks. I noticed the man was wearing a tiny tee shirt under his jacket that said "Daddy's Little Princess" and it had a picture of a child princess, a unicorn and lots of sparkles. The woman was wearing rags, really, that's about the only way I can describe it. The young boy, Flip or I guess Zeke is his real name, he was wearing a railroad baseball hat, a dirty red Isotopes tee shirt, black gym shorts and sneakers. I had to leave for a meeting before the three of them finished their meal."

"Is this him?" Officer Hanover asked showing him a picture of Zeke that he had printed from his patrol car printer and showed it to all three of them.

"Absolutely! He's a bright little boy. I was half expecting to see him tonight for dinner. We talked a little about him helping me to build a website for the church."

"Yes, that's little Zeke, for sure," Ethel said. "Are we in trouble officer? I told them that we had seen an AMBER Alert for the boy a few hours ago and the precious angel said that he wanted to send a text to his parents to let them know that he was fine."

"No, you did the right thing. You're not in trouble. But now we need to find this little guy and get him back home to his parents. We have your phone number, Ethel. You two, please stick around in town where we can find you until we wrap this case up. You weren't planning on going anywhere, were you?" Officer Hanover asked.

"No, we'll be around for a while. One more thing you should know," Ethel said while putting her hand on top of Ernest's in a gentle effort to keep his crazy energy under control, "they said they were on their way to harvest artichokes in California but that was probably part of the same tall tale Alan Wilson made up on the spot. These people are not criminals, I can tell you that for certain. Also, I don't think the boy was being kidnapped. I got the sense that they were all out having themselves a big adventure or something."

"Sure would be nice to have a K-9 unit to track these folks down. All we have right now is this phone with Zeke Wappinger's fingerprints. I doubt that's enough for a dog to sniff out. Officer Gonzales, I think we should put a call in to our dispatch office and have them send out the Tactical Team."

"Good idea. Father el del Dingo and you two, Mr. and Mrs. Gamble, if you hear anything else, here are a couple of my cards. Call me. One last thing, which way did they leave?"

Both Ethel and Ernest pointed towards the hallway.

"If they are in fact hobos, there really is only one direction they would probably think of heading—right through the tunnel and back to the switchyard. Let's quickly touch bases with the dispatch office and see if we can find this kid before he goes much further," Officer Hanover said as the two of them started heading down the hallway. "Thanks, folks."

Meanwhile, at the far edges of the Gallup switchyard, the soon-to-be dubbed Jackson family heard a siren coming in their general direction. It was first noticeable from about a mile away and even over the loud buzz from the interstate, all three of them knew that it was heading to the church that they had just fled moments ago.

"I'd say we're now in the final countdown," Captain Bix Pickles stated. "We could stay right here and get caught and let Freddie get a free ride back to paradise or we could try to flip a train in broad daylight and hope for the best."

"Or we could go hide in a dumpster somewhere," Poots offered, as it was probably true that this strategy might have worked for her in some sort of past situation.

"Or we could go jump in the back of that truck over across the street being loaded up with furniture and go wherever it's going," Flannel Freddie exclaimed, seeing their one way ticket out of Gallup.

Without a single additional word being exchanged, they grabbed their stuff and ran over towards the truck. Bix motioned for them to stay behind him as he crouched behind some cars that were parked nearby.

"Let's just see what the situation is here and see if there's a way for us to get inside before they close the doors," Bix Pickles whispered softly to Betty and Freddie who were huddled in close together.

From their vantage point, by looking through the car windows while still mostly hidden from view, they could see that the truck was mostly full and the two guys that were loading new chairs and tables were almost ready to head out for their delivery. Luckily, the Jackson-Wilson-Haskell-Poots-Ham-Wappinger family was close enough to hear most of the mover's conversation.

"One more couch and we'll be ready to roll, Hector. Last delivery of the day—finally! Any big plans for the weekend, man?"

"I'm taking my kids camping up on Tsoodzil, or Mount Taylor as you white folks like to call it. They've gotten more interested in their Navajo roots lately so I thought I'd take them to a place that my dad and grandpa use to take me when I was a little boy. She's a beautiful place."

"I go four wheeling up there sometimes. It is a great place to get away. Listen, before we head out, I'd like to grab a few water bottles for the trip. You cool with that?"

"Sure, I should probably hit the head first anyway."

Both men were dressed in the same outfits, matching black tee shirts with their company logo on the back, blue jeans, heavy work boots and both were rather large, tough looking guys. The man named Hector had brown skin, arms covered in colorful tattoos and was wearing a black skull cap. The other man was a Caucasian version of Hector but had a long blond ponytail all held in place with a worn and faded Red Bull baseball hat.

Captain Pickles ducked back down behind the car door so that he was completely out of sight and signaled for Burrito Betty and Flannel Freddie to do the same. They waited in silence until they heard the two guys return with the couch. Bix slowly raised his head enough to look through the car from the driver's window and whispered down to the other two that they were just about done loading the truck.

"Hey, don't close the doors yet," Hector said, "I need to grab two pillows from that sectional that we forgot in the showroom."

The two men then disappeared back inside the building and the time had clearly come for the hobos to hop in. They all did a quick three hundred and sixty degree scan of their surroundings and Bix gave the signal to go. Freddie was first inside, Poots jumped in right behind him and the Stinkbomb brought up the rear. The truck was mostly full but since it was large furniture, there were a lot of spaces to hide. They all worked their way as close to the cab as possible and positioned themselves in a way that they thought would make them invisible from the two large back doors, but were in a position where they could still all see each other. Within another few minutes, the two men returned and they could hear one of them climb up into the driver's seat and start the engine while the other closed and secured the doors. He got up into the passenger seat, slammed the door and the truck started moving.

Bix put his finger to his pursed lips and looked at both Betty and Freddie in the semi-darkness of the truck so if there had been any doubt, they knew not to make even a single sound. This become immediately obvious when the two men in the cab started talking and the hobos could clearly hear every word they said.

"So it's about 3:15 now. We should get to Tohatchi at about four, unload and be back here by five, five fifteen at the latest," the man named Hector said. "We timed today perfectly, wouldn't you say, Vince?"

"Right on, dude! Sure beats how things worked out yesterday. My girlfriend was really pissed that I got home so late. I tried to explain to her about all the things that went wrong with that delivery we made to Grants but she didn't want to hear anything about it. We were having a cookout at her sister's house and got there a little late. Not a big deal to me, in fact, I kind of liked getting there late so I didn't have to be around her annoying husband any more than necessary. That guy is such a fucking blowhard!"

"I hear ya, man! I've got a few relatives like that too!"

To get out of Gallup, the truck needed to make a few sharp turns and go through a series of traffic lights. In the back of the truck, the turns were somewhat challenging as the furniture shifted a bit inside and the hobos needed to use their bodies and various appendages to maintain their space without making any sort of discernable sound or having any of the furniture land on them. The same thing was true when the truck slowed down for a stop sign or red light and then accelerated again but at least this motion was more predictable.

"Shit, man, what's going on up here?" Vince asked after a few minutes of silence up front passed.

"Looks like a sobriety checkpoint or something like that," Hector observed. "You haven't been drinking today, have you man?"

"Not yet, but I can almost taste that first beer!"

"Okay, we're cool then. Just be sure to smile and answer their questions. Don't pull any shit this time, dude. Remember, we both want to get back on time today."

The truck slowed down to a full stop then periodically started and stopped a few times before they made it to the head of the line.

"What's happening, officer?" Vince asked, sounding as friendly as he could, even though he could feel the anger starting to work its way up inside him.

"License and registration, please. Where are you gentlemen heading this afternoon?" the police woman asked.

"Just delivering some furniture to Tohatchi. We just put in our last load of the day," Vince responded as he dug his driver's license out of his wallet that was resting on the center console while Hector rummage through the glove box to find the truck's registration.

"Where did your delivery originate, sir?"

"We just left Kokopelli's Big Furniture Mart on Roundhouse Lane a few minutes ago and we're driving straight north on 491 to the Tohatchi Chapter of the Navajo Nation building on Choos Gai Drive, " he said looking down at the delivery slip that was on a clipboard that Hector had just handed him.

"Could I see that routing slip please? Kokopelli's is near the railyard, right?"

"Yes ma'am, it is. What seems to be the problem?"

"We just received a report of a missing child in the company of two adults that were recently spotted in that general area, sir. Please pull your truck over into that parking lot. We'd like to take a look inside, if you don't mind," the police woman said after writing down Vince's license information and the truck's registration number. She pointed across the street to a vacant lot where two additional squad cars waited.

CHAPTER 8

"CAN'T WE DRIVE a little faster?" Roxanne asked Officer Ramirez as his cruiser was passing cars with a regular frequency.

"I'm sorry ma'am, I'm already driving a little faster than I should be. Just sit back and relax if you can. We'll be back in Belén in about forty-five minutes. Have you gotten any more texts from your son?" he asked hoping to divert her attention from the drive and her understandable anxiety for a moment.

"No, you would have heard about it if I had, don't you think?" she responded sharply.

Officer Ramirez quickly came to the conclusion that making small-talk with Mrs. Wappinger, at this time and under these circumstances, was going to be about as successful as trying to talk to his own wife when she was at her hormonal worst about most any topic but especially any topic having to do with finances, exercise, drinking, his poker playing, vacuuming or sex, and not necessarily in that order. In fact, the tone of voice that Mrs. Wappinger just used could have been his own wife if they did a complete body, hair, makeup and clothing swap. If it weren't for those differences, he could have closed his eyes and imagined it was his wife sitting in the backseat, which he did, only without the closing of the eyes part. He was starting to look forward to getting back to Belén and dropping the kid's high-strung mother off at her fancy modern subdivision mini-mansion even though it underscored the comparatively modest and possibly even, by some standards, dumpy ranch house that he and his family lived in across town.

The traffic on his police radio had been pretty steady, with all the usual things that police radios are used for to communicate between officers and the dispatch office. However, given the seriousness and urgency of a missing child situation, there was a lot of extra traffic related to the incident. Up until this point, it was mostly communication between the patrolmen and women on duty to keep everyone apprised of the latest developments, which at this point, amounted to nothing that he didn't already know. As the time got closer to 16:00 when the shifts changed in the Belén Police Department, Officer Ramirez assumed everyone coming onto the second shift had already been briefed on the situation at their shift meeting.

"Attention all units," the voice of the Belén police dispatcher began and immediately caught Officer Ramirez and Roxanne Wappinger's attention. "We have an update from Lieutenant Forsmark via Colonel Morgan from the NMSP Headquarters regarding the 10-57, Belén resident, six-year-old Zeke Wappinger. They report that three witnesses have provided positive identification of the missing child in Gallup, New Mexico at approximately 15:10 this afternoon. The missing child is believed to be in the vicinity of Wilson Avenue and North 4th Street and is described as wearing a red Albuquerque Isotopes tee shirt, black gym shorts, a baseball hat with a railroad insignia and sneakers . . ."

"Oh my God, that's him!" his mom cried out, sitting far forward on the edge of the backseat while Officer Ramirez tried to tactfully quiet her down so they could hear the full message.

". . . and is described as four feet tall, approximately forty pounds . . ."

"He's taller and weighs more than that!" Roxanne yelled at the radio.

". . . dark brown shoulder length wavy hair, brown eyes and is missing a front tooth. He is in the company of two adults, one male and one female . . ."

"Holy Christ!"

". . . ages estimated between thirty and sixty years old, both wearing outfits that can best be described as hobo-like and answering to the names Alan and Annie Wilson. Witnesses were reasonably confident that these are not their real names. They also told police that they did not seem to be dangerous persons and there was no indication that they were armed. The two suspects and the missing child were last seen at Our Lady of Saint Jorge and Geronimo de Gallup Catholic Church at a soup kitchen. 10-4."

Officer Cellucci, who was about twenty-five miles closer to Albuquerque than Officer Ramirez at the time of the radio broadcast but still ten car lengths behind Lieutenant Forsmark, heard the exact same message on her two-way police radio and knew that Roxanne Wappinger had just gotten the news as well. She had noticed Lieutenant Forsmark leaning over on occasion to grab his radio's microphone and appeared to be speaking into it and figured there might be some new developments. She was still trying to formulate theories about the two trains that went in opposite directions out of Belén, the one that transported his GPS watch to Tucumcari and the one that apparently transported Zeke to Gallup. Maybe the kid threw the watch onto the train just to throw people off his trail, maybe the two adult hobos did it for him, maybe it was somehow accidental or perhaps there was another explanation that she hadn't considered. What was clear to her and probably everyone else who was a part of this ordeal was how anxious she was to find out what really happened. Given the last message, however, she was extremely optimistic that soon everyone would know the entire story and the little boy would be back at home without experiencing any sort of harm.

Andrew Wappinger was still back at his house in Belén and trying hard to focus on having positive thoughts in spite of his heightened anxiety level. While continuing to monitor both the location of Zeke's GPS watch as it made its way west on I-40 in Roxanne's hand and the news on the television, he hoped it might possibly reveal some information that wasn't being communicated to him. He had the station set to KOAT, the Albuquerque ABC affiliate that did a pretty good job of covering national, state and local news. Not entirely to his surprise but with a jolt that was roughly the equivalent of a strong electrical charge to his nards, he saw a breaking news AMBER Alert message appear followed by a short news story on Zeke's disappearance, anchored by the overly coiffed and highly tanned Sheila Watkins. He always wondered why the makeup people at the television station made her look so artificial. He had met her in real life when she interviewed him last year on a controversial cattle-grazing plan that he had spearheaded and, like most things that he did at the BLM, pissed some large segment of the local population off and was therefore deemed newsworthy.

"An AMBER Alert for a six-year-old Belén boy was issued around 11:15 a.m. today out of Valencia County, New Mexico. Colonel Jack Morgan of the New Mexico State Police Headquarters in Santa Fe reports the boy is suspected to be heading east towards Tucumcari on a freight train. It is not known at this time if this is a kidnapping but the state police are treating it as one, as a precaution, even though Colonel Morgan says there is no evidence to indicate foul play. According to the boy's father, Andrew Wappinger, a natural resource planner for the Bureau of Land Management in Albuquerque, the boy, Zeke Wappinger, as you see in this recent photo, is described as Caucasian, four feet tall, forty pounds, long brown hair, brown eyes, missing two front teeth and has a few scrapes on his right arm. It is not known what the child was wearing at the time of his disappearance. Anyone with any information is asked to call the number of the New Mexico State Police listed at the bottom of this screen. We will be following this story to its conclusion and wish the best to the Wappinger family. Oh, excuse me; I was just informed that the boy's mother, Roxanne Wappinger, is a well-known, prominent attorney in the greater Albuquerque area. We will have further updates as they become available. Come home safely, little Zeke," Sheila added, completely off-script and her producer cringed off-camera as Sheila was prone to this sort of thing and he had asked her many times to stick to the teleprompter.

"Their information is already dated," Andrew said aloud to himself, as he had received the phone call from his wife saying they had found Zeke's watch in Tucumcari about half an hour ago and that the text message he sent to Roxanne had been traced to Gallup. He called his wife as soon as he saw this first AMBER Alert message on TV but for some reason, she didn't answer and he didn't bother leaving a message. He went back to his computer monitor and saw that she was still traveling along the interstate about forty miles or so east of Albuquerque. Remembering her last request of him, he decided to use this time to go into the kitchen and start making a lunch for them when he heard his phone play Roxanne's country love song ringtone.

"Honey, Zeke's disappearance was just on the TV news!" Andrew said excitedly, expressing both surprise and concern at the same time.

"I'm not surprised. That's a good thing though. Listen, Andrew, we just got information that Zeke was spotted at some church soup kitchen in Gallup. The police there talked to three people that Zeke apparently had lunch with. Absolutely a positive identification. Now, here's the kicker. Apparently, he's in the company of an older man and woman and the witnesses think that they're hobos!"

"Hobos? Are you kidding me? Hobos? What the hell is he doing with hobos? I know he's obsessed with trains and all but this is insane! You think that all along he just wanted to run away and become a hobo?"

"Andrew, calm down for a moment. I need to make this brief so shut up for a second and listen to me. I think the police are closing in on rescuing him. They know more-or-less where he is and I'm confident they'll find him real soon. I swear, if I get my hands on those people, they're gonna rue the day they kidnapped our son!" In the background,

Andrew heard a voice that he assumed was Officer Ramirez say that there's no evidence that your son has been kidnapped.

"He's been kidnapped?"

"Well, not officially, but why the hell else would Zeke just disappear in the middle of the night? Those damned hobos must have abducted him. It happens all the time and sometimes you just never hear about it. They're a shifty, untrustworthy bunch." There was a brief pause for a moment and Andrew heard a muffled conversation between his wife and Officer Ramirez. "Okay, well, Officer Ramirez doesn't want me jumping to any conclusions here, but regardless, I'll be home shortly. Make sure you've got the food and drinks ready. See you soon." She disconnected the call before Andrew could respond any further.

Andrew was used to Roxanne's alpha personality and her sometimes-volatile reactions. He usually went along with her approach to things but chalked up her latest theory of kidnapping to a simple overreaction to a very stressful situation. He thought back to when they had first met about fifteen years ago when she was a law student at Stanford and he was doing work on his Masters in Earth Sciences at the University of California at Santa Cruz about an hour away. Some friends dragged him along to a bar in Sunnyvale, not exactly kicking and screaming, where they had plans to meet up with some friends of these friends who were bringing Roxanne along to get her away from her books for a few hours. Unlike Andrew, she was figuratively kicking and screaming. Given Sunnyvale's location in the heart of Silicon Valley, the place was filled mostly with computer nerds and flashy high-rolling entrepreneurs who were just starting to see the fruits of their business labor take off in the early stages of the dot com bubble. The mood was rather festive as the taste and smell of money and success seemed to bring out the best in those most likely to benefit from the emerging technology boom.

Now the name of this place, as Andrew recalled and as Roxanne has reminded him many times since, was Butterball's Bikini Bar. Since their motto was "Better than any other bar or strip club combined," Andrew wasn't at all disappointed when he and his friends walked in and saw a whole bunch of super sexy waitresses all wearing bikini tops and tight little shorts. He also noticed various dance platforms with ceiling to platform poles currently being worked over by a bevy of scantily clad women wearing even less cladding than most of the waitresses, and in some cases, none at all. Twenty minutes later, when Roxanne walked in with her entourage, her reaction was one of supreme disappointment and disgust and she would have turned around right then and left if she had come in her own vehicle. Since she hadn't, she was promised by her friends that they would leave if things were too skanky or if the situation was uncomfortable for her.

Roxanne had been a super-focused law student. She intentionally dumped her previous boyfriend right after graduating from UCLA before coming to Stanford just to make sure that her distractions were minimal. Like Roxanne, Andrew was in his early twenties at the time and hadn't really had any serious long-term relationships in his life up until this point. Given the peculiarities of fate, Andrew and Roxanne ended up being seated next to each other at the far end of the table and were somewhat cut-off from the mainstream conversation that seemed to be in full force at the other end so it was logical that they would converse with each other.

Andrew's first impression of Roxanne was very positive. She was slender, tall, athletic looking, had gorgeous long wavy black hair, stunning sparkling green eyes slightly magnified behind stylish glasses, was dressed more conservatively than most young adults of their approximate age but had the most delicious, juicy lips and a big mouth, in more ways than one. As Roxanne told Andrew about a year later when they had both graduated and began dating more seriously, she was surprised that he looked less like a stereotypical Santa Cruz surfer-boy and more like an Ivy League privileged preppie-type.

He thought that was a fairly accurate description since he had grown up in New England and had been shipped off to prep school at a fairly young age until it was time to go to college. Having grown up with a single, unmarried mom and two rather wealthy grandparents, he liked to say that he was raised by two moms and an elderly but kindly dad. His mom married later in life but Andrew wasn't around enough at that point to develop much of a relationship with his stepfather, even though he ended up with his last name. The three of them took very good care of him but also watched his every move like three hawks. Even though he ended up at one of the premier preppie bastions of the Ivy League, Amherst College, he never really felt like one of the super-preppies. While he was at Amherst, he had cultivated what he thought was a more anti-preppie look and thrived in the Five College area counter-culture, post-hippie, post-grunge, post-Goth and post-punk eras and became active in various left wing environmental and political movements while also embracing the outdoor pursuits of mountain biking, snowboarding, back-country camping, white-water kayaking and various other adventure sports that western Massachusetts was known for. He probably still looked kind of preppie, though, and had sophisticated bookwormy good looks, was a few inches over six feet, in pretty good shape at this time of his life, had curly dark longish hair, blue eyes and his trademark soul patch which was a little ahead of it's time in the rise and fall of the soul patch popularity curve.

As he remembered, their conversation that night was mostly of future career plans and how they both wanted jobs and lives that made a difference in the world and continue the mostly progressive policies of the Clinton administration. However, Roxanne also made it clear to him how distasteful this strip club scene was to her and that anyone who enjoyed this sort of thing was a misguided misogynist. Andrew knew that if he was going to have any future with this lady, he had to agree with her and try to hide his ogling of the women. Andrew succeeded in letting her attitude wash right over him because he was quickly becoming enthralled by Roxanne's intelligence, assertiveness, attractiveness and humor. He was only barely aware of the busty bikini-clad waitress that came by periodically to take orders and then serve food and drinks to the table, leaning over into his face threatening to absorb his thoughts and words into her cleavage. This, too, became a recurring theme in their early courtship and subsequent marriage when Roxanne would accuse him of having a disrespectful wandering eye with this sort of distraction. However, he was certain that the night at Butterball's Bikini Bar was not one of them, because, despite how hard it was to give her his full attention, he felt he had passed with flying colors.

When the evening was wrapping up and it was clear to both of them that a connection had been made, Roxanne was the one to set the ground rules. They both had another full year of academia and she was very clear that law school was her number one priority. Andrew remembered feeling a little deflated by this proclamation, as it was clear even at this first meeting that Roxanne was someone he wanted to get to know better. Andrew was the one that usually set up the boundaries and barriers to fit his lifestyle and now she beat him at his own game. Perhaps they could get together for dinner sometime in a few weeks, Roxanne suggested, as she wouldn't have much free time between now and then. It was a take it or leave it offer which he couldn't in his right mind refuse. Her one condition, however, was that it wouldn't be a place that featured either bikinis or stripper poles.

After Lieutenant Forsmark had received the information update about Zeke's confirmed sighting from Ellen LaToya out of the NMSP Gallup office, he made his first call to Colonel Morgan at the Santa Fe Headquarters who then relayed the information to their dispatcher and eventually passed it on to the Belén Police Department dispatcher who broadcasted the message that Officer Ramirez and Roxanne Wappinger had just heard. Remarkably, unlike a game of "telephone," the message maintained its accuracy throughout the entire communication chain. His job done for the moment, he just sat back and enjoyed the thrill of driving at high speed back to the Albuquerque barracks knowing the cute ballgirl and her dog were following him and that they would soon be spending some extended and hopefully, quality time together. They arrived at the barracks around four in the afternoon, right around the time they both would be getting off work on a normal day, and if he had any say in the matter, this wasn't going to be one of them.

The two police officers pulled in next to each other in the parking lot. Lieutenant Forsmark told Officer Cellucci that he needed to quickly run in, use the facilities and grab some food before they continued on their next leg to Gallup and invited her to come in and do the same thing. Having never been inside the NMSP Albuquerque office before, she figured anything she could do to further her career was worthwhile. Plus, she really had to pee and knew that she had better grab some food, not knowing when the next opportunity would present itself. It wouldn't have made a very good impression on the lieutenant if she had wet her pants.

They entered through the side staff door after Lieutenant Forsmark swiped his ID on the card reader and they were immediately smack dab in the middle of the frantic energy vortex of the state police field office. Even though he worked out of the Clovis office, every police officer had access to each field office and considered all NMSP officers to be their colleagues. He introduced Daria Cellucci to a few of his Albuquerque counterparts and she got the feeling she had when one of her dates would show her off to their friends like a prized trophy or amazing treasure at a show and tell. She tolerated the attention but was somewhat tired of the responses she usually got from men just because they usually stepped all over themselves to bask in her attractiveness. Women, at the opposite end of the spectrum, often reacted with condescension mixed undoubtedly with jealousy, which was even worse when the women were other police officers who might not have taken her that seriously based solely on her looks.

Daria Cellucci was well acquainted with the mostly unwanted attention she received from her fellow officers but was almost always able to deflect it by maintaining a professional attitude in the atmosphere of the military-like police protocol. She would treat the male in question like she would treat any citizen she was interacting with out on the streets while on active duty in the real police world of Belén or wherever her duties took her. However, in her other world as the Albuquerque Isotopes ballgirl, where her working uniform consisted of a fairly skimpy tank top with the team's logo plastered across her undeniable curvy chest, short red shiny shorts with a yellow lightning bolt down both sides, an Isotopes ball cap and knee-high baseball style socks and running shoes, she received an extraordinary amount of attention. The protocol of the much more overt and rowdy ballplayers—from the new rookies full of big league dreams and aspirations to the seasoned veterans in the fading glory of their past successes and the harsh reality of closing out their once illustrious careers in the minor leagues - was more challenging for her. Not only did many of them feel some sort of imprudent entitlement to perhaps hook up with the sexy ballgirl but also they were less likely to interpret her direct refusals, body language, facial expressions and social cues as "no." Daria wasn't the sort of person that could be pushed around or bullied and she absolutely never did anything that she didn't want to do. She had had a pretty tough upbringing in a rougher part of Albuquerque and her take-charge personality was clearly honed from a combination of street smarts, native intelligence and a no-nonsense approach to people. Not that she turned down all advances but she was very selective and any relationship she started was on her own terms. In her own words, when speaking with one of her few girlfriends, especially when they went out drinking, "Guys are so easy, kind of like training a puppy. They just want to make you happy and have you pet them."

Lieutenant Forsmark pointed the way to the women's room and showed her where the break room was located. After using the facilities herself, she wandered into the room where she had been invited to help herself to anything and where she agreed to meet Lieutenant Forsmark.

"I would highly recommend the chicken pesto wrap," said a macho looking police officer that had followed her into the room. "Either that or the ham and swiss club. Both are in the refrigerator on the middle shelf."

"Are there any vegetarian options?" Daria Cellucci asked and it was probably one of the questions she asked more than any other. The other questions she found herself asking quite often were, "What part of 'no' don't you understand?" and "Did I say that you could do that?"

"Don't tell me you're one of those veg heads," he asked, seemingly oblivious that this choice of words with Daria was kind of like walking around with a sandwich board sign that said "I am an A-hole. Avoid me like the plague."

"I am. Do you have a problem with that officer?"

"Officer Darling, Bruce Darling. Pleased to meet you, officer . . . ?"

"Cellucci, Officer Cellucci."

"And no, I don't have a problem with that. We just don't have many fellow officers that are vegetarians but you might be able to find a tuna sandwich in there someplace if you root around enough. No guarantees on how old it might be, though."

"Let me clarify this. I'm a vegetarian. That means that I don't eat meat. Meat includes beef, pork, chicken, fish, ostrich, bear, wild boar, turkey, things that walk or fly, get the idea? I'm also a vegan, which means that I don't eat dairy products or foods that are in any way derived from animals, like eggs. I eat vegetables, beans, fruit, grains—you know, foods like that. Understand?"

"Slow down there, lady! I was just trying to be helpful. Would you eat a bean burrito? You might be able to find some of them in there."

"Now we're getting somewhere. As long as it doesn't have sour cream, cheese or yoghurt."

"Why would you restrict yourself like this?" Officer Darling asked but luckily Officer Cellucci was spared from yet another philosophical food discussion as Officer Forsmark came in and told her he was ready to blast out to Gallup.

She grabbed a bean burrito and a can of unsweetened iced tea and the two of them walked out of the building and to the Belén K-9 cruiser. Bullet was let out of the car to answer his own call of nature, given a little treat and had his bowl on the floor of the backseat filled with some water from a bottle Daria had filled up inside the barracks. They were soon on the road again and careening along I-40 west towards Gallup with Officer Cellucci behind the wheel and Lieutenant Forsmark riding shotgun.

"I see you met Bruce Darling."

"Is he always that clueless?"

"Clueless? Yes. I think that might in fact be his middle name. If anyone in our unit ever got called in on a two eighty-eight, I would immediately think that it must be Officer Darling. He's gone through all of the required sexual harassment and workplace tolerance training like all of us, hell, I think his supervisor even required him to attend the optional inappropriate work topics training but I'm not sure it really sunk in with him. There's something about attractive women that turns his brain to rotten tomatillos. He's a good officer but a bit awkward socially, as you discovered. Listen, getting off that topic for a moment, I'd like to ask you about this young child, Zeke Wappinger, since you were called to the scene soon after the boy was reported missing. Am I correct?"

"Yes, Lieutenant. Officer Ramirez was the first to respond to the 9-1-1 call but I was asked to assist at the scene with my dog Bullet to provide tracking services."

"And you met both parents?"

"Correct, I interacted first with the husband because he was the one who discovered that his son was missing while his wife was away working. She's a lawyer in the Albuquerque area. I'm not sure what he does, I think he told me, something to do with natural resources, I seem to recall. Anyway, both of them seem to have pretty demanding jobs."

"What is your feeling about this boy? Do you think he ran away or do you think he was abducted?"

"Good question. I got the sense from the mother that she is so wrapped up in her career that she might not be the most attentive or sensitive person in the world to the needs of a young six-year-old boy. I got the feeling that the father might be the more nurturing parent but it's really hard for me to pass judgment at this point. However, you got to meet the mother at the rail station in Tucumcari. What was your impression?"

"Yeah, kind of driven. A classic over-achiever and multi-tasker. I could see where a kid might feel that he has a lot of competition for some attention."

As the cruiser crested the Continental Divide a few miles west of Grants which was really only a low rise followed by a gradual descent towards Gallup, Lieutenant Forsmark tried to chat Officer Cellucci up with a bunch of personal questions but she stonewalled him as much as possible without appearing to be rude. Unlike Officer Clueless Darling, Lieutenant Forsmark read her answers, body language and tone of voice more accurately and kept the conversation on a more professional level and managed not to raise any of her hackles very much. In fact, Daria Cellucci was rather enjoying his company and semi-intelligent conversation as she barreled along the interstate at such a high rate of speed. As they passed a sign saying "Gallup 15," Lieutenant Forsmark received a call on his mobile police radio from Colonel Morgan in the Santa Fe Headquarters with an important update on the missing boy.

At the same moment, Officer Ramirez was just pulling into the upscale Ladera Drive neighborhood in Belén and dropped Roxanne Wappinger off by her front door. With a gentle reminder to let the police do their work without any interference, he also said that he would keep her and her husband up-to-date with any new developments. Roxanne thanked him, strode quickly into the house and greeted her husband as best she could considering she was experiencing such an enormous amount of worry and anxiety.

"Do you have the food and drinks ready? As soon as Officer Ramirez is out of the neighborhood, I want to drive out to Gallup and find Zeke," Roxanne said emphatically, leaving no room for discussion.

"Do you think that's a good idea? I heard what he said to you about not interfering with the police."

"This is our son, Andrew! He's with a couple of desperate hobos! We've got to go find him and bring him home before these low-life bums get crazy ideas about extorting a ransom or something even worse. I can't even think about what they're doing to him."

"Have you heard anything to indicate that his life is in peril?" Andrew asked with more than a hint of panic in his voice. "Is there some information that you haven't told me yet?"

"No, but I don't want to be too complacent here. Isn't it obvious that they tried to throw us off his trail by strapping his GPS watch to the inside of a boxcar going the opposite direction? These people are up to no good and we've got to go get him before they have a chance to pull any more stunts like that one."

"But you told me that his text message said that he was fine and that he'd be home soon. Why would he text that message if the hobos were mistreating him?"

"Geez, Andrew, you're so damned gullible. Do you really think he texted that message? It was clearly sent by those criminal kidnappers! Zeke's pretty good with his punctuation and that message didn't have any. It's got to be obvious, even to you, that one of those uneducated bums sent it."

"But how would they know your phone number?" Andrew challenged.

"Man, do I always have to supply all the brain power here? I'm sure they somehow coerced the information out of him. Listen, we can talk about this on our drive but let's get rolling. Time is wasting! Let's take your car."

Roxanne grabbed some extra clothing and a few personal items in case they were going to be away for an extended period of time while Andrew threw the food and drinks into a small cooler with a few ice packs. He then unplugged his fully charged cellphone, tucked it into his man purse along with his wallet and did one last check of his computer to see if there was any new information to report. He noted that Zeke's GPS tracking watch was at 398 Ladera Drive but knew it was because Roxanne had thrown it into the basket by the front door when she arrived.

"Got everything, honey?" he asked when they rendezvoused in their foyer. "More sirens? That's becoming an all too familiar sound today."

Officer Ramirez was only about a mile down the road and on his way back to the police station when he heard a broadcast from Lieutenant Forsmark and immediately put on his siren and lights, banged a tight U-turn, raced back to the Wappinger house and was about to knock on their front door. As he reached towards the ornate brass roadrunner door knocker, Roxanne and Andrew opened the door on their way out and almost bowled him over.

"Mr. and Mrs. Wappinger! They have your son and the two hobos in custody! Let's get into my cruiser and go to Gallup!"

CHAPTER 9

"**D**AMN, DUDE, I'M gonna get home late again. I just know it," said Vince, the blond ponytailed driver of the furniture delivery truck, looking over at Hector sitting in the passenger seat as he maneuvered the vehicle across the street into the vacant lot where other police officers were waiting to search vehicles. "You didn't see any stowaways in the back, did you, dude?"

"No, man, not unless they snuck in when we were inside getting our stuff. I threw those ugly sectional pillows in and shut the doors quickly so I didn't have to look at them any longer than necessary. I would have seen people if they'd been hanging out inside."

"Yeah, dude, but there are a lotta places to hide in there."

There were two other vehicles being searched and one of the officers pointed to where he wanted Vince to park his truck and wait his turn. One of the vehicles was a sparkly, fluorescent green 1968 Chevy Impala low-rider that was carrying four Latino men who were all now relegated to standing off to the side watching while one of the officers searched the trunk of the car. This turned out to be a pretty quick task since it was filled almost entirely with the hydraulics necessary to get the car to hop around to ungodly heights and to be able to drive around on two of it's wheels like a circus car. The other vehicle was an old Dodge van with a paint job that had been almost entirely oxidized by the blazing hot New Mexican sun. Two older people - a man in a tank top and shorts with his long, fuzzy white hair pulled back in a ratty sort of bun and a scruffy plus sized woman dressed similarly and cradling their pet Lhasa Apso against her barely contained massive bosoms - also watched from the edge of the parking lot. The officer that was searching the van was inside and probably had a bunch of potential hiding places to investigate.

The low-rider was cleared for departure and the officer apologized to the men for the inconvenience. He thanked them for their cooperation, which wasn't acknowledged by the men, and then walked over to where the Kokopelli's Big Furniture Mart truck was parked. He asked Vince and Hector if they would please step outside the vehicle and open up the backdoors. Hector walked around to the back, unlocked the doors and threw them both open.

"Thank you, sir. If you and your friend would please step aside and stand over there, I'd be most appreciative," the officer said without sounding too unfriendly. Both Hector and Vince dutifully followed his directions in spite of their frustration with the delay they were expecting for their last delivery of the day. It was a Saturday and they were anxious to start their already short weekend.

The police officer had already looked inside the cab of the truck while the men were getting out, confident that three missing people could not have been hiding in there. He went around to the back and pulled out his huge flashlight to root around inside the cargo area. After a preliminary search, looking under the legs of the chairs, couches and tables as best he could, he didn't see anything. His next step was to climb up into the truck to make a closer inspection. Still not seeing any missing child or hobos, he called the men over to explain his concern.

"Gentlemen, there are clearly any number of places for people to hide back here but without taking some of this furniture out or crawling back in there myself, I won't be able to give it a thorough search. Would you please remove a few of these items for me?"

Vince and Hector looked at each other and made faces that said "are you freaking nuts?" but instead, without a verbal response and realizing that they really had no other options, started removing the furniture piece by piece and arranging it in the parking lot in a semi-circle around the back doors until the truck was about a quarter empty.

"I'd be super surprised if anyone or anything unexpected were to show up," Vince said to the officer as his muscles started to glisten in the mid-afternoon heat and sunshine. "We were really hoping to get out of work on time today for a change."

"I'm sorry, sir. We'll make this as quick and painless as possible. I'll help you reload the furniture if that would help," the officer offered as a way to soften the inconvenience to the moving men. When the large sofa was out of the truck, the officer crouched down again but this time saw something of interest. "That looks like a little pair of sneakers and they seem to be attached to a pair of two little legs." He called over to his fellow officer who had just sent the couple in the van on their way and asked him to come over and provide some assistance. "I think we found what we're looking for."

The two movers came over to join the two police officers and everyone bent down to see where the flashlight beam was shining. Zeke, Bix and Betty now realized that a clean escape was not going to be the order of the day so they started moving around and began the process of extracting themselves. After some furniture readjustment, the three stowaways tried to start working their way towards the open truck doors. Both officers instinctively drew their guns, not knowing what sort of situation they were about to encounter but, as their training had taught them, were prepared for the worst.

Flannel Freddie, the Deviled Ham's cute little face was the first one to appear as he had the easiest time getting out of his hiding place and could fit through the smallest places. He poked his face out from under one of the upholstered chairs and looked directly at the gang of four, two with guns and two with their jaws dropping towards their shoes.

"Don't hurt me or my friends," Zeke yelled out. As he scooted on his belly towards the men, he added, "You can put your guns away. We're all coming out but it might take Captain Bix Pickles and Burrito Betty a few minutes. They're in there pretty tight."

What followed immediately after that was the sound of furniture being jostled around inside the truck and then the sound of a chair falling over, which was then followed by Burrito Betty, the Princess of Poots yelling out, "For the love of Christ, would someone come help me out of here? My legs have cramped up from being wrapped around these stools and I can't move!"

"Hold on, you loo loo. I'll yank your sorry ass out as soon as I can get my sorry ass out of this crack," Captain Bix Pickles Haskell yelled out and it caused Flannel Freddie to explode in a cascade of chuckles.

"What the hell are you dudes doing in our moving truck?" Vince yelled out. He was immediately asked by the first patrolman to go stand over by the edge of the parking lot with his colleague Hector. As soon as Zeke started laughing, both policemen realized that this wasn't a dangerous situation, nodded to each other and holstered their pistols.

The two officers jumped up inside the truck and positioned themselves on either side of the prone Zeke who was trying his best to pull himself through the four legs of a chair. They bent down, grabbed him by the shoulders and gently pulled him past the chair and in one smooth arc, got him into a standing position. Both officers were a bit surprised by the kid's tiny size.

"Are you Zeke Wappinger from Belén?" the first officer asked.

"Yes, officer, I am. These are my friends, Captain Bix Pickles Haskell, the Human Stinkbomb and Burrito Betty, the Princess of Poots. Can you please help get them out of the truck?" he asked in his little six-year-old voice that had taken on a road weary but worldly timber in the last sixteen hours of his jam-packed hobo experience.

The officers looked at each other and couldn't keep themselves from tittering at the hobo's names but tried to maintain a professional appearance. The second policeman stuck his head out of the truck and called the two movers over to get their help and advice. In the meantime, the first officer told Zeke that he needed to pat him down to make sure he wasn't carrying any concealed weapons.

"Gentlemen, there are two other suspects in the back of your truck that are having a hard time extricating themselves. Would you remove a few more items of the furniture to make it easier for them?" the second patrolman asked.

The two men jumped up into the truck and saw Flannel Freddie standing beside the policemen in his dirty Isotopes tee shirt and shorts, looking more and more like he was a street urchin from a modern day version of *Oliver*. From the back of the truck, they heard more grunting and groaning, followed by Burrito Betty's usual gaseous punctuations as she tried to move out of her hiding place. Captain Bix was about half out of his space when the mover's told him to just hold still for a moment so they could remove the two end tables blocking his way out.

"If any of this furniture gets scratched or damaged, it comes out of our hide. Just hold on there, old timer! We'll get you and your girlfriend out in just a second!" Hector said sternly, but then lightened up a bit when he got a better look at Captain Bix. "Can't be too comfortable back there, huh, grandpa?"

They repositioned a few pieces of the furniture to the side of the truck and helped the old hobo to his feet. Bix was a bit wobbly even though he had only been curled up in his hiding place for about ten minutes. The officers told him to come stand beside Zeke and not to try any funny stuff.

"That's the last thing on my mind, officer," he responded in a very dignified manner. "Betty, hold on just a second longer. The men are coming to get you out."

Extracting Burrito Betty was a bit more challenging. She had somehow managed to get some of her rag clothing stuck inside the mechanism of the recliner that she had been pressed up against. The movers shifted the sofa blocking her exit route to the side and it revealed Betty, in all of her hobo glory, and the four non-hobo men reacted with an audible sucking in of their collective breaths at the sight of her.

"Hold on there, sister," the first police officer said. "We'll get you out of there as soon as the recliner lever is pulled. That should release your clothing."

Hector gently pulled up on the recliner lever while Vince not-so-gently had to yank some of her shabby and grubby material out from the metal mechanism that operated the foot rest. By rocking the lever a few times, he was able to get her unstuck.

"I hope you haven't turned any lice or bedbugs loose in here," Vince admonished. "How did you three dudes get in here, anyway?"

"Sir, we'll take over the questioning from here. We appreciate your help but we need to take all five of you to the station for questioning. I'm sorry but that's the way this is going to have to work. This young boy is a missing child so all of you folks will have some explaining to do. Officer Danforth, would you please get on the radio to dispatch and tell them what we found and let them know that we'll be coming into the station shortly? You two, please put your furniture back inside, lock up, call your supervisor, do whatever you need to do because it's going to be a while before you're going to be allowed to continue on with your delivery."

Vince and Hector went about their task with less-than-sunny dispositions. What they didn't anticipate, however, was another unpleasant surprise that awaited them. Once the three hobos were out of the truck and standing together as a tidy but shabby little family unit in the parking lot, the officer who wasn't Officer Danforth pulled his set of handcuffs off his belt and strapped them on Bix and Betty, one on each wrist "until we find another set and can cuff you properly," the officer explained.

"Officer, these people didn't do anything wrong!" Zeke cried out when he saw what was happening. "I ran away from home last night and they were trying to help me get back. I swear! If anyone should be handcuffed, it should be me!"

"Sorry, son, you are the former missing child and these are the people that might be responsible. I wouldn't be doing my job if I let two prime suspects escape. In addition, once Officer Danforth calls this in and returns, the two movers are getting his pair of handcuffs and then all of us are going to the station to try to straighten this thing out. I'm sure your mom and dad are going to be pretty happy to see you. It may be up to them to see what sort of charges they might want to file."

"Wait a second!" Vince said really loudly as he positioned a couch into the opening of the truck and overheard the conversation. "We're getting cuffed too?"

"You two are potentially an accessory to a two-oh-seven since you happened to be driving a vehicle containing a possible kidnapping victim."

"Nobody was kidnapped here!" Zeke exclaimed.

"I would advise all of you to remain silent at this point while I read you your Miranda rights. All five of you listen up," the officer said and waited until everyone had gathered around him. "You have the right to remain silent. Anything you say can, and will, be used against you in court of law. You have the right to an attorney. If you cannot afford one, one will be appointed to you. Do you all understand?"

They all nodded and looked down at their shoes, each one undoubtedly wondering what sort of mess they just found themselves in. Officer Danforth returned from his squad car and helped the men finish loading the furniture back in the truck and waited until they had locked everything up before attempting to slap his set of handcuffs on the two movers.

"Wait! Before you do this," Hector said backing away from the incoming handcuffs, "we need to call our office and tell them what's happening. There are people up in Tohachi that are expecting a delivery this afternoon."

Officer Danforth permitted him to make the call and then put the cuffs on the two movers, which only barely fit around their brawny wrists. Both officers then searched each of the three men and called the female officer over, who was no longer stopping suspected vehicles, to search Burrito Betty. When all were found to be clean, at least from a weapons perspective, he led the movers over to his patrol car while the second officer escorted the hobo family to the other car. Once inside, he told his passengers that he was Officer Stanton and that they were going to drive over to the New Mexico State Police District 6 office for questioning. Burrito Betty, still attached to Captain Bix Pickles by their wrists, let out a series of nervous poots which again caused Zeke to start laughing.

"I'm sorry I got you both into such trouble," Zeke said before Officer Stanton again reminded them that it was probably in everyone's best interest to remain silent for the duration of the short ride to the station. Bix and Betty both turned to him and nodded and Bix mouthed the words "don't worry, kid." Burrito Betty, the Princess of Poots, trying unsuccessfully to get her pooting under control, gave Zeke a reassuring pat on his head.

The drive to the police station only took a few minutes. The traffic on the police scanner was full of the news of the moment, namely, the capture of the two possible hobo kidnappers and the rescue of the abducted or runaway missing six-year-old from Belén. Zeke wondered where his parents were, if they had gotten the news yet and how they were going to react to all this. He guessed that his dad was going to be more happy than upset and that his mom would probably be more upset than happy. The fact that the police seemed intent upon treating Captain Haskell and the Princess of Poots as criminals was a huge source of fear and anxiety for Zeke. If he had anticipated this possibility, he might have tried to go it alone and not involve them in his adventure. They were great people, colorful and odiferous, certainly, but both of them had risked their own comfort and safety to look after him and were helping him to return home. Apparently, he had a lot to learn about the ways of the adult world. Zeke resolved then and there to do anything he possibly could to make sure they were treated as heroes, not kidnappers.

The police cruiser was driving the speed limit back to the station without the siren going or the lights flashing, which Zeke could tell by looking at their reflection in the large storefront windows they passed on the busy main street of Gallup. They even stopped at red lights and didn't really seem to attract any undue attention from the pedestrians walking the busy streets. As they got out towards the edge of the downtown region, the storefronts transitioned to motels and fast food joints, the pedestrians largely disappeared except for the occasional homeless person pushing a loaded shopping cart along the local highway and the landscape started opening up to a vista made up of the distinctive brown, white and red cliffs and mesas off in the distance with scattered homes on the high desert sagebrush between them and the distant hills. Zeke was struck by how different this area looked than his surroundings in Belén.

Officer Stanton got on his police radio and talked to the dispatcher telling them their location and estimated time of arrival. They also heard Officer Danforth reporting nearly the same information from his vehicle with the handcuffed movers. The dispatcher told both policemen to pull around to the back entrance since a small army of the media was beginning to arrive and stake out their positions in the front of the police station.

"Did you catch that folks?" Officer Stanton asked while turning around to look at the three hobos through the metal divider. "Sounds like it's circus time back at the station. I'm not sure Gallup has had this kind of excitement since that melee at the county fair a few years back. We'll try our best to get you inside for interrogation without any interference from the press but that doesn't mean that they're not going to try to ask you some questions and snap some pictures. I'd imagine the local television stations will be there as well and will probably be filming the whole thing live and for their broadcasts later. My advice is to cover your faces and not respond to any of them. It will only complicate matters. Understand?"

"How did everyone find out about this so fast?" Captain Haskell asked.

"Any number of ways, sir. All the newspapers and TV stations have police scanners so they can follow any communication we have over the airwaves. Each one wants to be the first to know about any breaking news story and this is surely one of them. They can also listen on the internet through their computers or smartphones so they know just about anything that's happening around here."

"Couldn't that jeopardize sensitive police communications?" Bix asked.

"Yes, good observation, sir. If we have information that we don't want the general public to hear, we have our own restricted channels, but we really only try to use those in a few special situations."

The patrol car slowed down and turned into the entranceway to the NMSP District 6 station. As expected, the crowd had gotten fairly large and the three hobos could see not only the swarm of reporters near the front of the building but also two news vans with large, fully extended antennae on top and satellite dishes pointing in various directions. There was also a variety of other vehicles with the names of newspapers and television stations plastered all over the sides. As the two cruisers pulled into the station, reporters started running towards the vehicles, followed closely behind by two different camera people lugging around unwieldy-looking large video cameras perched on their shoulders to capture the arrival of the missing child.

Both reporters from the two television stations were broadcasting live and tried to quickly walk backwards while talking into their microphones and trying to stay between their cameraperson and the police vehicles that had slowed down to work their way to the back of the buildings through the crowd of people. Unfortunately, their legs got tangled up with each other and they both tripped and fell over backwards. The perfectly groomed male reporter, in a tailored dark pinstriped suit and flashy red tie with elegantly styled salt and pepper hair, fell first and landed hard on his rump while the woman reporter, wearing trendy black high heels, a satiny blue sheath dress that had gotten hiked up over her hips revealing a miniscule black thong, superb makeup and what looked like a helmet of blond hair, fell face first on top of the man. Their subsequent squirming and grinding to get unstuck and back on their feet all the while trying to maintain their running monologue was ten seconds of pure, unintentional comedic genius, especially when one noted the juxtaposition of the man's microphone and the woman's thong that only marginally covered her private parts. Luckily, both camera people caught it on tape from two slightly different perspectives and both videos went viral on YouTube within hours. It was probably the one thing that most people around the world remember when the topic of the little boy from New Mexico who ran away from home to become a hobo was brought up in thousands, if not millions, of casual conversations. These videos spawned a veritable cottage industry of spin-off videos that garnered even more views—one interspersed this footage with the scene from *Bridget Jone's Diary* where Bridget, as a TV reporter, slides down the fire pole while her cameraman is filming the thigh squealing and subsequent super-wedgie from below and the other one used the video footage and mashed it up with the "I Got Bronchitis (music video) feat. Sweet Brown" talking about the fire she witnessed and claims "ain't nobody got time for that" complete with her synthesized singing voice and even the piano playing cat. This video took full advantage of the two humping reporters with special attention to her thong ribboning down her butt crack and his microphone action and made liberal use of the "ain't nobody got time for that" tagline. This video was viewed more than two million times in the first week alone.

Officer Stanton rolled up all four windows in his vehicle and made his way through the reporters and then through a gate in a chain link fence to get access to the restricted area behind the station. The second police vehicle followed closely behind and was now also followed by another police car, the K-9 cruiser from Belén. The reporters were not to be deterred and walked quickly beside the vehicles yelling out questions that went unanswered while the photographers flashed picture after picture, hoping to capture some sort of image of Zeke for their print and online editions. The camera people stopped videoing their now embarrassed reporters and concentrated on getting footage of the three vehicles. One camerawoman was even able to get within a few feet of the window that Zeke was looking out of with wide-eyed wonderment.

Once they cleared the fence, the vehicles parked as far away from the throng of reporters as possible but were positioned in such a way that they were still partially visible to them. As the five captives were led out of the vehicle, with the two movers and the two hobos handcuffed together, while Zeke walked beside them, cameras flashed, video cameras rolled and reporters shouted out questions.

Zeke heard questions such as "Why did you run away from home, Zeke?" "Did the hobos mistreat you?" "Are you worried that your parent's are going to be really angry at you?" and "What's it like to be a hobo?" He wanted to answer their questions but Officer Danforth, who was walking between him and the field of reporters, told Zeke to just ignore them and look straight ahead.

The three occupants of the K-9 police car now joined the entourage as they were about to enter the building. Officer Cellucci, with Bullet on his leash, came right over to Zeke and the dog went absolutely crazy barking, whining, and eventually assumed his supine position to indicate that he finally found what he was looking for.

"You must be Zeke Wappinger. I'm Officer Cellucci from the Belén Police Department. My dog Bullet and I have been tracking you all day. I think he wants to be your friend."

"Hi Bullet! I'd love to be his friend! I love dogs! I've been asking my parents for a dog now for about five years but they keep telling me not until I'm older and more responsible," Zeke said while patting Bullet's head, which apparently was permissible under these circumstances.

"We're so happy that you've been found safe and in good spirits," Officer Cellucci said. "And it looks like you're a fan of the Isotopes."

"I sure am but I've only ever been to one game. I know all the players. I even entered the contest last year to be the honorary batboy but I didn't win. Do you like the Isotopes?"

"I do. Maybe I could take you to a game sometime if your parents would let me. I would really love to do that and maybe we could even get you a new tee shirt. That one looks a little worn out."

"That would be so cool! My friend's dad was going to take us to a game last week but it was rained out. It was mini-bat day."

Officer Stanton motioned that it was time for everyone to proceed inside the station and said there would be time to talk about these kinds of details later. Once inside, it seemed that all the police and support staff were waiting for their arrival and wanted to catch a glimpse of the five characters involved in this case. The office had been buzzing since word first went out that the missing AMBER Alert boy was known to be in Gallup and got even more intense when it was discovered that he was spotted at the soup kitchen with two adult hobos and then reached a fever pitch when they heard that he was captured at a road block hiding in the back of the moving van just a few miles down the road. The three hobos and two movers were shown into an interrogation room, their handcuffs removed and instructed to have a seat because Major Queznal and Detective Anders would be joining them in a few minutes to begin the proceedings. They were offered some food and drink from a small refrigerator in the corner of the room and given the opportunity to use the bathroom, with supervision, that was connected to the interrogation room.

When everyone was settled back into the room, Major Queznal and Detective Anders came through the door and introduced themselves to the crew of five. Major Queznal stated that none of them were being charged with any crime yet and that nobody was under arrest. Each person sitting at the table was asked in order of where they sat to please state their full name, age and address for the record. Vince and Hector did as they were told, as did Zeke Wappinger. When it was the two hobo's turn, Zeke wondered what names they would use since their hobo names often caused laughter, and as he had seen, it could be anywhere on the spectrum from mild to raucous. Captain Bix Pickles Haskell, the Human Stinkbomb was next in line to answer.

"Well, officers, my legal name is Robert James Rand the third. I was born on August 19th, 1959, which makes me fifty-three years old at the moment. You can list my address as the streets of North America because I haven't lived in an actual house now for about twenty years or so."

"Robert James Rand the third?" Burrito Betty asked incredulously. "Well, I'll be! In all the years we've known each other, I never knew you as anything other than Captain Bix Pickles Haskell, the Human Stinkbomb!"

This observation had the exact effect on the people in the room that Bix and Zeke were expecting. The police officers were trying not to laugh, given the seriousness of the situation, but all were unsuccessful, except for the detective.

"That's my hobo name, as you might have figured. I've been a rail rider for the last twenty years."

"Wow, that's a long time to be on the rails. I've known a few hobos over the years but that must be some sort of record," Major Queznal stated. "Your turn ma'am, if you would, please."

"Okay, my name, age and address. This might take me a while. My legal name is Rebecca Stone, at least I think it is. I never knew my parents, either they died soon after I was born or my mother just gave me up to an orphanage. I was given the name Rebecca Stone there but when a dognapping couple adopted me, they called me Tami Franklin, but I don't think they ever had my name legally changed. It was probably just to confuse the authorities. When I ran away from them after they got arrested, I went by the name Tiffany Spears, but I don't think that was a legal thing. I might have changed it but to tell you the truth, back in those days, I was usually too drunk to know much of anything. What else did you ask?"

"Your age and address."

"Right. Okay, now that could be a tough one too. I know that I was born on the fourth of July, that's an easy one to remember, at least that's when everyone told me I was born so I always would celebrate then. My address, hmm, like Captain Bix here, I don't really have an address."

"Do you know what year you were born?" Major Queznal asked.

"No, not really. I know that when I was first sent off to school, when I lived in the orphanage, my favorite song was about a girl named Rose Hannah. I wanted to change my name to either Rose or Hannah or Rose Hannah, I really liked both names but the sisters at the orphanage wouldn't let me."

"Are you talking about the song by Toto? That Rosanna?"

"Beats me. I just remember that I loved that song and that name."

"Can you sing any of it?"

"I'm not much of a singer these days but it had a line in it that I really loved that said something like 'All I want to do at night is screw you tight, Rose Hannah.' I loved it!"

"Yes, that's the song by Toto, with slightly altered lyrics," Detective Anders confirmed. "They played that song at our high school prom. The girls went wild for it. Must have been the year of my graduation, which was 1983, so let's say you were five or six then, that would make you about, um, let's see, about thirty-four, thirty-five. Sound about right?"

"Sure, I guess so," Betty agreed.

"Alright, Detective Anders has the information we need to run some background checks on all of you. While he's doing that, we're going to take each of you into another room, one by one, and have you make a statement, you know, tell us in your own words what happened and why you were all together in the moving van today. Now, you've been read your Miranda rights already so let me remind you that you don't have to do this without legal representation present, a lawyer if you will, and you have the right to not say anything at all if you choose. Our purpose for the statements is to find out if there is any reasonable cause to hold you and possibly charge you with a crime. If you wait for a lawyer to be present, and we will supply one to you if you don't have a preference or have the ability to pay for one, this might take some time, maybe hours, maybe a day or two. In the meantime, you will be kept in our holding facility until then. If you decide to cooperate and submit a statement now, we will determine if there is probable cause to arrest you and charge you with a crime. If we do, you will be transferred to the local jail until a hearing can be arranged before a judge. However, if you tell us a story that is believable and we can get independent confirmation of the details, there's a chance you could be released in the next hour or so. It is entirely your decision."

Both Vince and Hector knew they were completely innocent of any wrongdoing, even though they happened to be driving the truck that had the missing boy in it. Perhaps they should have been a bit more cautious about agreeing to give a statement without legal counsel but after discussing it amongst themselves in the presence of everyone in the room, weighing the pros and cons, they each decided to agree to give a statement.

Robert James Rand III, also known as Captain Bix Pickles Haskell, the Human Stinkbomb, decided to offer up his opinion. "I know what happened out there, fellas, I know the full story since I've been involved in it since Flannel Freddie here, I mean Zeke, hopped the train we were on in the middle of the night in Belén and we hopped into your truck an hour ago without your knowledge. All this is true and neither of you did anything wrong but I practiced law in Massachusetts for about ten years and even though I'm not your attorney, I would highly recommend that you not agree to give a statement without legal representation."

The police officers present in the room were visibly shocked by this revelation. Additionally, they were a little upset that Mr. Rand was trying to talk the movers out of giving a statement, especially since they had already agreed to do this. They were anxious to find out everyone's story and wrap things up.

"Everyone's certainly entitled to their opinion," Major Queznal stated, "and certainly Mr. Rand, the supposed former lawyer turned rail rider, has an opinion, but ultimately, the decision is yours. By the way, Mr. Rand, where did you go to law school?"

"Yale and I was in-line to be made a partner in Schwartz, Henley and Maples in Boston but for a number of reasons which I won't get into, that never happened."

"You're kidding me, right?" Detective Anders asked.

"I wish I was," the former Attorney Robert James Rand III responded, "but you can check it out if you don't believe me."

"That won't be necessary at this point," Major Queznal stated. "What will it be, gentlemen?"

"I think I'd like to get this over with so I can get home before my girlfriend blows a gasket again," Vince stated. "You hobos have already screwed up my day enough as it is. I might possibly be able to get back home before seven if we get going here."

"Me too. I'm taking my kids camping on Tsoodzil tonight and they were really looking forward to it. I think I'll take the chance on giving you a statement. Neither of us have anything to hide," Hector said. "I can't imagine anything I would say would lead you to think that we were in any way involved with this boy's disappearance. We have the delivery logs in the truck and lots of witnesses who will be able to vouch for our whereabouts today."

"Okay then, let's go into the other room and take your statements. Who wants to go first?" Detective Anders asked.

Vince volunteered and all of the police officers that had been involved in the case got up to lead him out of the room. As they left, another police officer who was out in the main part of the station, was asked to come in to make sure that Hector, Bix, Betty and Zeke didn't collaborate in any way to effect the details of the statements they were or weren't going to give. In fact, he told all of them up front that it would be a good idea if they remained silent for the time being.

"Is it alright to talk about things unrelated to this case?" Burrito Betty asked.

"I suppose but you should know that everything you say and do is being captured by that camera over in the corner and all of it is considered admissible evidence," he explained.

The three hobos and Hector, the furniture mover, sat around the table, not sure what to say or not to say so they chose to maintain their silence, that is until the door opened and a different officer came in to say that Zeke's parents were on line three and that he could talk to them if he wanted. There was a phone in the middle of the table with a flashing white light indicating which line was on hold at the moment. Zeke took a deep breath and said that he would like to talk with them. The officer told him that he would talk first and that he would be putting the call on speakerphone since the police monitored all conversations that took place in this room.

"Hello, this is Officer Biggles from the New Mexico State Police District 6 office. Who am I speaking to please?"

"This is Roxanne Wappinger and I'm here with my husband, Andrew Wappinger. We were just informed that my son Zeke has been found and is in your custody. Is that correct?"

"Affirmative, ma'am. I'm with your son Zeke right now. I should tell you that this call is being monitored and that you are on speakerphone at the moment. Your son said that he would like to speak to you. Here he is, ma'am."

"Hi Mom, long time, no see!"

"Zeke, honey? Are you there? Are you okay?" Roxanne asked. He then heard his father say, "Hey Zekie, it's your dad. How are you doing, kid?"

"Hi Mom. Hi Dad. I'm fine, really. Don't be mad at me! Where are you?"

"We're not mad at you, honey. We're so happy to know that you've been found," his mom said.

"Son, you gave us the biggest scare of our lives, times twenty," his dad chimed in.

"I'm sorry. I just got this idea to go out on an awesome trip. I can't really explain it right now. Are you coming to get me?"

"We'll be there in about ten minutes. We're driving on the highway right now with Officer Ramirez and are close to the Gallup exit. Can't wait to see you honey and give those two nasty hobos a piece of my mind," Roxanne said.

"You better not do that Mom, and they're not nasty. They're like my new best friends, you'll see. They didn't do anything wrong other than take care of me. You should be coming here to congratulate them!"

"We'll see about that, dear. Anyway, we're so happy that you're safe and we'll be seeing you in a few minutes. Is there anything you need? Anything we can pick up for you on the way?"

"No, I'm good unless you see a place along the way that sells ham sandwiches. Just kidding! I have to say, Mom, this whole trip has been really fun. We should all ride the rails sometime like on a vacation or something. I think Dad would love it too, maybe even you, Mom."

"I don't think so, Zeke. For one thing, it's illegal and for another, it's really dangerous. Plus, there are some pretty sketchy people out there."

"Let's talk about this some other time, okay? I've got to go now. See you and Dad soon. Bye!"

Zeke was getting excited about seeing his parents but was worried that his Mom was going to come down pretty hard on Bix and Betty, especially since everyone in the room had heard what she had said. He tried to explain to them that his mom could get agitated at the drop of a hat and hoped that he could get them to understand what role they played in his running away from home. Bix and Betty looked pretty worried and Bix, especially, was expecting the worst from their current predicament.

Vince had been gone for only about ten minutes when he came back into the room with Detective Anders. He sat down back at the table, looking like a big load had been lifted from his shoulders and had a big goofy smile on his face. Detective Anders told Hector it was his turn and asked him to follow him into the other room. On his way out the door, Vince told him to relax, tell the full truth and keep it simple.

"That should be easy, man, since there's not much to say," Hector said, looking like he was taking his last few steps towards the gallows.

Nobody in the room said anything but Vince took advantage of the time to begin consuming some of the sandwiches and cans of soft drinks from the refrigerator and supplemented it with a few bags of chips that were on the counter. Zeke had never seen anyone consume that large quantity of food so quickly.

"This food is for us, right dude?" he asked the policeman that was in the room maintaining order and discipline as he started on the second sandwich, second Coke and second bag of chips.

"Yes, it is, sir. And I'm Officer Biggles, not Officer Dude."

"Sorry Officer Biggles, dude, I mean Officer Biggles without the dude part. Just habit, I guess. Sorry, dude! Oops, see? Sorry again!"

Vince continued eating while everyone else sat in silence and stared at their feet. Burrito Betty put her head down on the table and seemed to be taking a little catnap when Zeke used the lull to start asking Officer Biggles some questions.

"Will I be asked to make a statement, too?"

"Yes, we would like you to do that."

"Will I have to go to jail for running away?"

"No, that's not a crime but once your parent's arrive, we'd like a chance to talk to all three of you. All of us will want to hear what happened before we release you to their custody, you know, stuff about your running away and then your travels with the hobos, things like that. Plus, there are some folks from another agency that will want to talk to just your parents. We'd like to hear your side of the story, as well as what your mom and dad have to say, before we decide if any laws have been broken or if any of the other people should be charged with anything. You and your parents might want to have a lawyer present."

"My mom's a lawyer. She works with people that have been hurt somehow so I think I'm all set."

"Perfect then. Let's just wait until your parents arrive before we take the next step."

They all sat in the room for what seemed like a long time to Zeke but was actually only about five minutes. Everyone was silent, except for the sound of Burrito Betty snoring and ripping an occasional fart, until they heard a commotion outside the door of the interrogation room. Zeke recognized the voices of his mother and father and glanced at Captain Bix Pickles with a worried look on his face.

"She can be a little intense sometimes. She's also probably pretty worked up at the moment so don't take anything she says or does personally. My dad and me will eventually be able to calm her down," Zeke whispered.

"I hope so," was all Captain Pickles said as the door opened and Zeke's parents came rushing in with several new police officers they hadn't met yet.

His mom came running over to Zeke and swept him up in a big bear hug while his father was a step behind and joined the happy reunion. This woke Betty up who must have been deeply in another state of consciousness and might have thought they were under attack.

"Bix, we're getting the bell! Let's cheese it before the flatfoots catch us!" she screamed.

"Now, now Betty. You're just dreamin'. We're at the police station. Calm down, you loo loo!" He took her hand and that seemed to bring her back to reality after the wild look in her eyes started to mellow a few notches. This commotion pulled Zeke's parent's attention away from their son and they had their first opportunity to have a look at the two hobos that had been Zeke's traveling companions. After the initial shock of what they saw sunk in, Roxanne sprung into action.

"How dare you two hobos run off with my son! You should both be locked up for the rest of your lives! I have half a mind to come over there and flatten you both!"

"You just try it, sister," Burrito Betty, the Princess of Poots said while jumping to her feet and taking a few steps towards Roxanne. "I could pulverize your scrawny ass even after a week long bender."

The police sprung into action and got in-between both ladies to keep the peace. Two officers led Roxanne, Andrew and Zeke out of the room while the other two officers stayed in the interrogation room with Bix, Betty and Vince, telling everyone to just settle down. Zeke turned and said goodbye to his hobo pals and gave a little wave as he was led out through the door between his parents and several police officers.

"I'll see you soon, I hope!" were his final words.

After they were gone and the door was closed, Betty rumbled, "That's the thanks we get Captain Haskell? What's this world coming to? I could have taken that bitch with one arm in a sling."

CHAPTER 10

AFTER MAKING THEIR statements to the NMSP, Vince and Hector were indeed released without charge since everyone the police talked to helped to corroborate their stories and their delivery log backed everything up. Neither of them made it home to their families or loved ones by seven that evening, but it wasn't much later than that. Vince's girlfriend was forgiving, especially when she saw the local "story of the year" on the six o'clock news that evening after he called to tell her what was going on and explained why he'd be late coming home yet again. He and Hector became minor celebrities for a few minutes, especially when the clip showing Zeke meeting Bullet and Officer Cellucci in the parking lot was picked up for rebroadcast around the country and various parts of the world. If you looked close enough, you could see the two movers walking towards the building in the background in handcuffs but from the distance and the angle, it almost looked like they were holding hands. Their friends and co-workers kidded them about this for years afterward. Vince basked in the attention while Hector kind of wished it had never happened. Hector did, however, manage to take his kids camping on Tsoodzil that weekend and he had a lot of great stories to tell around the campfire. His kids couldn't get enough of their dad's brush with the missing boy from Belén and his even briefer brush with fame.

Earlier in the afternoon, Major Queznal had walked outside the front door of the station to issue a statement to the throng of assembled media people. One of the civilian staffers at the office had gone out about half an hour earlier to set up a makeshift podium and informed the anxious press members that a statement would be forthcoming. News day deadlines were rapidly approaching and everyone wanted to get some sort of information from the police in order to make their evening broadcasts.

"Good afternoon. My name is Major Nicholas Queznal of the New Mexico State Police from the District 6 office here in Gallup. It is my pleasure to announce that the missing six-year-old boy from Belén, New

Mexico, Zeke Wappinger, has been located and returned safely to the custody of his parents, Andrew and Roxanne Wappinger. After a series of meetings with the parents, the child and staff from the Protective Services Division of the New Mexico Children, Youth and Families Department, we all determined that there was no evidence of child abuse, neglect or any indication of domestic violence, so we were able to reunite the family. The boy's two adult companions, Robert James Rand the third and Tiffany Spears, are currently being held in custody and are being questioned. No charges have yet been filed in this case. This is an ongoing investigation and we will have further statements to make as more information becomes available. The New Mexico State Police would like to thank both the Gallup and the Belén Police Departments for their cooperation and outstanding professional work to help us return the young boy unharmed and in high spirits to his parents an hour ago. I will not be taking any questions at this time. Thank you for your time."

The circumstances surrounding the judicial treatment of the hobo heroes, however, were a little more complicated. Captain Haskell eventually gave a statement to the state police the following day, after spending a very restful night in the lockup facility complete with a warm shower, hot meal, comfortable bed, and clean clothes. Before being led away, he advised the Poot Princess to hold off for a day as well, telling her that a free night with all the amenities in the "calaboose" was what they both needed to clear their heads and maybe even their bodies. They were led off in different directions to cells in different parts of the building to insure that they wouldn't be able to communicate. The next morning, dressed in a bland orange jail jumpsuit that was infinitely less interesting than his fetching hobo outfit, he was brought into the interrogation room to give his statement. Burrito Betty was sitting around in the waiting room in her jumpsuit and some might say that it was a fashion upgrade for her. Bix asked for special permission to act as Burrito Betty's legal counsel when it was her turn to give a statement. The police balked at this arrangement and ultimately failed to be persuaded by Robert James Rand III's somewhat complicated argument, which included citing several dated legal precedents.

The police were none-the-less impressed with his attempt, however, and Major Queznal said as much to his colleagues after Bix left the interrogation room. "I guess all that time spent leading the hobo lifestyle has only dulled his memory and intellect ever so slightly."

Betty decided to give her statement without any legal representation, in spite of Bix's warnings against it. After going more than a day without any hootch and receiving all the amenities that a day of jail-style pampering could possibly offer, she was feeling like a new woman. "Ready to tackle the world," is what she said when a police officer came to her cell the next day to ask if she was ready and willing to give a statement.

They were both returned to their separate holding facilities while the police reviewed their statements and compared them to the statements issued by the movers and the young boy. Since there were a total of six officers that sat in on all of the interrogations and heard all the statements, they each felt they had a good idea about what happened during the last eighteen hours and developed strong and clear opinions about how to deal with the two hobos. However, they were split down the middle - three were convinced that the hobos were good Samaritans and three were convinced that the hobos were petty criminals. None of them believed that Zeke was kidnapped since, after listening to everyone's statements, all six were convinced that he ran away from home on his own free will, contrary to what his mother believed. However, they did feel that the hobos could possibly be charged with aiding and abetting Zeke by encouraging him to become a hobo and illegally ride the trains with them. Their argument was that once the hobos understood that Zeke was a runaway, they should have immediately turned him over to the authorities.

Even though it was Major Queznal's final decision and he sided with the other two officers that didn't want to charge the hobos with aiding and abetting a minor, he felt that it would be prudent to question Mr. Rand and Ms. Spears individually about their actions and get a better understanding of the proper sequence of events to help them make this determination. They also wanted to question the only other people they knew who might have an opinion on the matter, the only other people that could describe the dynamic between the three hobos before they were captured, namely the Reverend el del Dingo and Mr. and Mrs. Gamble from the soup kitchen. They were able to schedule an interview with Reverend el del Dingo the following morning but it took a little longer to track down Ernest and Ethel Gamble. Even though they had Ethel's cellphone number, it took several calls and messages before she answered them, but she eventually agreed to meet an officer at the homeless shelter the next day to be brought in for questioning.

Meanwhile, Captain Bix Pickles Haskell and Burrito Betty luxuriated for a second night at the spa, or as others called it, the NMSP District 6 lockup facility, before they were brought into the interrogation room for a second time in as many days.

Bix Pickles, being even more rested and thinking as clearly as he had in years, and after his second shower which removed more of the road grime that the first shower hadn't managed to tunnel down into, was the first one to be called in. A lot of questions were asked that were more-or-less the same question, only asked from slightly different angles, and he was well aware that they were trying to trip him up about Zeke's time with him and Ms. Poots. Bix patiently explained a number of times that Zeke made it clear to him within the first few minutes of hopping the boxcar in Belén a few nights ago that he had run away from his parents. Their very first opportunity to get off was in Gallup, Bix explained, which they did. Captain Bix told his interrogators that Zeke said that he was homesick for the first time when they were sitting near the switchyard in Gallup and that he and Betty discussed getting him back to Belén. The challenge for them was trying to figure out how to do that and it was only a few moments later when they were caught stowed away in the van.

"One thing doesn't add up entirely, though, Mr. Rand," Major Queznal said. "When you knew that we were coming for you, because you admitted that you heard the sirens after Zeke Wappinger sent a text to his mother, you decided to illegally enter a moving company van to try to escape capture. Why would you do that if you were trying to get him back to Belén? Why wouldn't you just turn yourselves in at that point?"

"Two reasons. First, it was what Zeke wanted to do because he was having a ton of fun being a rail rider and second, being a hobo, with all due respect officer, we're used to being treated differently. I didn't think that we would get the benefit of the doubt if we were caught with a runaway child. Our hope was to get Zeke back to his neighborhood safely and then quietly slip away into the night. Gallup became a hot yard because we had gotten fired off by a bug slinger and they were on the lookout for us. Going back on the highway and becoming a rubber tramp seemed like the safest way to get him home."

They finished up their questioning and then called Tiffany Spears into the room. She was asked a series of very similar questions and, even without any of Bix's counseling, gave almost exactly the same answers and followed the same line of reasoning that he had, perhaps a bit less eloquently, but the content was nearly identical. It had to be apparent to all of the police that the two hobos were telling the truth and they eventually took them back to their cells where they basked for their second day in captivity.

While they were in their cells, dozing the day away, two other interviews took place. The Navajo-Latino-American priest arrived in the later part of the morning and told his story in a straightforward manner and impressed the police with his nuanced observations and character assessments.

"I wouldn't be a very good priest if I wasn't a keen observer of personalities and the human condition," he commented when Officer Danforth complimented him on his descriptions of the three hobos. "Even though they made up some almost believable story about being from Florida and having their car break down on the way to the artichoke harvest in California, and made up some pretty funny aliases, they really did seem like one big happy family. I knew something was up because ninety-nine percent of the people that come into our soup kitchen have pretty sad and, oftentimes, unbelievable stories to tell and I always take what they tell me with a grain of salt. But the bottom line on these three folks for me was that the two hobos were taking very good care of the young boy Zeke and he seemed to be having the time of his life. There was absolutely no indication that he was being held against his will, I'm certain of that."

Father Gaagii Jesus el del Dingo was thanked by the officers for taking time out from his busy schedule to come talk with them. They told him that his observations were quite valuable to their investigation and Detective Anders led him out of the building via the front desk. The detective quickly returned to the interrogation room and the group briefly discussed Father el del Dingo's assessment of the hobo family. Major Queznal said that the Gambles, the couple that also interacted with the hobo family, were due to arrive in a few hours and that he would let everyone know when it was time to reconvene. In the meantime, he advised everyone to "keep an open mind."

All the officers went back to their desks, processed some of the endless piles of paperwork that they usually put off until they had absolutely nothing else to do, made idle chatter with their colleagues and office staff and took note of the stream of reporters that came and went with regular frequency to make inquiries about the case at the front desk. The receptionist gave the same response to each new arrival, saying that it was an open, ongoing investigation and that Major Queznal would be issuing a statement later in the day to update them on their decision about the two hobos in custody. Everyone in the police station could see the major through his windowed office and open door and saw him answering his telephone with an astonishing frequency. The two local television stations kept their vans parked out in the visitor lot in anticipation of the upcoming briefing.

Around two-thirty in the afternoon, 14:30 in police time, Detective Anders set out to gather the two homeless alcoholics at the Little Helpers of God homeless shelter on Lincoln Street as he had discussed the day before with the eternally happy Ethel Gamble. The two were nowhere in sight so he went inside and spoke with someone who looked like he worked there. The man was apologetic when he told the officer that the Gambles had left hours ago according to the rules of the shelter, as it closed down every day from nine in the morning until six in the evening. He said that a likely place to find them was at the 4th Street Pub, three or four blocks away.

"I'm well acquainted with the place. If you happen to see them in the meantime, however, would you ask them to call me at this number?" Detective Anders said as slipped his business card into the man's hand. "They told me they would be here now, at this address."

"Okay, officer, maybe they were planning on coming back to meet you here and they're just a little late. Keeping close tabs on time isn't the strong suit of many of our clients."

Detective Anders walked back to his cruiser and did a slow reconnaissance drive of the route he thought the Gambles might possibly walk, either to or from the bar. He had met them a time or two over the years and from what he knew about Ethel and Ernie, they didn't reside primarily in Gallup but seemed to turn up there rather frequently, more often during the winter months. His last encounter with them was earlier in the year when they tried to participate in a turkey shoot at the Gallup Shooters range northwest of town. They showed up somewhat inebriated in the back of a pickup truck and Ernest insisted that they "let us shoot some damned turkeys before the aliens get to have 'em for dinner 'cause, damnation, there are people goin' hungry in this world and the least they could do is let some real Americans have a seat at the table for once!" This would have normally been a matter for the local police but since the pickup truck was being driven by a fugitive from neighboring Arizona, the state cops were called in. Ernest and Ethel Gamble were taken into brief custody for their own protection and dropped off back at one of the homeless shelters where they hadn't yet exceeded their maximum number of consecutive nights they were allowed to stay.

There was no sign of the two of them walking the streets between the Little Helpers of God shelter and the 4th Street Pub, so Detective Anders parked out front and walked inside. Sitting right near the door was a very red nosed Ernest Gamble, smoking a cigarette while nursing a half filled glass of some sort of clear brown liquor. The detective scanned the mostly empty bar, noticed a few other patrons in the back corners of the room but didn't see any signs of Ethel. Ernest did a double take when he became aware that Detective Anders was standing right next to him, momentarily lost his balance and was about to slide off the barstool if the officer hadn't been there to steady him by grabbing his shoulders and re-centering his butt back on the stool.

"Easy there, Mr. Gamble!" Detective Anders said while Ernest tried to regain his composure. "Did you forget about our meeting this afternoon?"

"Was that today?" he asked but it sounded more like "waschat due day?"

"Yes, we told your wife we would meet at the shelter. Is she here?"

"That lady don't never tell me nuttin', for crying out loud! I think she's here somewhere. Maybe takin' a piss or somethin'. I don't know. Hard to keep track of her sometimes."

As if appearing on cue, Ethel Gamble came blasting into the barroom through the door of the ladies room with her arm around one of her female drinking buddies, hooting and hollering like one of them had just told some sort of raunchy joke. When she noticed the police officer standing at the end of the bar with her husband, her howling came to an abrupt halt and she took her arm off her pal's shoulder.

"Oops, I think I forgot about our little meeting, officer. Ernest, finish up your drink because we need to go with the handsome policeman here to tell them everything we know about those two hobos and that nice little boy."

Ernest chugged the remains of his drink. Ethel did the same with the glass she was toting around at an awkward angle, rummaged around in her scruffy pocketbook for some money and settled up with the bartender. She made a big show of saying goodbye to all her pals and told them they'd "return as soon as they set the story straight about those sweet hobos that were looking after the cute little runaway boy that's been all over the news the last few days."

Detective Anders escorted the two tanked bar patrons into the backseat of his police car, making sure they didn't smack their heads on the way in and gently closed the door behind them, careful that all their body parts were safely tucked inside first. He also did a visual check for concealed weapons on both of them as he helped the Gambles inside. He had hoped that they would be a little more coherent since the fate of Mr. Rand and Ms. Spears might hinge upon what they would be able to tell them about their encounter the other day at the soup kitchen. Of more immediate concern, however, was to get them to the station without making a mess in the back of his cruiser. Driving slowly and trying to avoid any bumps or holes and taking corners extra carefully so they stayed upright, he managed to arrive at the station with everything nicely intact and relatively fresh except for the smell of the bar and cigarettes on their clothes and the aroma of alcohol that seemed to be exuding out of their pores and expelled into the car with each of their exhalations.

The Gambles were helped into the station, through a security scanner and past the receptionist behind bulletproof glass who buzzed them through the heavy metal door into the large office area. They were asked to take a seat in an empty meeting room while the other police officers gradually wrapped up what they were working on and reconvened in the interrogation room. When everyone was settled in, Major Queznal asked someone to go get one of the Gambles and Officer Stanton came back with the somewhat tipsy Ernest. He was asked his name, age and address and was able to supply everything but the address, which he decided was best described as "planet earth."

"Perhaps you could be a little more specific, Mr. Gamble," Major Queznal suggested.

"Okay, how about the planet Earth in the Orion-Cygnus Arm of the Milky Way Galaxy?"

"How about you get more specific about an address on Earth?"

"I am currently living at a place called the Tiny God Helpings shelter or something like that in the U S of A, at least until the FBI comes to get me. Does that answer your question?"

"I guess it will have to. Can you please tell us about your encounter two days ago at the Our Lady of Saint Jorge and Geronimo de Gallup Catholic Church soup kitchen with Mr. Robert James Rand the third, Tiffany Spears and the young boy Zeke Wappinger?"

Ernest Gamble was digging deep into his brain's recesses to recall the encounter and after a while said, "I don't remember meeting nobody with those names."

"Perhaps it will jog your memory if they were described as the two adult hobos and their six-year-old traveling companion. You might remember them as the Wilson family; Alan, Annie and Flip," Major Queznal suggested hoping something would click inside his brain as he looked down and referred to his notes.

That seemed to do the trick and he was able to at least talk about them like he had some vague sort of memory of the encounter. Unfortunately, given his mental condition, his intoxication and inability to say much of anything without talking about aliens or conspiracy theories, the police interrogators realized it was a waste of their time to try to get any useful information out of him. Major Queznal thanked him for his time and said that once his wife was interviewed, he would be free to go and they would be given a ride back to wherever they wanted to go within the city limits.

His parting words were "how about the planet Loki?" to which Officer Danforth was heard muttering under his breath, "how about the planet Wingnut?" Detective Anders guided Ernest to the other room and returned a minute later with what they hoped would be Ernest's better and more stable half. Now, compared to the general population, Ethel Gamble might be viewed by most normal citizens as someone who looked to be on the fringe of society, which she was. However, compared to her wild-eyed and wild-ideaed husband and the Princess of Poots in her normal hobo outfit of many layers of colorful and dirty rags, Ethel almost looked like a model from a Talbot's catalog. She had on a stylish broad rimmed black hat, a black and white striped party dress that flared wildly out at the bottom and might have actually been the dress she wore to her prom thirty or forty years earlier, leopard print high heels and enough cheap costume jewelry to keep a Salvation Army in business for a few weeks if she were to donate her collection to them. On top of it all, her attitude towards those around her, and the world in general, was "here I am, baby, ready or not."

Ethel came sashaying into the interrogation room like she was auditioning for the lead role in *Cat on a Hot Tin Roof*, as performed by the Gallup Community Players, which they had actually just staged the previous year. She clearly liked receiving the attention of the six police officers for whom she was about to perform. Even before sitting down

DAVID W. GOODWIN

and well before Major Queznal was able to ask his first question, Ethel launched into her version of her fateful lunch with the Wilson family.

"So officers and gentlemen, and I'm assuming you're a little of both, just like that dreamboat Dick Gere who I once saw in a Payless shoe store outside of Tucson, believe it or not, I was surprised to see him shopping there and he bought a pair of black loafers, by the way, I'm gonna tell you all about the little runaway boy. Where would you like me to start?"

"How about you tell us about the lunch you shared with him and the others at the soup kitchen two days ago unless you have any more relevant information to share with us," Major Queznal said, hoping to get her back on track.

"Well, here's what happened. Here's the dilly yo yo, homies. Me and Ernest, my husband, who you just met, and I'd be surprised if he remembered a whole lot about meeting the hobo family a few days ago. Hell, I'm surprised when he remembers something that happened a few minutes ago, unless it happens to involve his aluminum foil lined hat that he likes to wear most of the time to prevent alien brainwashing, or something like that, so I'm assuming you sort of catch my drift, if you know what I mean."

"I think we've got a pretty good understanding of your husband, ma'am. Back to the lunch, if you'd be so kind," Major Queznal said, prodding gently with his proverbial stick.

"Yes, officer, I'm getting to that part. So, we were just finishing up lunch over there at the church that that nice Native American priest runs and these three hobos walk in, just when it was about to close down. Well, I should clarify that, it was two grown up hobos, a man and a woman and they told some complicated story about their car breaking down while they were trying to get to the asparagus harvest in Mexico or someplace, which me and Ernest knew right off was a tall tale. No wait, it was the artichoke harvest in California, yeah, that's right, artichokes, that's what they said and it's not even artichoke harvest time right now. So Ernest and me started asking them some questions and the man sort of admitted that he had made some of the story up. I had also seen on my phone about the missing boy from near Albuquerque and I put six and nine together and realized that this was the boy. What a darling! So smart, sharp as a tack and he seemed to have a real nice relationship with the two hobos. I have to say, most of the families I see out there could learn a lesson from these folks. Maybe they weren't a real family but they acted better than some other families I run across. And he didn't really look like a hobo, if I had to guess."

"Did you get any sense that the boy had been kidnapped or was being held against his will?"

"None, absolutely none. When he realized that half the world probably knew about his disappearance, his first thought was to send a message to his real parents to let them know that he was okay. If the hobos were up to no good, do you think they would have let him do that?"

"Were they aware that he was sending his parents a message?" Officer Danforth asked.

"Yes, although to be honest, I'm not sure they understood modern phone technology very well. I got the sense that the kid certainly did. He was going to help the reverend with the church's website so he was pretty bright. Oh, one more thing I should tell you, the little boy told me and Ernie that the two grown ups were his new best friends."

"Thank you, Mrs. Gamble. Your information has been extremely helpful. Unless there are any additional questions, I think we've heard all we need to hear. Thanks for coming in today and being so forthright. Detective Anders will take you and your husband back to the shelter now if that's where you want to go."

After this task was accomplished and Detective Anders returned back to the station after driving the Gambles back to the bar, the six policemen met again to discuss their various options. They made a unanimous decision to release the two hobos without charge. Both were brought back into the interrogation room later that afternoon.

"Mr. Rand, Ms. Spears, we sincerely appreciate your cooperation and the fine way that you took care of Zeke Wappinger. This story could have had a very unhappy ending. Although we disagree with your decision to stow yourselves aboard the moving van and your continued trespassing on private railroad property which we would like to find a way to prevent you from doing in the future, we have decided to release you and not charge either of you with any crime. Even though Mrs. Wappinger may feel otherwise, we all congratulate you for the way you safeguarded and looked after Zeke Wappinger. We'll take you to the front desk clerk to process your release," Major Queznal said.

DAVID W. GOODWIN

A day earlier, a little while after Major Queznal's press statement late Saturday afternoon and a day before the hobo's release, Zeke was released to the custody of his parents. Both Belén police officers had waited around to see what was going to happen and to drive them home. Life back in Belén, after Zeke's grand escapade was going to be rather complicated, at least for a while, probably much more complicated than that of the movers, the priest, the Gambles and maybe even the Wilsons.

The K-9 cruiser had come to Gallup with Officer Cellucci, Lieutenant Forsmark and Police Dog Bullet while Officer Ramirez had come with Andrew and Roxanne Wappinger. It was obvious that Zeke was going to ride back with his parents, as his mother was stuck to her wayward son like epoxy and wasn't planning on letting him out of her sight any time in the foreseeable future. Roxanne was so overcome by the entire spectrum of human and, more importantly, motherly emotions that all she wanted to do was get back home with her son and husband as quickly as possible and interact with as few people as possible. After everyone had finished up their business at the NMSP District 6 office in the waning late Saturday afternoon hours that were by now transitioning into early evening, the group of three Wappingers, three police officers and one dog left the building and took note of the horde of reporters, TV cameras and press vehicles that were still clamoring around on the other side of the chain link fence.

The several print reporters were ready for action in a heartbeat and ran over quickly to the fence. The single Albuquerque NPR radio reporter, who had recently arrived on the scene after Major Queznal issued the statement, immediately started talking into his microphone, giving the expected play-by-play description of what was happening. The two television reporters, who were internet sensations already from their provocative falling incident a few hours earlier, unbeknownst to either of them yet, quickly sprung into action, fluffed their respective hairs, smoothed their somewhat rumpled clothing, put on fresh lipstick (yes, both of them), grabbed their respective microphones without any further plans to use them like that again and woke their camerapersons up who were both asleep inside their news vans. This put them at a distinct disadvantage for being first on the scene to question Zeke Wappinger. Both, however, were able to be patched in live as "late breaking news" at the tail end of their respective six o'clock news hours.

As before, Lieutenant Forsmark advised, "There will undoubtedly be plenty of time to talk to the press and it might be best to save it all for a later date under better circumstances." Steady barrages of questions were being yelled through the fence, perhaps twenty or thirty yards away, while the traveling arrangements back to Belén were being negotiated.

"I want to travel in the backseat with Bullet," Zeke stated. "I think he really likes me."

"I'm sorry Zeke, that's against our regulations," Officer Cellucci said smiling, "but I will let him out for a minute so you can play with him."

"And besides, little Zekie, you're going to be riding with us," Roxanne said as her heart broke just a crack.

"I promise that once things are back to normal in Belén and when Bullet is off-duty, we'll come over and play. How does that sound?" Officer Cellucci asked while letting the dog out of the car. He immediately ran right over to Zeke and got all wiggly in his hindquarters.

"Guess so," Zeke said a bit dejectedly. "Hey, wait a minute! What about Captain Bix and Burrito Betty? I need to see them before we leave! Where are they? Can't they come home with me? They're my friends now!"

"Over my dead body!" Roxanne blustered. "Those two kidnappers are in jail where they belong. I'm sorry, Zeke, you won't be seeing them ever again."

"Now, now, honey. First, it seems unlikely that they actually kidnapped our son, especially if you've heard anything Zeke has said and second, it would be nice if Zeke could at least go say goodbye to them. They've all been through a lot together. I don't see any harm in that. I'm assuming they're locked up inside, isn't that right Lieutenant Forsmark?" Andrew asked.

"Yes sir, that's true. And just for the record, ma'am, the various suspects in this case are all going to be questioned before any charges are brought against any of them. Innocent until proven guilty is the way I was taught."

"Mom, I wish you would stop calling them kidnappers. They didn't kidnap me! I've told you that already. I want to go inside to see them before we leave!" Zeke cried out.

"I'll only allow it under two conditions. First, they have to be inside a cell and second, I want your father and me to accompany you."

"Fine with me," Zeke said. "I won't leave here without seeing them first."

"Let me go inside and see if Major Queznal will allow a quick visit. I don't see why this would be a problem," Lieutenant Forsmark stated as he walked back into the building.

While they stood around waiting for permission to go back inside, the reporters let loose with a non-stop and overlapping stream of questions from the other side of the fence that were barely decipherable even if one were to try hard to focus on just one reporter with directable cat-like ears. The TV cameras were both positioned so that their respective reporters were in the foreground while all of the Wappingers, police officers and Bullet were in the background. Both live newscasts captured Zeke's encounter with the dog and both broke away from their long shots to zoom in up close on Zeke. One voiceover said erroneously, "and here you see the happy reunion of the young runaway child with the police dog that successfully tracked him down" while the other voiceover, narrating the exact same scene said even more erroneously "it is probably safe to say that you are seeing Jake Wappingly playing with the dog that in all likelihood, saved his young life just hours ago."

What all of the reporters failed to notice from across the parking lot was the argument that Zeke was currently having with his mom. What they saw were two parents overwhelmed with happiness to have their son back, apparently unharmed, as both of them took turns hugging him but they didn't notice the nuanced body language between mother and son as they watched Zeke pull away from his mom and argued about seeing the hobos while his dad kept his arm around Zeke's shoulder. Lieutenant Forsmark appeared a few moments later and escorted the Wappingers inside.

"The suspects have not yet been processed into a holding facility," he said. "They are still in the interrogation room under guard, if that is acceptable to you, Mrs. Wappinger."

"I suppose so. Just so they don't try any funny stuff."

"Mom, I want you to promise to not say anything mean to Bix or Betty when I say goodbye. In fact, you might want to say 'thank you' to them for taking good care of me and getting me here safely."

Andrew agreed immediately while Roxanne was less committal. A police officer led them back into the station and through the maze of hallways to the interrogation room. When they entered the room, both Bix Pickles Haskell and Burrito Betty had their heads on the table and were both sound asleep while one officer sat in the corner guarding them. By this time, both had on orange jail jumpsuits and Zeke hardly recognized them without their distinctive hobo outfits and the top few layers of dirt and grime that their first shower had already removed.

"Mr. Rand, Ms. Spears, wake up! You have a few visitors," the officer called out loudly.

Captain Haskell was the first to stir from his slumbers but the Princess of Poots required some additional prodding and added a few punctuations of her own in the process. Zeke stood in front of them with a big smile on his face while his parents waited at a respectful distance behind him. He waited patiently while Bix shook the sleep out of his head, stood up, eventually recognized Zeke and walked over to give him a hug.

"Flannel Freddie, the Deviled Ham! As I live and breathe! I wasn't sure if we'd ever get the chance to set our eyeballs on you again! How are you doin', son?"

"I'm fine, Captain Haskell, but I don't understand why you and Burrito Betty haven't been released from jail yet. I've told all of the officers what happened and they said they just wanted to talk to everyone before they decided if you would be released or not."

By now, Betty had roused enough from her sleep and realized that Zeke was in the room. She jumped up and gave him a proper greeting, saying, "Frankie! I'm so happy to see you. You've come to get us out, right?"

"Not yet, but I'm hoping it's soon."

"I hope you two know that you have one of the finest young men I've ever had the chance to meet. He's a real treasure and I hope you never let him out of your sights or give him another good reason to run away again," Betty said, unable to resist the urge to stick it to Roxanne again based on the encounter they had earlier in the day.

"I guess I'll reserve judgment on that until I hear all sides of the story. I just hope for your sake that you didn't do anything wrong here because if you did, you'll be sorry," Roxanne said in her threatening lawyer sort of way.

"Mom! Remember? I told you to be nice and maybe even thank them for taking good care of me?"

"We both would like to thank you for taking care of Zeke," Andrew said, assuming his usual role as peacemaker when his wife went off on some extreme behavior, although he had never seen her this worked up and unreasonable before. "I guess he's gotten a few new nicknames in the last twenty-four hours. Frankie and Flannel Freddie?"

"Well, actually it's just Flannel Freddie, the Deviled Ham. Burrito Betty, the Princess of Poots always gets it wrong and thinks that it's Frankie."

"It's Freddie?" she asked incredulously. "Why didn't you ever correct me?"

"We did, you loo loo! More than once, for the record," Bix said.

"Anyway, we're glad to have our son back where he belongs. Zeke wanted to come in here and say goodbye so let's get it over with," Roxanne said impatiently.

"Can I have a few minutes alone with them?" Zeke asked.

Andrew nodded his head and took his wife's hand. When she pulled it away, he took her by the upper arm and almost had to drag her out of the room. "We'll just be outside the door, Zeke, when you're ready to leave."

"For crying out loud, Andrew, you don't need to be so rough with me," Roxanne said loudly as she was being led away.

Once his parents were out of sight, Zeke started to cry. This caused Burrito Betty to start sobbing noisily and even caused Captain Pickles to tear up a little. He gave them a big group bear hug and took a couple of deep breaths before his sobbing started to peter out.

"It's no fair that you two have to go to jail. I should be me. I'm the one that ran away and all you two did was take care of me and help me go on the most awesome-ist adventure ever. I'm going to make sure that the police release you as soon as possible, okay?"

"Don't fret too much there, Freddie. It's probably not goin' to be so bad bein' in jail for a night or two. I'm sure once they hear all the stories people have to tell, includin' ours, we'll be released in no time. It's not like we've been hooked or nuthin'. Heck, we haven't even been ossified yet and I'm thinkin' that we won't be. It even felt purty good to scrape my mug with hot water and shavin' cream for a change. So, we'll be fine and back nailin' a hotshot in no time," Bix said reverting back to his hobo language.

"And besides, darling boy, you get to go back home with your family, such as they are, and hang out again with your friends," Betty said to console both of them.

"But you're my friends. I don't want to say goodbye."

Almost on cue, Roxanne's voice was heard from outside the door, "Come on Zekie, honey. It's time to go."

"In a minute, Mom!" he yelled back. "Promise me one thing. When you get out of here, would you come visit me at my home in Belén? We live at 398 Ladera Drive. Can you remember that?"

"Sure, son. No problem. We both have memories like a steel trap. Maybe a little rusty around the edges but they are made of steel, none-the-less. 398 Ladera Drive in Belén. Got it!" Bix said. "Can you remember that Betty?"

"Yeah, 296 Ladder Road in Boston."

"No, 398 Ladera Drive in Belén!" Zeke cried.

"Just kidding, Frankie. I'll remember your address," the Princess of Poots said with a soft chuckle. "How could I forget such an important piece of information?"

With that, she leaned over, put her face right up next to Zeke's face and gave him a kiss on his cheek. Bix squeezed Zeke's other hand and then let go to give him a pat on his head and tousled his unruly locks.

"We'll miss you, son. Take good care of yourself, you hear?" he said.

"I'll miss you both too, but remember your promise to come visit me. Soon! Okay?"

"You got it, Frankie," Burrito Betty said with a laugh and a sob that came out at the same time and sounded like a cow that got interrupted in mid-moo.

CHAPTER 11

THE WAPPINGER FAMILY was finally settled into the back seat of Officer Ramirez's Belén Police Department cruiser, cleared the tangle of reporters, gotten onto Historic Route 66 and were heading towards the interstate. In the space of five or six blocks, they drove past every conceivable fast food joint in the country except maybe an A&W. These weren't places that Roxanne ever took her son to eat but every so often, if he was out someplace with just his dad, the two of them might get to go to a KFC or Taco Bell under the condition that "we just won't tell Mom about it, okay?" As Officer Ramirez was now driving according to the various traffic laws and speed limits and there were approximately twenty traffic lights between the District 6 office and the entrance to I-40 East, Roxanne had some time to ask her little vagabond if he needed to stop anywhere for some food before they hit the highway.

"When was your last meal?" she asked.

"It was lunch today at the church. I have to say it was one of the best meals I've ever eaten. The food was really good, homemade, not take-out, and there were a bunch of people there to talk to. Everyone was super friendly. Not really like meals that we have at home very often. It made me want you and Dad there at the same time without your cellphones and not have to go rushing off to work or meetings or some other place. Just eating a meal together, that was really nice."

"Honey, did you know that when you sent me that text message that we'd be able to figure out where you were?" Roxanne asked, choosing to let Zeke's barbed comment glide on past her without getting hooked, but the tight smile on a face flushed red from the verbal slap her son had just intentionally or unintentional given her, gave her feelings away. She had never known him to be deliberately mean. In fact, he had such an endearing way of just telling the simple truth, his six-year-old reality, regardless of the consequences, that it was hard to ignore.

"Yes. I had already told Captain Bix and Burrito Betty that I wanted to go home and they were trying to take me there."

"Why didn't you just wait for the police to show up then?"

"I wasn't ready to go home yet. I just wanted you to know I was okay so you wouldn't worry too much."

"Did you know the people whose phone you borrowed?"

"Only from eating lunch with them."

"Did you know that they are going to be questioned by the police, too, because they're suspects now, as are the two movers?" his father asked.

"Yeah, I sort of figured that might happen," Zeke said with a soft mumble.

"We'll have lots of time to talk about this when we get home but this might be your last chance to grab a quick bite to eat. Want to stop somewhere before we get on the highway, Zekie?" his dad asked quietly.

Zeke had been leaning up against his dad, who had his arm draped over his shoulders and his large hand on his leg kept him close in the back seat. When Zeke didn't respond to his question, his father bent his head down, looked over and noticed that Zeke was sound asleep, snuggled up against him. He looked over at his wife, who was pushed off into the far corner of the seat and was working hard to keep her emotions under control. Andrew could tell immediately from her body language and breathing patterns that she was finally letting her guard down and the harsh reality of what had just happened to their son was slowly beginning to seep into her entire being. Andrew reached over without disturbing his son's now deep sleep and gently touched her hand. She flinched ever so slightly, sniffled, gave Andrew a sad smile that launched a few early tears over her upper lip and sent them catapulting onto her lap.

"I don't understand any of this," she said as her words quivered a bit, speaking softly through clenched teeth so that Zeke wouldn't be woken up by her anguished voice. "How could being a hobo be better or more fun than being with us, in our family, in our fantastic house, with great friends? You saw those two people, Mr. Pickles and Betty Boop, or whatever their names were. Come on, Andrew, I'm having a hard time buying his story about just deciding to run away in the middle of the night. I mean, what kind of kid just runs away to hop a damned train? What does that say about us as parents? What are our friends going to think of us? What are they going to say? I can well imagine what Chuck is going to say when I show up at the office on Monday. He's always ready to give me parenting advice and tell me that I work too many hours. If he ever developed any ambition himself and tried to become a partner and stopped spending all his money on his fancy cars and hussies, maybe he'd understand. He should try raising a kid and being a lawyer at the same time. That might shut him up for a few minutes!"

Andrew couldn't respond. This was a discussion he had tried to have with her many times but Roxanne would always just brush him off. The demands of Roxanne's profession were extraordinary, he knew that, but he often felt that she sometimes preferred working to being a mother. She would sometimes half-jokingly call Andrew a "househusband" when he would make the choice to hang out with Zeke instead of choosing to do some of his endless BLM work. Once they both got their careers on solid footing, she would often say, they could afford to put some more time into parenting. That would explain her insistence on using birth control just yesterday morning, which didn't really surprise him if he stepped back far enough to look at the big picture. Maybe this really was the wake up call she needed. Maybe this was the wake up call he needed too, if he was being honest with himself. Perhaps they hadn't been tuned in enough to Zeke's needs. No, he thought to himself, there was no doubt that they hadn't been tuned in enough. Why else would he run away?

"Things are going to have to be different when we get back home," Andrew finally said but by then Roxanne had turned away and was staring at the sagebrush dotted landscape rushing by in the fading light of the early New Mexican evening. She did, however, nod and sniffle a little and then squeezed his hand with the slightest of pressure.

Other than the constant chatter and beeping of the police radio, the rest of the trip back to Belén was in total silence. By the time Officer Ramirez pulled into the circular driveway with adobe and brick columns marking both entrances at 398 Ladera Drive, it was dark outside. However, their neighborhood street was filled with an assortment of cars and news vans, all wanting to capture on video the return of the six-year-old hobo to his home. The lights from all their vehicles and equipment gave their house and yard an eerie glow, like it was a house on a Hollywood set or was about to be decorated for Halloween or Christmas. At least they weren't bold enough to park in the Wappinger's driveway but weren't so timid that they hesitated using spotlights to illuminate the entire front of their large and long house.

Zeke's parents each exited their side of the vehicle and Andrew reached in and gently lifted his still sleeping son out of the car and cradled him in his arms. They both thanked Officer Ramirez and he said that he would be in touch tomorrow to go over some final paperwork.

Andrew nodded, quickly shook his hand while balancing Zeke in his other one and followed his wife towards the house. First, however, they had to get past the five reporters and camera people that had taken up positions between the Belén police car and the Wappinger's front door.

"Mr. and Mrs. Wappinger, can you tell us how it feels to have your son back?"

"Was your son mistreated by the hobos?"

"Are you expecting to file kidnapping charges against them?"

"Is it true that your son actually ran away from home because he wanted to become a hobo?"

Andrew and Roxanne tried their best to ignore all of the reporter's questions but Zeke was woken up by all the noise and had heard the last one. The reporter who asked the question was about three feet away and her cameraman was filming from almost as close. What she captured and what went out over the airwaves and, of course, onto YouTube, was the audio of the reporter's question and a sleepy-eyed six-year-old hobo still being held like a large, awkward forty-pound sack of loose potatoes in his father's arms. Zeke turned his head sideways, away from his dad and wiggled his body so that he was almost upside down when he answered the question.

"Those hobos are Captain Bix Pickles Haskell, the Human Stinkbomb and Burrito Betty, the Princess of Poots, and they're my new friends. I'm hoping my mom and dad will let them come live with us when they get out of jail."

"That ain't gonna be happening," Roxanne was heard off camera snarling to the night sky as the camera pulled back and followed the backs of the three Wappingers towards their front door.

Roxanne opened the door of their spacious house and they all disappeared inside without another word to the press. This, however, did not give a clear message to the reporters that it was time for them all to leave. Even after retreating to the relative safety of their kitchen, where they all had a little snack, they were aware of the lights and reporters hanging around outside hoping for a few additional opportunities to get more of the story. One reporter was even bold enough to ring the front doorbell.

"I guess I'll need to go out there and get them all to leave," Roxanne said, giving her son a little noogie on his head. "You've created quite a sensation, young man! Looks like everyone wants a piece of you. Both of you please stay here in the kitchen while I go deal with them."

Roxanne checked herself in the hallway mirror, quickly made a few minor adjustments and then opened the front door. The press corps had formed a small semi-circle on the walkway leading up to the door and were visibly happy to see Roxanne appear before them.

"I appreciate your interest in our son's safe return, but we've had an unbelievably long and stressful day and would like some privacy tonight. My husband and I will make a brief statement tomorrow afternoon here at two o'clock after we've had a chance to absorb all of the circumstances leading to the disappearance and return of our son. However, we will only do that if you all agree to leave right now," Roxanne stated, leaving no opportunity for discussion, and walked back into their house.

Zeke looked out of his bedroom window and saw all the reporters retreat to their cars and vans, turn off their flood lights and slowly drive away out of their neighborhood. Whatever his mom said seemed to work because within a few minutes, everything outside was dark and quiet like on almost any other night of the year. His dad witnessed the transformation as well since he was standing right behind him in Zeke's still messy bedroom.

"Why does my room look like this, Dad?"

Andrew explained to him about the various searches that he and the police had conducted and the need that Officer Cellucci and her police dog had for some smelly items of his clothing. He told him that he needed to give her something with his scent on it, like a dirty undershirt or something.

"I'm sorry, it's my fault that your room is such a mess. Too bad we didn't have the Isotopes tee shirt you're wearing now. It stinks to high heaven! Why don't I straighten things up a bit while you take a shower?"

"But I'm still pretty hungry, to tell you the truth. I'm thinking that it would be nice to have some dinner. It's only eight o'clock and it's Saturday. Remember, we usually go out for dinners on Saturdays? It's one of my favorite things we do all week!"

An absolutely spent Roxanne heard Zeke's request as she walked into his bedroom and did her best to try to talk him out of it, saying that she could whip together a meal for them at home tonight. Going out in public, she argued, might not be such a hot idea at the moment.

"Like what? Unless you went shopping, I doubt there's anything here that could be made into a meal," Zeke observed.

"Let's go into the kitchen and check it out. I'm sure I could find something, maybe even something that would be as good as the lunch you had today at the soup kitchen," Roxanne said and the hurt in her voice was obvious to Andrew.

A quick survey of the refrigerator, the pantry, the fruit bowl on the counter, their large freezer in the garage and various cabinets came up pretty slim. The truth of the matter was that neither Roxanne nor Andrew did much of what the rest of their neighbors might term actual cooking. Andrew would barbeque up some meat that he bought at Whole Foods for holidays, birthdays or other special events. Roxanne would sometimes make her own pasta with the help of a machine they had gotten as a wedding present and homemade tomato sauce, but both of these occurrences needed to be planned well in advance, both from a shopping and scheduling perspective. There were always the staples of eggs, whole wheat muffins, milk and cereal for Zeke and Andrew's breakfasts and various additive-free lunch meats, cheeses and organic fruits for their school and work lunches but most of their dinners were take-out from the handful of reasonable quality restaurants either in Albuquerque or Belén or someplace in-between - like their favorite teriyaki place in Los Lunas.

"How about I make us an onion and cheese omelet?" Roxanne asked while her upper body was bent over and her head buried in the refrigerator. "Or English muffin pizzas, except we don't seem to have any tomato sauce."

"I could go get some take out if you'd like, Zeke," his father offered.

"Could we go over to the diner in the old caboose on the other side of the tracks near the piss house? You've got some toadskins, right Dad?"

"The piss house? Zeke, please don't talk like that! Why would you use such awful language?" his mother asked incredulously like his six years of training in the proper use of English were all for naught.

"The piss house is the jail, Mom. That's what hobos call it."

"Okay, but you're not a hobo anymore and I'd appreciate it if you wouldn't speak that way."

"That place is kind of a dive. You really want to go there? Haven't you had enough of trains for a while? And what, for crying out loud, are toadskins?" his father asked with the tiniest fragments of laughter splintering his words.

"Money, like dollar bills. Coins are what we call thin ones, just so you know," Zeke explained patiently to his non-hobo parents and was taking great amounts of pleasure using some of his newly acquired hobo language. "Do you have some toadskins and thin ones Dad?"

DAVID W. GOODWIN

"Yes, son. I have some toadskins and thin ones. I'd be willing to risk food poisoning. How about you, Foxy Roxy?"

"I thought we were going to stay in tonight? I'm sure we could scrape something edible together for a meal."

"Like pizza without sauce or omelets without ham? Can't we just go to the diner? It would be fun! I've been asking you guys for the last two years to go there and you keep saying no. I think tonight is the night we should finally do it since it's kind of a special night, wouldn't you say? We could even dress up so nobody would recognize us, if that's what you're worried about."

His mother eventually gave into her son's request but would agree to go under the condition that he take a shower and put on some clean clothes. Zeke was marginally resistant to changing out of his hobo-ized outfit because, in a way, he felt by doing so, he was giving up on Bix and Betty. Eventually, he realized, he would have to make the switch since he was rather grimy from his night and part of the day as a hobo on the run. Roxanne told him that she wanted to throw his hobo outfit away but he made her promise not to after they were washed.

"Those clothes will always be special to me," he explained. "And besides, remember what Officer Cellucci said about getting me a new Isotopes tee shirt? That will be special to me too!"

"I can see that," his dad agreed. "Maybe she could get me one too."

"Like maybe one that she's already worn?" Roxanne sniped.

Andrew let her comment go and realized after it was too late that he probably shouldn't ever say anything again about Officer Cellucci. It seemed to push a powerful jealousy button in Roxanne, even though she had no real reason to be jealous. She was Foxy Roxy, after all, and Andrew knew that the nickname had zero percent irony and sarcasm. He was lucky to have such a babe for a wife. Just because the Isotope's ballgirl was a smoking hot, banging bodied twenty-something didn't mean he couldn't admire her, did it? Apparently it did.

Zeke had mixed feelings about being home. He certainly missed his family and friends and the comforts of home but he was really worried about his hobo friends. What was going to become of them? Would they end up spending a long time in jail? Would they be charged with kidnapping? And if they were released, where would they go, what would they do? How could they have lived like that for so many years? Why wouldn't they want to settle down someplace? Why couldn't they come live with him since they have a lot of extra room in their house? There were so many aspects of the details that his naïve six-year-old view of the world just couldn't understand. Now that Bix and Betty had been involved in his experience, he felt entirely responsible for their well being. What could he do to help them at this point? Their lifestyle wasn't very healthy. He saw some of the things that they ate and drank and smoked. Mr. Noriega, his health teacher at school, would have a lot of things to say about this.

These rapid-fire thoughts filled his head while he was changing out of his dirty clothes, showering and getting some fresh, clean clothes on for dinner. Searching through the clothes that his dad had just put back inside his dresser, he found just what he was looking for and then went out to the living room where his parents were waiting for him.

"That must have felt pretty good, eh Devil Boy?" his dad said, wrapping him up in his arms. He nodded while his mom tried her best to get some of the wrinkles out of his brown Las Cruces Railroad Museum tee shirt.

The three of them got into his dad's hybrid SUV in the garage. Andrew hoped there weren't any residual reporters hanging around in their neighborhood but if there were, he thought that maybe they could catch them by surprise if they made a quick get away. As soon as the garage door opened, he quickly drove out onto Ladera, closing the garage door behind them. Nobody noticed any suspicious looking cars or vans in their neighborhood so maybe they all kept their word and were planning on returning the next afternoon with their questions and to hear what the Wappingers had to say.

The drive down to the L'il Red Papoose Caboose Diner on Jarales Road only took four or five minutes and was pretty close to the place where Zeke had hopped the boxie just a day earlier, only on the other side of the switchyard. If it had been light out when Zeke had gotten into the hobo world quick, he might have even been able to see it. To get there by car, however, they had to cut north and take the East Reinken Avenue bridge over the tracks and then drive south on Jarales. None of the Wappingers had ever eaten there before but had seen it hundreds of times from their many trips to the bridge to watch the trains come and go. Zeke was excited to be having another adventure. It wasn't often either parent was willing to do something outside of their comfort zone.

Considering that it was close to nine o'clock on a Saturday night in June in the sleepy town of Belén, also known as "The Hub City" given it's railroad history and function, and coincidently, the Spanish word for "Bethlehem," they were happy to see it's shining lights from a block away, almost like a star guiding their way to a late evening dinner at the caboose diner. A red neon sign in the window indeed said "OPEN" and there were still many cars and pickup trucks in the parking lot. The harsh diner lights were blazing away inside, visible through the many extra windows that had been added to the caboose plus the glassed in cupola that extended upwards from the middle of the train car looking almost like a lighthouse. From where his dad parked, Zeke could see that the diner was almost completely full and even from their car, he could hear a lot of loud voices and music playing, both in Spanish.

"Are you sure about this, Zeke?" his mother asked tentatively. "I'm not sure we belong here."

"Mom, if there's one thing I've learned on my adventure with Bix Pickles and Burrito Betty, it's not to make any assumptions. Didn't you learn that in lawyer school? Other than one bad actor and one cinder dick, I didn't meet anyone on my trip that was mean and as it turned out, the cinder dick let us go and Bix easily took care of the bad actor."

"Okay, I'll bite, what's a cinder dick?" his dad asked.

"It's a galvanizer or the Bull, someone who will kick you off the train if you get caught. Captain Haskell says they usually just throw you off but he said some times, they send you to the piss, uh, the jail. You know, the slammer?"

"Got it, thanks for the explanation."

Zeke got out and started walking towards the diner but looked around and saw his parents still in the car. He came back to knock on the window and yelled "come on." They reluctantly got out and Zeke boldly led the way into the diner via the staircase that led to the covered platform at the end of the caboose and through the narrow door into the train car. As they entered the rather small diner, they saw a long counter with about twenty metal stools facing the long galley-style kitchen - half of which were occupied - and six narrow booths lining the other side, which were full of grown-ups and boisterous kids. The noise inside the restaurant dissolved into the ether as all heads turned to look at them standing in the doorway.

To make them feel more welcome, a chubby, short man wearing a baseball hat with the New Mexico state flag on it, a clean white tee shirt covered with an equally clean and white apron and blue jeans, came over to greet them quickly.

"¡Hola amigos, bienvenidos a mi restaurante!"

"Hola," Roxanne said. "Gracias. ¿Tiene espacio para tres de nosotros comemos la cena?"

"You speak pretty good Spanish for a gringa!" he responded with a laugh, teasing her a little.

"How could you tell I was a gringa?" she responded, returning his volley and knowing that she would never get mistaken for anything other than a white, upper middle class woman unless she spent a few weeks riding the rails with her son and his new hobo friends and got real dirty and a crazy hairdo and outfit like that woman he was with.

"Oh, just a lucky guess. Say, would you be okay with sitting at the counter? I could get a few of my pals here to slide over to free up three stools together if that works for you. Otherwise, it might be a half hour or so for a booth to open up."

"That would be fine, gracias," she responded.

The noise in the L'il Red Papoose Caboose Diner gradually increased back to it's previous level as the clientele adjusted to having the only non-Hispanic diners amongst them. It helped a lot that they had all heard Roxanne speak Spanish to their friend Manny. It was almost like passing the entrance exam and they were now accepted as if they were second cousins. After settling into their three stools at the counter, right in the middle of the caboose, directly under the cupola in which were hanging two large beautiful and colorful horse piñatas, they had a chance to look around at the diner's motif. It consisted largely of Day of the Dead skeletons, figurines and many sizes, shape and types of skulls. Zeke found it completely captivating. The menu, printed in Spanish, had some items the Wappingers were used to seeing like burritos, tacos and chimichangas, but included a lot of things that none of them had ever seen before like barbacoa, romeritos, machaca, cabrito and, ironically, gringas. Roxanne tried her best to translate the descriptions of them for Andrew and Zeke. Manny saw their struggles, walked over from behind the counter, gently took the menu out of Roxanne's hand, flipped it over and said that the English version was on the other side.

Both parents ordered Pacificos while Zeke was steered towards ordering horchata since he liked milk so much. While deciding what food to order, Manny brought over their drinks and some tortilla chips with an assortment of salsas of differing colors and intensity on a little serving carousel and gave them a quick description of each one.

"Do you folks live in Belén?" Manny asked as they began attacking the chips and drinks.

"Yes, we do. I've lived here all my life. We live over on Ladera Drive," Zeke said proudly.

"I see. Have you ever eaten here before, chico? You all look familiar to me."

"No, this is our first time. I've been trying to get my parents to bring me here but this is the first time they said yes."

"Then, welcome! That means the chips and salsa are on the house!"

What they hadn't noticed in all of the activity of the diner was a large television over in the corner. The station was showing an Isotopes game against the Round Rock Express, which had captured Zeke's interest, especially since the Isotopes were leading seven to three going into the top half of the ninth inning with two outs and the bases loaded. Both male members of the Wappingers were half paying attention to the game and half paying attention to their food and each other. It would be untrue to say that Roxanne didn't notice.

"Maybe you'll catch a glimpse of your favorite ballgirl, Andrew."

Needless to say, his full attention was back at the counter of the L'il Red Papoose Caboose Diner in a flash. They ordered their dinners and Andrew thought it might be a good time to start asking his son a few of the many questions that had been building up inside him since about ten-thirty this morning when he discovered Zeke missing. Roxanne had surprisingly restrained herself from asking her pile of questions, thinking that Zeke was probably not yet in the correct mindset to be on the receiving end of her distinct and relentless style of cross-examination. She had made a conscious effort to wait until they all had a good night's sleep. However, since they had heard Zeke's statement just a while ago at the Gallup district office, they knew the general sequence of events from the time Zeke left home until the time he was caught with those bums in the moving van.

"Zeke, I'm sure you've got a lot more to tell us about your experiences and your mother and I would love to hear every little detail that you can remember, but the one thing I'm dying to find out from you is why you decided to run away from home?"

"Andrew, I don't think this is the time or place for this discussion. I think it needs to be done in the privacy of our own home," Roxanne interjected.

Even if Zeke had been given the green light to answer and was able to articulate that answer since he had been percolating various responses in his head over the last three or four hours, the "Special News Update" on

KOAT that interrupted the Isotopes/Round Rock game at a critical point, causing their viewers to completely miss the Round Rock Express coming back to score seven runs in the top of the ninth inning, to go on to win the game ten to seven, changed everything inside the L'il Red Papoose Caboose Diner. Manny had just brought out their three dinners and was setting them in front of the Wappingers as the "Special News Update" started.

"Good evening. We are sorry to interrupt tonight's broadcast of the Albuquerque Isotopes baseball game but we have important breaking news on the capture and return of the six-year-old missing boy from Belén, New Mexico. If you would like to continue watching the game, please tune to KOAT affiliate station KOON on channel 784. Again, we apologize for the interruption," the newscaster said in a serious sounding voice while her name, "Tatiana Ruiz, KOAT Anchor," was displayed below the live shot of her sitting behind the station's glossy news desk.

"As you may have been following from KOAT's breaking news coverage all afternoon and evening, six-year-old Zeke Wappinger was found hiding in the back of a Kokopelli's Big Furniture Mart moving truck in Gallup in the company of two adult hobos. As you can see in this footage, the young boy is shown being led into the New Mexico State Police District 6 building by police officers from both the state police and Belén Police Department with the two furniture truck workers and the two suspected hobos behind him, in footage you might have seen live this afternoon. At this time, we do not yet know if any charges will be filed against any of these people and KOAT News will keep you up to date on these developments as they happen. However, the boy has since been released to the custody of his parents, prominent Albuquerque lawyer, Roxanne Wappinger and BLM Natural Resource Planner, Andrew Wappinger.

"As you see in this footage, filmed several hours ago, Andrew, Roxanne and Zeke Wappinger are being led to and now driven away in the Belén Police Department squad car allegedly, according to reliable sources, driven by Officer Ricardo Ramirez who was the initial respondent to Andrew Wappinger's 9-1-1 call at 11:15 this morning. Just moments ago, our own field reporter, Gloria McGloria and KOAT cameraman Stan Zuckerthong filed this report."

"I'm KOAT field reporter, Gloria McGloria, and I'm standing outside the home of Zeke Wappinger, the young boy who disappeared late last night and was found in Gallup, New Mexico in the company of two hobos this afternoon. We have been told that Zeke is to arrive at his home in Belén shortly with his parents, Andrew and Roxanne Wappinger. In fact, there is a Belén Police Department squad car driving up the beautiful street in this decidedly upscale neighborhood as I speak and appears to be carrying the three Wappingers. Yes, it must be them as they are now pulling into the Wappinger's driveway. Ladies and gentlemen, I'm not sure if I can describe this scene fully as it is emotionally laden with equal parts of happiness and sadness, joy and frustration, pathos and celebration. The young boy who, for whatever reason, ran away or some think might have been kidnapped by the two hobos you saw in the earlier footage, has now been miraculously reunited with his parents and is about to get out of the police car. You see the Belén officer, yes, there he is on the left, and now we see both of the parents out in their driveway but we have yet to see the young boy. They seem to have somehow lost him along the way! No, I'm sorry. I'm mistaken. Apparently, he was asleep in the backseat of the car because now you see his father lifting him out and carrying him into their house. Ladies and gentlemen, this is an unbelievable scene. I'm going to see if I can get in close enough to ask a question or maybe even get a statement from them."

The video went shaky and blurry for a few seconds but when the image was stabilized and focused properly, it showed a close up of an almost upside-down Zeke in his father's arms with Gloria McGloria off to the side with a microphone in her hand, asking, "Is it true that your son actually ran away from home because he wanted to become a hobo?" to which Zeke responded, "Those hobos are Captain Bix Pickles, the Human Stinkbomb and Burrito Betty, the Princess of Poots and they're my new friends. I'm hoping my mom and dad will let them come live with us when they get out of jail."

"About thirty minutes after the return of the Wappingers to Belén, Roxanne Wappinger appeared at the front door of their house and here you see the video footage we were able to capture of her promising to hold a press conference tomorrow, which would be Sunday, at two o'clock. I'm sorry not to have the audio on that due to technical difficulties. We will carry that press conference live tomorrow. Reporting for KOAT Albuquerque, I'm Gloria McGloria."

"And that brings you up-to-date on the capture and return of Zeke Wappinger from Belén, New Mexico. We will have more information as it happens. I'm KOAT anchor, Tatiana Ruiz, with this special report. We now return you to the regularly scheduled programming."

By then, the Isotopes had already lost and just about everyone inside the L'il Red Papoose Caboose Diner had been struck completely dumb, including Andrew and Roxanne, but not Zeke. All eyes were on the Wappingers, perhaps to see if these gringos that were sitting inside the restaurant with them were indeed the Wappingers they had just seen on the special report. This was probably clear to all of the diners and diner staff. Maybe they were expecting the Wappingers to say something in response.

"How many times do I have to tell everyone, they did not kidnap me!" Zeke cried out, putting any remaining speculation to rest.

"Excuse me," Roxanne yelled out to Manny, "could you wrap up these dinners to go? It might be a good idea for us to go back home."

"¡Dios mío! Es usted!" Manny responded. "You are welcome to stay. We would love to have your company tonight. It will be our way of saying 'Welcome home, Zeke.' Please? It sounds like you've all had a pretty rough day."

"I feel so raw, so exposed. Everyone in the world now knows about this! I can't believe this is the news story of the decade!" Roxanne cried out.

At that point, a spontaneous, rather remarkable and probably completely unheard of thing in the Anglo community happened. Without any warning or any words being spoken, everyone in the diner got up and came over to welcome the Wappingers both to the diner and back to their reunited family. Adults and children alike lined up to give Roxanne and Andrew hugs and everyone saved their most special hugs for Zeke. To the person, from the oldest of the old to the youngest of the young, each person came up to each Wappinger, gave them a hug and said something along the lines of "Nos alegramos de que ha venido a casa" or "Dé la bienvenida a casa a pequeño muchacho." After a few people said more-or-less the same thing, Roxanne told her family that they were saying that they were happy that you have come home. Once they had finished welcoming the Wappingers, everyone went back to their seats and continued eating, almost like nothing had happened. Roxanne motioned to Manny to not box up their food and said she would like to stay and finish eating if it was alright with Andrew and Zeke. It was, of course.

"Gracias a todos. Nos sentimos honrados," Roxanne said standing beside her stool with one hand on the counter to steady herself, one hand touching her heart and was starting to cry ever so slightly as she spoke. She spoke loudly and confidently so that everyone in that crazy little caboose diner could hear her. Zeke had never seen her like this and had definitely never seen her cry before, ever. She was always direct and business-like with others, no nonsense, straightforward, but he saw a new, softer side of his mom that night and he was overjoyed that she was capable of displaying a certain vulnerability, perhaps for the first time ever. Maybe Zeke didn't label it as vulnerable at the time because it wasn't a word he yet fully understood but he certainly knew the raw feeling of it, he could taste it that night, he could taste it forever, for the rest of his life. As his vocabulary and maturity increased, this was a moment he would keep inside his heart forever. The word vulnerable was inextricably tied to this memory of that night, his mom, her little Spanish sentence of gratitude and that meal at the L'il Red Papoose Caboose Diner.

CHAPTER 12

AFTER ERNEST AND Ethel Gamble had wrapped up their interrogation and were taken back to the 4th Street Pub; after Officer Ramirez had dropped off the Wappingers and wrapped up his business at the Belén Police Station and finally gone home to his family; and after Daria Cellucci had dropped Lieutenant Forsmark off in Albuquerque and also wrapped up her business at the Belén Police Station and gone back to her smallish four room house in Los Lunas and had given Bullet his dinner; they all were in front of a television and saw the same "Special News Update" from Tatiana Ruiz, Anchor at KOAT in Albuquerque that the crew at the L'il Red Papoose Caboose Diner had seen. Captain Bix Pickles and Burrito Betty were still languishing in their holding cells in Gallup at this point and did not have a television to watch, however intrigued they would have been by it. Even Chip Brockaway of Big Air Off Road Adventures saw it, as did Zeke's friend, Warren, his nemesis Nicole and his nanny, Pamela.

However, the day before Ethel and Ernest Gamble were going to be brought into the NMSP District 6 offices for questioning, they were hanging out at the Spread Eagle Bar and Grill on East Coal Avenue. Both of them had forgotten about their upcoming questioning by Saturday night when this newscast was aired. Ethel, indeed, was the life of the party, wearing her one and only festive outfit and dancing with her "new best friend in the entire world," Janice, whom she had just met that evening but seemed to be the only other person in the bar that wanted to dance to the song catalog of Gerry and the Pacemakers currently on the bar's sound system. Ernest, on the other hand, was holding court over in a far corner of the bar with some fellow conspiracy theorists and could be heard shouting out random phrases such as the moldy-oldie and not-so-current "do you have any real proof that the Holocaust really happened?" and "I know someone who not only knows that Jim Morrison is still alive but saw him being abducted by aliens" to some more current ones like "undoubtedly the government knows everything about you. Why do you think they implant an RFID chip in everyone when you get the flu vaccine? Never get a flu shot, if you know what's good for you."

The one old picture tube style TV that was tuned to the Isotopes game in the corner was going largely unnoticed, even when the "Special News Update" was broadcast that night. If not for the fact that Herb, the ornery bartender, who was upset that the game had been interrupted by the news of Zeke's return to Belén and made a big stink about trying to change the station to channel 784, Ethel might not have noticed. However, it caught her attention for the briefest of moments and she stopped frugging with Janice to *How Do You Do It?* long enough to come over to watch it at the bar.

"That's him! Holy shit! Herb, leave it here for a moment! That's the boy we ate lunch with today over at the soup kitchen with those two hobos I was telling you about! Hey Ernest, stop your crazy talk and come over and watch this!"

The bar got quiet immediately, except for *Don't Let the Sun Catch You Crying* playing loudly in the background. All of the bar patrons, except for a guy dressed in a full sailor outfit passed out in one of the booths, came over to watch while Ethel peppered Tatiana's and Gloria's reporting with a few comments of her own.

"What a nice house he lives in," was followed by "his mom seems kind of like an uptight bitch, if you ask me," and ended with "why the hell didn't you interview me? It was my damned cellphone that led to his capture!"

When it was all over and the Isotopes wrap-up show was on and the commentators couldn't believe that three Isotope relief pitchers combined to give up seven runs in the ninth inning to the usually anemic Round Rock Express batters, Ernest said, "Just so they don't finger us for this one like they did Lee Harvey Oswald."

It was an unusually long day for Ricardo Ramirez. Belén was a pretty sleepy town from a police perspective so Ricardo's shift was generally predictable. When he was on his way to Gallup with the Wappingers to go get Zeke, he called his wife to tell her what was going on so she knew that he would be getting home much later than four or four-thirty that afternoon. After all was said and done, he didn't arrive home at his ranch house on Fermin Chavez Road until after dark that evening. His wife and two young daughters had waited to have dinner until he came home. They sat down within minutes of Ricardo coming through the door, he was hungry and exhausted from the day's events but pleased that it had a happy ending. As the family ate, he entertained them with the story about the six-year-old first grader from their town that was now an instant media celebrity. After dinner, his daughters begged him to watch *The Vampire Diaries* with them, their favorite television show. The same "Special News Update" interrupted that program, being broadcast on a local affiliate of KOAT. The Ramirez family started going crazy when they saw their dad appear in the report twice, first leading Zeke, the two hobos and the two movers into the station in Gallup and next, when he got more of a starring role dropping the three Wappingers off at the driveway across town.

"Dad, I know Zeke or I should say, I've seen him walking around school a few times," his older daughter, who was a fourth grader, said when their excitement started to wear off a bit. "Do you know why he ran away from home?"

"I'm not sure anyone knows that yet, Briza, except for the little boy. I spent a lot of time with his mom, driving back and forth to Tucumcari, spent some time with his mom and dad driving out to Gallup and then, as you saw, drove all three of them back to Belén. If I had to guess, I might say that his mom is pretty controlling and maybe the little boy felt that he needed to get a little space from her and maybe a little fresh air. She seemed to be convinced that he was kidnapped by the hobos but I don't think there's any evidence at all to support that."

"What were the hobos like?" his younger daughter, Malia, asked.

"I didn't get to spend more than a few minutes with them but they seemed really nice, actually, very protective of the boy. He must have said five or six times while I was around to anyone that would listen that they were his friends and that they didn't kidnap him. I would tend to believe that."

"Where are the hobos now?" Malia asked.

"They're still back in Gallup, locked up awaiting further questioning, from what I understand."

"Why? Doesn't anyone believe Zeke?" Briza asked.

"I'm sure it's being done as a precaution. I think the only person at this point that thinks Zeke was kidnapped is his mom. What you probably didn't sense from the news coverage is that Mrs. Wappinger is a pretty aggressive lawyer, top notch. She's probably used to using some hardcore tactics to fight for her clients. Based on the time I spent with her today, I think it's probably safe to say that she would be one tough chiquita to deal with. Like I said already, maybe Zeke just needed to get out from under her thumb for a while. I could believe that."

"It will be interesting to see if he comes to school next week. We only have Monday and then half a day on Tuesday before summer vacation," Briza stated.

Daria Cellucci's day was just as long as Ricardo Ramirez's and she wasn't able to get to Isotope Park in time to watch their epic collapse. Luckily, her friend Lola was able to sub for her as the ballgirl sitting in foul territory down the third base line. In fact, most diehard Isotopes fans held Lola responsible for the Isotopes loss when she accidentally fielded a curving but fair rocket hit by Binx LaDuke of the Round Rock Express with bases loaded, two outs and the score seven to five, still in favor of the Isotopes in the top of the ninth. She made a fantastic catch of a two hopper that apparently had curved around third base making it a fair ball and tossed it to a young girl in the second row, which was then ruled a ground rule double. Some Isotopes fans were incensed because the runner on second, Wade "Juicy" Koontz, fell flat on his face rounding third after tripping on the base and would have been easily thrown out at home to end the game, ironically, by left fielder Mike Hunt. As it was, this tied the score and after the next batter hit a home run, the game was more or less over since the Isotopes went down in order in the bottom of the ninth. After the game, Lola was told by the Isotopes General Manager to never come back to the stadium again. This wasn't the worst screw up Lola had made in her twenty-two years but it certainly ranked up near the top, rivaled only recently when she thought it would be a good idea to get a tattoo of Orbit, the Albuquerque Isotope's mascot, on her left butt cheek to keep the tattoo of Ronald MacDonald on her right butt cheek company. The good news was that most fans watching on their televisions didn't see it live because of the special news update but, unfortunately, many more did see it later since it made almost every highlight reel for the next few months. The silver lining was that the attention and exposure she got from this incident led to a few modeling jobs, which led to a contract, which meant that she never went back to being a substitute ballgirl anyway.

However, when Daria got home that night to her modest house on the southern outskirts of Los Lunas, within a stone's throw of the Rio Grande that formed the eastern edge of the town, she had a lot of decompressing to do after her extraordinary day. Bullet's needs always came first so even before getting her mail or checking her phone messages on her land line, he was fed, given some fresh water and let loose in her spacious back yard to do his thing. She then did her thing, which meant taking a shower and then microwaving a vegan meal from her stockpile of meals in the freezer and finally sat down in front of her TV with a cold local beer to watch the fateful Isotopes game and, of course, the "Special News Update."

She was a little disappointed to only make a far background appearance in the news coverage from the footage in Gallup but very disappointed that there was nothing in the report that mentioned the Belén K-9 unit, especially since some visibility from such a high profile case would greatly improve her chances with the city council when they voted next month on making her job full time. Since she had spent some time with Zeke and his parents, the story warmed her heart because of the apparent happy ending. Once things settled down a little, she resolved to be certain to make good on her promise to take Bullet over to hang out with Zeke. Maybe she would even go over to their house tomorrow afternoon for Roxanne's statement, in an unofficial capacity, since she wasn't scheduled to work until Tuesday.

A ringing phone jump-started her back to the moment as she was daydreaming a bit after watching the Isotopes postgame show, complete with Lola's gaffe shown four times, twice of which were in super slow motion. Clearly, Lola wasn't the brightest bulb on the tree but she had such a good heart and just wanted to please everyone. Daria felt kind of sorry for her.

"Yeah, this is Daria," she said picking up her cellphone that was beside her on an end table. The number didn't have any name associated with it but she decided to answer it anyway.

"Hi Daria, it's Marc Forsmark. Hope it's okay that I'm calling you."

"Sure, Lieutenant. What can I do for you?"

"Please, call me Marc. I'm off duty. Say did you happen to catch the KOAT special report that just aired?"

"I did."

"Pretty cool being involved in a case that has such major traction, wouldn't you say?"

"Yes, I suppose it is. I'm really happy that Zeke was found so quickly and is now home safe."

"Yeah, me too. Say, I really enjoyed spending time with you today. Would you let me take you out for dinner sometime, like maybe tomorrow?"

"That's sweet of you. I've got an Isotopes game tomorrow night but thanks anyway."

"How about some other night this week?"

"Lieutenant, I mean Marc, I hope you don't take this personally but I generally don't go out with people that I work with."

"I could see where that would be a good idea if we worked together but we're not even on the same force. Maybe you could relax your rules a little and go out with me on a technicality."

"Listen, Marc. I'm pretty drained right now. It's been a long day for me. Let's talk about this some other time. If you press me for a definitive answer right now, you probably wouldn't like the outcome. Maybe if you catch me in a better mood some other time I'd feel differently. I'm sorry, but that's just how I'm feeling right now."

"Fair enough. I appreciate your honesty. I won't take it as a definite no then. Perhaps some other time, Daria."

"Yeah, perhaps. Good night, Marc."

Her phone was barely out of her hand when it rang again, this time she saw that it was Lola calling. She debated whether or not to answer it, knowing that it was undoubtedly going to turn into a therapy session and she wasn't sure that she had the energy to deal with Lola's fragile ego and probably lower-than-normal self esteem at the moment. Since she did fill in for her at the stadium today at the last moment, however, Daria felt that maybe she owed her one.

"Hi Lola. How are you doing, girl?"

"Daria! I blew it! Did you see the game?" she cried.

"I did, but lucky for you though, most of the ninth inning was preempted for a special report on the missing Belén boy's return home. Maybe you timed your mistake perfectly," Daria said, hoping to put a positive spin on it.

"Really? Preempted? What does that mean?"

"You know, not shown. Nobody saw the play you made."

"Okay, but then how do you know about it if nobody saw it?"

"Yeah, good point, Lola. They just showed it on the Isotopes Corner Post Game Show. What happened? Did you think that it was a foul ball?"

"I'm not sure. The ball just came right at me on two or three bounces and all I could do was react. How could the ball have been fair and come right to where I was sitting? I'm way the hell over in foul territory by the rolled up tarp, you know that. You saw it. Was it really fair?"

"Yes, I'm sorry. It clearly was. It hit about an inch or two inside the line on the grass past the third base bag. It had some wicked spin on it, for sure, to get over to you. It was an honest mistake, Lola. Don't take it so hard. Nobody will remember it in a few days."

"I just feel awful, especially since it had such a big impact on the outcome of the game."

"Let it go, girl. It's not such a big deal. It's not like this is the major leagues or anything. Keep it in perspective."

"Yeah, you're right, Daria. Thanks for talking me down. I appreciate your support. I'll talk to you later. Oh, remember that we're going out for drinks after the game tomorrow? I'll meet you by the player's entrance, okay?"

As the Wappingers drove back into their neighborhood from the diner and approached their house, there seemed to be a lot of people out wandering the streets, or more precisely, wandering their street. This was a bit out of the ordinary since once the sun set, people normally went inside and stayed inside. Andrew assumed correctly that a lot of folks must have seen the "Special News Update" and wanted to initiate a little investigation of their own. At the very least, they might be able to catch a glimpse of Belén's newest celebrities, or, for some concerned neighbors, welcome little Zekie back home.

Andrew pulled into the driveway and when all of the various pedestrians saw that it was indeed the Wappingers, they congregated by both sets of brick and adobe pillars. Roxanne felt it important to go assure her neighbors and curiosity seekers that everything was all right. She went out to the end of the driveway to talk to them. Zeke and Andrew followed closely behind.

"We're so glad you got back safely, Zeke," one neighbor cried out before Roxanne said anything.

"Thank you all for your support. It's been a long day for all of us. We'd just like to go inside and get a good night's sleep. My hope is that we just put this all behind us and go back to our normal lives again and I hope you can respect our need for some privacy. Thanks everyone!" Roxanne said like she was addressing the press corps on the courthouse steps after a particularly contentious trial.

"Where are the two hobos that you traveled with?" an unfamiliar looking person asked.

"Please, no questions. We'll have time to talk some other time. Good night."

"They're still in jail where they don't belong!" Zeke yelled while his mom tried to quiet him and guide him towards their garage.

"Honey, it's best not to engage with anyone at this point. Let's get all the facts before we start offering our opinions, okay?" Roxanne whispered as they walked into the garage.

The time was closing in on ten-thirty - way past Zeke's bedtime. Once inside, everyone went about their nighttime routines and Andrew asked Zeke if he'd like a bedtime story or just wanted to go to sleep. Zeke said that he'd like to tell him a bedtime story this time for a change and invited his mom to join them, contrary to their usual bedtime ritual. Andrew checked to make sure all the outside doors were locked, Roxanne quickly checked her voice and email messages while Zeke put on his pajamas and hopped into bed. Eventually, his parents settled around him, leaning back and getting comfortable against the wooden headboard.

"Okay, so this is going to be a story about a little kitten that gets lost when a big storm comes through and blows him far away from his brother and sister kittens and his mom and dad cats," Zeke began. "Wait, it was a little puppy that gets blown away by the storm. Yeah, that's right. So here goes. Once upon a time, in a place that looked a lot like right where we are right now, there was a little puppy that got blown away by a big haboob."

"A big haboob? What's that?" his mom asked.

"It's what folks in the Middle East call a dust storm," his dad said. "I learned that from playing a lot of Trivial Pursuit in college."

"Yeah, Warren and me like the sound of it so we like to use it a lot. So anyway, this haboob comes along and sweeps up the little puppy and takes him far away from his family."

"Does this puppy have a name, Zekie?" Roxanne asked while smoothing down his hair in a sweet motherly gesture.

"Yes, he does. His name is, umm, his name is," Zeke said, hesitating and looking around his bedroom for some inspiration, "oh, perfect, his name is Orbit the Dog and he's a little black mutt. The cutest little black mutt that was ever born. So this haboob picks little Orbit the Dog up and finally drops him off in a land far away, a place where nothing looks familiar and where he doesn't know anyone and he's totally behind the eight ball."

"Behind the eight ball? How do you know that expression?" his father asked.

"Captain Bix uses it sometimes. I think it means that you're in a tight jam," Zeke explained.

"Would you expect that a puppy might know other dogs in other places?" his mom asked pointedly, never quite able to put her lawyer ways behind her.

"Maybe. It's a story. You don't know what goes on inside the world of dogs, do you Mom? Besides, in a story, anything is possible. Do you actually think that the caboose in *Charlie the Caboose and the Great Divide* can really talk?"

"Good point, counselor. Objection withdrawn."

"So Orbit the Dog finds himself in a strange place and is scared. He's hungry, dirty and confused. All he wants to do is get back home but he doesn't even know which direction to go. He sits down beside the railroad tracks in the little town that he's in, curls up into a cute little ball of new puppy fur and decides to prone his body. In a short while, he's woken up when a train comes through and a one-eyed bandit stops right in front of him. He opens his eyes and sees a bunch of scruffy dogs of all shapes, sizes and colors sitting in an open boxcar. He asks them if they know how to get back to his home and family. They all make doggie laughs when they find out that Orbit doesn't know the name of the town he came from, but invite him to come along with them and have a really great adventure. He ends up having so much fun that he almost forgets about missing his brothers and sisters and parents for the longest time, weeks, maybe even months. One day, the train happens to be going through his hometown and he looks around and recognizes it. He invites all of his new friends to jump off the train with him and help him track down his family, which they do in no time at all. They all like each other so much that his new doggie friends stay with him and they all live happily ever after. And just like Charlie the Caboose, Orbit the Dog got his final wish. The end."

"That was a sweet little story, Orbit, I mean, Zeke," his dad said with a smile, trying not to break up. "Now it's time to say goodnight. We love you so much, my man, and are so happy that you are back here with us. We missed you more than you'll ever know until you have your own kids. Please never run away again."

He gave him a big hug and a kiss, as did Roxanne but since she was so overcome with her emotions, only managed to say good night to him before she walked out of his bedroom with her husband and turned off the light.

Andrew and Roxanne went off to their own bedroom and Andrew did his best to comfort his distraught wife. He had never seen her in such an emotional state and wasn't quite sure what sort of approach he needed to take with her to show his support. Eventually, he started talking when it was clear that she wasn't going to initiate any conversation.

"That was quite a story, wouldn't you say?"

"Andrew, that was about the saddest thing I've ever heard. A little puppy getting tangled up with a haboob and becoming a dog hobo and forgetting that he had a family somewhere waiting for him. And his new friends make his new life happy and complete? Andrew, I can't help but feel that we haven't been very good parents. Why else would Zeke run away? I mean, what six-year-old kid feels so neglected that living with some strangers who are hobos looks like the better life? For Christ sake, we have to pay someone to be a parent to him because we're at work all the time. That's nuts!"

"You're right, honey, that is nuts! But now we see that. Clearly, we need to do things differently, that is pretty obvious. The challenge is that both of our jobs demand that sort of commitment, that sort of time schedule. There really seem to be only two options; one is for one of us to quit our job. The other is for one or both of us to cut back on our hours and be around more. Do you see any other alternatives?" Andrew asked tentatively.

"Nope, that's pretty much it. I honestly can't even talk about this anymore, Let's talk more tomorrow. I'm just too exhausted right now," Roxanne said as she snuggled up behind Andrew.

By midnight on that Saturday, nearly everyone was finally sound asleep from their stressful and highly eventful day. Ethel and Ernest ended up leaving the Spread Eagle by eleven-thirty and managed to find their way back to the shelter without incident. Ricardo Ramirez and his family finished watching *The Vampire Diaries*, tucked his daughters into their beds, performed his Saturday night ritual with his amorous wife and they were out cold by eleven. Daria Cellucci's phone kept ringing for a while with various friends calling to hear what she had to say about the Belén story of the century and one additional potential suitor calling to ask her out, ironically the same Juicy Koontz, the left fielder from the Isotopes that had been involved in Lola's controversial play. Daria had gone out with him once about a month ago and deferred any definitive answer until he came back to Albuquerque following their short four game road trip that left after tomorrow's game.

It should be noted that not all of the people involved in the entire drama were asleep at midnight on that Saturday. There were two folks that, even though they were out of their element, were still living on hobo time. They weren't used to sleeping seven or eight hours at a stretch. All their years spent riding the rails meant that they were used to sleeping an hour or two here and there as their situation dictated. Being locked up in a jail cell since Saturday afternoon meant that at midnight, Captain Bix Pickles Haskell, the Human Stinkbomb and Burrito Betty, the Princess of Poots were wide awake. The lights had been turned off around ten that evening but the bright New Mexican moonlight was shining in both of their cell windows, giving a melancholy sort of ambiance to their surroundings.

They remained incommunicado Sunday night as well since they hadn't yet been interrogated and were separated by some distance in the Gallup District 6 station. However, after their interrogation but before their subsequent release out into the streets Monday afternoon, they were allowed to cohabitate the same cell for a few hours. Conversation was easy in these quiet confines.

"Bix, do you think they're going to keep us here for a while?"

"I can't imagine they will but it's out of our hands now. How are you doin', Betty?"

"I'm good. A little sad and a little lonely, for Frankie. He's such a darling I just want to eat him up. What do you make of his parents?"

"Well, his dad seemed fine but his mom, well, you saw what she was like."

"Yeah. I'm certainly not one to judge based on some of the mistakes I've made but, what's up with that bullshit?"

"You got me. If I was able to understand certain people better, I'd probably not be here in the calaboose in Gallup, I'll tell ya that."

"Bix, when we do get released, where do you think you'll want to go?"

"Probably out to Shakeytown to help Eduardo Buttsteak, the Cabbage Patch Man set up his beanery near the beach. Don't that sound appealin'? I hope you'll come with me. I actually wouldn't mind takin' a break from the hobo world for a while and maybe set down some roots."

"Thanks, honey, for wanting to include me in your plans. It's been a long, long time since I've heard you say you want to set down some roots. I'm never quite sure sometimes where we stand but, just so you know, I consider you my man. If that's where you want to go and you're looking for some company, I'm with you. But here's a slightly different plan, so tell me what you think of it. We just made a promise to Frankie that we'd come visit him. Maybe we should go do that once we get sprung from the slammer. As much as I dislike his mom, I'm missing that little boy already. Would you ever consider paying them a quick visit? I just want to know in my mind that he's okay and that he'll never run away again. I feel like I owe him at least that much."

"Well, Betty, to be honest, it wouldn't be my first choice of places to go. You saw how the parents were, especially the mom. I'm not sure we'd be welcome visitors but let's see how we both feel about it when we get out of here. Okay?"

"Fair enough, sweetheart."

And with that and a tender kiss, the two hobos sat in silence, relishing each other's company until a guard came to tell them that they were being released without charge. With the possible exception of Zeke, none of the people involved in this entire adventure probably realized the true importance of the events that had just transpired and dramatically altered the trajectory of the lives. Sometimes it's the big obvious things that are the important catalysts for change, sometimes it's the things that weren't so obvious at the time but, in retrospect, when one looks back with the benefit of hindsight, they can see perhaps why it led them to a certain place in their lives. In this case, the events that happened and changed everyone's lives could only be described as fate.

CHAPTER 13

SUNDAY WAS AN eventful day for just about everyone involved in Zeke's awesome hobo adventure. First, Ethel and Ernest Gamble had two nights left at the Little Helpers of God shelter and had to start thinking about where they might want to go when they maxed out their number of nights there. Second, in the afternoon, the Wappingers held a press conference on the front steps of their house but since they didn't take any questions, it was more like a press briefing. Third, Daria Cellucci attended the press briefing with civilian dog Bullet and got to hang out with Zeke. Later, she worked at the Albuquerque Isotopes game who were wrapping up their homestand and four game series with the Round Rock Express and even later, went out for drinks with the disgraced substitute ballgirl, Lola. Fourth, Andrew and Roxanne had to prepare for a busy upcoming week of work and make some difficult lifestyle changes. Fifth, Zeke got to hang out with Warren at the Isotopes game and prepare himself for the last day and a half of first grade before summer vacation. Given his newly acquired celebrity status, it was going to be an interesting few days at the HT Jaramillo Elementary School for him, his classmates and his teacher, Mrs. Edelweiss.

At two o'clock that afternoon, at 398 Ladera Drive in Belén, New Mexico, a large crowd of reporters with microphones, camerapersons, curiosity seekers, neighbors, satellite vans, a few police officers and one off-duty police dog stood around in the Wappinger's driveway waiting for the promised press conference. Bullet was so well behaved, even when off-duty and off-leash, that when a little lizard skirted across the concrete driveway in front of him, he looked at Daria for permission to chase it. She shook her head so Bullet had to content himself with sitting by her feet and watch it disappear into the landscaped rock and succulent garden next to the front door.

Zeke Wappinger could be seen inside the house since he kept popping up in the window of his bedroom and gave his parents a running commentary on the crowd gathering outside. When he spotted Officer

Cellucci dressed in her civilian clothes with her dog, he got very excited and asked his parents if he could go outside to say hi to them.

"You'll have time to do that later, after we give our statement," his mom said tersely.

At five minutes after the hour, Andrew gathered his family and said it was time to go face the crowd. They had rehearsed what each member of the family was going to say and had printed everyone's script out for them. Roxanne kept offering to make the entire family statement but both Wappinger men wanted to do their part and she finally relented. When the front door opened and the family filed out and stood on the spacious and pillared portico, everyone gathered in close, cameras started filming and reporters started talking into their microphones in loud whispers until the Wappingers started reading their prepared statements.

"We each have a brief statement to make and will not be answering any questions at this time," Andrew began and read directly from his notes. "I'm Andrew Wappinger, Zeke's dad. I would like to thank everyone who played any sort of role in helping us locate and return our son to us yesterday, unharmed, a little dirty, but in a great emotional state. Thank you to the Belén Police Department, Officers Ramirez and Cellucci, the New Mexico State Police and especially Colonel Morgan, Major Queznal, Lieutenant Forsmark, Detective Anders, and Officers Danforth, Stanton, Hanover and Gonzales as well as other support staff. I would also like to thank the numerous employees of the BNSF Railroad who helped out considerably and were very cooperative. My appreciation is also extended to Ernest and Ethel Gamble for their role in finding my son and finally, a hearty thank you to Robert James Rand the third and Tiffany Spears for taking such good care of Zeke while he was riding the BNSF train to Gallup. Thank you all."

Camera flashes popped, questions were shouted out and reporters resumed talking into their microphones while looking directly into the video cameras from their respective stations.

"Hello, my name is Roxanne Wappinger and I'm Zeke's mother," Roxanne began and Andrew noticed that she didn't have her prepared script with her. "I would like to echo my husband's appreciation to all who helped us find Zeke. Just like the rest of you, I'm still trying to understand why my son might have slipped off into the middle of the night and boarded a freight train bound for Gallup. We are still trying to fit all of the pieces together but are not yet able to make a lot of sense of it. I haven't yet ruled out the possibility that he was kidnapped by the two hobos currently being held in jail and I call upon the police to conduct a thorough investigation into the matter. That's all I have to say at this moment."

Andrew and Zeke exchanged a look that all four camera people were able to capture. It was a look of surprise, shock and disbelief at what Roxanne had just said. This clearly wasn't what she had agreed to say. Zeke snapped out of his reaction and realized, when his dad prompted him, that it was his turn to make his statement. He turned around and placed his paper on a chair behind him.

"My name is Zeke Wappinger. I've already said this about a million times to anyone who will listen, especially my mother, that I ran away from home on my own, hopped a train down at the BNSF yard, met up with two hobos who were already on the train and then in Gallup, decided that I wanted to go home. They agreed to get me back here so I sent my mother a text message saying that I was all right. Then we got caught trying to come back to Belén. Captain Bix Pickles and Burrito Betty are 'A-number-one' people, the Emperor and Emperette of the Hobo World and any one of you would be lucky to have them as friends and they shouldn't be in jail. They didn't kidnap me, Mom! Thank you."

Every reporter started shouting out questions but Roxanne herded her family back inside the house, repeating that they wouldn't be answering questions. Eventually, as Zeke observed from his window, the crowd dispersed, but only after he made eye contact with Daria Cellucci and through a series of pantomime and hand gestures, told her to go around to meet him in their backyard. Slipping out the side door, he found her and the dog standing beside their deck while his parents retreated to their own bedroom to have a heated discussion about Roxanne's deviation from her prepared statement and failed to notice, yet again, Zeke's disappearance.

"Officer Cellucci! Thanks for coming and bringing Bullet!" Zeke exclaimed in a very loud whisper so as not to attract any other attention from his parents or any hangers on around the other side of the house.

"Zeke, my little friend! Great to see you! But please, call me Daria. I'm off duty now and so is Bullet. He's been dying to see you again and now he's free to play!"

Zeke got down on his knees and started rubbing the bloodhound's ears and Bullet immediately rolled over onto his back to get a belly massage. Zeke was so happy he started to crack up and this set Bullet off on a sort of dog-giggling thing, which was part baying, part whimpering,

DAVID W. GOODWIN

and a part moaning sort of sound. This got Zeke giggling even more and he flopped down next to the dog to do some high octane dog belly rubbing. Daria got down on the grass with them and joined the fun.

"He really does seem to like you, Zeke. I've never seen him react to anyone like this before. How are you doing? You look nice and clean. Are you happy to be back home?"

"Yeah, for the most part but I'm really missing Burrito Betty and Captain Bix. I don't know why my mom doesn't believe me. Do you know how they're doing?"

"Yes, I do. I just had a conversation with Officer Ramirez about an hour ago and he told me that your two hobo friends are still being held in the Gallup lockup. He says that they are wrapping up their interviews today with them and the Gambles and will then make a decision about releasing them."

"Who are the Gambles?"

"Oh, they're the people that you ate lunch with at the soup kitchen yesterday. Remember them?"

"Yes, I just didn't remember their names."

"Anyway, he told me that Major Queznal called him a while ago and said that they would probably be releasing your friends later today without charge."

"That's totally rad! Totally awesome! That's great news!"

"Yes it is. That makes me happy, too. Listen, Zeke, I need to head over to The Lab, you know, Isotopes Park to get ready for the five o'clock game but I wanted to stop by and welcome you home. Are you still interested in going to a game sometime?"

"Are you serious? Of course!"

"Good, I'll track you down sometime soon and you'll be my guest. We can go in the clubhouse, you can sit in the VIP section, maybe even bring a friend and your parents; we'll have a ton of fun, I promise. Deal?"

"Deal! Bye Daria, bye Bullet!" Zeke said as the ballgirl and her canine colleague disappeared around the corner of the house.

Daria drove home to drop her dog off after taking him for a short walk along a pathway in the floodplain of the Rio Grande. She grabbed a quick snack, got her Isotopes ballgirl outfit and another change of clothes for her evening out with Lola and drove north up to the ballfield. With about an hour to spare before game time, she pulled into the lot reserved for players and staff and walked into the woman's staff changing room. The other ballgirl was there and was already changing into her uniform.

"Daria, good to see you. I was wondering if you'd be here today. From what I've seen on TV, you've had a hell of a weekend. You and that runaway boy are all over the news!"

"Hey Wendy. Yeah, I was just over at his house for a press conference. I'm hoping to bring him to a game sometime soon. He's a big Isotopes fan. Say, were you working the game yesterday with Lola?"

"Don't remind me! I can't believe she screwed up so badly. I take it you heard about it?"

"Impossible to miss. It's not only all over TV but it's also gone viral. Poor Lola. She can't seem to stay out of trouble in spite of herself. I'm pretty certain she'll never be allowed back here again. Say, I'm going out for drinks with her after the game. Want to join us?"

"Maybe. One of the players asked me out but I think they're all leaving for a road trip after tonight's game. I'm not sure he remembered that little detail. Maybe he and I will have to have a super quick quickie, depending on the timing," Wendy said with a wink.

The Isotopes—Round Rock game was played without a repeat of the now infamous ballgirl incident, in fact, Daria made a spectacular play on a one hop blistering foul line drive hit down the third base line that got a huge ovation from the crowd of close to eight thousand. After the game ended, Lola texted her that she was out in the parking lot and this was where they met up after Daria changed into her going out clothes. While they were drinking margaritas and nibbling on chips and salsa at a popular Mexican restaurant called El Guapo's, Lola received the call that would change her life. A Hollywood talent agent had seen the clip of her blunder and another of a post game, post blunder interview with her that night and offered to fly her out to LA to discuss a modeling/acting job. She left New Mexico the next day and only came back briefly the following day to pack up her few belongings and drive back to California.

Back on Ladera Drive, Andrew was steaming mad with his wife after the press conference. Why she decided to change her script from one of gratitude and relief, like they had talked about, to one of continuing accusations of impropriety on the part of the hobos, was beyond him. Clearly, they had a fairly major issue to iron out and the ironing out started the second they all got back inside their house. Zeke went off to his room to monitor the crowd while his parents went into their bedroom and closed the door behind them.

"What the hell was that all about?" Andrew demanded. "Why do you continue to want to twist this story around like that?"

"There are a lot of unanswered questions, Andrew. There's got to be a lot more to the story than our son running away from home and hopping a train in the middle of the night."

"Even though he has told the same story every time he's asked? Damn it, Roxanne, he's not making this stuff up! Why don't you believe him?"

"Because I think those people put this fantasy in his head and now he honestly believes it's true. C'mon, Andrew, would a six-year-old kid run away from home and become a hobo? Specifically, our six-year-old kid? He's got everything here he needs. He's got a great house, a great nanny, great friends, he's got a great life, wouldn't you say?"

"I think what he's missing, honey, are the great parents. I think what he was running away from and what he ended up running into were two adults that formed a nice little family in his mind, like the little haboob dog Orbit, one that he doesn't always have here. Don't you see it? All he ever asks for is more time with you, more time with me, more family time and we're so damned blinded by our careers that we're not seeing it. He never really asks for material things, he wants to go camping, he wants to go to a baseball game, he wants us to sit down and eat a meal together that one of us prepared, all three of us at the same time. That doesn't really happen very often. Hell, he even said a few days ago that he wanted a brother or even a sister. Roxanne, the kid wants a family! If we don't make some changes now, and I mean right now, he's going to keep running away, he's going to keep looking for a family that gives a shit about him and right now, he doesn't think that we do. We even made him do a Confession the other day and threatened to take him to a priest. How stupid was that? You saw how he reacted to it and we just ignored him. Do you hear what I'm saying?" Andrew exclaimed as his voice got higher and louder reaching a crescendo at the last rhetorical question.

"I think you're overreacting," Roxanne said using a dull and unaffected sounding voice.

"And I think you're in denial to think that he was kidnapped. There is zero evidence to support that theory, zero! The bottom line, Roxanne, is that this is our fault, entirely, and we are the ones that have to fix it. So here is what I'm willing to do. It's probably safe to say that I work, on average, say, fifty or sixty hours a week counting my normal weekly schedule, the night meetings and parts of the nights and weekend that I usually end up working. That's bullshit! I'm getting paid for forty and it's my own damned fault that I put in all those extra hours. Nobody is holding a gun to my head saying that I have to do this. I resolve, from this point onward, to only work a forty-hour week and to feel okay about only getting forty hours worth of work done each week. This is not life and death stuff here. If it doesn't get done, it just doesn't get done. If I have night meetings or things to do on weekends, I will take comp time off during the week. I might even be here when Zeke gets home from school some times. How about you? Are you willing to make some changes too?"

"That's all well and good Andrew but you've just started another round of meetings that will take most of your attention and waking hours. How are you going to deal with that?"

"Yeah, that's going to be a tough one. I will do my absolute best to hold to my new resolution starting right now. Clearly, once I get through these next two weeks, for sure, it will be a lot easier."

"But I'm in the same bind. We're committed to all of these clients and cases. I can't just say, sorry, I don't have time to meet with you or prepare for your trial, I need to go home to be with my son. You'll just have to plead guilty and spend some time in jail, sorry about that," Roxanne said, her words drenched with sarcasm.

"Maybe there are other options. Maybe you could hire more help and reduce your workload. We don't absolutely need the level of income we're currently making. We could get by on a lot less money if we wanted to. Our lives are more than what we own, Roxanne. I realize this might be more of a challenge for you in the short term but if you think long term, maybe you could take on fewer clients."

"That's true, I could but I love doing this kind of work. It excites me and I could be making a lot more money than I currently am if I had more support at home. How would you feel about quitting your job altogether and becoming a househusband? You could be with Zeke full time."

Andrew started laughing at the idea and eventually said, "It's not without merit but there are parts of my job that I like too. I'm not sure that I would want to be a househusband but I suppose it's an option to consider. Okay, I've laid out a few things here. Do you agree that we need to make some changes to become more of a family?"

"Yes, I do."

"Alright then, maybe we should leave it like that for the moment. I know what changes I'm going to make and maybe you could be thinking about some changes at your end and we can revisit the topic in a few days when we've had some time to think about it. You know that Zeke

DAVID W. GOODWIN

only has two more days of school and then he's out for the entire summer, right?"

"I do, but we've signed him up for a bunch of camps and Pamela is going to be with him some of the other time and then we have our vacation in August so that covers most of the summer."

"Yeah, see, that's what I'm talking about. Why do we have a kid if we're hardly ever around to do stuff with him? Speaking of which, I'm going to go find Zeke and see what he's up to."

Trying to keep to his word of being a more present father, Andrew was immediately faced with the challenge of trying to balance spending time with his son and getting ready for another round of public meetings that started again tomorrow night. This became even more urgent since he had lost most of the weekend already getting things back to normal with his son. He found Zeke in his room, having just returned from his encounter with Daria and Bullet in the backyard, and asked if he wanted to hang out and do something with the remaining hours of the day.

"The Isotopes game starts at five," he said. "Want to go? Warren just called and said that he and his dad are going and wondered if we could come with them but I know you're probably busy since it's Sunday."

"That means we'd be out until around nine tonight," Andrew said with some trepidation realizing that his resolve was already being put to the test. "Sure, Devil Boy, let's do it."

Sometime in the afternoon on Monday, Bix and Betty were released onto the streets of Gallup and were sporting a new set of duds that Officer Danforth had given them from a bag of donations that came from "Ghetto Fabulouz", Betty's favorite thrift store in New Mexico. Bix decided that his "Daddy's Little Princess" tee shirt was best left behind in the trash, as well as his torn and threadbare plaid pants. In their place, he found a nice sage green cotton oxford shirt and some comfortable blue jeans that fit him well. He retained his boots that were sporting brand new shoelaces, his freshly laundered cotton striped sport coat and trademark porkpie hat with the various bird feathers still in the hatband. Betty, on the other hand, with her clean hair that had required several hours of detangling with a brush and wide-toothed comb she was given at the jail, rummaged through her clothing selection and decided an entirely new wardrobe was in order. She ditched her rags, even though they had been cleaned and deloused thoroughly, and opted for a rather smart looking ensemble featuring stretchy black capris, a light blue silky blouse and topped off her new look with a grey cardigan and low ankle boots that fit perfectly. When Robert James Rand III saw her when she came out of the changing room, he almost fainted.

"My goodness, Betty. If I hadn't seen you walk into that room with your jail jumpsuit, I might not have known it was you comin' out. You look absolutely amazin'!"

Betty blushed and Bix Pickles, who still sort of resembled the old Bix Pickles only a lot cleaner and a lot more presentable to mainstream society, was freshly shaven and had clean and combed hair as well, came right up to her and gave her a big hug and major smack on the lips. The fact that Betty hadn't had a drink now for several days had certainly helped to clear her head significantly.

"You look pretty good yourself, old man! Maybe now you'll get the idea to show your best girl a good time in the big city."

The feeling they had must have been like they were both awkward high school kids going out on a first date. Captain Bix Pickles had taken three or four steps towards reassuming the look and swagger of Robert James Rand III back in his powerful and confident days in Brookline before he was cut to the quick. When he saw the unearthed sophistication and beauty of his traveling companion of many years, the former Burrito Betty, the Princess of Poots, and her almost magical transformation to Rebecca Stone or Tami Franklin or Tiffany Spears or whatever the heck her name was, his heart did a double take followed by a back flip. He had absolutely no idea that the rum dum, loo loo, bale of straw and booze hound could possibly have cleaned up so well. To say that he was overwhelmed was a complete understatement.

From Tiffany's perspective, Robert Rand was a vision of handsome elegance. She had never before seen him cleaned up like this either. Sure, she had many warm special feelings for him throughout all the years they had been hobos together, but to see him standing before her as a new man, a man that reeked of professionalism and promise, that looked like he could reintegrate back into normal society, well, that was never a thought that seriously crossed her mind until this very moment. Clearly, the possibilities were endless and it excited her like never before.

Robert reached out and gently took Tiffany's hand in his own. He raised it to his lips, gave it a tender kiss and said, "Tiffany, darling, will you allow me the pleasure of taking you out for dinner this evening?"

DAVID W. GOODWIN

"Why, Mr. Rand, how so very kind. I would be honored."

What they both understood, but didn't want to seep in to spoil the moment, was that neither of them had a toadskin nor any thin ones to their name. They both were flat broke and the details of having dinner, finding a place to stay for the night and traveling by any means other than hopping a train was a massive road block facing them down and staring them right in the eyes, not entirely unlike what a hog or a hotshot might look like, barreling through the end of a railroad tunnel with it's bright front light blazing a huge hole into the middle of the night. They were used to relying on the kindness of strangers or dumpster diving for discarded food and sleeping out in the open or in shelters or in a boxcar. The reality, sadly, was that Betty didn't know any other way to live her life and for Bix, it was a long ago forgotten memory. For the moment, however, the fantasy of being grown ups and living in a grown up world was rather powerful. Neither of them wanted to break that spell.

Walking hand in hand, they were escorted by a state police officer down the hall to process their paperwork, finalizing their freedom. At the front desk, they signed some documents, were given back their minimal belongings and asked if there was any place nearby that they would like to be driven. The woman helping them at the front desk asked where they might be heading.

"Your guess is as good as mine," Robert Rand responded. "We have a few options but haven't yet decided which direction we might go. We were given a sheet with the names of various shelters so at least we have that as a starting point."

"Do you have any money?" she asked.

"No, not really," Tiffany answered sheepishly.

"There's an ordinance in town against panhandling and we'd hate to hear that you got picked up by the Gallup PD in a few hours to face charges."

"Thanks for the heads up. Maybe we'll just hightail it outta here," Bix said.

"Listen folks, we don't normally do this sort of thing but given your circumstances and the way you took care of that young runaway boy, we all took up a collection to give you a few more options. I hope you'll accept this token of our appreciation," she said, handing him a sealed envelope with his and Tiffany Spear's name on it.

"That is so kind of you. Thank you so much!" Tiffany said, truly appreciative. "Maybe one of your cops could take us to the nearest shelter so we can figure out our next move."

With that, a police officer was summoned and they were treated to a door-to-door ride from the NMSP District 6 office on Historic Route 66 down to, of all places, the Little Helpers of God shelter. They checked in as husband and wife and were given one of the few private rooms that the shelter had to offer. As they settled into their relatively luxurious accommodations, at least compared to their recently vacated jail cells, or a shared dumpster or boxcar, or a patch of dirt in a hobo jungle with a few sheets of newspaper, they both felt giddy in a way they never had before. Tiffany bounced on the bed and fluffed up the pillows that had actual clean pillowcases and began giggling like a schoolgirl, which set off a few of her trademark poots. Robert started laughing as well and came over and sat next to her.

"I can't get over how incredibly beautiful you look Betty. Would you prefer that I call you Tiffany now?"

"Whatever you're comfortable with. I've been Betty with you forever; it would be kind of weird for you to all of a sudden start calling me Tiffany. I haven't been called that for many, many years. I'm not sure I could call you Robert. Are you okay with still being Bix?"

"That's fine, sweetie. Say, maybe we should look inside the envelope."

Betty reached over to the tiny pile of her possessions on the bed and grabbed the envelope off the top. After looking at it for a moment, she handed it to Bix to open. He carefully tore the end open, gently pulled out a small stack of bills and fanned them at Betty so she could get an initial appreciation for the enormity of the gift.

"Wow! There are quite a few bills here," Bix exclaimed as he slowly added them up. "Let's see, there are five twenties, three tens, five fives and seven ones. One hundred and sixty two dollars! Wow! That's huge! I can't believe they just gave this to us! What an amazing gift! Honey, I think I could actually take you out for dinner tonight, or you could take me out, or we could take each other out. Unreal! When was the last time we ever went out for a meal at a restaurant that we paid for?"

"I can't say I ever remember ever going out to a restaurant with you before," Betty said. "But I think we have to be careful how we spend this present so we can get some good mileage out of it."

After a delicious afternoon nap in one of the most comfortable beds they had slept in for years, they hit the mean streets of Gallup, which were actually pretty quiet and tame since it was Monday night and it was usually a not-so-mean place anyway. They had seen a few dining options on the drive over to the shelter and knew they had a few choices of places to eat that were all within a short walking distance. Out into the warm late June evening, dressed almost normally, as clean as they had been in years and with a sizeable wad of cash, the night offered many possibilities. Considering the food and drink they were used to eating as hobos, almost anything would feel like they were dining at a five star restaurant. The first place they ran across was the Spread Eagle Bar and Grill and the first people they saw inside were Ethel and Ernest Gamble.

Ethel and Ernest were sitting together at the bar with two other patrons. When Bix and Betty walked in, they both recognized Ethel and Ernest immediately but Ethel and Ernest wouldn't have recognized Bix and Betty if their lives had depended upon it. Not only were their memories fairly poor but the two former hobos were almost unrecognizable in their current manner of dress and attitude. Captain Bix Pickles Haskell and Burrito Betty decided to grab a more private booth off to the far side and sat down on the same side, wanting to keep as close to one another as possible. The woman who was bartending ducked under the counter and walked over to their table with some menus.

"Welcome folks, my name is Marge. Welcome to the Spread Eagle. Ever been here before?"

"Hi Marge. I've been spread eagled before but never here, as far as I know," Betty wisecracked.

"If I had a dime for every time I've heard that one, hon!" Marge said good-naturedly. "Can I get you some drinks to start you off?"

"I'm thinking champagne to celebrate. Is that alright with you, Betty?"

"You're on the right track there, big spender. You might even get lucky tonight if you play your cards right," Betty said as she put her arm around Bix and gave him a playful lick on his clean ear.

"We'll have a bottle of your finest champagne, as long as it's under twenty dollars," Captain Haskell said.

"What are you folks celebrating, if I may ask?"

"All sorts of things, Marge, but mostly just bein' here with my beautiful lady."

"That's sweet. I'll be back in a moment with your champagne."

In the meantime, the spiffed up hobos were able to eavesdrop on the loud conversation the Gambles were having with their drinking buddies.

All four of them seemed to be rather heavily under the influence. Ernest was off on yet another alien thing and was trying to convince their buddies that it was time to get the government to start protecting ordinary citizens from alien abductions, which, quite obviously, were becoming a bigger and bigger problem, at least in his mind. Ethel was bragging to her new friends about how she had helped the state police find that runaway boy from Belén a few days ago. Their buddies were a lot more interested in hearing about this than they were about hearing Ernest's nonsense, so he was quickly relegated to playing second fiddle to Ethel, something he had gotten used to many years ago.

"We were over at that soup kitchen on Friday and in walks this little boy and these two scruffy hobos. They made up some sort of cockamamie story about traveling to the artichoke harvest from Florida and I just knew they were making it up and I told 'em so, flat out. I also told 'em that all the world was looking for the little boy and showed them the AMBER Alert notice for him on my cellphone. They went white as ghosts and the boy, such a darling, asked if he could send his parents a text message to let them know he was all right. We got brought in for questioning today and from what I've seen on the news, the police let the hobos go without charging 'em with kidnapping or anything. They seemed like good decent folks, if you ask me."

The large, high definition TV at the bar was playing some sort of murder-detective-forensic-medical show and since Bix and Betty hadn't watched much television in their lives, it was rather mesmerizing. They were about a third paying attention to the TV, a third paying attention to Ernest and Ethel and a third paying attention to each other. Both of them were thinking to themselves that seeing the other person clean, groomed and in close-to-normal clothes was a powerful aphrodisiac. When their $15 bottle of Freixenet Brut Nature arrived with some champagne flutes and a clear plastic bucket with some ice in it, Burrito Betty thought she had died and gone to hobo heaven. She couldn't keep her rough, but spotlessly clean hands off her boyfriend and he was feeling the same way.

As Captain Bix Pickles Haskell, the Human Stinkbomb popped the cork out of the Freixenet, Ethel and Ernest's attention was immediately drawn to them. Bix poured both of them a generous amount and they toasted each other and their new found freedom and good fortune. As the two lovebirds were drinking their bubbly beverages, Ethel took it upon herself to wander over, introduce herself and ask what they were celebrating. Not wanting to give too much away, Betty said, "probably about the happiest day of my life."

"That's so sweet. I'm happy for you but what makes this the happiest day of your life?" Ethel asked as she got up closer to the two hobos.

"Oh, any number of things," Betty responded.

"Does any of it involve a six-year-old runaway boy from Belén perhaps?"

"As a matter of fact it does," Bix said, realizing they had been discovered and a bit surprised that Ethel recognized them.

"Ernest, come over here quick. It's the hobos that we had lunch with yesterday!" Ethel cried out. "My God! I barely recognized you! You folks look awesome! I guess prison life agreed with you!"

Ernest slowly wandered over and Ethel connected the dots for him after they sat down on the other side of the table. Bix and Betty then told the Gambles what their last two days had been like and Ethel told them about her experience with their police interrogations. She then brought them up-to-date on what the latest news broadcasts had said about Zeke and his return home and the press briefing the Wappingers had held earlier in the afternoon.

"It was unbelievable," she explained. "Maybe you can see a replay of it on the ten o'clock news tonight. You two went from being treated like kidnapping suspects to heroes. I think everyone except that bitchy mother of his knows that you both took really good care of the little boy. For some reason, his mom still seems to be ungrateful and is still pushing for some sort of inquiry, even though all the news channels have wrapped the story up with a happy ending. Anyway, congratulations to you, for doing what you did, getting out of jail and cleaning up so well!"

Glasses were clinked and everyone drank deeply in the friendly ambiance of the Spread Eagle Bar and Grill. The bartender/waitress came over and asked if they were ready to order and Bix graciously asked Ethel and Ernest if they would like to join them for dinner.

"Thanks, but we ate quite a while ago. Don't let us stop you though," Ethel said encouragingly. "We'll leave you two alone to enjoy your meal."

Captain Bix Pickles and Burrito Betty ordered like they hadn't eaten in a week. Appetizers, entrees, desserts and coffee were consumed, as was the entire bottle of champagne. The Gambles were still at the bar drinking, and even to the casual observer, it is probably safe to say that Ethel did most of the talking—she was certainly the life of the party. Betty got as close as humanly possible to Bix and the night just seemed to have a rosy glow to it, all around. When everything had been finished, Bix got up and asked the bartender for their bill.

"This really is your lucky day, sir. These fine folks have covered it for you," she said indicating Ethel and Ernest.

"That is really kind of you but I can't accept that sort of generosity. We can pay for our meal. Everyone at the police station chipped in and gave us a nice wad of cash on our way out to help us make a new start," Bix explained.

"No, we insist, really!" Ethel said, getting up from her barstool. "Just one condition, however. Ernest and me would like to come join you at your table and talk about an idea we have."

"Fair enough. Please, be our guests," Bix said bowing and indicating with his outstretched arm the way.

When they were all comfortably seated at the booth, Bix explained to Betty that the Gambles had covered their bill and wanted to discuss something. Betty was deeply touched and thanked both of them profusely, even letting out a little tear and a little poot at the same time, which went almost completely unnoticed.

"Where are you folks headed, now that the dust seems to be settling?" Ethel asked pointedly.

"That's a good question," Betty began when Bix didn't immediately jump on the question. "We're trying to decide which way to go. We might go out to California, not for the artichoke harvest like you know, but to help out a beachcomber friend that wants to start up a food cart near the beach. That's kind of where Bix is leaning. Me, on the other hand, I'm more interested in going to visit our new little friend Frankie, or Zekie I guess is his real name, to make sure he's okay back at home. He came to visit us while we were in the slammer, before his parents took him home, to say goodbye and made us promise that we'd come visit him soon. I'm not sure why but I feel I need to do that so we can wrap this whole episode up."

"How might you get there?" Ethel asked.

"Another good question. We're used to runnin' the lines, so to speak, but in this hot yard, I'm not sure if we could flip a boxie without getting nabbed by the Bull," Bix said, back in hobo mode for the moment, perhaps to impress the Gambles with his hobo pedigree.

"Listen, me and Ernest were kind of taken in by that little boy, too. We were thinking that maybe we'd go to his house and meet his parents and just say goodbye. We don't really have anything else to do. We just need to be in Gallup sometime next week to get the next check that my sister sends. Every month I tell her which post office to send it to. Me and Ernest been living off that check now for about eight or nine years. Maybe we could take you there."

"You could?" Betty asked. "How?"

"Oh, I guess I should have mentioned it before. We've got a car."

CHAPTER 14

MONDAY MORNING AT the HT Jaramillo Elementary School on Esparanza Drive was anything but typical for Zeke, his friends, classmates, the teachers and even his bus driver. As the yellow bus labored and rumbled up Velta Drive and came to a stop at the intersection with Ladera Drive, Zeke was the only student waiting. There were usually a couple of other kids from his neighborhood there with him, but not today. When Big Darl opened the door for Zeke to hop on, he was greeted with a huge cheer, led by Big Darl, but soon every single person was clapping, hooting and calling out little Zeke's name. Since he was usually one of the youngest and smallest kids on the bus and kept a pretty low profile in general, this was a big surprise. He didn't even think most of the kids on the bus knew his name, especially the big sixth graders who liked to harass pretty much everyone.

"Welcome back to Belén, Zeke Wappinger! You are one tough little dude!" Big Darl said as Zeke walked past him to grab an empty seat. His stop was near the end of the bus route so the bus was almost full of students at this point. Big Darl high-fived him as did nearly every kid in an aisle seat as he made his way towards the back. In fact, even most of the kids in window seats wanted to get in on the high-fiving action, even if it meant leaning onto the body of their seatmate. This violated one of the unspoken rules of the typical elementary school student who had pretty clear physical boundaries that did not include a whole lot of touching unless you were best friends with that person. This rule was thrown out the school bus door today for two reasons. First, because it was the penultimate day of school and the kids were kind of wired anyway; and second, and of much greater importance, they had a celebrity amongst them. The mood on the bus was high energy, similar to the type of energy one might witness if instead of being carted off to school, they were going on a field trip to a water park.

This energy was only going to escalate over the course of the school day. From the moment the bus arrived in the special bus lane in front of the school, to the moment Zeke was dropped off back at the corner of Velta and Ladera Drives at three-fifteen that afternoon, he was the center of attention. Even the stodgy, uptight and tight-lipped Mrs. Edelweiss, his first grade teacher, who only ever seemed to crack the slightest bit of a smile when the class was performing the Pledge of Allegiance each morning, welcomed him into the classroom with a hug and slightly moist eyes.

"Zeke Wappinger, you had us all so worried. My husband and I prayed for your safe return all weekend. Thank God you are home. That must have been a horrible experience," she said with a slight shakiness to her voice.

"Not really, Mrs. Edelweiss. I had a ton of fun!" Zeke exclaimed, while all of his classmates started laughing their tiny butts off, even Nicole.

Much to Zeke's surprise, the principal of HT Jaramillo Elementary School, a dynamic roly-poly white haired man of seemingly endless enthusiasm and optimism, had called a school-wide assembly for nine o'clock to welcome Zeke home, but more importantly, to call attention to the alarming issue of runaway children. He had even prepared a PowerPoint presentation complete with links to the various videos of the coverage from the local television news stations and even some of the YouTube snippets that had been posted over the weekend, all starring Zeke, obviously. These were a huge crowd pleaser. He then went on to link to the New Mexico AMBER Alert site and explained the workings of this network and the support services that the school had in place if any child had even the slightest inclination to run away. Without trying to scare the young students too much, he alluded to the growing problem of child abductions and warned all of the kids "to be on the lookout for such things."

"This is exactly what this network was created for, and over the weekend, it showed how beautifully and perfectly it can work. Now boys and girls, I hope that none of you ever run away from home but I want to know that if you or a loved one ever does, there is this incredible network of help and support out there. This story has a very happy ending and we have great news because today we welcome home first grader Zeke Wappinger, safe and sound. Come on up here, Zeke so we can properly celebrate your return!"

Zeke was not too happy to be getting this sort of attention but since Warren and Nicole, seated on either side of him in the cushiony auditorium seats, gave him a power assist up to his feet, he had no option but to make his way up to the stage to stand beside his grinning principal. The sound of the applause filled every corner of the room as he got a super-hearty handshake from his super-hearty principal.

"Is there anything that you'd like to say to your classmates and teachers?" he asked Zeke, pulling the microphone out of the podium holder and bending over to put it right in front of his mouth.

"Um, no, not really," Zeke said softly into the microphone that had been thrust into his face.

"Are you sure? Can you tell us what your experience was like?"

"Well, yeah, I guess so. I had a lot of fun, I got to go to some cool places, I met some awesome people and an awesome dog. Oh yeah, I also got to ride in a police car. And fixing a boxie with my hobo friends was pretty cool, too! And also, I just remembered, I met one of the ballgirls from the Isotopes and she's going to take me to one of the games soon."

"But what you did was so dangerous. Aren't you sorry that you ran away and caused so many people so much worry and concern?"

"No, I'm not really sorry that I ran away. Like I said, I had a lot of fun and met two really nice people who just got out of jail where they shouldn't have been in the first place. I'm really happy about that. And yes, I am sorry that so many people were worried about me though."

The principal realized that Zeke was undoing the message that he had just tried to instill in his young charges so he put the microphone back into the holder on the podium, welcomed Zeke back again and issued an adlibbed warning that "if you decide to run away, your story might not be the same as Zekes." He ended the assembly by telling everyone to return to their classrooms and pulled Zeke off to the wings of the stage and told him that he was hoping to convince the kids that running away might not be such a good idea.

"You asked me some questions and I answered them honestly," Zeke said, the picture of pure innocence and integrity. "You wouldn't want me to lie, would you?"

"No, certainly I wouldn't want you to do that," the principal said as he escorted Zeke off the stage to rejoin his waiting classmates. Under his breath, so Zeke couldn't hear, he said to himself, "except that was a total buzzkill of my message, you little brat."

DAVID W. GOODWIN

Tuesday morning at the Little Helpers of God shelter, the four conspirators, also known as Bix, Betty, Ethel and Ernest, packed up their belongings and said adios to the staff. They jumped into Ethel's old car that looked like it might make a good battering ram at a demolition derby and drove straight over to the nearest grocery store to stock up on provisions for their impending road trip from Gallup to Belén, a distance of about one hundred and fifty miles. Before Captain Bix and Burrito Betty were able to get into the back seat of what amounted to a trash heap on four mismatched tires, however, a significant amount of work needed to be done to clear away the heaps of trash and belongings that covered it.

"Sorry about the mess, folks," Ethel said as the foursome approached the mostly white 1990 Lincoln Town Car, with the exceptions being one of the doors and one of the fenders, which were black and red, respectively. Also noticeable was the back passenger side window, which had been replaced by some cardboard and a lot of duct tape. "Everything we own is either in the back seat or the trunk. I'm sure we can consolidate enough into the back to clear out some room for you."

"Sure beats traveling by rail," Betty said, sizing up the accommodations.

Ethel pulled a partially full black garbage bag, a full size ice chest and several ratty suitcases out of the back seat and made a neat mound in the adjoining empty parking space. Ernest, who up until this point hadn't done a thing, was instructed to see if he could find some room in the trunk. He started grumbling about something that sort of sounded like a reference to "worker bees" and "slave driver" more than once and eventually ended when he was able to complete the task to Ethel's satisfaction. Captain Haskell and Miss Poots got comfortable in the back seat while Ethel got behind the wheel and almost took off before Ernest had both feet inside the car.

"Hey, where's the fire?" he yelled out while pulling all of his body parts inside and managed to close the door right before it was about to sideswipe a telephone pole at the edge of the lot.

Ethel's driving style was, at best, erratic and at worse, downright menacing. She took corners so fast that everyone had to hold on for dear life. Stop signs and red lights were apparently optional as Ethel often chose not to pay them much attention. Plus, the speed limit appeared to have been a mere suggestion to her. Perhaps she was counting on the blue smoke coming out of the Town Car's tailpipe to provide some sort of camouflage but, miraculously, she managed to arrive at the parking lot of a Walmart off of Kachina Street without getting ticketed or arrested. Bix looked out the rear window of the car half expecting to see every police car in the Gallup Police Department following them.

"Before we go inside, let's have a quick discussion of our plan for the next few days," Ethel said turning around in the driver's seat part way so she could see all of them. "What do you want to do when we get to Belén? Will we want to stay there overnight? Do you think you'll want to come back to Gallup with us? How do you want to handle this?"

Tiffany decided to take the lead on this one and call the shots. She usually deferred to Robert James Rand III to make all their decisions but felt both empowered by the sudden lifestyle change and confident in her desire to go to Belén and see Zeke. She was also getting the impression from Bix that he was fine with letting her be in charge for a while. In fact, she sensed that he was encouraging her to do this.

"I think Bix and me would like to probably stay overnight at least tonight in Belén, maybe get settled somewhere, scope out the scene and then visit with Zeke the next day. After we wrap things up there, we'll probably go back to riding the rails. Belén is a great place to flip a boxie."

"So if we stock up on enough food and drinks for two or three days for the four of us, that would work out okay, you think?" Ethel asked Burrito Betty.

"Yes, Ethel, I think that would be perfect. We can cover the food expenses, right Bix?"

"Absolutely!"

With that decision under their belt, the four of them went into the Walmart and tried to find foods they could all agree on. This was a lot harder than it sounds. Hobo food, and this is what Bix and Betty's diet had consisted of for years, would hardly even be considered food to most people. If it wasn't half rotten or moldy or discarded, they barely considered it edible since this kind of food wasn't normally an option for them. By contrast, Ethel and Ernest seemed to subsist on alcohol and bar food, like peanuts, pretzels and beer nuts out of small bowls. There wasn't a lot of overlap between these two culinary preferences so they decided to split up. The Spears-Rand twosome went directly for the produce section while the Gambles naturally migrated towards the snack aisle, eventually reconvening up front at the checkout area with their assorted food and quasi-food items.

As Burrito Betty started placing their purchases on the short conveyer belt, the young cashier was having a conversation with the special needs older bagger. Given the events that had taken place in Gallup over the weekend, the topic of their conversation probably wasn't too surprising and was probably taking place in thousands of checkout lines, across the low partitions of countless office cubicles, in a sizeable number of taxi cabs, in most of the classrooms around the country and around innumerable kitchen tables.

"Did you see the press conference with that family yesterday, Verne?" the young female cashier said, smacking her large wad of bubblegum in her mouth, punctuated by a large bubble pop at the end of the sentence before she started scanning the items before her.

"Nope," he responded quietly, looking down at his feet. "What press conference?"

"You know, the family of the little kid that hopped the train and was caught here on Saturday with the hobos."

Apparently Verne wasn't up on current events. The cashier turned her attention to Tiffany when it was clear that the bagger wasn't going to be much of a participant in the hobo conversation. She asked if she heard the news about the little boy as Ethel got in line and began placing their snack items on the conveyor belt.

"Yeah, we know all about him," Tiffany said before Robert James Rand III was able to intervene and thwart the conversation. Ethel Gamble, however, wanted the world to know what role they had all played in this drama.

"Lady, you might not believe this, but standing before you right now are four of the people that played major roles in this story. Me and my husband over there had lunch with the boy on Friday and he used my phone to text his parents, which eventually led to his capture. These fine folks here are the two hobos that took care of the boy and probably saved his life," she said loudly and with obvious pride while Bix and Betty looked sheepish and embarrassed. Ernest had just wandered over to the checkout area and was preoccupied with reading a *National Enquirer* that he had picked up from another checkout rack.

"Ethel, this is big news. They found an alien baby in France, alive!" he shouted as he came into the checkout aisle, interrupting the current conversation.

"Not now, Ernest, dear, we're in the middle of something else right now."

"No way! You're shittin' me! That couldn't have been you! I saw the video on the news over the weekend and you two folks don't look anything like those hobos!" the cashier said with another perfectly timed bubble burst to mark the end of her sentence.

"Listen, honey, I'm not shittin' you, as you so delicately put it, these are them, I guarantee it! They got to clean themselves up, got some new clothes, I swear, these people are the true heroes of that story. In fact, we're on our way to Belén right now to pay the family a little visit," Ethel bragged.

"Can we just get checked out now?" Bix asked softly, not wanting to draw any additional attention to them.

"Sure thing, sir, but, for the record, you don't look much like the older hobo I saw on the news except, now that you mention it, you do have the same hat and jacket. I remember them because when I saw him on the news, I mentioned to my little sister that your outfit might make a cool Halloween costume this year, no offense, if that really was you. I remember what the woman hobo looked like too, and you don't look anything like her," she said looking right at the former Burrito Betty, the Princess of Poots.

"Thanks," Betty said as the cashier finally started scanning their items and popping some more impressive bubbles. "The folks at the police station had some pretty nice new clothes for us to choose from."

Ernest slipped his copy of the *National Enquirer* between a bag of chocolate covered pretzels and some apples, hoping nobody would notice but the cashier saw the headline and asked Ernest if he thought the story was true.

"Of course it's true. There are aliens all over the planet right now, probably more than a thousand by last count. And if there are aliens, there's gotta be alien babies, right? This shouldn't come as a big surprise to everyone," he said like he was talking to a child. "I've met a few of them right here in Gallup, just so ya know to be on the lookout, missy."

"Here? In Gallup?" pop pop.

"Here, in this store, in fact," Ernest said. He leaned in close to the cashier and whispered, "Your bag boy is one, but don't tell anyone."

"He is not!" she said loud enough for almost everyone in the checkout area to turn and look at them. "Why do you say that?"

"That's all I'm gonna say about that right now."

Without any further discussion, their food and near-food items and the tabloid were scanned through; Bix paid the total, took the five plastic Walmart bags and they all made their way out of the store. As they were about to walk through the automatic doors, the cashier yelled at them, "Hey, hobos, congratulations on getting that boy back home!" which caused quite a stir with everyone in the general vicinity.

The bizarre looking quartet got settled back into the Gamble's ramshackle Lincoln and Ethel, whose right foot seemed even more energized than before, burned rubber getting out of the parking lot, fishtailed onto West Maloney Avenue and made the turns that led onto I-40 East in a similar fashion. Captain Bix Pickles Haskell seemed more comfortable with her driving style than Burrito Betty, who looked down frequently to make sure her seatbelt was fastened. When she pulled on the strap to tighten it down a bit more, the entire strap pulled out of its floor anchor. Giving Bix a quick look of concern, he took the loose end and tucked it discreetly back into the space between the seat cushion and the seat back and mouthed the words "don't worry." It was an interesting thing for her to worry about considering how many thousands of risky things she'd done over the last ten or so years, seemingly without a care in the world or a second thought.

Once Ethel was up to cruising speed on the highway, at least cruising speed for a vehicle that probably had no right to even be on the highway, they all settled into an almost serene rhythm of motion. The car had a misaligned front end, almost bald, unbalanced tires, suspension that no longer suspended, as well as many other moving parts that may or may not have been functioning as they were originally intended. At least Ethel had the sense to drive in the right lane so that every other vehicle on the road that was driving at or above the speed limit could safely pass the blue smoke encased Lincoln. Since the strong wind was out of the west, the smoke seemed to keep pace with the car. The Lincoln Town Car seemed to have one speed, whether it was on city streets or on the highway.

They drove in silence for a while, each person, with the possible exception of Ernest, probably thinking about the new direction their life was taking them and what they might expect from the Wappinger family in Belén. Tiffany was surprised how her latent maternal instincts seemed to have kicked in so strongly and how nothing in the world could have prevented her from somehow making this trip to see Zeke. Even Robert was surprised how agreeable he was to doing this trip with his traveling companion and even felt a slight touch of paternal instinct for the boy. He felt a compelling connection to the little hobo so he was willing to follow Tiffany's lead. Ethel just liked to party and she loved meeting new people. Since she was in a position to help the hobos and possibly get some closure with the little boy, so much the better. Ernest had completely forgotten about the young runaway boy or even where they were going. He was in the front passenger seat reading the *National Enquirer* and mumbling to himself about baby aliens in France but became even more agitated when he read the article on page four that said a recent CIA leak proved that Dick Cheney was a robot.

"Hey, I've known about that for years!" he exclaimed to the confusion of the other three passengers who were hesitant to ask him any questions about it for fear of where the conversation might lead.

Puttering along the highway at about forty-five miles per hour, or about the same speed as a hot shot that Captain Bix and Burrito Betty were used to traveling in (or even slower if they were on a local), it gave the two hobos a slightly different perspective on the landscape. In a boxcar, the view was rather limited to what you could see through the open door. In a car, even one with a cardboarded-over passenger window, the view was much more panoramic, even though they couldn't see much out the back window either since the space behind the back seat was jammed with blankets and pillows. Neither Bix nor Betty had been inside a car, other than an occasional police car, for a long time and the novelty of it made the trip seem really fun and exciting, even though the risk factor with Ethel behind the wheel was exceptionally high and the condition of the vehicle was exceptionally poor. They both were like kids in the backseat, mesmerized by the scenery and didn't feel the need for any conversation.

Like many parts of west central New Mexico, the mostly flat terrain and lack of much vegetation of any substantial height meant that drivers on the interstate could see for miles and miles in every direction. The objects that would occasionally block one's view were the large number of billboards scattered along the highway advertising a diverse set of upcoming services, from Bruce Bender, "New Mexico's TOP Divorce Lawyer" to Jose's Auto Mall on Business 40/East Santa Fe Avenue. Railroad tracks paralleled the highways on the north side so any driver heading east or west along Interstate 40 saw mountains, cliffs and mesas off in the far distance and sagebrush, low lying juniper bushes, and scrubby pinyon pine trees interspersed amongst the billboards. Trains would go barreling by the Gamble's car in the opposite direction at regular intervals but were traveling only slightly faster than the Lincoln Town Car when they were making their way east.

What did get everyone's attention, however, was the police car that came up behind them with its lights flashing like a gaudy Christmas tree and an earsplittingly loud siren as they neared the exit to Grants.

"Don't pull over, Ethel! Just gun it as fast as you can! We can outrun them!" Ernest yelled out when the sound finally broke through his *National Enquirer* haze.

"Ernie, really? This car probably couldn't outrun a motor scooter, even if we were going downhill," Ethel said with a laugh. "We don't really have anything to worry about except, well, maybe the smoke. Oh wait, I guess we also don't have any insurance and I haven't registered the car for a few years and I think maybe my driver's license expired a while ago. Other than that, I think we're fine."

"In that case, I think we're not so fine," Bix Pickles said softly, over the sounds the Town Car made and the screaming police siren.

Ethel slowly eased the junkyard-on-wheels over to the shoulder and opened her door to go outside to talk to the police officer who had just pulled in behind them.

"Ma'am, please stay in your car!" the officer's voice said really loudly over the speakers mounted somewhere on the police car.

Ethel got back in the car and sheepishly said, "This window doesn't roll down so I thought I'd go out to meet him."

The four travelers sat quietly in the car and waited for the NMSP officer to come up to the car where he motioned for her to roll down her window.

"I'm sorry, sweetie, it doesn't work. That's why I got out of the car to meet you," she said loudly through the window with her usual friendly nature and approach to social interactions.

"Ma'am, then, if you would please step out of the car. I'll need to see your license and registration," he responded in kind to make sure that she heard him.

Ethel instructed Ernest to rummage through the glove compartment and find whatever documentation he could while she grabbed her black and white shiny faux leather pocketbook off the center console. As she opened the door to get out, Ernest handed her a pile of mangled looking pieces of paper that he found mixed in with various maps, used food wrappers, lipstick, napkins and some doggie treats.

Considering that Ethel's New Mexico drivers license had expired several years ago, that the car's registration was about four years overdue, that she had no proof whatsoever of insurance, that the car had not been inspected since it was purchased and clearly failed all vehicle emission standards, and that there were numerous outstanding tickets for her car, the options for the trooper were extremely limited. Once he realized who the other occupants of the Town Car were, he tried to be as lenient as possible with the way that he dealt with the situation but really had no option other than to issue a pile of tickets for these various violations. In addition, he said that he was going to impound the car and would call a tow truck to take it to the nearest facility where it would be held until she could update all of the necessary paperwork. She'd also have to pass a vehicle inspection and that might take a fair amount of time and money before her car would be released back to her.

"I'm sorry, but I can't let you get back into this vehicle. I'll give all of you a lift into Grants where you'll have a bunch of things to do before you can take ownership again," the officer said kindly. "Luckily for you, there's an MVD branch office there. By the way, where were you folks heading?"

"To Belén, to visit with the boy," Bix Pickles said.

"That's kind of what I thought. I can't say as I blame you. That was a pretty touching story and what you folks did sounds incredible. How will you get there now? This process could take a while, like maybe a week or two if everything goes well and your friends have the funds for all the licensing and registration updates and repairs, not to mention the outstanding tickets."

"Not sure about that. We're somewhat limited ourselves in the funds department at the moment. Getting a ride with our new friends here was pretty good luck. I guess we'll just have to play that one by ear," Bix said, not wanting to mention their penchant for rail riding, even though the officer must have known that was their usual chosen mode of transportation, especially since he seemed to be familiar with their story.

Bix and Betty grabbed all of their worldly possessions from the car, not knowing if and when they might see it again. The four travelers arranged themselves in the police cruiser and Bix was offered the front seat, which was usually against department policy but the officer made an exception in this case. He wedged himself in among all the electronic devices and was infinitely more comfortable in the police car than he had been in the Lincoln. In addition, the view was a lot better. The officer called in their situation to his dispatcher and asked that a tow truck be sent to mile marker 79.6 eastbound along the interstate, saying he would return there shortly with the keys after he dropped his four passengers off in Grants. They were only about a mile and a half from the first of three Grants exits.

"I talked to Detective Anders yesterday. He's a good buddy of mine. Do you remember meeting him this weekend?" the officer asked Robert James Rand III as he slowed down to take the exit off the interstate.

"He's the nice officer that tracked us down at the bar and brought Ernie and me in for questioning yesterday," Ethel piped in from the backseat. "Remember him Ernie? He's the one that kept you from falling off the barstool and then took us back to the shelter after we had given our statements."

"I thought that was Commander Cody and His Lost Planet Airmen," Ernie said and nobody was sure if this was his attempt at humor or if he was being serious.

"No, that was him. Our families are good friends, in fact, we got together last night for a cookout at our house in Thoreau. He had nothing but good things to say about you folks. Listen, we're about to arrive in Grants. I was thinking that I'd drop you off at the MVD office there so you could start working on your paperwork to get your vehicle back. How does that sound, Mrs. Gamble?"

"Sure, dear, that sounds like a fine plan," Ethel said sweetly.

"Okay, so once you get all the details ironed out and are ready to get your car out of impoundment, it will be over in that lot," the officer said, pointing out a parking area surrounding by an industrial-strength looking chain link fence. "Right behind our field office and just a few blocks down from the MVD branch office. I'm not sure what sort of accommodations you all might find here since there aren't any shelters in Grants but I can show you where the local social service office is if you're interested. There's also a great mechanic in town, a gentleman by the name of Rusty who runs 'Rusty's Auto Repair Shop.' He's on West High Street, just around the corner from that tanning salon over there. He's another good buddy of mine and if you tell him that I sent you, he'll give you extra good service," he said slipping his business card out of a shirt pocket and handing it over his shoulder to Ethel.

"Officer Bruce Van Vlaanderen, New Mexico State Police, Grants," Ethel read. "Did I say your last name correctly? It sounds Dutch or something."

"Belgian, actually, and yes, you did a pretty good job pronouncing it. A lot better than most people do. Okay, so here's the MVD office. I'm going to let you folks off here and wish you the best of luck. Please get all those details taken care of so you can go visit that boy in Belén safely. The Cibola County Family Service's office is over on East Roosevelt Avenue so you might want to check in there to see what sort of help they might be able to give you."

Officer Van Vlaanderen pulled into the MVD parking lot on Nimitz Avenue and let his passengers out. Three of them, not including Ernest, thanked him for his help and advice, even as he handed Ethel her tickets for her various violations. Ernest was making noises that a few astute observers might have recognized as the guitar riff to the Commander Cody hit "Hot Rod Lincoln" and was lost in his own world for the moment.

"You'll have to pay all of these tickets as well before you pick up your vehicle. I strongly suggest you take this seriously," Officer Van Vlaanderen said as he put his cruiser into reverse. "Just so you know, most folks in your situation would have been taken into custody with all those violations."

"Thank you, officer. I will take care of this immediately!"

Their trip to Belén, which about a half hour ago seemed to be right on track for an easy later-in-the-day arrival time, now required a major revision. Given the multitude of issues facing the Gambles, it seemed clear that they were stuck in Grants indefinitely. The Spears-Rand twosome needed to decide their next course of action and assess their various options and modes of available travel if, in fact, Tiffany was still committed to seeing Zeke and his parents. In her mind, abandoning the Tiffany persona and getting back into Burrito Betty mode was always an option. The one thing, however, they could all agree on was that the situation could be dramatically improved by having a drink or two. Ethel, not surprisingly, was the one to suggest this as the obvious first step.

"Maybe you should just check into the MVD office first and see what kinds of things need to be done before we get too sidetracked," Robert Rand suggested, thinking perhaps that one of them needed to espouse a more rational approach and he seemed the most likely person to do this.

"Oh, what fun would that be?" Ethel said with a forced laugh. "I think I have a pretty good idea what needs to be done and it will undoubtedly involve filling out a lot of forms, making a bunch of phone

DAVID W. GOODWIN

calls and spending a lot of money and I'm not sure we have enough right now to cover everything. That's kind of why I've put it off for so long."

"But wouldn't you want to know sooner rather than later what you'll need to do to get your car back?" Tiffany asked.

"I'm not sure it would be worth any amount of money to fix that old heap! Maybe we should just cut our losses and start fresh," Ethel suggested to Ernest who was still making odd guitar-like sounds.

"What? Are you crazy? Everything we own is in that car!" he responded when he realized what his wife was suggesting.

"Exactly! Other than some clothes, what really do we have in there that we couldn't do without?"

"I'll tell you what we have. We have my magazines, my acid nebulizer, my gamma ray deflector, my thought screen helmet . . ."

"Ernie, you're wearing your thought screen helmet, you never take that thing off," Ethel reminded him with an embarrassed laugh and made a funny face while looking at Bix and Betty.

"Right, I kind of forgot about that but I also have my 'Area 51' tee shirt. I'd hate to lose that," he lamented.

"Okay, it was just an idea. If it makes you feel better, I'll go inside and see what it might cost us to get everything straightened out. Ernest, I want you to come inside with me and stay where I can see you. I don't want you wandering off someplace. Neither of us have ever been here before and I don't want you getting lost again. Bix and Betty, I don't want to slow you folks down or have you change your plans on account of us. If you want to make other plans, we'll understand but we'd still love to somehow find a way to go to Belén with you two."

"We can hang out with you for a while, right, Captain Haskell?" Betty asked.

"Sure thing, darling. We'll come inside with you and then can discuss our options later, once we have a better picture of what needs to happen."

It was now late in the morning on another beautiful day in late June. The scene inside the MVD office in Grants was quiet and mellow. There were two older women working behind the counter and only one customer, who was being helped by one of them and appeared to be taking a vision test on a shiny new instrument sitting to the right of her on the counter.

"I can help you," the other woman said as Ethel walked into the brand new facility and towards the woman behind the counter. Her three buddies took seats nearby in comfortable wooden Mission-style chairs with colorful Navajo print cushions. Ethel explained her situation to the MVD employee.

"Oh my, that's a lot of details to work out. Can I see your expired license, dear?"

Ethel had to rummage around in her large purse, which, as you might imagine, had absolutely no organization to it. Even though she had recently produced her driver's license for Officer Van Vlaanderen, it was well hidden back inside the purse somewhere and apparently, not anywhere near the top because she had to remove most of the contents to locate it.

"Here it is!" she finally exclaimed proudly and handed the woman her license.

"Wow! This expired years ago! How long have you been driving on this one, Mrs. Gamble?"

"Pretty much all along. I just got a ticket for driving on an expired license as well as a bunch of other violations. As I explained, that's why I'm here. I'm ready to dance to the music." This musical reference got her involuntarily humming the Sly and the Family Stone song of the same name and even caused her to dance around a bit while the woman behind the counter rummaged through a big stack of forms to find all the ones that Ethel would need.

Ethel remained at the counter dancing her heart out for quite a while, trying to wrap her hands around all of the various tasks that were ahead of her and that didn't even include getting the "Non-Hot Rod Lincoln" Continental roadworthy again, if it ever had been in the years the Gambles had been driving it. Ernest occupied his time moving his head around ever so slightly like he was trying to find the best position to tap into the cosmic transmissions that must have been particularly strong inside the building. Captain Bix Pickles Haskell and Burrito Betty were having a quiet conversation about possible ways to get to Belén if the Gambles were going to be tied up in Grants indefinitely. When at last Ethel wrapped up her exploratory information gathering session, she came over to join the others with a fistful of papers.

"Looks like we got a crapload of things to do if we want to get ol' Connie back on the road, lover."

"Like what?" Ernest asked.

"Pretty much everything. A new license for starters and I need to pass both the written and the road test since it's been so long. Insurance, of course, ours expired a few years ago and they'll need proof that we're actually insured from our company. I've also got about three hundred dollars of outstanding tickets plus another two hundred dollars in late fees. Then we'll have to get our car fixed and Lord knows how much that might cost and then we need to pass a vehicle inspection. All told, we might be looking at three or four thousand dollars."

"That doesn't sound too bad," Ernest said to the surprise of Bix and Betty. "Hell, we've got twice that amount in cash alone, right Ethel?"

"No, not really. I'm the one that handles all the finances," Ethel responded and was addressing the two cleaned-up hobos. "We've got a lot of money but it's in our bank account, not in cash."

"You do?" Bix asked, even more surprised than before. "How is that possible? I thought you were homeless folks like us, just travelin' around livin' hand to mouth."

"No, it's more complicated than that. I told you a while ago that my sister sends us money each month. Well, Bix, honey, the truth is she sends us quite a bit of money each month on account of a family settlement from a long time ago. We just prefer this lifestyle."

"So why do you eat at soup kitchens and live out of your car? Why don't you settle down somewhere?" Betty asked.

"Probably for the same reason that you two are hobos. I'll tell you the story sometime if you're interested but only if you tell me your stories, too. Maybe this would be a good time to go get a drink - our treat!"

CHAPTER 15

Z EKE GOT OFF the bus at the end of Ladera Drive as the driver, Big Darl, yelled out, "see you tomorrow, Zeke. Don't run away again tonight!" As he made his way up the road to the cul-de-sac, he was not too surprised to see a news van, a cameraman and a familiar looking, smartly dressed and heavily made-up woman holding a microphone standing at the end of their driveway. Before he had left for school this morning, his parents instructed him not to talk to any reporters without one of them being there. It was going to be tough not to answer questions that were directed at him, as this just wasn't his style. He saw his nanny, Pamela, looking out the window of their living room.

"Zeke Wappinger, this is field reporter Gloria McGloria from KOAT TV News in Albuquerque. Our viewers have been flooding our phone lines and website with questions about you. Can I ask you a couple of questions?"

"My parents told me not to talk to any reporters without them here with me," Zeke responded. "Sorry."

"I've really just got one question and it's the question that everyone wants to know. Why did you run away from home?" she persisted as Zeke walked past her and was halfway up his driveway. He noticed that Pamela had come outside and was standing on the front porch making motions for Zeke not to say anything. Before Zeke had a chance to respond to the question, which he was considering doing since he realized that the press wasn't going to leave him alone until they had a sufficient answer, his mom's red Miata came screaming up the road and pulled into the driveway right next to him.

"Please leave my son alone!" Roxanne shouted at Ms. McGloria as she blasted out of the driver's seat. "I thought I made it clear that any interviews with my son were to be scheduled through me! I'm asking you to respect that and I'm also asking you to leave our property at once!"

This flustered Ms. McGloria immensely and she tried to find a dignified way to wrap up her aborted and highly unsuccessful interview with Zeke. She turned to face her cameraman and said, "And so, ladies and gentlemen, that will wrap up my interview for the moment with the young six-year-old runaway hobo from Belén. There are clearly many questions that still need to be answered. Reporting for KOAT News, I'm Gloria McGloria reporting live from Belén, New Mexico."

This snippet was used on the five-thirty newscast that afternoon, including a two second shot in the background of a very agitated, angry and out-of-focus Roxanne Wappinger walking towards Gloria McGloria with all of her cannons firing. She was clearly yelling something at the reporter that couldn't be made out unless one was a highly skilled lip reader. However, Zeke, Pamela and the cameraman, Stan Zuckerthong, heard Roxanne say something quite threatening and very off-color and included a reference to a female body part that wasn't usually spoken of in polite company. Roxanne herded Zeke into the house without another word like a border collie, making sure that her body was between the camera and little Zekie.

"Mom, what are you doing home?" Zeke asked once they were inside and after letting Pamela give him a super-big hug and spun him around a few times in the air and kissed both of his cheeks several times.

"Zeke! Homie! So happy to see you!" Pamela said before Roxanne had a chance to answer. "You've become quite famous! It's all anyone was talking about this weekend! Welcome home! I was so worried about you when I heard what happened. Are you okay?"

"Yes, Pamela, I'm fine. Mom, you're never here when I get home from school. Is everything alright?"

"Yes, dear. Your father and I talked yesterday about making some changes around here. We want to be around more often for you, and I also know that the press is probably going to follow you around for a while until this whole thing blows over. It's not going to blow over until they get an answer about why you ran away from home, if you really did run away. Is that what that idiotic reporter asked you?"

"Yes it was, Mom, and I did run away. You're going to have to accept that fact sooner or later."

"Alright then, listen Zeke. I need to go back to work for a while. Mr. Filborn has agreed to meet me at the Chili's in Los Lunas at four so I don't have to go all the way to the far side of Albuquerque Your father has another meeting tonight so he won't be home until after you go to bed but Pamela will be here until I get home, hopefully before six. I want to have a good heart-to-heart talk with you at dinner tonight and we can talk about having one more press conference and, hopefully, that will be the last one we have to do. Okay?"

His mom grabbed a few things and Zeke and Pamela watched through the window while she roared off in her red convertible, just as the KOAT news van, too, was leaving the neighborhood but not before Roxanne pulled up alongside them and said something that Zeke couldn't hear. Pamela was very excited to be spending time with Zeke and offered to make him a special snack. She didn't want to leave his side, even when he excused himself to change into his play clothes after his almond butter, banana and Fluff sandwich (which Pamela smuggled into the house in her large bag knowing that Roxanne would throw a fit if she knew that she had done this and also knowing that this was one of Zeke's most favorite unauthorized snacks in the world). Zeke had made a plan to ride his bike over to Warren's house three blocks away.

"I don't want you to leave, Zeke! I just want to eat you up! Will you tell me the story of your big adventure sometime?" Pamela asked through Zeke's closed bedroom door.

"Yes, how about tomorrow? I just need some time with my best friend today. We have a lot to talk about," Zeke yelled through the door. As he walked back into the kitchen in his clean play clothes where Pamela was hanging out, he said, "Tomorrow's the last day of school and they let us out before lunch. Will you be here then?"

"Yes, I will sweetie. Your mom asked if I could come here at noon tomorrow."

"Okay, I'll tell you the full story then," Zeke said, grabbing his Isotopes baseball hat and his kid sized Derek Jeter signature Rawlings glove while Pamela gave him another adult sized hug. "I promise! Bye, Pamela!"

"Be safe my little friend and no running away again, okay?" Pamela said with a nervous laugh.

Zeke laughed as well and walked out through the kitchen door to the garage, put his bike helmet on over his hat, put his glove over the end of the handlebar, opened and closed the garage door, sneaking out with his bike before it began it's closing motion, and pedaled off to Warren's house over on Hansen Drive. The houses in that neighborhood were a lot more modest than the hacienda's in his, mostly a mix of small ranch houses and mobile homes with permanent foundations, but Warren's house had a big vegetated open lot behind it and an abandoned lot next door where they liked to play baseball. He could either follow the streets to Warren's house

DAVID W. GOODWIN

or take a shortcut and ride his bike across a huge chunk of undeveloped land that separated their neighborhoods, but it meant getting across two fences. That was a challenge since he was about four feet tall and had a new bike that was still a little big. Additionally, he would run into a sidewinder every so often back there so he opted instead for the longer but easier and safer route along the sidewalks of Velta and South Mesa Roads. When he rode up into Warren's driveway, he saw not only Warren, but also his two younger sisters and aunt.

Warren and his two sisters, aged four and two, were temporarily being taken care of by Aunt Samantha, his dad's sister, since his mom ran off with Raul, the Zumba instructor, a few months ago. Warren's dad was a carpenter, and like his own dad, was away a lot of the time. Aunt Samantha, who was single without any children or even a job that anyone knew about, had a bunch of time on her hands and loved having the opportunity to spend time with her nieces and nephew. The girls were playing some sort of make believe fantasy game in their carport with Aunt Samantha while Warren was throwing his baseball against a springy mesh backstop in the vacant lot. It would return the ball right back to him on a fly if he managed to hit the backstop somewhere in the middle. If not, the ball would either fly over his head or bounce a time or two, or get sent off to his left or right and sometimes roll out into the street.

"Hey, Zekeballs!" Warren said by way of greeting. "How are things in Hoboland?"

"Little Zekie, honey, come over here and give your Auntie Sammy a hug!" Aunt Samantha said as Zeke parked his little mountain bike over by the carport. She always seemed to give him special treatment and told him often that he was her favorite friend of Warren's. "We saw you all weekend on the news and are so happy that you got home safely. What a crazy story!"

After getting wrapped up in a two hundred and fifty pound hug and almost being smothered by Aunt Samantha's fleshy abundance, Zeke grabbed his mitt and ran over to the vacant lot and played catch with Warren. His two little sisters barely looked up from their play when Zeke arrived, as they were wrapped up in the world of "My Little Pony Princess Palace." The two boys started throwing Warren's fluorescent yellow hard ball with the Isotopes logo on it back and forth, fairly close at first to give Zeke a chance to warm up and got farther and farther away from each other as their throwing session progressed. Warren was also six years old but wasn't as coordinated as Zeke so their game of catch often times turned into a game of fetch, especially as the distance between them increased. Zeke had better aim but less power to throw the ball over the longer distances while Warren could throw farther but with much less accuracy. Once they tired of playing catch, Warren suggested they get on their bikes and ride over to their secret hideaway. Zeke strapped on his helmet while Warren, in spite of Aunt Samantha's ineffectual suggestion, rode away wearing just his Isotopes baseball hat for protection.

Their secret hideaway was over at the nearby Our Lady of Belén Memorial Gardens Cemetery, a short two blocks away. Once they rode their bikes into the cemetery, through the almost always open entrance gate off of West Reinken Avenue, it was a short distance to the grassy area surrounded by towering skinny Italian cypress trees that reminded the boys of green candlepins, waiting to be knocked over by a team of giants with huge bowling balls and garish matching team outfits. Inside the space the trees defined was a gazebo and several large stone memorials with a tiny space between them. Zeke and Warren locked up their bikes and then crawled between the "Saint Francis" and the "Passion of Christ" memorials, a space that only two six-year-old boys might want to enter—physically, since they were still small enough to fit and psychologically, since most older people would immediately become claustrophobic. Once they crawled the ten yards or so back between these two structures, there was a little protected chamber of sorts. It was completely hidden from the rest of the world, as the crawlspace was the only way in or out. They sometimes brought contraband back here, like cans of soda or candy bars. It was also their special place to talk about any topic that might not be acceptable anywhere else in their world and they had shared many a secret while in this chamber.

"Okay, Zeke, time to tell me about your train trip," Warren said, cutting to the chase the moment they got settled in.

"What parts do you want to hear?"

"All of it. The running away part, the train part, the hobo part, the getting caught part. All of it. Start to finish."

"Okay, if you say so. It might take a while," Zeke said and recounted every detail that he could remember starting with slipping out the backdoor on Friday night and ending up with their press conference on Ladera Drive yesterday. It probably took about an hour to complete the entire story. Luckily, they both brought in their water bottles from their bikes so Zeke could keep his mouth and throat well lubricated.

"Holy freakin' moly, Zekeballs! That is awesome!" Warren, who had remained silent for the entire hour, said when Zeke finally wrapped the story up. "But the one thing that you didn't ever say was why you ran away in the first place. Everyone keeps asking me about it since I'm your best friend and I don't really have an answer for them."

"Yeah, that's about all anyone seems to want to know, especially the news people. I know my parent's want to know but they haven't actually asked me directly yet."

"So why did you do it?"

"It's not so easy to answer. Sometimes, I just get tired of waiting around for them to do something with me. They hardly ever want to do stuff. You know how much I love trains, right? You and me love hanging out by the Harvey House Museum and watch the trains come and go. You know how many times we've joked about hopping a train. Remember that time we saw those three hobos jump off and they saw us and then they came over and asked us where they might find a free meal? Between the two of us, we were able to give them about five dollars, remember? Well, I wanted to have an adventure like that and now you know what happened. Warren, it was so much fun! I met these two hobos that seemed more interested in me than my parents do! I really miss Captain Bix and Burrito Betty already and I'm worried about them. All I can think about is what they're doing now, if they're safe, where they are, you know, stuff like that. My mom thinks they kidnapped me, even though I've told her they didn't. I don't think she gets it that I just ran away because I wanted to do something completely different and crazy. My parents are always staring down at their phones and then don't seem to notice anything else. I could be running around with a chain saw inside the house and they wouldn't notice. They're always texting someone, or looking something up on Safari, or playing with some dopey app or checking their email. You know, I've told you about how crazy they get trying every phone app that has ever been made, especially my dad? Well, the night I ran away, he downloaded some sort of stupid app where you went through something called a Confession, like at a Catholic church. They asked me these really stupid questions, most of them didn't seem appropriate for kids, and then said that we had to go to church the next day to do a Confession with a priest for real. It felt like they had gone insane, so I decided to run away."

"That was a pretty brave and retarded thing to do," Warren observed. "But why didn't you ask me to go with you?"

"I thought about it. It would have been fun to go together but it was just something that I decided to do that night. Plus, I didn't think that you would have wanted to go with me. I knew I'd get into trouble and didn't want you to get into trouble too."

"Yeah but it's usually me getting you into trouble, like that time with the BB gun or when we decided to call up Nicole and pretended to be the principal and told her that she flunked kindergarten again."

"Right, or the time you suggested we let the air out of that kid's bike tires from fifth grade because he knocked you over on the playground and then he saw us doing it."

"But you convinced him that he was riding with too much pressure and we were just trying to help."

"And then he knocked both of us over anyway."

"I might have become a hobo with you if you asked," Warren said like the great friend that he was.

"I know Warren. That would have been super-cool!"

The boys sat in their secret place for a while longer, not saying much, just soaking up their friendship and cracking a joke every so often and then both collapsing in a heap of laughter over things that generally weren't all that funny. Somehow being in their hideaway, just the two of them, with Zeke back in Belén after such a grand adventure and having gained such widespread notoriety for his escapade, made this a golden moment for them. Eventually everything either one said was extremely humorous. After a while, they heard some other kid's voices outside and figured it was time to head back home, but they waited until after their voices had disappeared. They wouldn't want to reveal their secret place by crawling out where they could be seen in broad daylight, especially by some other kids.

When Zeke got back home, it was getting close to six o'clock. Pamela was starting to worry that he might have run away again and then she'd be in a heap of trouble. Zeke saw her sitting on the top step by the front door with her boyfriend and she looked visibly relieved when he came riding up the driveway.

"I thought maybe you decided to become a hobo again," Pamela said, only half kidding. "I was worried that you might not come home."

"I think my hobo days are over for a while, although if Captain Bix Pickles Haskell, the Human Stinkbomb and Burrito Betty, the Princess of Poots were to show up here right now and ask me to get back into the world quick, I might consider it."

DAVID W. GOODWIN

This cracked Pamela and her boyfriend up and eventually the boyfriend asked, "Are those the names of your hobo pals?"

"Yeah, pretty funny names. Their real names are Robert James Rand the third and Tiffany Spears - although she has a lot of other names too that I can't remember. My hobo name is Flannel Freddie, the Deviled Ham."

This set both of them off again and caused Zeke to start howling along with them. They were still in the midst of their laugh-fest when Foxy Roxy came driving up Ladera Drive and pulled into the driveway and three-car garage with a little toot of the Miata's horn.

This meant it was time for Pamela to leave and she stopped laughing long enough to give Zeke her usual spirited hug and welcomed him home again, saying she would see him tomorrow around noon. Roxanne came out of the garage and said goodbye to Pamela and her sidekick, thanking them for looking out after her little wandering hobo. She asked Zeke if he would come inside with her to tell her all about his day back at school.

The kitchen was usually their first choice for a hangout place and each grabbed a glass of water before settling onto the bar stools at the counter. Zeke told her about his big reception on the bus ride, Mrs. Edelweiss's prayer comment, the school assembly and his being called up to the stage to say a few words and then about the time he had just spent hanging out with Warren. Zeke then politely asked his mom about her day and she talked mostly about her clients before mentioning all the people that asked her about him and his weekend exploits.

"I have to say, Zeke, it was a little embarrassing. I just know all these people must think that I'm a terrible mother. I mean, really, what sort of mother must I be if my very own son runs away to become a hobo?" Roxanne lamented, as her voice went from controlled to a little warbley to slightly hysterical and then to full out sobbing when she added, "I can't believe you just ran away, Zeke! What were you thinking? Why did you do it? Do you hate me and your father?"

It wasn't until that very moment that Zeke understood the full, deep, dark implications of his actions. Of course he didn't hate his parents, he just wished they loved him as much as they seemed to love their jobs and their phones. When he ran away, he honestly didn't think that his mom would take it personally, as a flat out indictment of her failure as a parent. It was just an adventure, a lark, but it really wasn't anything more than that in his mind. As he had told his hobo friends and now his best friend, he was hoping that his parents might stop being such bozos and start being normal parents that had a normal relationship with their child. However, to see his mom in this agitated, self-loathing sort of state, he suddenly got it, suddenly saw it from her perspective, at least as much as an intelligent, sensitive six-year-old could. And at that moment, for the first time since he ran away Friday night, he felt some remorse.

"Mom, I don't hate you and Dad. I hope you believe me when I say that. I'm sorry that this whole thing makes you so sad. I didn't run away to make you look like bad parents and I'm sorry that some people might think this. I like to do things, lots of things and you hardly ever seem to have the time to do the kinds of things I like to do. I sometimes feel sad because I think that maybe you and Dad didn't really want to have a kid and that maybe you'd be happier if I wasn't ever born so you could work more at your jobs."

This sent Roxanne up through the stratosphere of human emotion. Her sobbing was coming from the deepest abyss of maternal worry imaginable, thinking that her precious son didn't feel loved or wanted and it made her feel like she had just been shot in the chest with a shoulder mounted grenade launcher from about ten feet. Clearly, this was the lowest point in the trajectory of the Wappinger family dynamics during the entire crisis, and the only direction it could go from here was straight up. In that regard, it was a wake up call for both of them. They were now both wide awake and came to an understanding in this brief moment that was going to guide their thoughts and actions for the rest of their long lives together as a family.

Zeke, for the second time in his young life, saw his mom cry and she needed to go into the bathroom to grab some tissues. When she came back, her eye makeup was ridiculously smeared and the scary sight of it caused Zeke to immediately roar with hysterical laughter. This had the unintentional effect of breaking the tension in the room, something that might not have happened under any other set of circumstances. Roxanne felt she had a better understanding of Zeke's worries and needs and Zeke knew their relationship had just shifted significantly. Perhaps they were starting over with a clean slate.

"I'd like to use my one 'get out of time-out' pass now from doing that Confession thing the other night," Zeke said with a straight face. When his mom looked at him quizzically, he added, "you know, for running away and all."

"Oh, Zeke. I love you so much!" Roxanne said through her sniffles and laughter.

DAVID W. GOODWIN

Eventually, after sharing a few tender moments, Zeke broke their embrace and told his mom that he was hungry. Roxanne asked where he might want to do for dinner and Zeke asked what she could cook. What he really wanted to do was stay at home and cook something together, "like something hobos might make, only better."

"Well, I'm not sure what hobos eat but let's see what we have in the fridge," Roxanne said, managing a slightly wobbly smile. "By the way, what did you eat when you were with them?"

"We had a great lunch at a soup kitchen one day but the rest of the time we ate whatever little things we each had with us. I had an apple, some baby carrots and a few fruit rollups, while Bix had a Slim Jim and a hunk of moldy cheese. Betty had a bottle of water and some crackers."

"And that's the sort of dinner you want me to make tonight?"

"No, not really, but it's kind of fun seeing what sort of meal you can put together based on some random ingredients. Let's look around the kitchen and see what we've got."

Roxanne pointed out the fruit that was on the counter in a large wooden bowl and then listed off an inventory of the refrigerator items, a few things in the freezer and some canned stuff in one of the cabinets.

"I could always do up some pasta, like I usually do."

"Or we could do a bean dip with cheese and onions and peppers and those avocados. The only thing we're missing are chips and maybe some olives," Zeke observed.

"No, we've got a few bags of chips out in the garage and we can probably make do without olives, wouldn't you say? We could also get some cilantro from your father's garden. That sounds like a great meal, honey."

In no time at all, the makings of an acceptable bean dip were assembled and the meal came together quite easily. Roxanne surprised herself with three things. First, was what a clear sense Zeke had about what ingredients might go well together for a bean dip; second, was how much fun it was to improvise to create an edible concoction; and third, much to her amazement, was how much fun it was to work on the meal with her son and then experience the joy of spending some leisurely time around the table eating it. She even turned her cellphone off when they started on the meal. It wasn't turned back on until Zeke was safely tucked into bed, after reading not only his favorite story about Charlie the caboose but also, as an added bonus, one of his favorite books called *The Stray Dog* about a little mutt that appears at a family picnic. The story has a happy ending and Zeke always asks if he can get a puppy when the story is over. "Maybe one like Bullet," he qualified.

"We'll think about it honey. I love you, little Zekie. Don't ever run away again, darling boy!" Roxanne said as she kissed her little hobo goodnight and turned off his bedside light.

"I won't Mom, I promise."

Later than night, when Andrew returned from his second public meeting on his Rio Puerco Resource Management Plan in much better spirits than he had been in when he got home from the meeting held last Thursday, Roxanne recounted as closely as she could, word for word, what had transpired with their son that evening.

"I get it Andrew, I understand now why he ran away and I think he gets it now how deeply it has affected me," Roxanne said while fighting back tears. Andrew just comforted her and nodded his head and was impressed that she really did seem to get it. "I wish you could have been here Andrew. Our little boy is so articulate, so mature, so clear about his emotions. It's hard to think that all of this is coming from a six-year-old boy. Sometimes, I think he's more in touch with life than we are."

"He's a special kid, for sure," Andrew said softly. "Did you have a chance yet to hear about his ordeal with the hobos?"

"No, not much of it yet. I think we had to get all of these raw feelings out in the open first. We'll have lots of time for that soon, I imagine."

True to his own personal resolution, Andrew was home around noon the next day to meet his son as he got off the school bus for his last time as a first grader. Also there to greet Zeke was Pamela, since Andrew wasn't able to stay home all afternoon with his son as he had a whole pile of things to do in preparation for his next meeting on Wednesday night. Just the fact that his dad was there when Zeke came running up Ladera Drive, free as a kid who was about to embark on a summer vacation, was something beyond belief for Zeke. His dad was never seen at home during a weekday so this was pretty special.

"Happy summer vacation!" Andrew yelled out as he walked down the driveway with Pamela to meet his restless son.

"Dad! I didn't expect to see you here! Is everything alright?" Zeke asked with a hint of worry in his voice.

"Absolutely! It's more than all right. I'm taking some time off from work today to hang out with you this afternoon. Pamela will be with us too until I need to go to a meeting at three and then she'll be here until Mom gets home. Do you have any plans?"

"I was hoping to go for a bike ride with Warren after lunch. Wanna go?"

"Yeah, honey, that sounds like a great idea. Maybe we could even stop at the fish taco shack along the way and get some lunch," Andrew suggested.

"I'd love to join you boys but my bike's at home," Pamela said. She was a hardcore road cyclist who raced a lot and, as such, was quite particular about the type of bike and setup she felt comfortable riding.

"You could ride my mom's bike. It's pretty nice," Zeke said. "That would be really cool to all go riding together. Dad, since you and Pamela are coming with us, maybe we could go riding down by the river. I know that you never want me to go down there without an adult. Let me send Warren a text to tell him not to eat lunch yet! Dad, you never want to go there to eat!"

"That's true but today's different, in fact, it feels special to me. I'm not sure I could convince your mom to eat there but we certainly can."

So with his one significant and epic hobo adventure, Zeke went from being a child who wasn't sure that his parents even wanted to hang out with him and the prospect of hopping a train and becoming a hobo was a desirable option, to becoming a six-year-old kid with parents that were willing to take some time off from work to do things with him. It made him very happy, clearly, and he thought that maybe this outcome might have actually been worth all the risks he took and the heartaches he caused. His tidy compact world, however, had been greatly expanded in the last four days. Before he fixed a boxie, he had lived all of his life in the cushy small-town confines of Belén where he was mostly surrounded by people more-or-less like himself, to living in a world where he was now aware of the reality of hobos and their challenging lifestyles, perpetual homelessness, unhealthy diets and marginal living conditions. He was also witness to other people that were down and out and living on the outer fringes of society and, for a little kid with a big heart, his big heart ached for them, especially Captain Bix Pickles Haskell and Burrito Betty. When he got back from his bike ride, he was resolved to make some phone calls to see if he could find out some information about where they were and how they were doing. Maybe Officer Cellucci or Officer Ramirez would know.

The three-person peloton of Andrew, Pamela and Zeke soon became four when they swung by Warren's house. There was a little negotiating with Warren, helped by Aunt Samantha and driven by Andrew, that involved a bike helmet. Andrew insisted that if Warren was going to join them for this bicycle ride, he would have to wear one like the rest of them. Warren was resistant at first but eventually conceded the point and strapped it on. They rode slightly downhill, first through the small Belén downtown area, then over the railroad tracks, through Officer Ramirez's neighborhood and eventually hooked up with a network of trails that had been worn in along the Rio Grande and it's wide floodplain. This, not surprisingly, was a popular walking and bike riding area but also a popular hangout for older kids looking to avoid detection by their parents, and sometimes the police, to engage in a variety of anti-social and mildly-illegal behaviors. It was also a place where some older people, most notably homeless types, and perhaps an illegal rail rider or two might set up their own semi-permanent camp, or, if you will, hobo jungle.

It was just the previous day that Robert James Rand III and his stylish traveling companion, Tiffany Spears, had been stranded indefinitely in Grants with Ethel and Ernest Gamble. The logistical and mechanical challenges facing the Gambles were enormous. The two temporarily reformed hobos' natural inclination to rely upon railriding for transportation, and indeed, their habit of not staying in any one place very long, beckoned them towards Belén. After hanging around with the Gambles for lunch and then through dinner, the dark of night called out and drew them to the easy switchyard of Grants. It was easy because, first, it was such a small switchyard, second, because the only trains that stopped there were local freight trains that stopped pretty much at each and every town and switchyard, and third, because there was really only one nighttime cinder dick and he was an old doddering duffer who was years past retirement age and was really only a figurehead to give the BNSF enforcement staff a small amount of comfort knowing that any human presence there was probably better than none. Plus, he was usually asleep in his office, or buzzard's roost, as Bix or Betty called it, most of the night.

Slipping onto a train in Grants on a beautiful moonlit evening, after thanking the Gambles and promising to meet up with them in Belén somehow once they had their car legally back on the road, was a piece of cake. Even if the train stopped a few times, it was only an hour or two to Belén, so they weren't too picky about the type of car they hopped- they'd even ride the bumpers between cars if necessary. The transformation back to Captain Bix Pickles Haskell, the Human Stinkbomb and Burrito Betty, the Princess of Poots, really only took a few minutes, especially after Betty changed out of her nice office-casual outfit to a more hobo-friendly ensemble that she carried in her turkey - or was it balloon? Before they had left the NMSP District 6 office, she had taken two changes of clothes that were offered, in addition to the nice outfit she left the building wearing. After dinner in Grants at the Pig-a-Rama, she excused herself to the sow's room and made the transformation back to Burrito Betty complete. Hopping a flatcar, loaded with pallets of lumber, was easy as there were convenient people-sized spaces between the pallets and the pallets themselves blocked the hobos nicely from the wind and gave them something comfortable to lean against. Two hours later, in the dead of night, they jumped off the flatcar in the Belén switchyard and made their way towards the hobo jungle down in the floodplains of the Rio Grande, a place Bix and Betty knew very well.

The hobo world was changing. In the past, it had been composed primarily of dyed-in-the-wool hobos who spoke a common language, honored a certain code and ethic, and generally looked out for one another. This was the world that Bix and Betty lived in and loved. They had a lot of friends they trusted and looked forward to seeing them in their various travels around the extensive rail network of the country. More recently, however, the dyed-in-the-wool hobos were becoming more the exception than the rule, as the hobo world was becoming largely infiltrated by both a younger generation and a different caliber of person that could sometimes be described as flim-flam artists, druggies, petty thieves, Flintstone kids, bad actors, hooligans, scalawags, and people living on the lam due to past criminal activities. It was clear that the life of the rail rider was becoming a lot more dangerous.

When Bix and Betty got off the flatcar in the well-lit freightyard of Belén, they noticed evidence of two of their friends who were in the area, based on some markings on a nearby telephone pole and yesterday's date, and added their own mark with a chunk of chalk Bix always carried in his coat pocket. This made both of them happy, especially Burrito Betty, since she really liked them and hadn't seen either of them for about a year. They also knew exactly where to find them.

It was only about a half hour walk to get from the Belén freightyard to the hobo jungle down in the Rio Grande floodplain. They had done it any number of times in the past and could have done it even on a cloudy night. As is was, it was a clear night, the moon was close to full and the two hobos meandered their way to the camp quite easily as they were well rested, well fed, had their turkeys packed with enough food and drink to last several days, were relatively clean and were wearing fresh clothes. It was hobo paradise in just about every way possible. They arrived at the camp around midnight.

Approaching a remote hobo jungle outpost such as this one required a little strategy. You couldn't just burst into the area without warning as this would scare the bejesus out of it's inhabitants who were generally on high alert anyway, unless they were sufficiently elevated on hooch or sneaky pete. You needed to approach slowly and carefully and make your presence known in the most non-threatening way possible. This was the hobo way.

Captain Haskell and the Princess made their way to the edge of the hobo jungle and did a quick survey of the situation. They saw a small fire that was down to just embers, two blue tarps strung up between several trees, a folding table set up under one of the tarps with some old crates underneath, a bunch of plastic lawn chairs scattered around the camp, and two bodies lying under the other tarp on a pile of air mattresses and some worn out, ratty old blankets covering them. There were a few dead soldiers lying on the ground nearby, a sure sign that they had consumed a fair amount of whisky already.

"Hey Jazzie, hey Roadkill, it's Captain Bix and Burrito Betty. Is that you?" Bix yelled out in a loud whisper. After getting no response, he walked a little closer and yelled the same thing only louder. Still, getting no response, he walked into the camp and said it again even louder. This finally got a reaction.

"Wha, who's out there?" a man's sleepy and slurry voice responded, trying to become alert enough to protect his turf.

"Is that you Roadkill?" Burrito Betty asked.

"Who wants to know?"

"It's Burrito Betty, Roadkill. I'm here with Captain Bix Pickles."

"You're shittin' me, right?"

This realization brought Roadkill Ronnie back to consciousness and he struggled to get out of his sleeping setup to greet the new arrivals and his best buddies. When he managed to get upright, he stumbled over towards them, fully clothed in a comical hobo outfit and gave each one a big welcoming hug.

"Well, I'll be! If it ain't the Captain and the Pooter! Hey, Jazzie, wake up, darlin'. We got visitors!"

Jazzie Jugs O'Reilly was still out for the count. It took the combined efforts of the other three hobos to rouse her out of her sleep and then it had to be explained to her several times where she was and who had come to pay them a visit. When she finally got on the same page, she was over the top with excitement.

"Captain Bix and Burrito Betty! This is freakin' awesome! We've been hearing all sorts of stories about you and some gunsel. I can't believe you're here! We was plannin' on goin' to Gallup tomorrow to come look for you two. Holy smokes! Welcome!"

The fire was given some fresh wood from a nearby pile, a new bottle of hooch was produced, four chairs were rearranged around the fire and the four hobos swapped stories and swigs from the bottle well into the night. When the first light of day began to filter in from the east and the sun made it's first appearance over the river, the hobos finally wrapped up their reunion with their friends and eventually passed out in their makeshift beds under the tarp.

Zeke, Andrew, Warren and Pamela were having a great time riding their bikes on the very same network of trails that eventually went right past this hobo encampment early that afternoon. Zeke and Warren, with the youthful exuberance of six-year-olds and the utter joy of recently mastering their skills as competent bike riders, kept getting ahead of the adults. Pamela was struggling with riding a bike that didn't fit her very well and had to stop from time to time to make a few adjustments. Andrew rode back with her to make sure she was okay and to help change the height of her seatpost twice until she got it dialed in just right. Zeke and Warren were busy bombing around banked, sandy berms worn into the trail and jumping over the occasional branch blocking their way or popping wheelies over little bumps. They waited at every intersection to make sure the stragglers knew which way they were going.

As they got closer to the river, they rode ahead again right after Andrew and Pamela had just caught up to them. This time, however, Andrew rode through a pile of broken glass and metal shards that Zeke and Warren had bunnyhopped over and he flatted instantaneously. Zeke and Warren kept going, unaware of the flat tire and, as fate would have it, rode right into the hobo jungle, much to everyone's surprise. The four hobos had recently awoken with serious hangovers and were drinking cowboy coffee while sitting around the blazing fire when Zeke came skidding right into the middle of their camp after rounding the last corner of the trail at a really high speed.

"Oh, excuse me," Zeke said, somewhat embarrassed by infringing on someone's personal space as Warren skidded right into Zeke's rear tire since he was carrying a lot of speed too. This caused both of them to fall over into a heap on top of their bicycles and it took a little while to get everything sorted out.

"Flannel Frankie, the Human Ice Cream Cone?" Burrito Betty cried out. "I can't believe it! Is that really you?"

CHAPTER 16

THE REUNION OF Zeke, Captain Bix Pickles Haskell, the Human Stinkbomb and Burrito Betty, the Princess of Poots had to be brief. Zeke told them that he needed to quickly ride back on the trail since his dad was going to be coming this way at any minute and he didn't want him to know about this discovery.

"How long will you be hanging out at the jungle?" Zeke asked.

"At least for a day or two, son. We're here to see you. Both Betty and me wanted to make sure you're okay and maybe we can have a little powwow with your parents."

"That's cool! I think my mom has finally let go of the whole kidnapping thing. I'm out of school now for the summer so I can come back here later today and tomorrow and bring you anything you need, like food or supplies," Zeke said.

"We're good for now, Frankie, but we can't wait to spend some time together," Betty said. "Don't get yourself into any more trouble though, okay?"

"Don't worry about that. I can't believe you guys are here. That's totally awesome! There's so much I want to talk about. Oh yeah, I forgot to tell you that this is my friend Warren."

"Hi Warren. Zeke talked a lot about you when he was travelin' with us," Bix said. "Maybe you'll come visit with him sometime. I'd feel better knowin' that you two was bein' safe and lookin' out fer each other. Not everyone who hangs out down here is friendly."

"Except for these two," Burrito Betty said. "These are our two best friends in the entire hobo world, Jazzy Jugs O'Reilly and Roadkill Ronnie."

"Nice to meet you. We've got to scram right now before my Dad catches up but we'll be back soon," Zeke said as he and Warren hopped on their bikes and rode away.

With that, the boys disappeared and pedaled furiously back up the trail, meeting up with Andrew and Pamela within about a hundred yards of the camp, just as his dad finished inflating the new inner tube in his tire. Zeke told his dad that they were hungry and maybe this would be a good time to go have some lunch at the fish taco stand. They rode the shortest way out of the trail network and navigated the various streets and bikepaths to get back to the food stand in Belén. Zeke was almost bursting with excitement but tried to act normal so that his dad wouldn't realize that something out of the ordinary had just happened. Warren, too, was about to squirm out of his skin but realized the importance of keeping this secret. After placing their order, the four cyclists sat down at an empty picnic table underneath a big yellow umbrella. While waiting for everything to be ready, Andrew looked casually down at his cellphone under the table.

"That was a lot of fun," Andrew said. "I haven't been down at those trails for quite a while. Looks like it might be kind of a party site. I'm surprised that people would smash up some bottles right in the middle of the trail like that. Good thing I had my patch kit with me in the seat bag."

"Yeah, that was fun," Pamela said. "I train so much on the roads around here that sometimes I forget to just go out and ride a bike for the heck of it. I should do that more often. Once we got your mom's bike adjusted properly, I had a blast riding with you guys. Maybe I could bring my mountain bike over sometime and you could show me more of those trails. One of my teammates says those trails go for miles and miles. Zeke, do you know them very well?"

"No, not really. You know that my mom and dad don't like me riding down there without an adult. Dad, does Pamela count as an adult?"

"Yes, of course she does, ZZ. She's a grown up woman and we trust her judgment very much. Are you twenty yet, Pamela?"

"Not until next month."

The man inside the stand yelled out "order ready for the Addams family." Zeke's dad always liked to make up some sort of fictitious name so he knew the order was for them. Once they had consumed every last morsel, Andrew said that he needed to get back home, so they retraced their steps back to Ladera Drive. The boys were planning on hanging out at Zeke's swimming pool together for the rest of the afternoon so Pamela took over the supervision after Andrew changed his clothes, picked up his briefcase and went driving off to his meeting.

"Thanks for lunch, Mr. Wappinger!" Warren cried out when he was getting into his car.

DAVID W. GOODWIN

"My pleasure, Warren. Anytime!"

As soon as his dad was out of sight, Zeke and Warren ran into the house and into Zeke's bedroom to change into their bathing suits and talk about the recent developments, while Pamela went out on the back deck to call her boyfriend. Zeke closed the door behind them but told Warren that when Pamela was on the phone, you could rip the world's loudest fart and she wouldn't even notice. This got both boys laughing like six-year-old boys after a great fart joke, which was just about any fart joke for that matter, and their giggling become nearly uncontrollable yet again.

"Wait until you get to know Burrito Betty, the Princess of Poots! She's the best farter I've ever met. She should be called the 'Queen of Poots', not the Princess," Zeke said, barely able to get the words out between his gasps and their childish silliness.

The two best friends had some serious plan-hatching to do. There were a number of issues to iron out concerning the logistics of visiting Bix and Betty at a place where Zeke wasn't allowed to go without adult supervision. Given Zeke's recent exploits, you might think that breaking a relatively minor rule like riding his bike in the floodplain trails without a grown up wouldn't phase him much compared to running away from home, hopping a freight train and hooking up with some hobos. However, this ethical decision was causing him a fair amount of angst.

"That's why I asked my dad about Pamela, to make sure he considered her an adult," Zeke said. "I definitely want to go visit Bix Pickles and Burrito Betty this afternoon after we swim for a while but I know I'm not supposed to go there without a grown up. Maybe we should tell Pamela about them and have her go with us. What do you think?"

"I guess so, but why don't you want your father to know about them?" Warren asked, still somewhat confused about Zeke's logic.

"Because if he finds out they're here in Belén, Mom will find out and if Mom finds out, she'll freak out and might report them to the police. I don't think she trusts them yet and I'm worried about how she'd react if she knew I was spending time with them. I'd rather she not know yet. I don't know why she doesn't like them. They're really cool!"

"Maybe you could have the hobos come here to your house. That way you wouldn't have to break any rules. Your parents are away at work so much that there are long stretches of time that they could be here," Warren reasoned. "Plus, Zekeballs, I heard them say that they wanted to have a powwow with your parents. Does that mean that they want to dress up like Indians and dance around a fire making funny noises?"

"Maybe, but I'm pretty sure it means they want to meet my parents. Bix has kind of a funny way of talking sometimes and I know they want to meet with them so that must be what he meant."

Warren then started pretending he was a Native American and started dancing around Zeke's backpack like it was a fire and did the best imitation of what he thought an appropriate dance would be, including the stereotypical "woo woo" effect made by slapping his open palm against his open mouth. Zeke joined in the powwow and started dancing and chanting in a comically choreographed scene. Their chanting got louder and louder, the dancing more and more spirited and was only interrupted when they looked up and saw Pamela standing in the doorway filming the scene on her iPhone.

"You guys are really amazing!" she said when they stopped dead in their tracks. "Keep going!"

Naturally, any six-year-old would know that the presence of a recording device, an interloper, and the interloper's urging for them to keep going wasn't going to inspire them to actually keep going. They flopped onto Zeke's bed and waited until their breathing returned to normal.

"I heard you two from way outside on the back deck and just wanted to make sure everything was okay," Pamela said in her defense. "I wasn't trying to make you stop."

"That's okay," Zeke said, "but usually my parent's knock before they come into my room."

"I did. You were just shouting so loud you didn't hear me!"

"Pamela, we want to talk to you about something but you have to promise not to mention it to my parents, okay?" Zeke asked tentatively, shifting the conversational gears. "Warren and me might need your help but I don't want my parents to know about it yet. They'll find out soon because I'll tell them but not yet. Can you promise?"

"I guess it depends on what it is, Zekie," Pamela said, putting her phone down and coming to sit on the bed with the boys. "I can't promise to not tell them something if I think it's really important that they know. They've given me a responsibility to take care of you and that's the job they pay me to do. Can you understand that?"

"Yeah, but I think this is something that you could keep our little secret for a day or two. Are you willing to listen to what I have to say before you make a decision? If you can't keep it a secret, that's okay. It's not a big deal, just something that's really important to me."

"Sure, sweetie, I can agree to that. You know you can trust me, right? You're not planning on becoming a hobo again, are you?" she asked.

"Yes, I trust you and no, I'm not going to get into the world quick again. I'm glad you're my nanny!"

"And you're very special to me. I would never want anything bad to happen to you. I was so scared when I heard about your trip with the hobos but so happy that you came back home safe. We were all so worried about you."

Zeke laid out the situation for her, including Bix and Betty's desire to meet his parents, running into their hobo jungle camp along the river when his dad's tire flatted, and his parent's rule about not riding down by the river without a grown up, which she already knew about. He told her that he wanted to take some supplies to them but also wanted to hang out for a while and talk with them.

"It is very important to me to do this," Zeke concluded.

"That sounds entirely reasonable, Zeke. I have to say that after seeing all the news coverage and interviews and special reports and all, I would love to meet these two hobos too. If you are willing to introduce me to them, I'm willing to keep it a secret from your parents for a little while. How would you feel if I invited my boyfriend along? He keeps telling me that he wants to meet them too."

"I'm not sure if that's such a good idea. I'm worried that it might scare Bix and Betty off if too many people are in on this. How about just the three of us meet with them first and then we decide?" Zeke suggested.

"Fair enough. When do you want to go?"

"How about right now? I'll go grab some food and water bottles to throw into my backpack for them and then we can ride down there. Warren, are you okay with not going for a swim right now? We could go when we get back."

Warren agreed and with that, the two little Indians, one of which was a former hobo, and their adult co-conspirator jumped on their bikes and made their way down to the Rio Grande for a little powwow of their own with the two adult hobos and their two hobo friends, Jazzy Jugs O'Brien and Roadkill Ronnie. When they arrived at the hobo camp, they found two additional mammals they were not expecting to see - one human and one canine. Bullet, the off-duty police dog, greeted them with unbridled doggie excitement, compounded exponentially when he caught a whiff of Zeke Wappinger, who was apparently still fresh in his olfactory memory.

"I tell you, the remarkable coincidences just keep piling up! Zeke Wappinger, what a great surprise!" Daria Cellucci, dressed in a fetching running outfit, said as she stood up from one of the plastic molded chairs arranged around the fire. The other four hobos were not quite as quick to respond.

"Hi Officer Cellucci, I mean, Daria! Hi Bullet!" Zeke yelled out getting off his bike with Warren and Pamela close behind while Bullet came running right up to Zeke and started wiggling like crazy and licking his hand. "Hi Captain Bix and Burrito Betty and hi to your friends! I know they have some great hobo names but I can't remember them right now."

"I'm Jazzy Jugs and this is Roadkill Ronnie, my friend, hunter, chef and all-around main man," Jazzy said with a flourish and even Zeke and Warren took note of the two obvious physical attributes that probably were responsible for her hobo monika since she was wearing what looked like her summer hobo outfit in the warmth of a June afternoon in New Mexico.

"And you remember my friend, Warren, and this is my nanny, Pamela. I asked her to come here with us because my parents have a rule that we can't ride our bikes down here without an adult. What are you doing here, Daria?"

"I was just out running from my house in Los Lunas for a few hours. There's a great trail that I try to run once a week or so along the river and make it a point to check this area out every so often, just to make sure there's nothing bad going on. I just happened across your two friends. I didn't recognize them at first, if it wasn't for Robert's unique hat and the feathers in the band, I might have just kept running. I know that I didn't recognize Tiffany. Isn't that funny? I had a feeling that I might possibly run into them down here. They were just telling me what they've been up to since their release from Gallup. Sounds like quite the experience. And I'm glad to meet you, Pamela. I think it's a really good idea that you came along with these two wild boys."

"Nice to meet you too, officer. I've seen you and your dog on TV a few times. My boyfriend is a big Isotopes fan and he always seems to want to get tickets along the left field line. Now I think I know why. You're even more beautiful in person," Pamela said, and not in a catty way.

Bix and Betty had stood up by this point and walked over to properly greet Zeke with various hugs, handshakes and gentle pats on the back. Zeke leaned his bike up against a tree, took off his backpack and told the hobos that he had brought some supplies for them. He emptied his contents onto the table under the tarp while the four hobos oooh'ed and aaah'ed as each item was revealed.

"You are such a darling boy!" Burrito Betty proclaimed when the last item was added to the growing pile of cheese, fruit, bread and various water bottles. "We've got enough supplies to last us most of the week now!"

"Okay, there are three things that I think we need to talk about," Zeke began, holding up three fingers and counting them off as he spoke. "First, I want to hear what your time was like in the pisshouse. Second, I want to know how you got here and third, I want to talk about how we should go about you meeting my parents."

"It seems like you all have a lot of ground to cover," Daria said. "Maybe Bullet and I will continue on with our run and leave you folks alone and try to overlook the fact that you're camping illegally. We've got about forty-five or fifty minutes to run back home and I'm on duty tonight. Zeke, I was serious about wanting to take you to an Isotopes game sometime. You could even bring Warren if he wants to come."

"Awesome!" Warren exclaimed.

"Yeah, super-awesome!" Zeke added.

"I'll contact your parents next week to set up a time. Great to meet everyone. Bye!" Daria said as she and Bullet headed north on the dirt path along the big river.

Once they left, everyone settled in around the fire. Pamela and Warren sat on a big log nearby while the four hobos and Zeke each took one of the plastic chairs. First, Bix Pickles and Burrito Betty told their Gallup-Grants-Belén story, with special emphasis on their time spent with the Gambles. It was then Zeke's turn to tell them about his time since leaving Gallup in Officer Ramirez's car and his subsequent adventures at home and at school. Jazzy Jugs and Roadkill shared a brief history of their friendship with Bix Pickles and Burrito Betty, which was highly entertaining.

"I guess that leaves the discussion we need to have about you two meeting my parents. Are you sure you still want to do that?" Zeke asked.

"Unless you don't want us to," Captain Haskell said.

"Oh, Bix, honey, I think we need to do this. I think we owe it to little Frankie. Remember, we talked about wanting to make sure our man here was in good hands? I don't want to have to spend the rest of my life worrying that he isn't being well cared for or that his parents ever let him slip away again. Remember? And I'm curious to find out what they're like. I just have a strong feeling that this is something that we need to do. I'd hate to think that Frankie's mom is like that mean person we met in Gallup."

"Just so you know, Burrito Betty, I'm pretty certain my parents have changed a lot in the last few days. My dad actually met me at home today when I got off the school bus and my mom took some time off work yesterday and we had a really good talk. She cried a lot but at least she now understands why I ran away. I'd love for them to meet you so they could see what great people you are but I'm not so certain that you'd like them a lot. They're very different than you."

"Freddie, we're different from most people," Jazzy Jugs interjected with a hearty laugh.

"I'll leave it to you, though, to let us know what the best way might be to go about this. What are your ideas?" Bix asked.

"I was thinking of asking them if you could come live with us. We have lots of room."

"Whoa, hold on there a second! Let's not put the clown wagon before the engine!" Bix exclaimed to the delight of the hobo crowd and Zeke. Warren and Pamela probably had no idea what he was talking about. "We're hobos for a reason! Livin' in a house ain't my idea of a good time, kid. Why, I'd rather ride the blinds for the rest of my life than live in a house."

"We have a really nice one," Zeke said looking right at Bix with a twinkle in his young eyes. "With a pool and a hot tub!"

"How about we just focus on meetin' your parents first before we go about playin' house together?"

"Just for the record, Bix, I seem to recall you talking not so long ago about settling down sometime soon. Remember that?" Betty asked sweetly.

"That might have been the hooch talkin'," Bix responded.

"Okay then, here's an idea. How about tonight around dinner time, you and Betty come walking by our house, just so it looks kind of like an accident and I'll be out in the yard playing catch or something with my dad and I'll pretend I didn't even know you were in Belén and I'll invite you in and we can all have dinner together," Zeke suggested, clearly off the top of his head.

"By accident? Why would we be just be walkin' through your neighborhood by accident?" Bix asked.

"Hmm, I don't know. How about if we set a time where I could go down to the freightyard with my dad to watch the trains and you two be hiding somewhere close by on the other side and when a train comes by and stops, you pretend you just got off and then I'll see you and then we can get together and you can meet my mom and dad?"

"Or how about Bix and me just come knock on your door tomorrow night when both of your parents are there?" Betty suggested.

"Or how about we get Officer Cellucci to arrest you for being hobos and Zeke's parents bail you out from jail and then you have to go live with them until your trial?" Warren offered.

"No more jail for a while! That was enough for now," Captain Bix said laughing.

Everyone was so wrapped up in this brainstorming session that they failed to notice what was happening above their heads. Sheets of big, dark storm clouds had quickly moved in, obliterating the ever-present sun and off in the far distance, they heard the first crackle of thunder. Jazzy Jugs O'Brien suggested that if the cyclists were to leave soon, they might have a chance to get home in time before the storm hit.

"Or we could just huddle under the tarp with you," Zeke said. "These storms usually don't last very long."

"No, I think that's a good idea," Pamela suggested. "Zeke and Warren, I think we need to quickly ride home before things get too wild. Your mom will probably be home soon anyway."

"But what about you guys?" Zeke asked. "You're going to get drenched!"

"Don't worry about us, big guy. We'll be fine. We've been through a lot of storms like this one before. Ain't that right, Roadkill?" Bix asked his pal.

"Okay, but first thing tomorrow, I'm going to ride down here and make sure you're alright. I'll also have a plan for you to meet my parents by then. Bye everyone!"

The three riders got back to Ladera Drive, late in the afternoon, just as the first raindrops started to fall. However, unlike most June storms in New Mexico, this one wasn't over quickly. It was still raining the next day when Pamela arrived before Zeke's parents left for work. The storm covered the entirety of the upstream watershed of the Rio Grande, including all the area surrounding Santa Fe and north into a sizable chunk of the river's headwaters in the San Juan Mountains of Colorado. It was a deluge. Flood warnings had been up since early that morning and the level of water in the Rio Grande was rising steadily and racing towards flood stage. Residents near the floodplain were told to take precautions and houses in the floodplain were ordered to be evacuated by ten that morning. With the forecast calling for more rain throughout the day, the river was expected to hit the one hundred year flood levels by early evening and probably not crest until the day after that. Zeke was worried out of his mind for his friends and talked Pamela into driving him and Warren there late in the morning with blankets, raingear, food and some clean, dry clothes Zeke took from his parent's closets. She drove in the downpour as close to the trail as possible and then they walked the last muddy half-mile to the hobo jungle.

Unfortunately, they couldn't even get close to where the hobo camp had been located because it was already under water. From a nearby rise in the local topography, the three Samaritans were able to see down towards the river where the jungle had been. The startling reality of what they saw underscored the danger the four rail riders must have been in. Zeke and his pals could see where their camp had been as it was clearly marked by the two blue tarps that were still suspended and visible between the trees. However, where they had once been high enough for a full size adult to easily stand underneath, now the water of the river was within a foot from having the tarps completely underwater and was probably going to be swallowed up by the mocha colored, detritus-filled, fast moving water really soon.

Zeke was on the verge of becoming hysterical and there wasn't anything that Pamela or Warren could have done to assuage his fears as they, too, were experiencing the same feelings. The reality was even grimmer than any of them had imagined, even in their worst-case scenarios.

"What if they were drinking all night and were really elevated and didn't notice the rain or the rising floodwaters? What if the water just came and took them away in the middle of the night while they were asleep? Oh no! This is terrible! We need to find them! They might be dead! We need to contact the police right now!" Zeke cried out to his friend and nanny and into the teeth of the relentless driving rain.

DAVID W. GOODWIN

Even in the short few minutes since they had been standing on the low hill, looking out at the hobo jungle, the water level of the river had risen visibly. The waters were now occasionally splashing, in fact, were now licking the undersides of the blue tarps. The rise of the water was of biblical proportions and had an intense, angry sort of energy about it that absolutely scared the devil out of the Devil Boy. He was filled with a pain so sharp that he almost wasn't able to breathe, like breathing might somehow take the air away from his hobo friends whose very lives might depend upon that very breath. Were they under water drowning? Were they clinging to some downed tree for dear life? Were they already dead? One thing was clear, Zeke needed to take immediate action.

The three of them ran back to the car as fast as their six legs would take them. As soon as they got back to her car, Pamela dialed 9-1-1 and reported the situation to the person answering the call. The Belén Police Department was immediately on high alert as this was their first flood-related emergency call. Pamela suggested to Zeke that he might want to call his parents to explain the situation and get them involved in some way. He decided to call his father first, feeling that his reaction would probably be the most rational.

"Hello, Andrew Wappinger, BLM Resource Planner, how can I help you?"

"Dad, it's Zeke! There's an emergency and I need your help. I think Bix Pickles and Burrito Betty and two of their hobo friends might have gotten swept away in the flood down at the river. Can you come home now and help us find them?"

"Whoa, wait a second! How do you know this?"

"Because yesterday when the four of us were riding our bikes and you stopped to fix a flat, Warren and me rode right through the hobo jungle and right into Bix and Betty. They had come to Belén to see me and to meet with you. We took stuff to them yesterday after you went to work. Pamela, Warren and me just went down to where they were camping and the entire area is under water. Dad, I think they might have been swept away."

"Yes, that's possible. These are some serious floods we're having. Have you called the police to report this?"

"Yes, Pamela just did. Can you come home with your SUV so we can go search? Pamela just has her Honda and can't go places that your car does."

"Listen, Zeke. Whatever you do, don't go out searching without me. I'll leave my office immediately. Meet me at home. I'll be there in less than half an hour, okay?"

"Okay, Dad. We'll go there now."

"Son, one more thing. Do you have any of their clothes?"

"No, why?"

"I'm thinking we might want to call in the K-9 Unit."

Zeke had Pamela's phone on speaker so they could all hear what Mr. Wappinger had to say. When Zeke ended the call, without a word, Pamela started up her little car and began to carefully drive back to Ladera Drive. Some of the low-lying intersections already were beginning to flood around the edges so she had to drive very slowly through the unflooded middle part. Police barriers already blocked some of the intersections off so she had to take a round about way to get back. None of the passengers were able to speak the words they were thinking.

The first thing they did when they got to Zeke's house was to turn on the television news to see if there was any information being broadcast that might be helpful. Less than ten minutes later, Zeke heard a car pull into the driveway, followed soon thereafter by a forceful knock at the front door. He jumped off the couch in the family room and looked out the clear sidelight beside the front door and saw Officer Cellucci standing there in her uniform.

"Come on in, Daria. How did you know to come over? Did my dad call you?"

"Yes, Zeke, he did. He said Robert and Tiffany were missing from the camp we met them at yesterday. Is that true?"

"Yes, it is true. It's completely under water. We were just there. I'm worried something happened to them," Zeke said, clearly on the verge of tears and it caused Daria to break police protocol for a moment and wrap him up in her arms while she tried to reassure him that they would do everything to find them. "There's a good chance that they are someplace right now, safe and sound, so let's not lose hope. Let me go get Bullet from the car and bring him inside."

While she was doing this, another vehicle pulled into the driveway, a yellow Jeep with the company logo on the side that said "Big Air Off Road Adventures" and their crazy logo of an airborne Jeep going off some sort of major bump while the passengers were partying down. A big, blond haired surfer dude of a guy got out and followed the officer and her

DAVID W. GOODWIN

dog up to the front door. By this time, Zeke, Warren and Pamela were standing in the open front door watching their arrival.

"Howdy folks, my name is Chip Brockaway of Big Air Off Road Adventures. Is Andy Wappinger here?"

"Um, no, not yet. But my dad will be here soon and just so you know, he hates to be called Andy," Zeke explained.

"Yeah, okay, that's fine. He just called me to see if I could, you know, come meet him here to help with an off-road search and rescue mission, so here I am. I was already in the area so was able to get here lickety-split."

"I'm not sure that will be necessary, sir. A 9-1-1 call has already been placed and the Belén PD is about to start conducting a search for the missing persons."

"From what I understand, the missing persons, as you say, might have, you know, been swept up in the river, is that correct?" Chip asked, looking directly into the lovely eyes of Officer Cellucci.

"Yes it is," Zeke exclaimed.

"Zeke, this is a police matter. Would you please allow me to do the talking? We don't want too much of this information to get out to the public yet," Officer Cellucci said, trying not to make it sound too much like a reprimand. "And we don't want a bunch of inexperienced civilians out in dangerous conditions and create an undue risk to themselves and others who might then have to be rescued."

"I'll have you know that I've been certified for search and rescue by, you know, NASAR and I have a Jeep that can go just about anywhere, even through three feet of water. Can any of your police vehicles do that, officer?"

"No, I don't believe so, sir. Can you tell me what NASAR is?"

"Sure, it's the National Association for Search and Rescue and I've taken three courses, one basic search and rescue, one advanced search and rescue and one specialty course titled, you know, 'Search and Rescue Tracking Fundamentals.' Passed them all with the highest score in my class so I might, you know, be an asset to your team."

While Officer Cellucci and Chip Brockaway were busy having their pissing match, Andrew pulled into the driveway and joined the group in the living room where the Cellucci-Brockaway grudge match was still underway. Neither of them even paused long enough to greet him.

"Thank you all for coming," Andrew said to get their attention. "Officer Cellucci, Bullet, Chip Brockaway, Warren, Pamela, Zeke—thank you all. Pamela and Warren, if you two would like to go home, this might be a good time, not that we don't want your help but I don't want either of you to feel obligated to be a part of this. Your families might be more comfortable if you were at home."

"Are you kidding? I want to help out in anyway possible!" Pamela cried out. "I'm sure they'd be cool with this."

"Me too!" Warren chimed in. "I already called my dad and told him that I might be home late tonight and he's fine with that, as long as I'm with a responsible adult."

"Okay, everybody. Let me fill all of you in, then, on the current situation," Officer Cellucci began, clearly used to being in charge when the situation called for her to be assertive. "Every available on-duty police officer has been instructed to do a systematic search of the area surrounding the site where the four missing people were last seen. Unfortunately, this isn't the only flood-related emergency at the moment so resources are being stretched a little tight at the moment. Each officer has been assigned a quadrant north of East River Road centered on the missing person's last known location. Our team, under my supervision, has been tasked with a reconnaissance of the section of the river downstream, or south of East River Road all the way down to railroad bridge near Trujillo Road. We have mugs shots of Robert Rand and Tiffany Spears from a few days ago in Gallup but no police information at all on the other two, a woman who goes by the name of Jazzy Jugs O'Brien and a man by the name of Roadkill Ronnie."

This revelation certainly broke the tension in the room as both Chip and Andrew started cracking up, in spite of their efforts to remain serious.

"We do, however, have a physical description of them," Officer Cellucci continued over the snickering of the two men, "based on my face to face with all four yesterday as well as the clothing each one was wearing at that time. In addition, Zeke, Warren and Pamela, you all met them yesterday as well, so your help in this search could potentially be quite valuable since you know what they look like. Correct?"

They all nodded their heads, except for Warren, who blurted out, "Jazzy Jugs has huge boobies!" which caused all the members of the assembled search and rescue team to roar with laughter, even Daria Cellucci.

"Thanks for that astute observation, Warren," Officer Cellucci said while giving Warren a few noogies. She then went on to describe all four of the hobos in as much detail as she could remember, with Zeke, Warren and Pamela adding a few miscellaneous tidbits. "Hopefully that gives you all enough to go on. We'll split up into two groups. My group will stick to the roads that my cruiser can drive on and Mr. Brockaway's Jeep can explore the off road sections. I'd like us to travel together as a team and make our way systematically down the west side, until we come to the railroad bridge. We'll then retrace our steps back to East River Road and then repeat the process down the east side of the river. I'd like the two boys, Zeke and Warren, to stay with me in the backseat of my cruiser with Bullet. Andrew and Pamela will be with Chip in his Jeep."

"I'll just warn you," Chip said, "that the backseat and the way back of my Jeep are filled with, you know, a lot of rescue equipment but there should be room for you if we slide all the stuff over."

"Okay, that's good. Any questions before we begin?" Officer Cellucci asked.

"We should get each other's, you know, phone numbers, just in case we get separated," Chip suggested.

"Good idea, but let's try our best not to let that happen. Having civilians as part of this search mission is stretching the rules already so we need to make absolutely certain that it proceeds without incident."

Numbers were exchanged and the final preparations were made before the vehicles ventured out into the stormy wilds. Andrew toyed with the idea of calling Roxanne to let her know about the current crisis but decided to put it off for a while, at least until later in the afternoon when she might be getting ready to come home. If she knew what Zeke and him were up to, he reasoned, she might put her foot down and insist that they not participate. Better to leave her out of it for the moment.

The Jeep followed the K-9 cruiser through the streets of a very soggy Belén. The rain was still coming down at a steady rate and the town had the feel of one that was about to be invaded or was ramping up for war. Cars were rushing around as people were getting supplies stockpiled in case of power loss or if their access was blocked getting out of their homes. Emergency shelters were being established at two local schools. People in homes that were evacuated were moving to higher ground with friends or family. The state and local police presence was greatly increased, including patrol cars from surrounding towns that weren't along the Rio Grande and could spare the resources to help out. The National Guard was beginning to arrive as were government vehicles from FEMA. Flatbed trucks were seen here and there with loads of already filled sandbags going towards the river. Dump trucks full of sand were making their way to private residences that had the resources to buy a load and the person power to begin their own sandbag brigade to try, despite the odds against them, to protect their properties. News vans were out filming the flooding around the downtown area and from the East River Road bridge. It was like a scene out of a low-budget disaster film.

There are drainage ditches that run alongside both sides of the river, north and south, through all of Belén and extend far north up past Albuquerque and to the south for miles through Socorro and, in bits and pieces, towards El Paso and the Mexico border. These ditches are themselves paralleled by slightly elevated, well-established and maintained access roads that generally form the boundary of the floodplain on both sides. On the other side of these drains is development; houses, businesses, apartment complexes, ranches, agricultural fields and barns. These access roads are gated at each public road intersection and are not open to the public but dirt bikes, hikers, cyclists and ATVs can easily get around them. Just like the area north of East River Road where the hobo jungle had been, the area to the south is a dense network of hiking and biking trails and wider off-road vehicle paths. Driving a Jeep on most of these primitive roads, under normal, dry conditions, is not a problem and is a very popular activity.

When the police car and the Big Air Off Road Adventures Jeep arrived at the gate on the west side of the river, it was immediately obvious what sort of challenges the search party was going to face. Additionally, it was clear that the rushing torrent of the Rio Grande floodwaters created catastrophic conditions for anyone unlucky enough to be caught up in them. Looking south, the floodplain was about four hundred feet wide under normal flow conditions but now the water was within about a hundred feet of the access road and most of the tall floodplain cottonwood trees had a lot of their trunks submerged in the murky and swirling waters. Already, there were a bunch of trees that had been uprooted upstream and were either floating quickly by or getting caught up on other trees and debris along the edges where the water was moving more slowly. This debris edge formed numerous dangerous impoundments until something would shift around within the pile or something coming downstream would ram it just right and everything would get released back out into the raging waters, like the Log Jam app that Andrew liked to play.

Officer Cellucci pulled up to the gate and unlocked it using one of the keys on the large key ring hanging from her belt. Chip Brockaway's

Jeep was waved through. Daria had put on her police rain gear back in the Wappinger's driveway and looked ready for action. She noticed that Chip, as well, was dressed in a shiny yellow waterproof outfit from head to toe.

They approached the missing hobo search systematically. Chip and Andrew drove the Jeep down each side road until they got to the water's edge, scanned the area for any evidence of people, used Chip's blue megaphone to yell out "is anyone out there?" and then listened to the best of their ability for any response over the roar of the river and the sound of the driving rain. While one person was calling out, the other person would be scanning the surroundings for any indication of someone in trouble. While the Jeep was doing this, Officer Cellucci's cruiser was driving very slowly down the access road doing the same thing through her police car loudspeaker while her tiny backseat occupants were keeping a close eye on the water's edge. Bullet, too, was active, running from one window to the other, jumping onto and over the laps of Zeke and Warren while making excited doggie sounds.

In the course of about thirty minutes, they ended up down at the two railroad bridges, about a mile and a half from their starting point on East River Road without finding anyone or any clues that might help lead the way to any missing persons. They retraced their steps back north to the road, still keeping a watchful eye. After crossing the bridge over the Rio Grande, they repeated the process on the other side. This was much easier and went more quickly since, due to the slight curve of the river and the more pronounced topography along the eastern riverbank, the floodplain on this side was much narrower. In fact, the distance between the access road and the floodwaters was generally only thirty or forty feet. They drove together towards the south since any road or trail that angled off from the access road towards the river could be seen in its entirety and there really wasn't any strategic gain to be made by driving such a short distance except for a couple of roads that needed closer investigation.

As they worked their way toward the railroad bridges, the access road got further away from the water. Closer to the bridges, the floodplain was at its widest point in this whole river segment. Other than a lot of debris and vegetation piling up along the forested floodplain, they didn't notice any signs of human life, that is, until they took a smaller dirt road that paralleled the railroad track where it came in perpendicular to the river. From this perspective, they got a good look at the area around the bridge abutments.

CHAPTER 17

WHEN THE RAILROAD bridge abutments were in sight, the two boys, with their small faces pressed up against the windows on either side of Officer Cellucci's police car, were worried out of their gourds. But they were also feeling important to be a part of this effort and were on extremely high alert. All of the people in the police car knew there would be a lot of flotsam and jetsam smashed up against the various railroad bridge abutments from their previous reconnaissance when they were on the other side of the river. Ten of the abutments were now in the water instead of the usual six under normal flow conditions. What they hadn't expected, however, was how much wider and deeper the floating pile was on this side. The river at the bridge crossing was now so flooded and swollen that when they were standing on the other side, they weren't able to see much of the detail that was now apparent. Warren, sitting by the cruiser's passenger side window closest to the water, was the first to notice something out of the ordinary.

"Look over there!" he exclaimed, pointing to the middle part of the debris dam out in the river. "That looks like someone!"

"You might be right. That looks like more than one someone!" Officer Cellucci said as her demeanor changed from someone leading a low probability, casual search detail to a police officer responding to a crisis situation. "Let's go investigate. I want you boys to stay right near the car. Do not go near the river. It is very dangerous. Do you understand?"

The two best friends nodded and Officer Cellucci said, looking each one directly in his eyes, "No, I need you both to answer me with words. This is very important that you follow my instructions exactly. One false step and you could easily be swept into this flood. Plus, I need you to stay and keep Bullet company because he gets lonely when I'm away."

The two boys, realizing the tone of absolute seriousness in her voice, responded verbally. She parked the car right near the upstream side of the bridge and motioned for the Jeep to pull in right behind her. Pulling out her binoculars from a box in her trunk, she quickly focused on the area that looked promising.

"I think we've located two people," Officer Cellucci said to the assembled occupants of the two vehicles. Turning to the other three adults, she said, "Here, let me know what you folks think."

As the binoculars were passed around, each person in turn said that it looked like two people holding on to the trunk of an entire tree that was part of the pile. What none of them could say with any certainty, however, was if they noticed any signs of life.

"I'm going to call this in immediately," Officer Cellucci said over the loud roar of the rushing floodwaters passing by with an extremely high velocity underneath the bridges. "In the meantime, Mr. Brockaway, would you pull out of your Jeep whatever rescue equipment you have?"

While she got on her radio, Chip set about piling up his equipment in the dry area under the railroad bridge on the upstream side. He had a few bundles of climbing rope, some harnesses, a bunch of carabiners, a yellow helmet, a bow saw and a two-headed axe. When Officer Cellucci had completed her call to dispatch, she added her equipment to the pile which consisted of more ropes plus a large first aid kit, a few space blankets, a headlamp, some straps, bungee cords, goggles, yellow reflective safety vests, an orange helmet and a small rescue pad spineboard with a molded foam brace for a victim's head. She noted that Chip's Jeep had a powerful looking built-in winch in the front bumper and instructed him to drive his Jeep as close to the water's edge as possible as it might come in handy for their rescue effort.

"Support will be here in about ten or fifteen minutes and I asked them to also send out an ambulance. In the meantime, I'd like to assess the situation as best as we can without putting ourselves in any danger. Mr. Wappinger, I would like for you, Pamela and the boys to stay around this pile of equipment with this walkie-talkie while Mr. Brockaway and I get as close as we can to those people out there. I may call you with instructions and want you to be able to assist us if necessary."

"Okay, Officer Cellucci. We'll do that," Andrew responded.

Both Officer Cellucci and Chip Brockaway put on their safety vests, stepped through a harness, tied the end of a rope to a carabiner and attached one end to one of the two hooks on the front bumper of the Jeep and the other end to another carabiner in their harness. Both then donned their helmets, Chip in yellow and Daria in orange, and carefully knotted the other end of their ropes so they wouldn't accidentally exceed the rope's length and lose their protection completely.

"I'd like to carefully walk out onto that debris mat as far as we can safely to get close enough to see what's going on out there. If you could walk out the cable on your winch with us, it might come in handy," Officer Cellucci instructed.

Chip turned his Jeep's engine back on and flipped the switch on the winch motor. This allowed the cable to be released and he called Andrew over to show him which button to push to reverse the switch in case they needed to haul something in.

"I think I can handle that," Andrew said flatly, a bit disappointed that his role in this crisis was so minor at this point.

The two rescuers slowly made their way out onto the pile, much like lumberjacks must have done in the past when they were driving logs down a river to the sawmill and had to deal with the numerous log jams that happened along the way. They didn't have calks on their boots for traction and stability or a peavey or even a pickaroon like the old-timers so they had to rely upon their own athleticism, balance and good sense to negotiate the tangled mess of trees, bushes, construction debris and trash to get close enough to the victims. As they walked along, each slowly pulled their safety rope though the carabiner on their harness to give them enough slack to move carefully while still maintaining a lifeline.

"This heap seems pretty stable but make sure you're confident with each step before you take the next one," Officer Cellucci yelled out to Chip over the wall of sound the water was making as they inched out. "Things are tightly packed in this close, but I think as we get out further, things may become more unstable."

In the short space of a few minutes, as they were walking, crawling and climbing at roughly the same speed, they managed to get about twenty yards out onto the pile. From this location, probably another ten yards from the victims, Officer Cellucci, if she got a good angle, could see two people through the branches of the very uneven mess. Both had their arms draped over a large tree trunk with their heads down on the log like they were sleeping. They were somehow wedged into this position from behind by more trees, branches, furniture, buckets, barrels and splinters of lumber from some sort of structure upstream that had been washed into the floodwaters, mixing with everything else that met a similar fate. Officer Cellucci's heart started racing when she realized that the material behind them might have crushed these people because she hadn't seen either of them move a muscle the entire time since they arrived. In a few more minutes, she thought, they would be close enough to touch them.

Daria Cellucci was a strong woman, physically and mentally, and a top-notch police officer. In her four years working part-time as the Belén K-9 officer, she had responded to a whole range of situations where Bullet's superior sense of smell was a huge asset. Naturally, she worked on a lot of drug-related cases, but she had also worked on tracking various criminals from the scene of a crime back, in more cases than not, to the criminal's living room where they were usually found watching TV while drinking a beer and eating popcorn or potato chips and were absolutely dumbfounded when they were caught so quickly. She was also called in from time to time to deal with cases involving the poaching of wildlife, as Bullet could smell a wild animal being transported in the trunk of a car from about a mile away. Bullet was also very good at finding spent shell casings from firearms and could locate them quicker than any human, even one armed with a powerful magnet on a string or a metal detector. What Officer Cellucci had never dealt with before, however, were dead bodies and the thought of finding these two people dead almost made her legs quiver and buckle as she got within a few yards of them.

"Hello! Hello! Can you hear me?" she shouted into the wind and rain and over the cacophony of the rushing water. Not getting a response, she steeled herself to the fact that maybe this was going to be a body recovery situation, not a rescue. Chip Brockaway decided to make the final push towards them and crawled over the last tree that stood between them and the two bodies. "Careful, Mr. Brockaway! That tree looks very precarious!" Officer Cellucci cried out into the roar of the floodwaters.

As he straddled the trunk, much like the Slim Pickens character Major T. J. "King" Kong riding the atomic bomb to its target in the Soviet Union in *Dr. Strangelove*, Chip's two hundred plus pound body caused a shift in the dynamics of the log pile, resulting in a sudden realignment of the tree pick-up sticks. Much like Major Kong, Chip Brockaway was immediately sent on his way elsewhere and in this case, that elsewhere was downstream towards the railroad bridges. Just as he was beginning his journey, his safety rope went taut in his harness and he was immediately yanked off the log. He landed right at Officer Cellucci's feet with a soggy thud. She had the wherewithal to tighten down on her rope when she saw the situation unfold in one heartbeat, which prevented her from losing her balance and getting yanked downstream too. Chip was able to steady himself enough to stand up on Daria's log. What happened next, however, was that the log the two bodies were wrapped around was freed up as well and as it started to rotate slowly, it also began moving downstream. Luckily, the rotation was towards the two rescuers so instead of the bodies being dumped backwards into the drink, the movement of the log caused their bodies to rotate out of the water and also deliver them near the feet of Officer Cellucci and Chip Brockaway.

Officer Cellucci reflexively bent down and pulled the body closest to her up by their shoulders and made sure they were stabilized on two parallel logs. Chip Brockaway did the same thing to the body near him. They could now hear sirens approaching the water's edge and looked up to see several police cars and an ambulance coming down the dirt road towards their own vehicles. Both bodies were still face down on the logs so it was impossible to tell much about them, They looked to Officer Cellucci like a man and a woman based on their waterlogged and debris-laden hair and the style of clothing each one was wearing. It only took a few seconds, however, before she recognized Captain Bix Pickles Haskell's cotton striped sport coat. She reached down, took his wrist and felt for a pulse while Chip followed her lead and did the same thing to the other person.

"He's got a weak pulse. How about her?" she yelled with urgency.

"I'm not getting anything right now. Let's roll them both over and see, you know, how their breathing is. They may be badly injured so we'll have to be extremely careful not to inflict any further damage."

With considerable effort, they were able to roll Bix over onto his side and then managed to get him on his back. He was pretty banged up, clearly had some broken bones given the unnatural angle of one forearm and foot, a few visible gashes to his head and exposed legs, since his pants had been mostly torn off. Bix began groaning and moaning loudly, clearly in a world of pain, but at least he was breathing well, now that his chest had been opened up from lying on his back. Officer Cellucci managed to wedge him into a safe position against another log while they focused their full attention on the woman.

"What is the situation out there?" a voice boomed out to them over a megaphone. Officer Cellucci and Chip Brockaway looked over and saw a policeman who had just arrived and was standing at the edge of the water with everyone else from all the vehicles that had gathered.

"We need help! Both people are in bad shape but at least one of them is alive. We're just about to see about the other one. We'll need to get them out of here on stretchers, for sure!" Officer Cellucci shouted out at the top end of her voice across the jangled mass of material.

Even Zeke could tell from where he was standing that the man was Captain Bix Pickles. He would have recognized that jacket anywhere. In his head, when they first arrived, he knew there was a good chance that it was him but his heart was of two hopes. One was that it wasn't him and that he and Burrito Betty were somewhere else, warm and dry and safe. Two, if the choice was between finding him alive versus finding him dead, this was indeed the better option. He could only hope, too, that the other person was Burrito Betty and that she was going to be found all right as well and hopefully, not injured, or at least, not injured too badly. It was a best-case scenario, he realized, and felt a little greedy for having these wishes. He knew the implication that if this was Bix and Betty, the fate of Jazzy Jugs and Roadkill might not be so rosy. Zeke took his father's hand and buried himself in his arms while trying to fight off his tears. Right at that moment, a news car and van came barreling down the dirt road and screeched to a stop near the police cars. There was also an ambulance that was in the process of turning around and backing up as close to the water's edge as possible.

With Captain Haskell stabilized and relatively safe, and the crew onshore mobilizing for action, Officer Cellucci and Chip Brockaway turned their attention back to the other person lying face down on the logs. Given her small size, it was much easier for the two of them to roll her over onto her back. She looked awful - her skin was a pasty dull white color, her eyes were open and starring up into space and she didn't seem to be breathing. Officer Cellucci immediately started mouth-to-mouth resuscitation on her, entirely expecting that she was a lost cause, but she had been trained to do everything in her power to save lives. She immediately recognized the woman as Burrito Betty, having just seen her the day before. Since both of them were wearing the same clothes as yesterday, there was no doubt that these people were the two hobos. Chip Brockaway knelt beside Betty as best he could, given the position of all four people in a very awkward space and took her wrist in his large hand.

"I'm feeling a very weak pulse, officer," Chip said, timing his comment between two of Officer Cellucci's breaths into Betty's mouth. "You may be able to, you know, save her!"

After a minute of this, much to Officer Cellucci's surprise, Betty turned her head sideways and threw up about two cups of brown river water and took a huge gasp of air. Officer Cellucci and Chip gently stroked her head and arm to calm her down enough to take a few shallow, tentative breaths on her own. Color started to return to her skin and her eyes looked like they were now focusing on her two rescuers. She violently coughed a few more times, spitting up more water, took some more gasps of air and started to breathe almost normally.

"Where the fuck am I?" she cried with slurred speech through her gurgling and then noticed Captain Bix Pickles lying nearby, looking like a scarecrow that had fallen off his supports, but also looking like he was sound asleep. "Is my Bix dead?" she managed to say through her understandable panic and pain.

"No, Ms. Spears. He's not dead. He's pretty banged up but I think he's going to be alright," Officer Cellucci said softly and reassuringly.

"How do you know me?" Betty asked tentatively, still looking sort of wild-eyed and not yet fully conscious.

"I'm Officer Cellucci, ma'am. We met over the weekend and again yesterday with Zeke Wappinger. In fact, he's standing right over there with his dad and if it weren't for the fact that he came looking for you and Mr. Rand this morning, we would have never known to come out here. I think he might have saved both of your lives." She wasn't sure how much of this Ms. Spears was comprehending as she seemed to be going in and out of consciousness and Chip had to hold her to keep her from rolling over and falling back in the raging waters.

Burrito Betty very slowly turned her head towards shore and saw Zeke standing about fifty yards away with a large group of people and by now, a large assortment of vehicles. She tried to wave but the pain of moving her arms caused her to scream a string of profanities out into the wind. Moments later, the other officers and emergency medical technicians arrived with two portable aluminum stretchers and blankets to deal with the hobo's expected hypothermia and started their journey out onto the pile. Daria and Chip got up out of the way and carefully made their way off the heap to give the others more room to do their jobs and carry the two hobos to safety. This was a huge task given the slippery footing, the driving rain and the obstacle course created by the jumble of debris. The McGloria-Zuckerthong KOAT field reporting team was again reporting live and seemed to have a magnetic attraction for any story involving this cast of characters. They eventually became known in journalistic circles as the "hobo team." Really, what were the chances that the two hobos and the six-year-old runaway boy from Belén would be the stars of two stories in less than a week that so captured the world's interest? It was almost like a public relations firm had choreographed it all to perfection.

Gloria McGloria was busy doing her running commentary while the final stages of the rescue were being filmed. As Officer Cellucci and Chip Brockaway took their first steps onto the saturated sandy floodplain where the river water had probably risen another half foot or so in the short time since they had arrived, Ms. McGloria asked them if they would be able to stick around for an interview as soon as the hobos were taken off in the waiting ambulance. Officer Cellucci wasn't very enthusiastic about the prospect, knowing how the press liked to both sensationalize everything (although, she admitted to herself, this was a pretty sensational story) and they asked some of the most inane, almost insulting questions imaginable. On the other end of the spectrum, Chip Brockaway of Big Air Off Road Adventures, knew this kind of attention and publicity was almost a once-in-a-lifetime opportunity for his company and self-promotion. Ms. McGloria, too, was aware of the coop she was making to be the only field reporter on the scene at two such important stories and knew that it had the potential to make her a much more valuable commodity in the field if she did a good job. It was with this motivation that she asked the Wappinger men if they would stick around as well for an interview.

It took a lot of time, concentration and energy to get the two hobos safely off the debris mat and onto solid ground. A crowd of policemen, civilians and the press gathered around their stretchers and greeted the bundled up hobos. Zeke was beside himself with joy that his new friends were apparently going to be okay.

"I was so worried about you two. I knew something bad had happened," Zeke said, clearly in shock by how badly battered and bruised his two friends looked.

"Now Freddie," Bix said, his voice laboring through clenched teeth from the pain he must have been experiencing and responding with the fewest words he could to convey his feelings, "thought it was pie-in-the-sky time for your buddies!"

"Frankie! You saved our lives. How did you know we were washed overboard?" Burrito Betty asked, clearly in better shape than Bix in spite of how she was just moments ago.

"Me and Warren and Pamela went down to the hobo jungle this morning to look for the four of you and it was completely underwater. We called 9-1-1 and with Officer Cellucci, we found you! But I'm really worried about Jazzy Jugs and Roadkill. I don't know if they've been found yet."

"Yeah, they might be half way to Mexico by now. Maybe they survived the flood too," Betty said as she was being loaded into the ambulance right after Bix. "Thanks for looking for us! You're a true angel!"

"I'll come visit you at the hospital. Soon—I promise!"

In no time flat, the hobos were being rushed away. Gloria McGloria talked about the heroic rescue and that the hobos injuries, miraculously, were very serious but didn't seem to be life threatening. She then turned her attention to the rescuers, Officer Daria Cellucci and Mr. Chip Brockaway.

"Office Cellucci, if I could get a word with you, ma'am?" she asked. Daria was off under the bridge talking to the Wappingers, Warren and Pamela, no doubt telling them what the situation had been like out on the floating log mat and what the conditions were of Bix and Betty.

"You were the first officer at the scene. Can you tell us what is was like?"

"You can see the conditions out here. It's terrible. The water's rising, the rain hasn't let up; this is a very dangerous place to be. We were doing surveillance in response to Zeke Wappinger and his nanny, Pamela's, 9-1-1 call about his missing friends. You may recall that this is the same young boy who ran away to become a hobo, right?"

"The entire world knows Zeke Wappinger by now, officer!"

"So we were assigned to search this stretch of the Rio Grande and as luck would have it, we found Mr. Rand and Ms. Spears out in that mass of vegetation and debris. Mr. Brockaway, who was assisting our efforts out here today, went out there with me and together, we were able to pull the two victims out of the water until backup support arrived from the Belén PD as well as several very talented paramedics."

"Thank you, officer. And you, Mr. Brockaway, can you tell us, in your own words, what happened out here today?"

"Sure can, ma'am. That's Chip Brockaway. I own Big Air Off Road Adventures out of Albuquerque, on Central Avenue, NW, right across from, you know, Elmo's Tiki Bar. We specialize in a variety of awesome off road Jeep trips, you can visit out website at www.bigairoffroad. com . . ."

"Thank you, sir, for that information but can you get to your description of the rescue. I'm sure our viewers are dying to hear about that."

"Yes ma'am, I was getting to that part. So I was down in Belén anyway, getting some, you know, welding done on one of my other Jeeps when I get a call from Zeke Wappinger's dad Andy, you know, the six-year-old hobo? Anyway, I teamed up with the sexy Officer Cellucci here, and I have to say, she could pose for Playboy for their 'Girls in Uniform' spread . . ."

"Mr. Brockaway, please. Just stick to the story if you would!"

"Yes, ma'am, like I said, I'm getting to that part. So, we come out here and Zeke and his best buddy over there, Barry or something, I forget his name, sees these people out on the, you know, junk out there, holding on for dear life. I've got extensive training in, you know, searches and rescues, so me and the police babe here geared up and hooked up our safety ropes and used the cable from the winch on my Jeep to go out to see if we can rescue those hobos. Man, I tell you, Officer Sex-ucchi, damn if she didn't, you know, save that woman hobo's life. She was knocking on heaven's door when we got out there - was barely breathing, couldn't find a pulse - so we yanked her out of the water and she starts giving her mouth to mouth and brings her back, you know, to life. It was awesome! Almost made me want to pretend that I couldn't breathe if she'd give me, you know, that sort of treatment, if you know what I mean."

"Thank you, sir, for that colorful account of the rescue. Maybe we can get a word with Zeke Wappinger, someone who's been in the news a lot lately. Zeke, can you come over here and talk to me, dear? That is, if your dad is willing to let you. Zeke, you've had quite an exciting few days here. Can you tell us how you discovered that the hobo's lives were in danger?"

"My friend Warren and me were down in the floodplain yesterday riding our bikes with my dad and my nanny, Pamela, when I ran across a hobo jungle and saw my super-awesome friends Captain Bix Pickles Haskell, the Human Stinkbomb and Burrito Betty, the Princess of Poots. They were hanging out with their hobo friends, Roadkill Ronnie and Jazzy Jugs O'Brien, sitting around a campfire, eating and drinking, sleeping out under a tarp, you know, doing cool stuff like that. They had just come to Belén to visit with me after our awesome train adventure. Anyway, we went down to visit with them later yesterday and it started to rain so we took off to come back home. When I got up today and saw that it was still raining, we pulled together some dry clothes and some food and got Pamela to drive us down to the river to give it to them. When we got to their jungle, it was under water and I knew they were in trouble so Pamela called 9-1-1."

"Did you ever think you would find your hobo friends alive?" she asked.

"Yes, I did. I'm very happy for them and hope they aren't too badly hurt though. But I'm wicked worried about Jazzy Jugs and Roadkill. If anyone knows where they are, call me or my parents or the police! Please!"

"Thank you, Zeke Wappinger. And that will wrap up our live coverage of the rescue of the two hobos from the treacherous floodwaters of the Rio Grande River. As you may know, these are the same two hobos who were found and released without charge in Gallup, New Mexico just days ago in the company of six-year-old runaway hobo Zeke Wappinger, who I just interviewed. It would appear that we have a lot of heroes out here today, from young Zeke Wappinger, to Officer Cellucci from the Belén Police Department, to Mr. Chip Brakeaway from Big Roads Air Enterprises, to the numerous other people who played a part in today's dramatic rescue, including Zeke's nanny Pamela who declined my interview request, saying she was too overcome with emotion right now to talk about the rescue on camera. I have the feeling that this story might not yet be over. Reporting live from the banks of the Rio Grande River in Belén, I'm KOAT field reporter, Gloria McGloria."

The soaked news people tried to dry off after packing their wet equipment back into their van. Chip Brockaway and Officer Daria Cellucci gathered up all of their rescue equipment and did their best to clean it off before stowing it back inside their vehicles. Zeke, Warren, Andrew and Pamela tried to help them out as much as possible without getting in their way or getting too close to the dangerous waters of the river. The rain seemed to be letting up slightly, although the water level was still rising, but it seemed to give everyone hope that, perhaps, the worst might now be behind them.

"We should probably call your mother and tell her what's been happening," Andrew said, turning to Zeke who was engaged with Warren in some sort of sign language thing that his dad had never seen before. "She likes to be kept in the loop on things like this, especially if they involve her son being interviewed on TV again. You've become quite the celebrity, my little Devil Boy! She's going to have a hard time believing what's been happening out here today."

It was Wednesday afternoon by now and already Zeke's summer vacation, only one day old, had been a memorable one. Roxanne Wappinger was up at her swanky third floor law office in Albuquerque with a killer view of the Sandia Mountains, talking to one of her colleagues about the unusual amount of rain they were having. The colleague was more interested in talking about her son's hobo escapade than she was in talking about the weather but that is where Roxanne kept steering their conversation.

"Roxanne, your family has become minor celebrities around here. What does that feel like to be recognized now everywhere you go?"

"Kind of annoying to tell you the truth. Valerie, you've lived in New Mexico most of your life, right?"

"Not my entire life. My parents moved to Santa Fe in the early eighties from Ann Arbor because they got this crazy idea that they just had to live in an adobe, so they just packed all us kids up and moved here. I was probably around five or six. Why do you ask?"

"Have you ever seen rain like this before? It hardly ever rains like this where I come from near LA."

"Not too often. I hear the river is going to top out near record flood levels later today or tomorrow. It's nuts! So, how is your son doing? He went through quite an ordeal as I understand things."

"We all have some changes to make, I'd imagine. I know you live up in the northern parts of the city near the Los Poblanos place. Are you guys in the floodplain?"

"Close, but not in it, as far as I know. At least that's what my husband tells me. We're on the eastern side of Rio Grande Boulevard Northwest, near the Casa Rondena Winery, so I think we're fine. Have you ever been there?"

"Yes, Andrew and I are members so we go fairly frequently for tastings and events, things like that." As she was saying this, her cellphone started playing a few measures of reggae music. "Say, speak of the devil. Excuse me, Val, I should probably take this call. Hi Andrew, what's up?"

"Roxy, big developments. Zeke's been all over the news again today!"

"Don't tell me Pamela let him out of her sight and he became a hobo for a second time? Please don't tell me that!"

"No, Zeke's fine. It's a long story but I wanted you to know what's been happening. Do you think you'd be able to come home early today?

There's a lot going on here and I think it would be best if you came home to be with us."

"You're at home? At 1:58?"

"Yeah, again, long story. Zeke called me mid-morning to say that his hobo friends were camping out down along the river. With all this rain, he discovered they'd been washed downstream, called 9-1-1, there was a big rescue and they found them almost two miles down by that double railroad bridge hanging onto a cottonwood tree for dear life. After a huge rescue effort, they were pulled to safety and just got taken away by ambulance to the hospital. Zeke is being called a hero and was just interviewed on the scene by your pal Gloria McGloria from KOAT. We're there right now."

"Are you kidding me, Andrew? You're being serious? This is totally out of control! When did the hobos arrive and how did Zeke know about them?"

"It's a long story, honey, and yes, I'm being totally serious. This is big news, I swear. Can you come home early? I left work around ten this morning when Zeke called to tell me what was happening and I've got another public meeting to run. I've got a ton of work to do to get ready for it."

"That's what Pamela is for. Can't you just go back to work and have her take over?"

"Honey, it's a lot more complicated than that. Zeke's going to want to go visit his hobo friends in the hospital, there's going to be more press issues, he's got a whole pile of emotional needs right now and I think we both need to be there for him. This has been one intense day so far! He's the one that found Mr. Pickles and Mrs. Burrito and I think he just needs us to pull together as a family right now. I'm thinking I might just have to cancel the meeting tonight, because of this and also because of the rain and all the flooding. It's really insane out there, very dangerous! You think about it and come back home if at all possible. Zeke needs you right now and I think I do, too."

Andrew, Pamela and the boys had been hanging out with Officer Cellucci and Chip Brockaway right after their interviews ended. Chip was on a major high, given his big interview; shameless plugs and what he thought were flattering references to Daria, who thought otherwise. In fact, the two of them began hashing it out so Andrew herded his charges away from them while he made his call to Roxanne, thinking, wisely, that the two of them might need some privacy to sort a few little details out.

"While I appreciate you telling everyone about my role in this rescue, Mr. Brockaway," Officer Cellucci was saying to him, right up in his face, with a finger pointing right at his jugular vein, using a voice filled with controlled anger that would have been obvious to even a single cell organism.

"Please, call me Chip," he interrupted.

"As I was saying, Mr. Brock-a-way, your blatantly graphic and juvenile references to me were both insulting and disrespectful, and I'm really angry that you would have thought that was an acceptable thing to do, especially on TV!"

"No, Daria, really, it was totally out of respect for you that I, you know, said those things."

"Do you honestly believe that? You don't know me; you don't know anything about me. And my name is Officer Cellucci and I expect you to address me as a professional."

"Okay, Officer Cellucci. By what you said is not true! I know that you are a brave police officer and I know that what you did out there today probably saved two lives. Plus, you know, you're totally hot!"

"See, that's the problem, Mr. Brockaway. The fact that you think I'm totally hot is all well and good but it was completely inappropriate for you to say that, to me or the people watching the newscast. Don't you get it?"

"No, not really. It was totally intended as a compliment."

"No, what you said about my actions were compliments. Those other comments were degrading. It reduces me to an object, not a person, and I'm really offended by that."

"Okay, my apologies. Listen, when we get this whole thing wrapped up and you get off work, you want to go get, you know, a drink or something?"

Roxanne turned on the television set that she kept in a corner of her office for the express purpose of monitoring breaking news and an occasionally episode of *Oprah* if she was doing something that didn't require much of her ample brain power. Turning to KOAT, she found that the most recent hobo developments were still being discussed by the two afternoon news anchors and they must have had the footage of the rescue and the various interviews on a repeating loop since Roxanne was able to catch all of the action from watching for about ten minutes.

"It really is quite remarkable how these three people, the two hobos and the six-year-old Belén boy, Zeke Wappinger, who achieved international notoriety when he ran away and illegally boarded a freight train, are now at the center of another incident, just a few days later," co-anchorman Tad Bunglebaum remarked while the Daria-Chip-hobo-log-rescue footage was being shown.

"To quote our ace field reporter, Gloria McGloria, who was live on the scene, I think we've got a lot of heroes out there today. She has quite the nose for news, I would say, especially when it comes to hobo stories," Tad's co-anchor, Charise Zonnie, chimed in. "Let's show you, yet again, the interviews she conducted with the hobo's two rescuers and the young Zeke Wappinger who we're hearing made the 9-1-1 call and is being credited with helping to save the lives of his two hobo friends."

All three interviews were again played in their entirety and Roxanne's remarks, spoken directly to the TV and no one else, in response to Officer Cellucci, Chip Brockaway and her son were, "how does she look that good after being out in those conditions?" "what an A-hole!" and "Jazzy Jugs O'Brien and Roadkill Ronnie? Who the hell are they?" respectively. Now she really felt out of the loop and quickly glanced at her iPhone calendar to see what commitments she had already scheduled for the afternoon.

Roxanne Wappinger's career as a personal injury lawyer was both overwhelmingly stressful and time consuming. It was also often highly unpredictable. In addition to having a schedule packed with meetings with clients and colleagues, time in court, time spent doing research and building the foundations for multiple cases, supervising the work of several paralegals who reported directly to her, and piles of paperwork; last minute scheduling changes and the need to shoehorn in new activities at the drop of a brief were often the rule of her day. However, after her recent conversation with Andrew and seeing the latest breaking news involving her son and, yet again, the hobos, she realized that she had to try to change her afternoon schedule and be at home with her family. Maybe she could spare a little time for her son without suffering too many consequences.

She walked down the hall towards the large, open office that was shared by all of the support staff and walked over to the corner where her paralegal's desks were, arranged face to face to facilitate collaboration, as Roxanne liked to point out to them. Before she even had a chance to say a word to them, the firm's office manager, Darlene, had something to say to her.

"Roxanne! Have you heard the latest news about your son?"

DAVID W. GOODWIN

"Yes, Darlene. Andrew just called and I just watched the rescue and interviews on my TV."

"He's a pretty remarkable kid! You should bring him to work someday. We'd all like a chance to meet this amazing traveler and hero!"

"Some day, Darlene. Listen, James and Molly, I need to go home for a while and make sure things are under control with my two men. I need you both to continue working on the documents we talked about for the Filborn case and, Molly, if you would begin researching legal precedents for sexting with a prostitute while in a public place and on company time, that would be a big help to me. I'll check in with you later this afternoon. Gotta run!"

Even in Albuquerque, there was a fair amount of street flooding. As Roxanne navigated the side roads and made her way to the interstate, her Miata, with minimal ground clearance, was experiencing some hydroplaning through many of the intersections. The rain was still coming down but wasn't as intense as she experienced that morning on her drive north to her office. Crossing the Rio Grande on I-25, halfway to Los Lunas, she saw a lot of cars pulled over in the breakdown lane just before crossing the bridge and people were out en masse gawking down at the extremely swollen chocolate waters. It was significantly higher than what she had seen five hours earlier and gave her a little feeling of panic about what it must have been like to get caught up in such a torrent.

Thankfully, she made it home safely but, again, was greeted by the familiar sight of a bevy of reporters milling around in front of her house. Standing on the front steps, her two family members and Pamela, who seemed to have recovered from the trauma of the rescue, were being interviewed by a small army of people while a few camera people were filming. Since Roxanne wasn't a part of this caper and probably wasn't of much interest to the press at this moment, she was content to pull into their garage, close the door behind her and head right into the house through the door inside the garage. She watched from Zeke's bedroom window, which was open a bit, and could hear what was being said without being too conspicuous.

The interviews were wrapped up after ten or fifteen more minutes. She heard the two Wappingers and Pamela come into the house through the front door and she watched as the news folks packed their equipment back into their cars and vans. Hopefully, she thought, this would be the last excitement for a while.

"Mom! You came home! I've got so much I want to tell you!" Zeke said running through the house looking for her. Roxanne came out of the bedroom and greeted him and her husband with big hugs. Pamela was surprised when she got one, too.

"Zeke, my little celebrity! What in heavens name have you been doing today? You're all over the news again. I saw it with my own eyes. I want to sit down here on the couch and hear all about it."

"Pamela, you're free to go now if you'd like. Thanks for all you've done. You were a huge help today in all of this craziness. We've got this kid covered for the rest of the day. Roxy, I need to go make some calls about canceling tonight's meeting. See you tomorrow, Pamela. You're one of today's big heroes!" Andrew said.

Little Zekie told his mom the complete story, beginning with the fateful bike ride yesterday and ending with the last round of interviews. Roxanne did her best to just let him tell the tale without interjecting any of her own commentary or opinions, which was a big challenge for her, especially since she still had a fair amount of distrust of the hobos and their motives. When he was finally done, his entire six-year-old body seemed to deflate; he got a very sad look on his face and snuggled up to his mom on the couch, resting his head in her lap while she stroked his shaggy hair. Andrew came over and joined them on the couch, sitting next to his wife.

"Mom, I'm so worried about Bix and Betty but also about Jazzy and Roadkill. It makes me feel all funny and yucky inside. Can we go visit Bix and Betty at the hospital? I don't know yet if they're going to be okay."

"Sure, honey, I think that would be fine. Or we could just call the hospital and ask what their condition is."

"No, I need to see them, I promised. They were pretty badly hurt. And besides, I want you to meet them and then you'll become their friend too, and then maybe you'll agree to have them come live with us."

Roxanne didn't say a word, but Zeke could tell that her entire body stiffened up.

CHAPTER 18

NIGHTTIME VISITS AT any hospital can be kind of eerie and the hospital in the bustling metropolis of Albuquerque where there was more action than other typical Wednesday nights was no exception. The green ghoulish glow of the industrial lighting, the labored zombie-like breathing of the patients, the grim faces of the visitors, the beeping of laboratory equipment and patient monitors, the mummy-like movements of the nurses and doctors all looking down at their clipboards and walking around randomly, the smell of urine and disease and death and hospital food. All of these factors made it the sort of place where a person generally did not feel light, happy and hopeful. The Presbyterian Hospital on Central Avenue in the southern end of the city was the closest full service hospital to Belén, so that was where Captain Bix Pickles Haskell and Burrito Betty had been taken. It took Andrew a few phone calls to figure this out and another few phone calls to ascertain the condition of the two hobos. He was a bit hesitant to tell Zeke that both of them were currently in the intensive care unit since he assumed it would cause him to worry even more and he was already emotionally fragile anyway. The hospital telephone receptionist recognized the Wappinger name and gave Andrew a thorough rundown of the injuries that both Bix and Betty sustained on their ride-from-hell down the swollen and chock-full-of-large-debris Rio Grande. "They're lucky to even be alive," is how she characterized and summarized their status after reading to him their laundry list of problems.

After the Wappingers stopped for a meal at the teriyaki restaurant in Los Lunas, they made their way to the hospital - past flooded fields, overflowing drainage ditches and backed up storm drains in the roads. Seeing the overtopped Rio Grande from the interstate was a harsh visual reminder of the extremely dangerous and terrifying situation the hobos must have dealt with. By the time the family arrived at the hospital in the early evening, the rain had finally stopped, even though the sky was still a dark sheet of thick clouds. However, as they were walking across the parking lot, a cerulean blue clearing appeared on the western horizon, just as the setting sun managed to find the hole in the sky and gave everyone a spectacular sunset to witness. It was the first time the sun had been seen in about thirty hours. The entire landscape, both natural and artificial, was bathed with an incredible illumination and golden glow, that was made even more intense and rich by the still dark storm clouds overhead and off to the east. It was almost like a giant box was suddenly lit with a cinder dick's flashlight, shining through a small hole with the dark sky, the dark surrounding hills, and the dark wet pavement creating edges and boundaries that the sun was able to spectacularly fill. It immediately gave Zeke a ray of optimism. Even though he probably wasn't aware of it on any conscious level, he suddenly felt hopeful and strong as he led his parents through the automatic doors of the visitor entrance.

Andrew asked the person sitting behind the large information desk where they might find Mr. Haskell and Miss Burrito and was given a look that maybe he thought Andrew was putting him on. Zeke let loose with a little chortle.

"He means Mr. Rand and Ms. Spears," Zeke said. "Or maybe Captain Bix Pickles Haskell and Burrito Betty or maybe Robert James Rand the third and Rebecca Stone or Alan and Annie Wilson or Tami Franklin, or some combination like that."

"Let's see, are we talking about the hobos that were fished out of the river earlier today?"

"Yep," Zeke said.

"They were checked in as Robert Rand and Tiffany Spears. You'll find them in room 302. They were just moved out of the Intensive Care Unit about an hour ago. There's a note here to ask any visitors if they know of any family or friends to contact or any insurance information because they didn't have any form of identification. Say, aren't you the boy from Belén that jumped onto a train and joined them to become a hobo and then helped to rescue them from the river?"

"Yes, that's me. I know a little about them and heard them talk about some family members but don't have any names or addresses to give you. Sorry," Zeke said.

"Maybe after they're rested, they'll be able to give us some of that information. So far, other than the police and some journalists, you're their first visitors."

The Wappingers were directed to the elevator but Roxanne, characteristically, insisted that they take the stairs. In the staircase,

Andrew told his son that the injuries to his friends were quite substantial and that he should be prepared to be a little shocked. Zeke nodded and kept walking up the stairs without saying anything. As they made their way down the hallway on the third floor, past the empty nurse's station and approached room 302, Zeke saw two uniformed officers standing in the doorway and immediately recognized them as Officers Ramirez and Cellucci.

"Well, well," Officer Cellucci said when she noticed the Wappingers walking toward her. She turned her head back into the room and said to the patients, "it looks like you've gotten your wish, folks. One of your favorite people in the whole world is here!"

Daria gave Zeke a full Pamela-like embrace. Officer Ramirez was next in line to greet Zeke with a hearty handshake and slap on the back. He then turned it into a full on hug and said, "You deserve that, Zeke! These folks would probably not be here right now if it hadn't been for you."

"Or for Officer Cellucci. What she did to save my friends was awesome!" Zeke exclaimed.

"Hey, Frankie, are you ever going to come in and say hi to me?" Burrito Betty's weak voice called out from inside the room.

Zeke strode into room 302 as quickly as his short six-year-old legs could take him while Andrew and Roxanne greeted the two officers. Andrew was a lot friendlier than Roxanne but was careful not to pay too much attention to Officer Cellucci, hoping not to provoke the animal jealously that his wife felt towards her. Zeke was indeed shocked at what he saw inside the room, nothing could have prepared him for this. Bix's head was wrapped in white gauze, he had two black eyes, numerous abrasions on his face, his leg was in a full length cast and suspended in a harness that was connected to a cable hanging from the ceiling that kept it off the bed and one arm was in a sling. Betty's face was covered in bruises too, and one of her arms was in a full cast, from her wrist all the way up to her armpit and bent at the elbow. However, both were all smiles when Zeke walked into their shared room, thanks, no doubt, to some serious pain medication.

"There's my little Frankie," Betty slurred, not unlike how she sounded the times Zeke saw her when she had been drinking heavily. "Don't be scared, honey. It's me, Burrito Betty. Might be kind of hard to recognize me at the moment. We'll be out of here and back on our feet in no time, but in the meantime, it kind of looks like we're ready to go trick-or-treating, don't you think? These would make great costumes!"

Zeke went over and tried to give her a hug without disrupting her too much. This was a little challenging given her plaster and the tenderness of her banged up face but he managed to wiggle into her a little and give her a quasi-hug. He then did the same to Captain Bix.

"There's our little hero!" Bix cried out, also sounding like he, too, had consumed a bit too much sneaky pete or white lightning and was temporarily feeling no pain. "Great to see you, son!"

Zeke noticed that his parents and the two police officers were watching their reunion from the doorway and giving him the space he needed to reconnect with his injured hobo pals. They chatted for a while about what things had been like for them since they'd been at the hospital, the friendliness and attentiveness of the staff, the endless stream of reporters coming in for interviews with the celebrity hobos, the great hospital food and certainly, the comfortable living arrangements.

"To tell you the truth, Frankie, they got us so hopped up on meds, as they call them, that mostly what we do is sleep and when we're awake, it's almost like we're still asleep anyway. I'm kind of looking forward to getting out of here and clearing my mind out some," Betty said.

Zeke looked over to see if his parents were going to join their conversation but noticed that they were out in the hall talking to the Belén Police officers in hushed tones. It was his hope that they would get to know his friends a little and would see what great people they were.

"Do you have any background information on these people?" Roxanne whispered to the two officers.

"Yes, actually, we wanted to talk to you about this. We searched all of our available databases and were able to find out a few pieces of information about them. Robert James Rand the third was a lawyer in Massachusetts back in the late '80's, early 90's as he claimed but we weren't able to find any surviving family members or next of kin - just a lot of dead ends," Officer Ramirez said. "And we were able to locate some information about Rebecca Stone, aka Burrito Betty, from an orphanage in Connecticut twenty-five years ago but again, after that there was nothing."

"Mr. Rand was a lawyer in Massachusetts?" Roxanne asked incredulously.

"Brookline, specifically, for the firm Schwartz, Marbles and Henderson, or something like that," Officer Ramirez said.

"Do you mean Schwartz, Henley and Maples?" Roxanne asked.

"Yeah, that could be it, why?"

"They're only one of the best law firms in New England! A friend of mine hoped to intern there when he got out of law school but didn't get picked. Are you sure this is the same Mr. Rand?"

"All indications are that it is the same person," Officer Cellucci said.

Eventually, Officers Cellucci and Ramirez stuck their heads through the door and Daria said it was time for them to leave. They wished Robert and Tiffany a speedy recovery, said that they'd check in with them from time to time, said goodbye to everyone and were gone. Zeke's parents came into the room and his mom took a chair while his dad leaned against a windowsill.

Betty asked Zeke's parents how things were at home with all of the crazy events of the last few days. Roxanne relaxed a little and talked about her endless questions from her friends and colleagues about her son's adventure and a stream of phone calls from reporters wanting to talk now about both the hobo trip and the hobo rescue.

"Hopefully, this will die down soon and we can all go back to our normal lives," she said.

"That's been my experience, too," Andrew added. "We're trying our best to shield Zeke from all of this attention but it's been a pretty big challenge."

"Well, he is a pretty special kid, wouldn't you say?" Betty asked.

"That's for sure!" both parents said at the same time and everyone had a little chuckle.

A nurse walked into the room and went over to check on her two patients. She said it was time for their meds and asked if there was anything that either of them needed.

"Just some time to heal up and get the hell outta Dodge," Bix said loudly and with a grimaced laugh.

"I think it's time for you folks to get some rest. Maybe it would be a good idea if all of your visitors wrapped things up here and gave you some quiet time. It's been a busy day for all of you, from what I've heard and seen on the news. And you, Mr. Zeke Wappinger, you are quite a young man. Your parents must be really proud of you," the nurse said kindly while giving Bix and Betty small plastic cups containing a few pills.

Within moments of taking their pain medication, Bix and Betty quickly slipped into semi-consciousness. As he was fading out, Bix made Zeke promise to come back for another visit when they were more alert.

Betty's last words were, "We love you Frankie! See you at the jungle!" Bix managed to say "Happy rails!" before falling asleep.

Out in the hallway, the Wappingers had a brief chat with the physician-on-duty who had just arrived on the floor to make her rounds. She impressed upon them how badly injured her patients were but considering what they had been through, she was surprised that they were in good enough shape to be moved out of the ICU. In addition to the visible injuries, she told them that Ms. Spears had some broken ribs and possibly a punctured lung while Mr. Rand had a fractured leg and a broken collarbone but that his internal injuries were relatively minor.

"I'm pretty certain they'll make a full recovery," she said, "but it's going to take some time. Their hobo days might just have to be over because they'll need a bunch of physical therapy once their contusions and broken bones heal."

"What will happen to them when they get released from the hospital?" Zeke asked.

"Not sure about that," the doctor said. "They'll be able to go wherever they want and my guess is that they'll go back to being hobos since that's the only life they seem to know."

"Zeke, the police ran a background check on them and found out that Mr. Rand used to be a lawyer in Massachusetts. I find that hard to believe. Did you know anything about that?" Roxanne asked.

"Absolutely!" Zeke responded. "In a town he called Brooklyn or Brookfield or something like that, near Boston. He told me all about when he worked there and how the people there set him up on some phony charges to take the rap for something illegal that one of the company's owners did. He was totally screwed out of his job, his wife and all of his belongings and became a hobo after that."

"Zeke, honey, your language!" Roxanne admonished. "I'm going to have to look into that one. It sounds too unbelievable."

"It's true, I'm sure. Bix and Betty are completely honest people. If Bix said he was a lawyer once, I'm sure he was. You'll see when you get to know them. Doctor, have you tried talking to them about how they ended up getting swept up in the flood?"

"No, not yet. You see what condition they're in. I haven't had much of a chance to talk to them yet although I'm pretty sure the police have already asked about those circumstances. I think they'll need a few more days to recover to the point where we'll be able to have a clear conversation," she said.

DAVID W. GOODWIN

Andrew thanked the doctor and the attending nurse that was over at the station filling out some paperwork and left the hospital with his family. They had a somber ride back home to Belén, mostly because Zeke fell asleep in the backseat of Andrew's Escape. Roxanne was especially distant and in her own world while Andrew drove them home. When he pulled onto Ladera Drive, Roxanne spoke her only words for the entire drive, "Schwartz, Henley and Maples?"

The next few days were close to business-as-usual for Andrew and Roxanne. Both put in their usual ten hour days at their respective offices but Andrew checked in with Zeke every two or three hours to see what he was up to. Pamela had previously agreed to be with him for the remainder of the week to supervise his activities until his soccer camp started the following week. Mostly, Zeke wanted to hang out at the Presbyterian Hospital in Albuquerque with Bix Pickles and Burrito Betty, but Pamela was under strict orders not to take him there. Instead, he and Warren spent most of the next few days playing catch, riding their bikes around, hanging out in the pool, and on Friday afternoon, got up the courage to ask Pamela to join them for a ride down to the hobo jungle to see what it looked like.

The sun had been out now for all of Thursday and Friday, allowing the desert soils to absorb the entire deluge pretty quickly and the floodwaters of the creeks, ditches and river were slowly receding. The National Guard had wrapped up their work in town and now concentrated on clearing roads and trails along the river and its various tributaries. Within a week, after the state of emergency was lifted, they would disappear, like the floodwaters. As the two bicycling boys and Pamela approached the recently muddy floodplain trails that led down to the former location of the hobo jungle, they were surprised to see how dry the landscape had become. What was immediately different was all of the vegetation and material that was stacked up in discreet piles parallel to the river, in random patterns. When they climbed over the first mound they encountered, they could see more parallel bands of material, all the way to the current water's edge. Pamela warned them to be extra careful as they climbed over each band of riverside accumulation.

By the time they made it down to the area that Warren thought was the spot where the jungle had been, it was subject to a rather spirited debate about if they were actually there or not. He was certain they were standing right near the spot, even though he said the exact spot was about ten feet out and still under some water. Zeke thought the spot was further downstream, closer to the bridge on East River Road while Pamela argued that it was a bit more upstream. They walked up and down the edge of the turbid water looking for any clues that might be helpful when Warren spotted something.

"Look, Zekeballs, over there! See on those trees! Ropes, from the two tarps!"

Sure enough, at the edge of the Rio Grande, still under four or six inches of water, were the trees that once supported the two blue tarps. They saw the frayed ends of ropes hanging from the trees at about the right height and, from their collective memories of what the place once looked like, agreed that this was indeed the right spot. The ropes were the only indication that this had been their campsite since everything they remembered was either still under water or had been swept completely away.

"Let's walk downstream a little to see if we can find anything from their camp," Pamela suggested after a moment's hesitation, worried that perhaps this might not be such a good idea. She wasn't absolutely certain if Zeke's parents would be upset if they knew they were down here but on the other hand, they didn't say anything specifically prohibiting it - only about not going to the hospital.

The bands of junk along the river were arranged such that it was pretty easy to walk between them, following the general course of the river. The areas between the piles were mostly scoured clean so they could walk downstream without too much effort. The material consisted mostly of natural vegetation, whole trees, branches and shrubs but there was also a fair amount of human-made material mixed in like lumber, garbage, clothing, small appliances, a few bikes, roofing, carpet remnants, chunks of concrete and asphalt - pretty much anything that was unfortunate enough to be in the hundred-year floodplain when the deluge came. The searchers glanced at the piles, looking for any clues and in some ways, afraid of what they might find.

"What if we saw Jazzy Jugs or Roadkill in one of these piles, our just one of their heads or a leg," Warren said with a shudder which freaked all three of them out. "Zekeballs, maybe we shouldn't be doing this."

"No, I think we do," Zeke said. "I'd imagine that Bullet or some other police dog might have already been down here looking for people or body parts. I saw on the news last night about the searching they were doing, including those army-looking dudes driving around in tanks and

Hummers. Some of them had dogs with them and they were running around sniffing their heads off."

Warren took that image and it gave him the idea to pretend to be a dog, running around helter-skelter, wagging his imaginary tail, going up to each pile and sniffing like a possessed fiend. He was doing such a great job of it that Zeke and Pamela both started laughing. This egged Warren on even more and he started rolling in the sand on his back like he was a dog rolling in some sort of pungent treasure. Zeke picked up a stick and threw it over a low debris pile and told Warren to go fetch. Warren started barking and howling and, on all fours, ran around the pile and disappeared from sight.

"That friend of yours is pretty funny, Zeke," Pamela observed.

Warren stopped making doggie sounds and Zeke wondered why he had given up on the dog imitation and hadn't returned with the stick. He and Pamela continued walking downstream a little while longer until they had cleared the pile that Warren was behind. Zeke called out, "here doggie, come here, doggie!"

"Come here you guys, quick!" Warren's little voice yelled out and he sounded very serious.

As Zeke rounded the pile, he saw Warren kneeling on the sand and he was white as a ghost, unable to move or speak. Instead, he pointed to a spot about ten yards away. It looked like a naked pair of legs stuck into the deep sand. The legs formed a roughly shaped "V" as both knees were bent at slightly different angles, kind of like something you'd see on a rabbit with two floppy ears.

"Boys, don't go near it. We need to call the police!" Pamela cried out, clearly startled and scared out of her wits.

"Do you think it's a dead person?" Zeke asked.

"What else would it be?" Warren responded.

"I don't know, it doesn't look quite right to be a person," Zeke said tentatively.

"Zeke, no, don't go near it!" Pamela commanded.

Zeke inched closer to the legs while Warren walked closely behind him, making sure his line of sight was always blocked by Zeke's body. Pamela kept calling out for him to stay away but the attraction of such a thing was too great for a boy with Zeke's level of natural curiosity. When he was finally right next to them, he grabbed both legs by the ankles, gave them a big yank and pulled the bottom half of a mannequin out of the sand with hardly any resistance but the motion of pulling out something that he expected to be a lot harder, sent him falling over backwards, landing right on top of Warren with the bottom half of a bisected mannequin landing on top of both of them. This set the two boys off laughing yet again, wet-your-pants, rolling-in-the-aisles sort of laughing, working their way into hysterics with what just happened and the relief they felt at finding what they did. Pamela came over, clearly relieved as well, and let her laughter join the boys. It helped a lot to dissipate everyone's tension.

"I could tell that it wasn't a real person when I got close to it," Zeke said in his defense.

"You boys are crazy!" Pamela said once they had laughed themselves out. "I think it's time to get out of here and go home to get something to eat. What do you say?"

They retraced their steps, hopped back on their bikes and rode the two miles back to Zeke's house. The boys hung out in Zeke's room for a while and told six-year-old boy stories about what just happened, eventually joining Pamela in the kitchen where she offered to make them a snack. Zeke noticed that his cellphone was lying on the counter, right where he left it hours ago, and he checked for messages. Both of his parents had left voicemail messages and both were just checking in to find out what he was doing this afternoon. His dad said he'd try to be home around five while his mom told him that it wouldn't be until seven or so, to make up for time she took off yesterday.

The hobos were still recovering in the hospital. It wasn't clear how long they'd be there. Zeke had only seen them, ever so briefly, on Tuesday night and here it was Thursday already. He decided to call his dad and ask him if the two of them could go for a visit tonight.

"Zeke, you know that's a ton of driving. I'd have to go from Albuquerque, back home to get you, then back to Albuquerque and then home again. I know you're anxious to see your pals but can't you wait until the weekend? I promise we'll go then."

Zeke was having this phone chat in the kitchen and both Warren and Pamela could clearly hear his side of the conversation. Pamela started making time out signals so Zeke asked his dad to hold on a second.

"Mike and I are going out to dinner tonight in Albuquerque and could drop you off at the hospital around six, if that helps," she said.

"Dad, excellent news!"

"Yes, I heard Pamela's offer. Tell her that's very kind of her but I'm not sure that would work out."

"What do you mean? That way, you could work a little later and wouldn't have to drive around so much. C'mon Dad, say yes! It's a perfect idea. Mom's not getting home until seven, probably later if I know her."

"Yeah, you're probably right about that. My little Devil Boy! Always working some sort of scheme. Okay, tell Pamela that we'll cover her time and expenses and thank her for offering. I'll meet you at the hospital entrance at six o'clock, okay?"

"Okay, Dad, thanks, see you then! Maybe if you bring some toadskins, we could go out for dinner afterwards."

"Toadskins? Oh right, money. Yes, honey, I'll be sure to bring some toadskins."

Warren said it was time for him to go home. Zeke walked him outside to his bike and heard Warren bark twice as he rode away down the driveway. Pamela called her boyfriend to tell him about their slight change in plan, which was fine with him. He was a very adaptable and agreeable sort of person - one of the top ten best characteristics he possessed, according to Pamela. Zeke called his mom's phone and left her a message telling her about his plan to visit the hospital tonight. "Let me know if you want to join us, Mom." He also called the hospital to check on the status of his friends and to give them some warning that they'd be coming by for a visit around six. The phone rang about ten times before someone picked up.

"Room 302," an unfamiliar voice answered.

"Hi, this is Zeke Wappinger. I'm calling to talk to Mr. Rand or Miss Spears. Are they there?"

"They're both asleep at the moment. Can I leave them a message?"

"Sure, tell them that me and my dad are coming for a visit tonight around six, okay? Do you think they'll be awake then?"

"Probably, wait, let me check their chart. Um, hmm, yeah, okay, so they were given their last meds at noon and don't get their next round until seven tonight. Yes, I think they'll both be awake soon."

"Okay, thanks, bye."

Zeke had a little over an hour before he was going to drive up to the hospital with Pamela and her boyfriend. He decided to call Officer Cellucci and ask her if there had been any news on the two missing hobos, Jazzy Jugs and Roadkill. She had given Zeke her Belén Police Department business card and had written her private cellphone number on the back when she came over for their press statement last Sunday afternoon, telling him to feel free to call her if he had any questions or even if he just needed to talk. This would certainly qualify for that, he surmised.

"Hi, this is Daria."

"Hi, Daria, this is Zeke Wappinger."

"Zeke! My bud! How are you doing?"

"Pretty good. I'm calling to ask you something and I hope it's okay to be calling you."

"Absolutely! That's why I gave you my number. What's up?"

"Well, Warren and Pamela and me were down by the river today, looking for any evidence of the hobo jungle and maybe even of Jazzy Jugs or Roadkill. We didn't find anything but me and my dad are going to the hospital tonight to see Bix and Betty and I was wondering if there was any news about them, I mean, Jazzy and Roadkill."

"Not that I've heard about. Sorry, I know how worried you are about them. We're continuing our searching and you know that the National Guard is helping too. Nobody found any evidence of them and there's been nothing that's come in over our network so I'm afraid I don't have any news for you. I'm really sorry, Zeke. You're such a fine boy with a heart of gold, so sweet and caring - I wish there were grown up men like you out there. You have the kindest, most innocent and gentle heart of any person I've ever met. If I thought I could help you in any way, I would in a heartbeat. You know that, right?"

"I do."

"Listen, I need to go now but give my regards to Robert and Tiffany. I know they look to be in pretty bad shape right now but I guarantee they'll be a whole lot better in a week or two. Bye, sweetie."

"Bye Daria, and thanks for everything."

Zeke spent the rest of his afternoon just lying on his bed, staring at his ceiling and thinking back on the last few days. He thought about the hobos, of course, and of the Gambles, the priest and the two movers. Then there were the police officers he met along the way and the people from the press. His thoughts then turned to his mother and father and he knew that they loved him. His father seemed to be acting differently and making more time in his busy life for him but he wasn't so sure about his mom. She talked like she was going to make some changes and try to put more time into being a family but so far, it wasn't that different from before he ran away. What would it take for her to see things differently? It was then that he hatched a plan and it was so obvious, he couldn't believe that it took him this long to think of it. This gave him such a peaceful feeling that the next thing he knew, Pamela was sitting on his bed saying it was time to get up and drive to the hospital.

Pamela's boyfriend, Mike, was a nice enough guy and he had a big car with a big engine and he liked to drive fast. He was a cyclist too, like Pamela, and they trained together a lot for weekend road and mountain bike races. He drove his car like he was in a bike race, always looking for a way to get around the person in front or to slot in behind someone to draft for a moment and then put in a big push to slingshot around them. Bicycle racing is all about the judicious use of one's limited amount of energy and the crafty use of strategy to be the first one across the finish line. When these principles were applied to driving, however, it was mostly a waste of gas and Pamela was constantly telling him to drive more slowly and consistently and "maybe use cruise control." Zeke, on the other hand, loved driving with Mike because it became more of an experience. His dad was a careful, law-abiding driver while his mom was closer to Mike's style, but when Zeke was in the car with her, she tried to set a good example.

Mike's car happened to follow Andrew's car into the hospital parking lot so Zeke just hopped out, said goodbye to Pamela and thanked Mike for the ride. He then walked over to meet his dad as he was getting out of his car.

"Hey, old man!" Zeke said, which was kind of funny since he'd never used that expression with his dad before.

"Old man? Where did that one come from, Devil Boy?"

"I just thought it was funny. That's what Mike calls his dad."

"Interesting! How was your day, Zeke?" Andrew asked as they started walking towards the automatic doors of the hospital.

"Kind of crazy. Pamela took Warren and me for a bike ride down near the river today to see how things looked and as we were walking along by all the junk from the flooding, Warren was pretending to be a dog and I threw a stick for him and he didn't come back so I went around the junk pile to find him and Warren was all freaking out so I went over to look and he thought it was a naked dead person buried upside down in the sand with just their legs sticking out and then I went over and pulled the legs out and it was just a dummy and I fell on top of Warren and the dummy fell on top of both of us and Pamela screamed and then we all just laughed for about an hour or two. It was really fun!"

"Good heavens! That sounds nuts!" Andrew said as they entered the hospital and told the receptionist who they were and where they were heading. "Room 302, right?"

When they got to the right room, Zeke did a quick little knuckle wrap on the door to give his hobo pals a moment's notice before they walked in. He was pleasantly surprised to see that both Bix and Betty were wide-awake, seemed to be in good spirits and were eating their dinner.

"Hey, it's Zeke Wappinger!" Bix cried out.

"Captain Bix! How are you doing?"

"Frankie! Great to see you! Hi Mr. Wappinger!" Burrito Betty said.

"Hi Tiffany, or do you prefer Betty?" Andrew responded. "I much prefer Andrew to Mr. Wappinger, please, let's not be so formal, okay?"

"That works for me, Andrew. Either Tiffany or Betty are fine, but I guess I'd prefer Betty. I feel more like Betty, at the moment at least."

"You both are looking a lot better than two days ago," Zeke observed. "How are you feeling?"

"Yes, quite a bit better, actually," Betty said, "and I think Bix is, too. Right, honey?"

"Yep, we'll be out ridin' the rails in no time. Well, maybe we've got some more recovery ahead of us but they told me they're gonna get me out of traction tomorrow and then I can get up and start learnin' how to use those crutches you see over in the corner. Guess its gonna be a while before I can flip a one-eyed bandit or anything like that, especially on the fly."

"Bix, I was kind of hoping that your days of being a hobo might have come to an end anyway so maybe this would be a good time to think about doing other things," Zeke suggested gently.

"Like what? Bein' a hobo is about all I know how to do."

"You were a lawyer once, right?"

"Yep, and look where it got me! Say, why don't you two men pull up some chairs and make yourselves a bit more comfortable. We can talk about that sort of stuff later."

Andrew got a chair from the corner, put it between the two hobo's beds and offered it to his son. He then grabbed another one from Betty's corner and positioned it so the four of them could all see each other.

"Just as long as we actually do talk about it later. I've got some ideas about that," Zeke said, "Right now, however, I'm really anxious to hear about what happened to you and Betty the night the floods came and washed you away. What do you remember? Warren and Pamela and me were down there today and your hobo jungle is still under water with no signs of anything you left there. What happened?"

"Well, Frankie, we don't really have a lot of details to tell you but I'm going to lay it all out for you as best as I can remember. I hope you don't mind, Andrew, if I tell you son here the entire truth because that's just sort of my way anyway."

"No, Betty, that's fine unless you were doing something illegal or immoral that I wouldn't want my son to hear about," Andrew said tentatively.

"No, other than camping illegally, I don't think so. The story does involve some drinking so I just want to warn you in case you'd rather me not tell that part of the story."

"Fair enough. I think Zeke is mature enough to handle that. Go ahead," Andrew responded.

"Okay then, here goes. Bix, honey, you feel free to add any details you think are important or if I miss anything," Betty started and Bix nodded his head. "We've had to tell this story to the police a few times already. So, a few days ago, you and your friend, Wally is it?"

"Warren."

"Right, you and your friend Warren rode your bikes right smack dab into our jungle the same afternoon that the storm began, right? You remember that, don't you?"

"Yes, and it was looking bad so you told us to go ride home before the rain started, which we did," Zeke said, wanting his father to see that he could be an obedient kid and Betty could be a responsible adult.

"Right, so the four of us old friends, me, Bix, Jazzy Jugs O'Reilly and Roadkill Ronnie - we hadn't seen them in a long time - went back to our little fire, heated up some food that we brought with us and that you gave us, and were passing around a bottle or two of some hooch. The rain had been falling for a while and by the time it was dark, it was falling pretty hard. We had moved our chairs under the tarps early on and the two boys, Bix and Roadkill, managed to move the fire closer to our shelter, using a few big branches, so we could continue to eat and drink and be close to the flames. We were kind of celebrating our little reunion so we broke out another bottle or two and before you knew it, we were all out for the count. I remember proning out on a nice rubber air mattress under the tarp that Jazzy had scrounged somewhere. In fact, each one of us had an air mattress and it was really cozy and comfortable. They even had a few extra blankets. The next thing I remember, it's the morning of the next day sometime and I'm holding onto a log in the middle of a raging river and Bix here has his arm around me and he's holding both of us on this log and we're shivering our asses off, pardon me, Frankie, we're shivering our butts off. Anyway, there's junk battering into us from all sides and we're absolutely getting hammered by the water and other logs and dead floating cows and all sorts of crap and I keep spitting out water because it's hard to breathe when your head keeps going under water and then we finally get caught up on a huge pile of other stuff down near that railroad bridge. There's more stuff ramming into us from behind and we got trapped in it all and couldn't get out. We were both so tired and cold at this point I just figured that this was the end of the line and we were just going to probably cash it in, right then and there. And then we were rescued by you and Andrew and that woman police officer and that big guy with the yellow Jeep. It was truly a miracle!"

"That must have been one hell of a river ride!" Andrew exclaimed. "I can't believe anyone survived such an ordeal!"

"Maybe the fact that we were so elevated, and I mean elevated by the booze, not by the terrain, in some ways might have helped us," Captain Bix Pickles Haskell offered in their defense. "But I'm wonderin' if we hadn't been havin' such a big party with our pals, if we'd a had enough sense to get outta the rain, so to speak, and maybe even move to higher ground, we might have avoided takin' a ride on the log plume ride from hell. So Freddie, let that be a lesson to you. Don't ever go campin' in a floodplain durin' a huge storm! Very dangerous! Oh, and don't drink like fish like we was doin'."

"Do you remember any more details, Bix?" Betty asked.

"No, that's a purty good description. I think those air mattress might of actually kept us afloat and out of the water until we were out in the river and rocketin' downstream. Maybe if it hadn't a been for them, we might have woken up when the water was lappin' in our faces and had enough sense to move out of the flood. Crazy thing!"

"Bix, Betty, I hope you don't mind me saying so, but the crazy thing is that given your lifestyle and all the drinking and living out in the open and the food you must eat, it's remarkable that you're even alive," Andrew said.

"Hard to argue, Andrew. Maybe this is a sign to me and the Princess that it's time to change our ways. To tell you the truth, I'm getting kinda old for this sort of stuff. Betty's been after me for a while to settle down somewhere and now that our injuries are gonna prevent us from bein' 'bos, for a while anyway, maybe we could give it some thought."

"Oh Bix, I think I'm finally ready to give it a try. Little Frankie here tried to guess my age the other day and he was off by quite a bit and what girl wants to look a lot older than what she really is?"

"I'm sorry Burrito Betty, but I was just trying to make an honest guess."

"No, sweetie, you did the right thing. I don't get a chance too often to look at myself in a mirror so maybe it's time to make some changes."

"Where do you two think you'll go when they let you out of here?" Andrew asked.

"Me and Betty talked some about goin' out to the coast to help a friend startin' up a food truck," Bix said while Betty gave him a sideways glance with her eyebrows raised.

"You know, after all you and Betty and Zeke have been through in the last week, I'm beginning to think that all of these adventures might just have happened for a reason. I know that Zeke wants you to come live with us and I see how much you all care for each other but the logistics of such a thing might be a bit too much for us, especially Zeke's mom. Maybe we could help find you a place to stay for a while until you're all healed up, like at a local shelter or something. I'm sure Belén has some places like that," Andrew said, trying to divert Zeke's enthusiasm a bit.

"Dad, we could talk Mom into having them come live with us! I'm sure she would eventually say yes!" Zeke exclaimed.

"Zeke, I appreciate your idea but I'm thinkin' that might be a purty hard sell with your mom," Bix said. "Betty and me wouldn't want to impose on your family. But, sadly, the bottom line for us is that we really don't have anyplace else to go right now. The doctor was talkin' about us being released from here in a few days so if you can help us find a shelter or something, that would be much appreciated. Just on a temporary basis though."

"Dad, listen to this idea. If Bix and Betty came to live with us, me and Pamela could help to take care of them and I wouldn't have to spend the entire summer going to camps. That would be so cool! Think of all the great things we could do, all of us, together!"

"The idea certainly has its merits, I agree, but why don't we slow down and we just take things a day at a time, Devil Boy. Nobody wants to see your friends thrown out onto the streets, especially considering all they've been through lately, not even your mom, trust me. We'll find a way to help them, don't you worry, honey," Andrew said, trying to reassure his son without upsetting him or making the hobos feel too uncomfortable.

"But Dad, we've got an entire apartment in the basement with it's own kitchen, bathroom and bedroom. It would be perfect for them!"

"Zeke, I hear you but let's talk about this later, with your mom. If anything like this is going to happen, it's going to have to be her idea," Andrew said, hoping to bring some closure to the discussion.

CHAPTER 19

I T TOOK ANDREW a few days to even lay the foundation for discussing the topic with Roxanne. She ended up putting in a full day at her office on Saturday to catch up on things that had accumulated up since she had taken parts of a few days off when Zeke was busy being a hobo fugitive from justice and then to be with him for a few moments here and there when he was busy saving the lives of two hobos. By dinner time on Saturday night, the Wappinger's traditional time to go out for a meal at a nice restaurant together, Roxanne arrived home around five-thirty and said that all she really wanted to do was take a hot bath, have a glass or two of wine and settle into the couch for the night, suggesting they get something delivered. She really didn't care what it was as long as it was something Zeke would eat. Zeke saw the evening as an opportunity to have the discussion with his mom about the hobos coming to live with them so he asked his dad to join him for a private meeting in the basement while his mom delighted in the Jacuzzi.

"So Dad, here's how I see it. First, we've got to get Mom in a really good mood. That's where the wine will come in and I think you and me should cook something really awesome for dinner; something she really likes, and we'll surprise her royally with our skills. Second, we talk about Bix and Betty and both say how awesome they are. This will be especially important coming from you because she already knows that's how I feel about them."

"I can do that but you're getting way ahead of yourself here. I'm not convinced myself that having them come live with us is a good idea. However, I have to admit that as I'm getting to know them a little better, I'm feeling a pretty strong connection with them, especially Captain Haskell. It's kind of strange."

"Great, Dad! I had the feeling that you'd see that this was a good idea. So the next thing we need to do is talk about what their future holds for them if they're just sent back out to be hobos again and how awful that would be at this point in their lives, especially since they're going to need some help doing things until they get all healed up. Finally, we need to talk about the kinds of things they're good at. Mom has to be the one to come to the conclusion that they should move in with us, like you said at the hospital, and we act like we hadn't thought about it before and pretend to give the idea some thought before agreeing with her."

"What kinds of things *are* they good at?" Andrew asked, aware of Zeke's skills manipulating him to sympathize more with his side of the argument, even though he was beginning to realize that he was probably right.

"Oh, a ton of things. The Stinkbomb used to be a lawyer, you know that already. He's a Boston bum and was a mouthpiece. They're great campers and know how to spear biscuits and how to avoid the pussy footers and use a number ten gunboat can and chuck a dummy and hunt a wampus, you know, cool things like that. They're not cabbage heads, Dad, and Bix ain't no wolf! Both of them are really smart people."

Andrew was highly entertained by his son's display of his newfound hobo lingo and just let him bandy about as long as he wanted and began laughing as his son got deeper into his description. Andrew then asked Zeke what meal they should make.

"You know, Dad! What's her favorite food in the entire world?"

"Same as mine. You know, I think this is a great idea. Let's quickly run out and get what we need. I'll go tell Mom that we'll be out for a short while. I'll take her in a glass of wine and light some candles first, suggest she take a really long soak and then we'll go shopping."

Andrew set the dinner table like he was trying to woo her, poured a glass of wine and took it into her, along with some candles. He told her to take her time because they'd be cooking dinner tonight but first had to go out for a few items.

"Now that's more like it. I could get used to this sort of treatment," Roxanne said, clearly unused to such pampering.

Andrew drove Roxanne's little Mazda to the Krogers on North Main Street because it was such a fun car to drive when it was only two of them. Zeke went right over to the fish counter and picked out the three nicest looking lobsters he could find from the tank and had them cooked while he and his dad stocked up on all of the other ingredients they needed to a special meal to set the proper tone for the evening, including another bottle of wine. They were home and working in the kitchen before Roxanne had even gotten out of the large tub. Andrew went in to fill up her voluminous wine glass, which was almost empty. This brought

DAVID W. GOODWIN

another smile to her face, especially when she was told that dinner would be served in about fifteen minutes.

By the time all the preparations were set, Roxanne came into the wonderfully decorated dining room in her white silk robe, looking like a lobster herself from the Jacuzzi and from a couple of glasses of wine. The table was neatly set and there were covered dishes containing their meal - everything except the main course.

"This is very nice of you boys. It kind of makes me wonder what's going on around here."

"Nothing out of the ordinary, dear, we just wanted to make the night special for you. It's been a tough week for all of us, especially your son, the international six-year-old boy of mystery and saver of the downtrodden and the nearly drowned. We're celebrating him, you, me, our family - the works. He came up with the idea for tonight's menu," Andrew said as he assisted Roxanne into her seat and topped off her wine glass. "Mr. Devil Boy, if you would please do the honors and present the pièce de résistance."

Zeke, wearing one of his mom's barely used aprons, went into the kitchen and pulled the platter out of the warm oven containing the three beautiful red crustaceans. It was all he could do to get his hands to reach the two ends of the tray but he managed to deliver them safely to the trivets that Andrew had set up on their dark cherry Queen Anne table. Roxanne oooh'ed and aaah'ed at the sight of the lobsters and, combined with the wine, the soak and the attention, was already in a fabulous mood.

"Oh my! Lobsters! What a treat! I feel like a princess!"

Andrew uncovered the dishes containing corn-on-the-cob, the microwaved potatoes and the Kroger deli-prepared cole slaw, and the Wappingers dug into the feast with gusto. The big glass bowl in the center of the table began to fill up with lobster shells, legs and three heads. Andrew, being from New England, ate the green tomalley from all three lobsters since Zeke and his mom wouldn't touch it. Roxanne, being a roe connoisseur, gladly ate the red eggs from the female that Zeke got. Now that she was in a really good mood and as the feast was finishing up, Zeke skillfully approached the second step of their plan.

"Mom, you know that Dad and me visited Bix and Betty at the hospital a few days ago, right?"

"Yes, we haven't had a chance to talk much about them lately. How are those hobos doing?"

"That's because you've been working so many hours lately," Andrew stated, trying to make it sound more like sympathy than an indictment. "They're pretty interesting people once you get over their rough exterior."

"You know, I still can't get over the fact that Mr. Rand worked at Schwartz, Henley and Maples. I had Molly do some background research on your hobo friend, Zeke, and sure enough, his story checks out. I won't get into the details but it certainly seemed plausible that he got railroaded, literally and figuratively, if you'll pardon my unintentional pun. Kind of makes me feel sorry for the old man."

"And I didn't even tell you Burrito Betty's story about being raised in an orphanage and being adopted by some people that made her join their dognapping ring at a young age! She's such a nice lady, Mom, I think she's somewhere around your age. I'll bet if you two were switched at birth, there'd be a good chance that she would be a big important lawyer like you and you might have become a hobo," Zeke hypothesized.

"First of all, she looks a lot older than me, and I mean a lot, and second, I seriously doubt there are any set of circumstances that would have resulted in me becoming a dirty, drunken hobo," Roxanne said indignantly.

"Mom, you saw *Trading Places*. It could happen to anyone," Zeke argued.

"Yes, honey, I suppose it's possible," Roxanne admitted with a little laugh. "Since you put it that way."

"Zeke and I spent a good hour, hour and a half with them Thursday night. It was really an amazing time, really fun. I thoroughly enjoyed my time with them. But pretty soon, they're going to be released from the hospital and I'm not quite sure what's going to happen to them. As far as the police know, they don't have any family to take care of them and they certainly can't go back to being hobos since Mr. Rand will be on crutches for a few months. Ms. Spears's arm is in a full cast since it broke in more than a few places so she'll be hobbled for a while, too. Plus, the hospital administrators told me that they don't have any insurance or really any money to speak of."

"What a surprise! Don't they have an account in the First National Hobo Bank of America?" Roxanne asked facetiously.

"Roxanne, you're sounding a little callous, don't you think? These are good people who just might be responsible for saving the life of our son and, due to circumstances somewhat beyond their control, ended

DAVID W. GOODWIN

up homeless and penniless and yet, have found a way to make a life for themselves."

"I'm sorry, Andrew, I wasn't trying to sound mean, really. I'm still struggling with accepting them as saints considering some of the life choices they've made. I mean, look at the way they live. They eat out of dumpsters, or live off handouts or eat at soup kitchens, they've got a serious drinking problem, and I mean serious. I'm sure they're alcoholics."

"I think that's the part you're missing. I'm not sure they've actually made all of these choices. Even the other day, both of them were talking about maybe settling down somewhere and getting jobs and trying to integrate back into normal society. This is a pretty big step for someone like Mr. Rand, who's been a homeless hobo now for a long time, maybe twenty or twenty-five years."

"And Mom, they have a lot of skills that could get them good jobs."

"Like?" Roxanne asked.

"They're great with kids. You know that Bix was a lawyer and he's pretty smart. He also told me that he's been a carpenter, a truck driver, I think he said he was a jack-in-the-box for trades, or something."

"And Ms. Spears?" Roxanne asked with a slight chortle.

"She was a teacher and a dancer, I think is what she told me. She's also been a cook."

"Sounds like the kind of people who could be a big help to us," Roxanne said sarcastically.

"Mom, that's interesting that you say that. I hadn't thought of that," Zeke said, entirely missing his mom's tone.

"You're in on this too, aren't you Andrew? Why don't you two just come out and say it. You want them to move in here, maybe even into our empty downstairs apartment, perhaps? C'mon, guys, the wine, the candles, the lobster, I got it a while ago. Don't get me wrong, this whole setup was a great idea and a great treat that I really appreciate. I'll admit that your idea has some virtues but do you really think it's a good idea to take two badly injured homeless people into our house who we don't even know and try to nurse them back to health and reform them? I don't have time for that, your father doesn't have time for that and Zeke, you're a six-year-old kid who should be spending his summer playing with friends, not taking care of some alcoholic hobos, plus, I really don't think I want them living in my house!"

"But Mom, it's a great idea! I've got the whole summer off and to tell you the truth, I don't really want to go to all those camps anyway.

Pamela's got another month before her real job begins and she could be here with me for some of that time. The two of us could take care of them until they get better. Once they're healed, there are a million things they could do. Mom, I'll bet Bix could help you with your job since he was a pretty sharp lawyer once and then maybe you wouldn't have to work so much. Betty could help around the house with cooking and cleaning maybe, and lots of other things, oh yeah, like shopping and maybe even help Dad with the yardwork and garden. They could both get their driver's licenses and take me places. It could be super-awesome! We could be one big happy family!"

"I know, sweetie, I know you feel that way and it is really, really sweet of you. You are such a sensitive and caring person. I love that about you, but this is something your father and I need to discuss. I think our lives are just a bit too busy and complicated at the moment to take on a project like this."

"You know, Roxy, Zeke actually raises some very good points. We hardly have time to do the kinds of things we want to do around here and it's kind of ironic that Mr. Rand and Ms. Spears have some of the skills and experiences that we don't, but more importantly, they have time and lots of it. Like Zeke says, it might even be a way for us to get more time to be a family. I just get a good solid feeling from both of them. They just seem like good, honest people and I find myself liking them both, a lot. It's kind of weird, considering how different they are from us."

"They are certainly different from us, I'll grant you that. Listen, guys, I'm not going to say definitely no to the idea right now. Let me mull it over for a day or two but I have to be honest with you, even though your crazy plan has its merits, I'm definitely thinking that it's a bad idea. I'm sorry, big honey and little honey, I just think it wouldn't work out the way you are picturing it but I'll try to keep an open mind. Let's talk more about it later. Say, did you guys by chance get a dessert?"

Zeke was deflated. Even through his favorite dessert of Boston cream pie, he adamantly maintained his hurt and angry disposition. Why couldn't his mom set aside her attitude for a few minutes and see what a great idea this was? It was the absolute perfect solution to almost every problem they had. They hardly ever had time to go shopping or to cook or clean or work in the yard or work in the garden or work on their house. They had to hire people to come in and do most of this stuff. Plus, Bix Pickles was probably a really great lawyer in his day, Zeke sensed, and could help his mom on some of her cases. Plus, they could

DAVID W. GOODWIN

drive him around which would free up even more time - maybe so much time that they could actually hang out together and do family stuff. The shortsightedness of his mom made his blood boil.

"Zeke, Zeke, don't you hear that?" Roxanne said numerous times while looking at her son who was completely glazed over from being inside his own anger.

"What?" he eventually said through the thick haze of disbelief and disappointment.

"Your cellphone's ringing, honey," Andrew said, trying to sound cheerful.

Zeke got up from dessert and walked over to the hallway table where he kept his phone when he was in the house and noticed that it was Daria Cellucci calling.

"Hi Officer Cellucci, I mean Daria. How are you?"

"Hi Zeke! I'm great. How are things going?"

"Alright. My dad and me have gone to visit Bix and Betty twice now and they're doing pretty good but I'm worried about what's going to happen to them when they get released from the hospital sometime next week. We're trying to talk my mom into having them move in with us because it would be a perfect thing to do but she doesn't want them to live here for some reason."

"I didn't say that, Zeke. I said I would think about it," Roxanne yelled from the dining room table.

"Yeah, I could see where that might cause a little tension with your parents. That's a pretty big step for everyone if you went through with it. I could understand the hesitation your mom might be feeling. Maybe we could all get together and talk about it sometime, like, maybe tomorrow. Listen, Zeke, that's why I'm calling. I've got five tickets for tomorrows Isotope game, box seats in the VIP section; right behind the dugout for you, your parents, your friend Warren and his dad, if you're interested. It's a one o'clock game. You'd be my guest and we could go into the clubhouse afterwards and meet the team if you'd like."

"Mom, Dad! Daria is inviting all of us and Warren and his dad to be her guest at the Isotopes game tomorrow. Can we go? Please? It would be way rad! She got box seats for us!"

"That's so nice of her," Andrew said. "What about you honey? Want to go?"

"Maybe she'll let you sit on her little stool with her," Roxanne whispered and then said out loud, "Sure, Zeke, that would be great."

Zeke confirmed that his parents would like to come to the game and said he'd give Warren a call to see if they wanted to join them.

"I'll have the tickets waiting for you at the box office and then I'll come get you after the game. Sound good?" Daria asked.

"It sounds fabulous!" Zeke said as his dark cloud lifted a little. "Bye Daria, see you tomorrow!" When he hung up, he walked over to his parents, still eating their pie at the table and said, "Maybe the three of us could go visit Bix and Betty after the game. We'll be right nearby and Mom, I want you to get to know them a little before you make a decision about them coming to live with us."

Zeke's parents slept in late on Sunday morning. As usual, Zeke was up for hours before his parents and used his time to take pictures on his cellphone of their basement apartment so that he could show Bix and Betty what the place looked like, to try to whet their interest and enthusiasm a bit in an effort to put a little more pressure on his mom. After leaving a note saying where he was, Zeke jumped on his bike and rode over to Warren's house to play some wiffle ball. The note also said to give him a call when they were awake and he'd come back home and have breakfast with them before it was time to go to Isotopes Park. His parents would be happy to know that he took his phone with him for a change.

After playing catch with Warren and after going home for breakfast with his rejuvenated parents, the Wappingers prepared for their afternoon together. After driving to Isotopes Park, after seeing his name on the JumboTron with the message "Welcome Home Zeke Wappinger" and then seeing a live shot of Zeke and his parents, which was met with wild applause from the entire stadium, after the Isotopes game which they won with a walk off inside-the-park home run that was made possible by the ball taking a crazy bounce on the sloping hill in center field that caused the center fielder to fall flat on his face, they were scooped up by Daria and taken into the clubhouse. They were able to briefly hang out with some of the Isotopes players who all knew about Zeke and gave him tons of attention for his recent exploits. When they parted ways with Warren, Warren's dad and Daria, they went over to visit the recovering hobos. However, the two boys didn't make it out of the clubhouse without Isotopes hats, tee shirts, a few bobbleheads and several signed bats. "It was pretty awesome," to quote the two six-year-olds.

Roxanne wasn't too jazzed about spending another part of her one day off during the week at a hospital, especially now that she realized the plan the Wappinger boys had hatched. Seeing the Isotopes, while an enjoyable way to spend three hours, wasn't exactly her idea of a good time. Spending time with her husband and son, however, made it a lot more worthwhile. Zeke's spirits had been lifted significantly by the trip to Isotopes Park and it elevated his mood back up to his normal positive level.

"I'd like to limit this visit to under an hour, if possible," Roxanne said on the short drive over to Presbyterian Hospital from the large parking lot by the stadium. "If we could get home by six, it will give me a chance to do a quick shop so we could throw some dinner together tonight. We can't just eat lobster every night!"

Luckily, when the three Wappingers arrived at room 302, Bix and Betty were both awake and sitting up watching a golf tournament. He had just heard Bix yell out something like, "I can't believe he shanked it!" when they approached the room so he knew he was awake.

"Captain and the Princess!" Zeke called out as he entered their room.

"This day is shapin' up purty good, now that I see Mr. Flannel Freddie, the Deviled Ham!" Bix responded.

"Hey Frankie! What brings you to our little corner of the universe? Did you miss us? We haven't seen you for a few days!" Betty said with an ear-to-ear grin across her clean and close-to-normal looking face.

"I wanted my mom and dad to get to know you a little better, well, especially my mom. We've all been talking about what's going to happen to you this week when they let you out of here," Zeke stated, "and I want her to see what great people you are."

"Zeke . . ." Roxanne said, giving her son a serious, disapproving sort of look.

"Now, don't you kind folks worry yourselves about us. We'll be fine. I'm startin' physical therapy to learn how to use those crutches tomorrow and I'll be limpin' around here in no time. Really. You've all done more than enough for us. Its me and Betty that need to somehow find a way to repay you for all you've done for us," Bix said.

"Mr. Rand . . ." Roxanne began, pulling up a chair next to his bed.

"Please, Bix or Robert. Mr. Rand sounds way too formal."

"Okay, Robert, I've been told that you were with the law firm Schwartz, Henley and Maples back in your younger days and my sources have confirmed that. I'm guessing that my son has told you that I'm a lawyer, too. Is that right?" Roxanne asked breaking the conversational ice.

"Yep, I sure was. You've probably heard the rest of the story too, so all that's just ancient history. Tell me, Mrs. Wappinger, tell me about your background. I'm sure that's a happier story."

"Not much to say, really. I grew up in Burbank, went to UCLA and then Stanford Law and have been a practicing attorney ever since. Well, also a wife to two of the most terrific men I've ever met, I'd say."

"I'll vouch for Frankie!" Betty responded. "How about your parents? Are they around?"

"Yes, both of my parents are alive and kicking, last I knew, and they still live in the Burbank area. My dad is a Court of Appeals judge, my mom sells real estate, nothing too out of the ordinary. I've got a younger brother and sister. He's a stockbroker in New York and she's a professional volleyball player. Made the Olympics the last two times. I don't see any of them all that often given our work and travel schedules."

"That's too bad. Family is pretty important. If I had one, I'd probably be with them right now. How about you Andrew?" Betty asked. "Zeke tells us that you grew up in New England, is that right?"

"Yes I did, actually. Not too far from Boston. I was raised mostly by my mom and grandparents in Marblehead. Great place to grow up with the ocean being right there," Andrew said. "Do you know the North Shore very well?"

"Not me," Betty admitted, "but Bix probably does. Right honey?"

"Yep, purty well but it's been a long time since I've been there after they ran me out of Brookline. Anyway, I was born in Newburyport, went to college at Brown in Providence and then to Yale Law School. I took the job at Schwartz, Henley and Maples, was workin' my way up the ladder for about ten years and then things kind of went downhill from there, as you know."

"Newburyport? That's where my mom was from too! Maybe you knew her. I think she might be about your age, Robert. Let's see, if she were still alive today, she'd be about fifty-one, fifty-two, something like that."

"What was her name?"

"Amanda, Amanda Wappinger," Andrew said. "Did you know her?"

"I knew a few Amandas from back in those days. I don't think I knew any Amanda Wappingers though. That's the kind of name that might stick in your memory, especially since I met this special young man here," Bix said.

"The Wappinger was my stepdad's last name. My mom got pregnant in high school and my grandparents pulled her out of school before she graduated. They moved all of us down the road a bit to Marblehead to have me. Her maiden name was Freemont, Amanda Freemont."

Captain Bix Pickles Haskell, the Human Stinkbomb, and Burrito Betty, the Princess of Poots, went white as ghosts and slowly turned their heads to look at each other like they had become marble statues of hobos in hospital gowns sitting up at an awkward angle in adjustable hospital beds. Betty began crying and pooting and laughing, all at the same time. Bix didn't say a word because his entire body had locked up and he couldn't physically say a word. Roxanne figured out immediately what was going on since she was intimately familiar with Andrew's personal history and the names of various family members. Andrew was a step behind and had a pretty good guess about what was going on as well. Zeke had absolutely no idea what the implications of his dad's statement were.

"So what's so special about the name Amanda Freemont, is she famous or something?" Zeke asked, noticing that his mom had taken his dad's hand and was pressing it to her heart.

"Well, son," Andrew began slowly, "Before your grandmother was Amanda Wappinger, her name was Amanda Freemont until she married my stepdad. You just know her as Nana Amanda, also known as Amanda Wappinger since she was about thirty years old. And I have the sneaking suspicion that Mr. Robert James Rand the third sitting here, your friend Captain Bix Pickles Haskell, the Human Stinkbomb is my long-lost biological father who I've never met in my entire life, but based on how he's reacted to the name Amanda Freemont, I'm guessing that I'm guessing right."

"I don't know what to say," Robert James Rand III spoke as the tears started streaming down his face. "I didn't think in all of my wildest dreams that I would ever in a million years, ever get to meet my child, my son. I gave up on that dream so long ago."

Andrew began sobbing as well now that it was all revealed and confirmed. He walked over to his dad and buried himself carefully in his embrace, an embrace that he, too, had given up on ever experiencing so long ago, almost as long as Robert had. His mom never would talk about him even when he pressed her for details. Her standard answer was always, "that's the past and we're living in the present so let's keep moving forward." His grandparents would always say, "that's between you and your mother." Even when she died unexpectedly a few years ago, preceded by his grandparents five years before that, he couldn't find any information about his father from all of her personal papers that he went through. His stepfather didn't know anything about Robert so he was never able to give him any information.

The hug between father and son expanded to include Zeke and Roxanne. Nobody spoke for minutes or hours, really, since time became inconsequential. Betty would have liked to join in but wasn't yet able to get out of her bed. She knew what a monumental moment this was for the only man in the world that she had ever loved and her heart was filled with so much joy, she thought it might burst. Bix had buried his longing for his child for such a long time that it was hard to even dredge up a tangible thought about the possibility of having one. He had no memory of a child since he was never given the chance to meet them or even to know anything about them. This was the first time in thirty-five years that his past reality merged with his current reality and it was a completely overwhelming sensation.

The wooing of Zeke's mother to talk her into allowing the hobos to come live with them was now obviously moot. Zeke was absolutely beside himself with joy, understanding the seismic shift in all of their lives but also with the discovery that he had another grandfather and all along it was Captain Bix Pickles Haskell, the Human Stinkbomb. He knew his mom's parents from the occasional visit here or there but they never seemed to have much interest in kids. Nana Amanda was a real grandmother in the sense that she doted on Zeke and loved to visit. Sadly, her death when he was three and a half was a huge loss for everyone. Andrew's grandparents, died before Zeke was born. This new revelation was of monstrous proportions.

Burrito Betty was over in her bed blubbering like a whale. It was almost too unbelievable to imagine that the last week's events had happened and even more unbelievable to understand that it happened for this very reason. She was happy beyond belief for Bix, happy for Andrew and without a doubt, happy for Frankie. What she was curious to see, however, was how Roxanne was going to handle the discovery. Sure, she was part of the family hug but Betty couldn't read her emotions. Was she just going along for the ride? Was she still going to be a jerk about them or was she going to embrace the entire concept? Surprisingly, she was the first one to speak when it seemed like the hugging session was starting to wear down and the crying had run its course, at least for the time being.

DAVID W. GOODWIN

"Isn't life funny sometimes?" she said as she pulled out of the cluster and stood up beside Bix's bed. "Here you two Wappinger men were wining and dining me last night to talk me into taking these two hobos into our house and then this happens. This is the last thing in the world I could have predicted. I thought for sure I was going to have to play the bad cop and put my foot down on this idea. Robert, Tiffany, in light of these newest developments, Andrew, Zeke and myself would be honored if you were to come live with us when you are released from the hospital."

EPILOGUE

NOW THIS COULD easily be the end of the story and the beginning of the next one. The sequel could be called *The Seven-Year-Old Contented Child That Didn't Ever Run Away Again* or *The Seven-Year-Old Hobo's Grandfather's Redemption* or maybe even *The Seven-Year-Old Former Hobo* or even broaden the franchise out to *Hobo's Salvation*, but the truth of the matter is that there are still a few loose ends that one might want to be tied up while Zeke was still in the waning months of his glorious and noteworthy sixth year. There must be some curiosity about all of the various police officers that appeared in the story, especially Daria Cellucci and how the family reunion might have affected her life and career, if at all. Maybe Chip Brockaway from Big Air Off Road Adventures was forever changed by, you know, being a part of the Belén rescue-of-the-century. What about the handsome priest, Reverend Gaajii Jesus el del Dingo whose kindness and welcoming nature might have played some small part in altering the course of events. Perhaps the rookie BNSF train engineer Priscilla Barbados was so traumatized by thinking that her train was carrying a runaway six-year-old boy that she quit on the spot and went back to working at Walmart. And what fate might old Phony Phil from Philadelphia have come to as a rec rider without a clue about the hobo code? Is it possible that the movers, Vince and Hector, from Kokopelli's Big Furniture Mart in Gallup never thought again about the hobo's short-lived escape using their delivery truck and went on to live the sort of lives they would have as if this whole thing hadn't happened? Perhaps. And did Lieutenant Forsmark ever convince Officer Cellucci to go out on a date with him? Maybe Corn Dog Dougie, the Underpants King and/or Muffin of Destiny and maybe even her kid sister Doornuts Sue Piglet, might have found a way to wiggle their way into the story. And what about Pamela, the heroic nanny and, not to be overlooked, whatever became of Jazzy Jugs O'Reilly and Roadkill Ronnie?

Certainly, anyone is free to imagine what they will and even draw their own conclusions. For the time being at least, there are two characters that, for sure, were a part of the story after Bix and Betty were released from the hospital and moved into the plush basement apartment on Ladera Drive in Belén where they had a fabulous convalescence. Within weeks, they were mobile and actively contributing members of the extended Wappinger family.

So the story has to back up a little to Grants, New Mexico where the curtain opens on the adventures and misadventures of Ethel and Ernest Gamble. As you may recall, they were stuck in automotive and administrative purgatory due to a large number of time consuming and costly details to pay their outstanding fines, get Ethel's driver's license up-to-date and valid, get a new vehicle registration, get automobile insurance and get their multicolored 1990 Lincoln Town Car roadworthy enough to pass a safety inspection. These were all weighty tasks and, as you might have guessed, Ernest Gamble was not only of little help, he was a complete and utter liability. Their story line picks up right after dinner when Bix and Betty bid a fond farewell and hopped the local bound for Belén in the middle of the night before the rains came.

The total outlay of cash to accomplish all of the aforementioned tasks was close to four thousand dollars, which they were able to scrape together without too much trouble given Ethel's steady flow of monthly checks. The total amount of time for the Gambles to get back on the road in their mobile trash dump was about two weeks. It might have been a little quicker but Ethel ended up failing her written New Mexico driver's test once and her road test twice, largely due to three different factors. One was that she hardly even looked at the driver's manual so she failed miserably to grasp the nuance of the New Mexico driving laws, or any driving laws for that matter. For example, on one test question that asked, "What is a safe distance to allow when passing a bicyclist?" she was given the choices of "A. an inch, B. a foot, C. 5 feet or D. other." She chose "D. other," and wrote in "the damn things shouldn't even be allowed on the road." The second factor that contributed significantly to her multiple failures was a wicked hangover and she just wasn't thinking clearly. And finally, she wasn't able to fight her natural impulse towards extreme flirting and her hunky uniformed driving test officer had to ask her to stop driving altogether so that he could strap her into the backseat while he drove back to the MVD building. Once informed that she had failed the test, her response to Officer Handsome was, "maybe there's something I could do for you to change your mind?" There wasn't.

Two weeks later, however, after spending most of their sleeping hours at the $47 a night Travelodge and most of their waking hours at Dusty's Watering Hole just a few blocks down the main drag, they packed up their trash into the Town Car, which no longer spewed blue smoke and was now able to drive in a straight line, and headed to Belén, hoping to connect back up with the hobos and that cute little boy. Ethel was closely monitoring all of the news coverage of Zeke's return from the televisions both at the bar and at their cramped Travelodge room and even knew about the hobo's dramatic water rescue. Ernest, as you might suspect, was fascinated by the story of the four hobos who apparently were swept away in the Rio Grande and was obsessed with the two missing hobos, Jazzy Jugs O'Reilly and Roadkill Ronnie. He was one hundred percent convinced that they had been taken captive or killed by the legendary weeping woman of the southwest, La Llorona, who was thought to wander the region's rivers and arroyos in search of any children or small adults to snatch up and either throw to their deaths in the flowing waters or hold hostage to atone, in some weird way, for the drowning of her own children, depending on which interpretation of the story you chose to believe. "Mark my words, La Llorona is behind this," he told all of his buddies at the bar who quickly learned to tune him out.

What they didn't know was that Andrew and Bix had discovered their true relationship and that the hobos had just moved into Ladera Drive a few days before the Gambles blew into town. As Ethel was barreling south on I-25, just passing the exit to Los Lunas, Ernest came out of some trance that he was in and asked where they were going.

"To Belén, dear, to try to find our two hobo friends and that sweet boy we had lunch with back in Gallup at that Catholic church food kitchen, remember?"

"No, not really. Are they the ones that got taken captive by La Llorona?"

"No, Ernie, they're the ones that got rescued by the little boy, Zeke, and his dad. Remember we saw them on TV? You're thinking of their two hobo friends, Jazzy Juggies and Ronnie something-or-other," Ethel said patiently, "and why do you think this La Llorona person got them?"

"It's so obvious, Ethel, do I have to explain everything?" Ethel had learned over the years never to respond to any of Ernest's rhetorical questions and just kept driving south.

At the second Belén exit, number 191, the one that pointed the way to "Camino Del Llano" and had a water tank decorated with the words

"Home of the Eagles" and flanked by matching eagle heads snarling at each other, Ethel eased the massive Town Car off the highway and had to panic break as she approached the "T" intersection at the end of the off ramp. Much to her surprise, the car could actually go close to the speed limit so she now had to learn how to properly decelerate the immense hunk of steel to a stop and ended up hitting the brakes so hard that it forced Ernest face first into the dashboard. He had a few choice words for her driving style and they weren't very complimentary. The Gambles hadn't actually discussed their plan of action once they got to Belén but Ethel assumed that if she asked Ernest, he would have said something like "wherever there's a pot to piss in" or something equally as unhelpful, so she knew it was up to her to be the decision-maker.

Little did Ethel know, once off the interstate, she was a mere half-mile from the Wappinger-hobo fortress. Not having a GPS or really even knowing what a GPS was, she decided to do what any self-respecting vagabond, settlement-funded alcoholic, fun-loving party girl, new-in-town stranger might chose to do. She steered the Town Car downtown and stopped at the first bar she saw as she eased off Camino Del Llano and followed the signs to downtown Belén. There, like a flashing neon sign in the desert announcing an oasis, was the Becker Street Pub on Becker Avenue (it was unclear who had it wrong, the town calling it an avenue or the pub owners calling it a street), in the heart of downtown Belén, their new home away from home and ironically, only a block and a half from where Zeke hopped a boxcar in the middle of the night two and a half weeks ago.

After parking the colossal, but now functional land yacht in the head-on parking in front of the pub on Becker Avenue, the Gambles extricated themselves from the car and sauntered into the bar at roughly eleven in the morning. Finding the place nearly empty, except for the sleepy bartender and two ranchers intent upon helping the day turn into a forgotten memory, Ethel announced her presence with a big "howdy folks" while Ernest scuffed along behind her and took a stool at the bar while Ethel introduced herself to the bartender and the ranchers. The place was surprisingly upscale, with a beautiful curving bar and a small raised stage with fancy stage lighting. In her usual flouncy black and white party dress, gobs of makeup and half a ton of cheap jewelry, the patrons and man behind the bar weren't sure what to make of her.

"Are you folks from around here?" the bartender, a man named Dwayne, asked Ethel.

"No, we're originally from Fargo and I've never been here before in my life," Ethel responded, adding, "and I'm pretty certain the same goes for my husband, Ernest. Is that right, honey?"

"I might have been here once before when I was time-traveling but it's hard to keep track of all the places I've been," Ernest responded, immediately setting the tone with the other three for all future conversations.

"Okay, so what brings you to Belén?"

"Zeke Wappinger. You know who he is?"

"Yes, of course. Everyone knows him now. He's made quite a name for himself lately. I'll have to warn you though that the police are keeping a pretty close eye on their house and neighborhood to try to keep the reporters and curiosity-seekers at bay. They've been flocking to his house like swallows to Capistrano the last few weeks, looking for interviews with any family members or the hobos or just to catch a glimpse of the boy. What's your business with them?"

"We're the ones that led to his capture in Gallup," Ethel stated matter-of-factly.

"You're shittin' me, right?" one of the ranchers, sitting a few stools down nursing a beer and now getting up to confront Ethel directly, said. "It seems like everyone now is jumpin' on the bandwagon and is telling the press about some role they played in the ordeal. Hell, half the town has been interviewed by now for the newspapers or the radio or TV. I doubt you're tellin' the truth, lady."

"Well, I am. Why would I lie about it?"

"Why would anyone lie about it?" rancher number two said pounding his empty Coors glass on the bar and nodding to the bartender for a refill.

"I don't know," Ethel answered, "but do you want to know the whole story?"

Naturally, they did. What else did they have to do on a late Tuesday morning? Ethel told her tale, Ernest chimed in from time-to-time which tended to cloud the facts a bit but Ethel would do some damage control and then continue on with the story, eventually arriving at the present time.

"So, that's why we're here in your fair city, to pay a visit to the Wappingers and see how they're all getting along and also to check in with our two hobo friends and see how they're recovering. The problem is, we don't know where they live and we don't know where the hobos might have run off to or even if they're still in town."

"This might just be your lucky day, ma'am," Dwayne said. "Rumor has it that the hobos went to live with the family in their basement and, get this interesting twist in the story, there are folks saying that the hobo man is the long lost father of Andrew Wappinger, the boy's grandfather, if you can believe that one!"

"My God!" Ethel exclaimed. "Are you serious?"

"That's what people are saying. Listen, if you're who you say you are, and I'll admit, your story sounds pretty water tight, you might just be able to go see the family without the police blocking your way."

"The police can't stop us, all we gotta do is become invisible and we can sneak right by 'em," Ernest said dismissively, reducing his credibility even more, if that was possible.

"What we don't know is where they live," Ethel said.

"Why don't you just look it up on your smart ass phone like you do everything else?" Ernest suggested. "Those things will rot your brain, for sure."

"Or you could just go up to 398 Ladera Drive where they live," the seated rancher said. "Everyone knows that address now. They've got one of the nicest houses in town, one of them crazy fake adobe ranches with all the modern conveniences known to mankind."

Ethel started tapping away on her smartphone and entered in the address in her map application. After a few seconds she said, "I see it. That's not very far from here."

"Right, lady, ain't nuthin' very far from here. Belén's a pretty small town and most of us know each other," the standing rancher said. "Those Wappingers are newcomers. Nobody knows a whole lot about 'em since they don't really have any roots or friends here as far as I know. I think the dad is from New England and the mom is from California. I'm not sure why they ended up in Belén since they both work in Albuquerque."

The Gambles ordered up some drinks and settled in at the bar for a while, talking to the bartender and the ranchers about the town, cheap motels where they could stay for a few days, and just passing the time of day while Ethel formulated a few options in her mind about how they might approach the family and what exactly they hoped to accomplish. Ernest, meanwhile, knocked back a few shots of whisky while being relegated to the outer fringe of the conversation, a place he was used to inhabiting.

The ranchers left after a while and a few more patrons came and went throughout the afternoon. Dwayne, the bartender, did a good job as host, introducing each regular as they came in for a drink to the Gambles and stressing the importance of their role in the Zeke Wappinger story, so Ethel, at least, was treated like barroom royalty, a position she absolutely basked in. She and Ernest even got a few free drinks out of their notoriety. Word apparently began to spread around town who the Gambles were and this brought in a higher number of patrons than was typical for a Tuesday afternoon. Ethel was introduced to a regular stream of residents who wanted to know more about her role and she gladly obliged. The story got a little more dramatic with each retelling and with each fresh rum and coke that was placed before her.

"The one piece of the puzzle that seems to be missing," Ethel said with an inebriated slur late in the afternoon after finishing off her fourth drink of the day, "is whatever happened to the other two hobos that got washed away. Does anyone know about them?"

Ernest didn't miss a beat with his theory about La Llorona, which got a good round of yucks from the surrounding group of about ten patrons at this point. A recently arrived middle-aged woman, who came into the bar with two of her fairly well-dressed colleagues, celebrating the end of the working day with cosmopolitans, which was apparently a tradition for them, advanced the theory that since their bodies weren't ever discovered downstream, maybe they hadn't been swept away in the flood after all and simply were going about their hobo business elsewhere.

"But the thing is," Dwayne said, "from what I know about the woman named Jazzy Jugs, she'd be hard to miss, even in a crowd, and nobody has reported seeing them."

"Yeah, but if they snuck off in the middle of the night and hopped a train, they could be almost anywhere by now," another suggested.

"Right, but since the other two hobos, the ones that were saved, floated off in the middle of the night on air mattresses, like I heard on Eagle 98 FM, I'd be willing to lay odds that this Jugs woman and her boyfriend must of met the same fate, they just weren't as lucky as the other two," another theorized.

More theories were proposed and Ernest, seeming to abandon his La Llorona theory for the moment, or maybe he was getting so blitzed on whisky that he had forgotten that this was a theory that he had been advancing for most of the day, offered an alternative explanation—alien abduction. This was written off by most of the current patrons except for one recent arrival, a fellow alien believer apparently, and he and Ernest went off to the side to share their thoughts with fellow kindred spirits.

Throughout the day, the Gambles would order up dribs and drabs of bar food—fries, nachos, beer battered pickles—enough to sufficiently call it a meal and eventually figured it was time to go in search of a dive motel to crash at for the night since there weren't any homeless shelters in Belén, their preferred accommodations. After taking recommendations from everyone in the place, Ethel settled on the Super Eight since it was the cheapest and closest to the downtown area. A few folks lobbied for one of the handful of abandoned buildings nearby saying they were often occupied by squatters but it might be a bit dangerous, given the spat of drug violence that had taken place there recently. Ernest was almost literally dragged out of the bar around seven by Ethel but she vowed to return later in the evening after they were settled in. At the Super Eight, Ethel asked for a room that was on the first floor and had a good view. They did get a room on the first floor but the view was of the parking lot and the back side of the China King restaurant. After unpacking their essential supplies and taking a nap that lasted until about midnight, they both woke up around the same time, somewhat sober, or at least less drunk, and fairly well rested.

"Hey, Ernest, this might be a good time to go scope out the Wappinger's house," Ethel whispered in the glare of the artificial parking lot light that shown in onto their bed. "We might even be able to look in some windows since everyone will be asleep. That might give us a better clue about what's going on there."

"Ethel, I think that's a crackpot idea. What if we get caught?"

"Don't be such a wussie! We'll be super careful. We'll both wear dark clothing and not take any stupid risks. According to my phone, we're only six or seven blocks away. We could walk over in a few minutes and not raise any unnecessary suspicions like we might if we drove. Want to?"

"No, not really but if you go, I'll go with you to make sure you stay out of trouble."

With that as their "A" plan, the two not-so-stealth, vaguely tipsy, darkly dressed Gambles tried to follow the directions on Ethel's phone and follow the recommended route to Ladera Drive. The phone app said it was 0.8 miles and should have taken thirteen minutes but it obviously didn't take into account Ethel and Ernest's condition or Ernest's propensity towards believing the software had some sort of hidden agenda to take them the wrong way for some reason that was only apparent to him, so the walk was a bit longer and took more like half an hour. Regardless, in the bright moonlight, they found themselves eventually standing before the Wappinger's house on one side of their circular driveway.

"Nice little bungalow," Ethel whispered to her sidekick.

"Now what, Herr Commandant?"

"Let's walk around the house and see if we can see anything in the windows," Ethel suggested.

They walked to the right of the Wappinger's garage, sticking as closely to the detached carport of the nextdoor neighbor and encountered a chain link fence that surrounded the entire backyard. They could see a large patio back there with a hot tub and inground pool and Ethel soon realized that the gate was closed but unlocked. Carefully opening it up, the Gambles walked right into the sloping backyard and got a full view of the entire house from the far side of the pool area. What they saw was an upstairs with all the lights off and a downstairs, which looked like a walk out basement, with all the lights on. They could see two people moving around inside, one with a full cast on their leg and the other with a full cast on her arm.

"I think that's Bix Pickles and Burrito Betty!" Ethel whispered excitedly.

"That don't look like either of them. Those aren't the hobos we met in Gallup," Ernest observed.

"You're right, they look different but I'm pretty certain that's them. Let's go let them know we're here."

Trying to be as quiet as two slightly drunk mice, Ethel and Ernest tiptoed around the pool, crossed the patio and walked up to the sliding screen door that was a part of the sliding glass doors. Ethel could hear Bix and Betty talking softly inside and was worried about startling them if she called out their names. Instead, she started out with a whisper, transitioned to a louder whisper and when that didn't get their attention, she cupped her hands over her mouth like a mini-megaphone and cried out, "Bix Pickles and Burrito Betty, come to the door!" from just out of sight in a bush beside the slider.

Betty heard that one and for a moment, was convinced that the ghosts of Jazzy Jugs O'Reilly and Roadkill Ronnie had tracked them down. "Bix, did you hear that? Someone's calling our names from the patio! I think it's JJ and Roadkill!"

Bix grabbed his crutches and hobbled over to the slider. Before he got there, though, Ethel walked into full view in the middle of the screen and in a soft voice said, "Don't be afraid, it's your pals Ethel and Ernest Gamble!"

"Well, well, what a great surprise! Betty, it's okay, they're not ghosts. Come on in folks!" Bix said as he opened the screen for them. "It's our friends Ethel and Ernest!"

The hobos had changed a lot since the Gambles had last seen them. In spite of all the plaster they were wearing and the various bandages and visible contusions that were in the process of healing, both Bix and Betty looked well rested, well fed and had a certain peace and serenity about them that they hadn't before. Ethel thought to herself that they didn't seem like wild caged animals anymore, almost like a normal couple living a normal life. Bix's proficiency with his crutches was improving exponentially and Betty had gotten to the point where she could move around pretty well without much discomfort.

The four friends exchanged greetings, hugs, stories, food, drink and things must have gotten a little loud because after about ten minutes of their reunion, Andrew Wappinger appeared at the bottom of the steps.

"Hi Dad, what's going on down here? I heard all these voices."

"Oh, Andrew, hi! I'm sorry. Some of our friends just showed up. We kind of forgot about the fact that it was the middle of the night and you all might be asleep." Turning to the Gambles, Bix said, "Andrew is Zeke's dad and, as we just discovered a few days ago, my long lost son who I'd never had the pleasure to meet. Andrew, these are my friends Ethel and Ernest Gamble."

"So it is true! We were at the Becker Street Pub today and some of the folks there told us about this most amazing coincidence. Congratulations to all of you. That is absolutely remarkable! Andrew, I don't know if you know this but your son Zeke used my cellphone to send his mom the text message from Gallup to let you both know that he was alright. That's how we're involved in this story," Ethel explained.

"What a freakin' cowinkydink!" added Ernest.

With that, Andrew's attitude lightened up some and he welcomed the Gambles again but asked if they could all keep the noise level down since both he and Roxanne had long days and had to get up pretty early this morning. "I'll look forward to talking more to you folks about this and I'm sure Zeke would love to say hi to you both. Will you be around later today?"

DAVID W. GOODWIN

"Yes, Andrew, we will. That's really why we came here was to see our friends and also to see Zeke and see how he's doing," Ethel said kindly.

"Just so you know, he's doing really well and couldn't be happier that he now has a grandfather and a sort-of-grandmother, although Tiffany is about the same age as his mom, my wife Roxanne, so that's a little weird, but we're one big happy family. We all are thrilled with what's happened here! Anyway, goodnight folks, goodnight Dad and goodnight Betty - Tiffany. See you all tomorrow or, I should say, later today."

"Betty - Tiffany?" Ethel asked quietly when Andrew was up the stairs.

"Yep, I think that Tiffany might be my legal name," Betty whispered, "and that's what Andrew's wife Roxanne seems most comfortable calling me so sometimes Andrew will call me Betty but sometimes he wants to throw in the Tiffany part too. I don't mind, really, in fact, I think it's kind of sweet. By the way, do you folks need a place to stay tonight? I'm sure it would be alright if you stayed here, don't you think, Bix?"

"We've already got a place at the Super 8, but thanks, Betty," Ethel said before Bix had a chance to respond. "It's probably best, in fact, that we head back. We don't want to keep you folks up too late."

"We're still on hobo time," Bix said, "but we should probably start adjusting to normal people time."

Ernest, who was keeping his usual low profile asked if by chance this basement room was a fallout shelter. The two former 'bos laughed nervously - they were mostly used to Ernest's off-the-wall view of the world and Bix told him that he didn't think it was, but would ask his son next time he saw him. With that, the Gambles were gone but they made plans to get together around lunchtime later in the day and hoped to get a chance to hang out with Zeke.

Bix and Betty figured they, too, should put a wrap on the long day and snuggled up in their new, amazingly comfortable bed together, trying to arrange their casts in a way so they didn't bump into each other too much and quickly started to drift off to dreamland with smiles on their rapidly healing faces. Before succumbing to their dreams, however, Bix murmured to Betty, "I'm glad we're doing this. I think it's gonna work out just fine." She smiled in the radiance of the bright New Mexican moonlight and made a humming sound followed by a little tiny poot exclamation point.

Upstairs in his large but cozy bedroom, Zeke slept deeply knowing that he absolutely couldn't have been happier. And with this new arrangement, with a new extended family and with parents that finally were one hundred percent committed to being parents, he felt just like his favorite storybook character, Charlie the Caboose or Charlie the Clown Wagon, as Captain Bix Pickles Haskell, the Human Stinkbomb and now, his beloved grandfather, would say when he read the book each night to Zeke. Fate really did seem to intervene in all of their lives. The railroad company, at least metaphorically, if not literally, really did give him his final wish.

DATE DUE

			PRINTED IN U.S.A.